Blood from the Air

Gemma Files

Blood from the Air

Gemma Files

New Orleans, Louisiana

CONTENTS

Little-Ease

It came out of the dark, and into the dark it has gone again.
—E.F. Benson

M Y NAME IS Ginevra Cochrane, and five years ago I was roughly eighteen months into a gig as a freelance exterminator, doing unregulated pest control jobs for a private contractor who moved me from placement to placement, always keeping stuff off the books. It was shit-work, basically—sometimes literally, always figuratively—and I'm not exaggerating when I say I took it on for lack of anything better.

You're probably thinking: "I'll bet she must've been on drugs, or drunk, or both." Well, you'd be right. Shorter version of an already short story, without all the boring explication: car accident, dead best friend, botched recovery, painkillers, and alcohol plus the side effects thereof, a truncated education, infractions to misdemeanors to a felony charge plea followed by a shortish stint in jail, crapped-out credit and an ex-con stamp on my resume. In the end, it took the events I'm about to recount to finally break me out of that overall downward spiral, for which I should be grateful, in retrospect.

My last foster-mother, Zillah, used to claim people eventually find the job they're most suited for, as though employment was some kind of moral refining process you'd really have to put your back into fucking up. She believed that to allow yourself to work simply for money, swap time for cash in order to walk away at the end of shift and spend the rest of the weekend thinking about anything other than Monday morning, was like you were cheating yourself on some cosmic level—that not giving a fuck about work was an insult to the universe, so you couldn't claim to be surprised when the karma incurred through that sort of deliberate perversity came back to bite you in the ass.

I got my exterminator work through a woman I'd met in prison, whom I'll call Leonora. She was a high school equivalency instructor, later admitting she used our test results to figure out which of us short-termers might be worth recruiting for her little side-business. She once told me I had the highest scores of anybody she'd ever passed, but I'm pretty sure that was glad-handling B.S.; pest control isn't exactly full of geniuses—it's something any moron can learn to do, and I do mean that literally, given how consistently dumb everybody I worked with in that area turned out to be. I'm talking people who never read anything longer than the back of a cereal box or couldn't calculate fifteen percent for tips, people who thought being a Muslim should be made illegal, people who called their pets "fur-babies." They were good enough to go out with for drinks on occasion, when the loneliness got too hard to handle, but that was about it.

Personally, I've always had a hard time *not* thinking about things, even when I know damn well I'd be better off if I didn't.

Dreaming can be a kind of drug, especially when you can't afford anything better. Throughout my life, whenever things get *really* bad, I've felt this overwhelming urge to lie down and open myself up, abandon myself to whatever might present itself—just turn off the light, shut my eyes and let my own unconscious boil up from inside until it presses back down upon me, rendering me slack, heavy, irresponsible: guiltless in the face of my own choices, or lack thereof.

Let it all wash over me, would be my last thought, before submerging; *let me sink down, like a rock in the river. And lie there untouched, 'til the morning*

I don't come up again.

Around the same time the events of this story took place, I started having a series of seemingly infinitely nested dreams that started one night only to cross over into the next, sometimes spilling into naps or reveries. Each new episode of the overarching narrative appeared to emerge from elsewhere, entirely outside myself; I'd wake with my sense of personal reality bruised and aching, actively questioning whether or not I'd actually experienced any of the things I devoutly felt I had.

Though these dreams varied widely in content, they always involved me finding a door somewhere no door existed, opening it, and going through. Once it was in the corner of my bedroom, lurking beneath the wallpaper; I only noticed it because the outline of its edges disrupted the pattern ever so slightly, a glitch in the design. Another time I got out of bed, crossed towards the bathroom and heard something squeak beneath me—when I glanced down, I caught the glint of hinges, realizing only then that someone had cut a trapdoor in the floor without me knowing, leaving it waiting for me to stumble into. And once the door manifested itself inside my hall closet; I pulled aside the coats to reach for something deeper, paused, then saw the shadow between them was a hidden portal, barely cracked onto a deep expanse of black.

Doors, doors, everywhere. Wrestling through them before crawling on, unable to go back, afraid to go forward. After which I would wake from darkness into darkness and lie there sweat-covered, pressing my hand down so hard it hurt over a hammering heart.

Pest control is a quotidian venture, at best; you can cull the overflow, but there's always more, lurking inside the walls. Everybody assumes—correctly—that the bugs are there, but nobody really cares, so long as they don't have to *see* them. And when you *do* see them, that's when you know you've got an infestation.

Similarly, the type of site you get sent to as an exterminator is usually determined by whether or not you're okay working with rats, as opposed to whether or not you're okay working with bugs. For myself, I find rats ten thousand times more disgusting than insects, mainly because they're far more unpredictable. Didn't help I'd once come across a nest full of newborn ratlings, all pink and squirming, blind eyes visible through their slightly transparent eyelids; *really* didn't help I'd found it the same moment a bunch of male adult rats were chowing down on what might have been their own kids, while the mothers were off scavenging for dinner. After that, I was totally an insect person. I think most of us are, in context—almost nobody I've ever met has a problem with killing bugs.

Another thing I learned is that each site has its own peculiar ecology, which means that knocking out one insect type only replaces it with another—so that's what you aim to do: maintain a careful natural balance that renders the inherent process of predator and prey invisible once more, without eliminating it entirely. Like managing climate change (supposedly), but restricted to one particular neighborhood, one block, one apartment building.

The sites I got sent to had a lot more in common than insect infestations, however. Inevitably, they were owned by one of a small, tight knot of local slumlords, while the buildings themselves ran the gamut from mildly run down to outright decrepit. We're talking exposed wiring, cold-water plumbing, bucket toilets, broken everything. Garbage piled up in the corners, sometimes rotting—the easiest fix, so long as I could find somebody English-fluent to translate my suggestions about better hygiene equaling fewer bugs. The residents I interacted with tended to be nomads and refugees, seasonal workers, people too old, broken, or poor to move, the illegal and the indigent: a constantly exploited floating class of paperless, voteless, voiceless drones who the city's legitimate social infrastructure probably wouldn't piss on if they were on fire.

I tried to tell myself I was doing *something* positive for these people, at least indirectly. That by ridding these places of pests, I was playing intercessor between these unfortunate residents and the system trying to game them, not just greasing the machine's wheels in mid-crush.

Leonora had deals with a bunch of different pesticide companies, buying expired products in bulk at a discount to keep her overhead down, and handing them out to us like they were brightly colored poison candy. One night, after being dumb enough to casually Google the names of the various sprays and powders I routinely handled, I discovered that almost all contact insecticides are literally nerve agents, organophosphates specifically designed to interfere with the enzymes that enable bugs' systemic impulses. Even the most benign have more in common with sarin gas than anything else, and multiple exposures only amplify their toxicity, creating a cumulative effect that can denude a whole area.

Our on-site safety protocols were put-on-rubber-gloves-and-hold-your-nose-type shaky. If we wanted masks, we paid for them ourselves, so most people went with the molded cotton kind plasterers use. I combed through military surplus stores 'til I came up with a chemical warfare rig from Desert Storm, but soon found out nobody made filters for it anymore. So I just cobbled my own together out of reconstituted, cut-down sanitary pads, and hoped I wasn't breathing in anything too permanently damaging.

Because it felt like I had no other choice, I sucked it up; played through the grime and the itchiness, the sore spots and intermittent waves of queasiness, the head-to-toe stink that never quite went away. I refused to chart symptoms, convinced stress was just as likely to cause everything I was experiencing, even as my shower's drain clogged up with hair and my face took on a hectic rosacea-patterned glow, flaky-flushed across the forehead, the thin-skinned arch between eyebrow and lid. Like I'd been trying to tan using a microwave.

Thirteen weeks in, however, I hit the wall hard, forced to admit what I really should have known all along: I was hip-deep in toxins and risking my health for a pittance, stuck fast, with no immediate way I could figure out to extricate myself.

"C'mon in here, Ginnie," Leonora told me one Monday, when I came in to load my car up with whatever awful shit they were handing out that week. "Need to talk to ya about the job you're on . . . Dancy Street again, right?" I nodded. "Yeah, okay; won't take a minute. And shut the door, will ya?"

Inside Leonora's office sat a tall woman she introduced as the "Dancy Street Project's" general manager, whose name I recognized from all my previous paychecks, but who I'd never seen in person. She wore a suit and a little too much perfume, both probably expensive.

"Nice to meet you, Miss Cochrane," she said, smiling wide. "Leonora tells me you're a pretty smart cookie."

"I like to think so," I agreed, already wary. People say women are more empathetic than men, which is why we socialize quicker and get along better. But most of us only learn to fake that empathy to deal with men's egos, rather than each other's; some of the worst jobs I've ever worked had all-female crews, especially when you got somebody ambitious enough to want credit but too shameless to put in any effort, yet duplicitous and clever enough — as Suit-chick already struck me — to shove any blame for the ensuing eff-up onto ground-level cannon fodder like me.

She nodded. "You've been on site how long now?"

"At Thirty-three? Well, I started last Tuesday —"

"— But Ginnie's been our point gal on a number of jobs in the area, over the past few weeks," Leonora chimed in. "So she's more than familiar with the current state of the Project."

I moved my head, noncommittally, while Suit-chick just kept on smiling. "Mmmm," she said. "And what've they got down there, in your opinion?"

"Basic infestation," I replied. "I'd guess roaches, by the damage."

I waited for her to ask if I'd seen them myself, but she didn't, which struck me as weird, even then. As it happens, I'd seen everything but: black pepper-flake feces with a musty, pungent odor, plus oothecae — oblong casings like a caterpillar's cocoon, housing fifty eggs each. I'd found them all over Thirty-three, fresh-popped and ready to go, either glued up under counters, clustered 'round the groins of pipes or in the dusty corners of ceilings where nobody thought to check, especially people too frail to crane their necks that high.

"Looks like they came out of the walls," I continued. "I've been laying down poison, but I'm still not seeing carcasses. What I really need to do is knock a few holes and look around inside, get a handle on what they're doing back there. I put in a request."

"Yes, we saw that."

"Um, okay, great. So . . . can I?"

Her smile didn't change, at all. "We'd actually prefer that you didn't."

The Dancy Street area — *Project* — was a weird little cul-de-sac jammed between a slow-dying semi-industrial area and pre-gentrification's encroaching decay. Their nearest neighbor had once been the Winnick Brothers Camp-out Cookery plant, home to a defunct brand of easy-heat tinned stew; "pet food for people," a guy I once dated used to call it. But they'd been gone since the short-fall crash, leaving nothing behind but a few crumbling buildings, a bunch of equipment too heavy to move and too obsolete to sell, plus a ground-in smell of dead flesh that emerged whenever the heat climbed too high, strong enough to make a hyena gag.

Number Thirty-three was an apartment building dating back to the 1920s, a moldering gray-brown brick box put up for the Cookery's live-in staff housing, then given some shoddy build-on action and sold as a combination halfway house and backpackers' drop-in. Now it was a crapped-out three-story inhabited by maybe fifteen extraordinarily old people, all of whom I'd run into in the halls, by this point. I'd see them stringing laundry up between the bottom balconies inside the all-concrete courtyard as I came out of the basement, shoes crunching slightly over its cracked and broken areas; they'd smile, or seem to, and I'd try to smile back.

Most I couldn't have described if you'd paid me extra, not even to tell the (presumably) men from the (presumably) women—just a bunch of hunched little figures at the corner of my vision, all with the same sort of wispy gray hair, gray teeth, gray faces.

The sole exception was a lady I called Great-Aunt Chatty, if only in my head. She'd sidled up behind me my second day on site, taken a long, squinty gander over my shoulder, then asked: "Are you sure you should be using that *indoors*, dear?"

"That" was Leonora's latest load of whatever-the-hell, a vile pink paste I was currently spooning out of a bucket and smearing along the baseboards on either side of the cellar door. "Just doing what it says to on the label, ma'am," I lied, without looking up.

"Miss," she corrected, gently. "Are you from the property office?"

"Um . . . sure."

"Then you'd be able to pass along a message for me, if I asked."

This, however, was further than I felt comfortable going, in terms of polite bushwah. "Not really," I replied, forcing myself back to a standing position, so I could seem slightly more official. "I'm just here to deal with the bugs. You'll need to talk to the superintendent about anything else."

"Oh, truly?" I nodded. "Because none of us have seen that particular gentleman in quite some time now, you know; three months, perhaps even six."

"I can't help you with that, ma'am — Miss."

"What a pity." Adding, after a pause: "I wasn't aware we *had* insects."

"Seriously?" She raised one surprisingly well-kept brow. "Well, my boss wouldn't've sent me out here if you didn't."

"I suppose not, no." Indicating the paste: "Will that help?"

"Hopefully."

"And if it doesn't?"

I sighed. "We switch to something else." Half to change the topic, I turned to face her and saw she fit the pattern of an Orthodox spinster, Jewish or otherwise: no makeup, long hair in wound-up braids, collared shirt, and a dark skirt to the ankles, her once-good black shoes gone dusty and cracked with age. "Miss, no offense, but what's someone like you still doing . . . *here?*"

"Someone like me? I'm not quite sure I know what you mean, dear."

"It's just . . . you seem —" Sane? Human? "—like you might have options."

"Ah, well. I've spent the last few years working on a private concern, a very particular line of inquiry; a scholarship, one might say. And despite its difficulties, this is the single best location for it I've found, as yet."

Sounds legit, I thought. But at that same moment, it was like a scrim dropped down over my eyes, like the hallway itself gave a single, slow, rippling blink. Two thoughts at the same time, superimposed: an image from my dreams sharpening quick into focus, darkening the daylight. The idea of crawling further and further in through successively smaller spaces, tunnel narrowing 'til it touched your skin, only to find you no longer had room to turn 'round, even if you wanted to: just stuck there, hot and close, jacketed in your own flesh like a ready-made coffin. Neither here nor there, forever.

"Oh yeah," I heard myself answer, from far away. "I know how *that* goes. Like when you get *so* far into a thing, dig in so deep, you just, you can't . . . get back out again."

"Something like that, yes."

"Like—an enthusiasm. Or an obsession."

"More a vocation, but yes, dear, yes. How perceptive."

Standing there smiling, studying me, her dim eyes vaguely satisfied, oddly proud. And then I was back to myself once more, world realigned with a sort of shrug—gloved hands poison-smeared, wavering slightly next to Aunt Chatty in the world's shittiest excuse for a hallway. Who reached over to pat my arm, announcing—

"Much as I appreciate your concern for my welfare, I certainly couldn't abandon this work just yet. So I'll leave you to yours, shall I? But if you *should* get a chance to speak to the management, do let them know that assigning a new superintendent wouldn't go amiss."

And with a raised eyebrow, as though letting me in on the joke, she walked on past, slow but upright.

We'd crossed paths a few times since, she always pausing to gift me a nod, no matter what else she might be in the middle of—shepherding someone even older to the elevator, or scribbling vigorously in a flip-top notebook she'd quickly tuck away, like she thought I might grab it. I didn't even know which unit she belonged to; I had no reason to wonder, let alone ask.

The last time was a few days before, at the top of Thirty-three's basement steps, while I trudged up them with a load of empty roach-traps. "No progress yet, hm?"

"Yeah, no. I just don't get it."

"Oh, evidence of things unseen is always difficult to compile, I'm afraid. As I know, from personal experience."

For all she said it lightly, the words rang true, flat, cold. Maybe that was what prompted me to throw a glance over *her* shoulder, as I reached it; the notebook was out again, and this time she wasn't quite fast enough. I glimpsed heavy black calligraphy that filled every page top to bottom, all thick curves and jagged angles—neither English nor Cyrillic, kanji or ideographs. Here and there I thought I saw numbers:

algebra? Some even higher mathematical form?

"Do you mind?" Chatty asked, flipping it shut.

"Sorry," I replied, automatically. "Your project?"

"Elements *from* it," she snapped back—then gentled her tone. "I'm sure they wouldn't interest you, dear."

Try me, I thought, but held off. And after a moment, she sighed, admitting: "These aren't mine, exactly. I transcribed them from papers belonging to an historical figure relevant to the overall subject of my investigation, a fairly obscure gentleman, by most standards. Have you ever heard of Doctor John Dee? An alchemist and natural philosopher, at the court of Queen Elizabeth the First . . . you've heard *her* name before, surely." I nodded. "He had a theory about language, you see. About the very first iteration of all primordial speech, the ur-type; that if you stripped every other language away, raised a child never teaching them even the rudiments of human speech, then if they finally spoke, *that* would be what came out. Whatever language Adam and Eve might have used in Eden, when they had no one to talk with but animals on the one hand, angels the other."

"And what—that's it, there? That tangle?"

"No, no. This is a cypher cobbled from something a seer he knew named Edward Kelley claimed was Enochian, the dialect of all Heavenly Choirs, Powers, Thrones, Dominions, etcetera. No one knows how to pronounce it, though many have tried."

"What would be the point of that, exactly?"

Chatty rocked back a bit, smiling slightly again. "The *point*, dear, is that whoever speaks Enochian with all its proper emphases intact—like a *native*—might, in theory, be able to parlay directly with those it was designed for, with no sadly outdated religious relics necessary. No prayers, no supplication . . . no clerical intervention, at all."

"Talk to angels."

"Oh, yes. Their names are Enochian, after all. And as Adam would have known, to name something—the way God Himself once commanded him to do, with every beast that creeps and crawls—is to take possession of it. To *own* it."

I looked at her, but she didn't look back. She was definitely somewhere else now, deep inside, contemplating her own mind's slow-etched wallpaper, whose pattern—I could only speculate—probably looked a lot like black mold at this point, incipient aneurysm's dull red craquelure.

"So how're we supposed to do it?" I'd already asked, out loud, before I could catch myself.

"We aren't," Chatty replied, briskly. "Not since Eve's mistake, the apple, the Fall. Not since original sin entered into every one of us, born or unborn, binding death fast to our DNA."

. . . okay.

This was getting a little weird, as she seemed to know, dialing things down from Slightly Scary Stranger to Mildly Eccentric Distant Relation almost immediately. "But, as I said, Dee had a theory. And it's that theory from which *my* work proceeds, more or less."

"Which was . . . ?"

The smile slanted, twisting to show just a peep of teeth. "Ah. Well, that would be telling."

I used to wonder what my dreams of squeezing through tiny doors into ever more tiny rooms were about, forever worming my way through cracks and crevices, face-first into the dark. But then I remembered that back in England, at the Tower of London, they used to have this punishment cell they called "Little-Ease." I'm not sure where I first heard about it, but it's stayed with me ever since: an airless, windowless space, four feet square, within which prisoners could neither entirely stand up nor entirely sit down. Instead, they'd do their time crouched over in ever-increasing agony, suffocating on their own breath until finally released, often by death.

Little-Ease no longer exists, supposedly. It was torn down, or maybe bricked in; became an entirely liminal space, rendered conceptual by history's tricks, retroactively denied: *it is not so, nor was it so, and God forbid that it should be so.* But it was, so it still is, continuously—like a penal system, Little-Ease will endure as long as any living person remembers it, even if they never experienced its horrors directly.

For anybody who's ever been in jail, these things become just a tiny bit more immediate, I suppose. Which, now I think about it, probably has some bearing on what happened next.

So now we were back in Leonora's office, me still contemplating Suit-chick in the wake of her announcement, uncertain how I was allowed to react. I glanced at Leonora, eyebrow hiking; she shrugged. Utterly unhelpful. But then again, it's not like anything needed to be outlined in neon for me to see what Suit-girl was getting at—job title aside, her own bosses didn't want her to *manage* the property around Winnick Brothers Cookery's dead shell at all, but to force a mass exodus so they could knock everything down and get to the far more profitable land it stood on. And to attain that goal, she'd gladly screw over what few residents might remain stranded on site right in their saggy old butts, Chatty included.

Not that I felt sorry for her, exactly, the crazy old bitch—except for how I suddenly *did*, so much I almost wanted to cry. Like I'd already be doing so, if my eyes weren't so damn dry.

This job, I thought, straining not to frown even with that rash between my brows rubbed raw, and all my mucous membranes tightening at once. *It's gonna kill me for sure, this fucking job. But only if I let it.*

"All right," I said, finally, prompting Suit-chick to nod, like I'd successfully jumped through some hoop. Then she leaned forward a bit, voice lowering confidentially—never a good sign—and explained.

"Truth is," she began, "we've been trying to clear Number Thirty-three for quite some time now, using all the regular methods. But the people who live there . . . well, let's just say they don't respond to the carrot *or* the stick, and leave it at that."

"What is it you *do* want me to do, then?"

Now it was Suit-chick's turn to look Leonora's way. "Obviously," she said, "I can't order you to make the infestation at Thirty-three *worse*—"

"Obviously," Leonora repeated.

"—but if you can just hold off on sealing the deal, shall we say? Clock your time, draw your pay; do what you have to, or rather, don't. Let nature . . . take its course."

"For how long?"

"You tell me."

I swallowed, considering my options. "Well," I replied, at last, "if I only *could* get inside those walls, there might be ways to accelerate the process: put down food, raise populations . . . " I trailed away, then added: "If that sounds like something you'd find useful, I mean."

Leonora gave me a narrow look over Suit-chick's shoulder, half assessing, half impressed: *nice bullshit you're shoveling there, Ginnie.* But the lady in charge must have felt willing to cut me some slack in the plausibility department, because the next thing I know she's shaking my hand and smiling, grip soft-skinned yet unrelenting in its pressure.

"Well, that'd be just great," she told me. "Pull *that* off, you can certainly write your own ticket, from now on." One last, slightly harder shake. "Or not."

In other words: *don't screw things up, especially after claiming you can un-screw them, or suffer the consequences.* I didn't hugely want to think about what those consequences might be, since nobody felt like elaborating.

"Yes, ma'am," I said, willing myself not to look away. And waited for her to let go first.

That night, when the tiny door in my dreams opened and I crawled inside, I found myself stranded, surrounded. The papery rustle of wings was everywhere, a general creep and rattle—some sort of hum, some sort of whirr, a big machine starting up in the distance, reduced to mere resonance. A vibration felt right against the eardrum, like something tongueless trying to talk.

I lay down on my dream-room's floor, in the dark, and waited for whatever it was to swarm over me in a chittering, clicking wave, its many mouths open. Didn't even close my eyes. *Let it come,* I remember thinking, incoherently. *Let it come.*

I spent most of that morning packing up my apartment, which was easier than I'd anticipated—just clothes, food, my computer and I.D., with everything else left behind. Didn't seem reasonable the Dancy Street Project would bother tracking down one lowly ex-con exterminator, but given I *was* just about to scuttle the fuck out of their little entomological warfare campaign, I also planned to dump my company phone right after. Before disappearing between the cracks, that is, like the metaphorical insect I was.

Because that was what I'd been thinking, of course, listening to Suit-chick's spiel: how since I wasn't on parole, there was literally nothing tying me to this job, no earthly reason I *had* to keep it. I mean, yes, the fees were good, and money is always better than no money (another Zillahism). But every under-the-counter disposal was one more stream of revenue I had no receipts for, one more potential audit—and predictable as my work could be, job satisfaction *was* an issue, increasingly, seeing how nothing I did was ever really, truly *done.*

Always more vermin, lurking; some fresh deposit, just breeding and waiting, right where you could never get permission to get at it. Who would you ask, after all? God? The—

(*angels?*)

So instead, I was going to do the exact opposite of what I'd promised: my *job*, the *right* way, then walk away—*fast*—and reinvent myself somewhere else, somewhere they probably wouldn't think to look, free and clear. One last suspect act of kindness, weaponized into a double middle finger on my way out the back door.

By the time I got on site, it was already afternoon. I drove into the Cookery parking lot, parked kitty-corner to Number Thirty-three, and suited up, hauling out a tub of Leonora's latest kill-'em-all mix. Glancing up slantwise, I caught a few residents peeping down on me from the building's upper areas: just backlit heads and shoulders mainly, with an occasional whitish-gray oval shoved so close against the glass it sprouted a mild suggestion of features. None of them seemed to be Chatty, but I wasn't at all sure I could tell, at this distance.

God knows what they thought I was doing, especially when I got out the sledgehammer.

I stuck the tub on my hip, haphazardly, and humped towards the building like Quasimodo. I'd already scouted out a place to start knocking in walls earlier that week, trying to determine what I was working with, the extent of the damage. I needed to know where the things leaving shit and egg-casings were actually coming from, not to mention scurrying back to, so I could reckon how many of them I'd need to kill in order to keep Thirty-three livable a tiny bit longer.

One way or the other, getting inside those walls would be the breakpoint, and whatever I saw there would determine exactly where things went next.

I began at what I assumed was the base of the garbage chute, a dumping channel running vertically down through all three floors to the basement garbage room. Thirty-three was old enough there were no assigned city garbage skips outside, mainly because the alley was far too narrow. Instead, once the garbage room was sufficiently full, the on-site superintendent—had he existed—would have carried bags full of the crap up a small, side-access stair opening directly into the same alley. I'd been down there a couple of times already to lay poison, only to find it surprisingly empty; maybe old folks just didn't generate much waste, or hoarded most of it, which probably went a ways towards explaining the insect situation in general.

The shaft was any colony's most easily accessible food source, so it made sense to start there. Since I'd still never seen any bugs during my earlier forays, however, I decided it might be more a matter of looking *around*, rather than into. Which is why I took a two-handed grip on the sledgehammer, swung it back as far as my biceps would allow and proceeded to knock a me-sized hole in the corner just outside, that deepish groin where the wall containing the garbage room door opened out from the next wall over.

Plaster flew, wood cracked. After ten to fifteen good hits, enough to open a hole big enough for head and shoulders, I thumped hard against concrete, shivering what I took to be a support; I pulled out my flashlight, stuck in between my teeth and squirmed in. I wasn't expecting much more than enough room to fit my head, a narrow cavity perhaps floored with nests and eggs where the insulation had shrunk back after drying out. But the beam of the flashlight plunged startlingly far into the blackness on either side, and the air had the thin dank chill of old stonework. I looked around, realizing this was no accidental architectural gap but a deliberately constructed passage: three feet wide at most, running *inside* the wall separating garbage room from storage room.

Holy shit, I remember thinking. *No wonder these walls looked so thick on the plans.*

It's due diligence to review blueprints for every urban site you service, but I think I might have been the only one left still doing it on Leonora's crew. That said, there was no way I'd expected something like *this*.

Before I knew what I was doing, I'd already crawled entirely inside.

There wasn't quite room to stand, so I had to move carefully, neck at an angle. I followed the passage further in but was startled to find it debouched even further into another cross-passage, this one clearly running the length of the building's outer wall. Transferring flashlight to fist, I ran its light down the floor left and right, yet could not find the end.

Concrete on the inside, brick on the out-. Pipes running overhead, occasionally T-junctioning out through the walls; plumbing, electrical, something. Cobwebs festooned everywhere, dusty as the walls themselves. They hung down like crusted lichen from the floorboards above, feathering gritty-stickily across my shoulders, my arms, the top of my head — 'til I thought I felt something tickle the nape of my neck as if it was trying to squirm between hot plastic mask and my cheek beneath, that is, and pulled my hoodie up high with a grunt of disgust.

Halfway in, I stopped and listened, breathing quiet, then nodded to myself: the sounds of insects rattled up and down the passage, getting closer. So I half-turned back to the hole, thinking to trade my hammer for the insecticide tub and slap whatever emerged with it, like I was poison-painting a fence . . .

Which is exactly when something finally *did* scramble right into my flashlight's beam and froze: grayish-brown mottled, protective coloration almost exactly matching the wooden "roof," both sorts of walls, the dust. And *big*, shit. Like rhino beetle big, a hissing cockroach crossed with a damn preying mantis. Big enough you'd need your whole hand to scoop it up and crush it.

The same way I wanted to, basically, the very second I spotted it.

It was primal, revulsion boiling up over me, making me gulp and shiver. The thing just looked wrong to me, in every possible way — how it moved, how it *was*. The way some malign and alien brain had apparently slapped its various parts together, so haphazard as to seem cruel, then dropped it to let it creep away into other people's nightmares.

Beneath a carapace-brow like a crab's, multiple eyes glinted, bulging. I stared at it, not moving. It stared back.

Then it reared up erect on its hind four legs, wings flared out like filthy cellophane, to give a distant, grinding trill. On its belly I glimpsed what almost looked like markings, far too fast to fully register, let alone read—but I saw them, somehow; I *knew* them. Recognized them, in a way that made my brain wrench.

The speech of angels, Chatty's voice murmured, soft, in my inner ear. And I felt my arm whip out again, up and back, one-handed; felt the hammer already coming down, heavy enough to wrench my shoulder 'til it screamed.

The bug whipped away, feet audibly clicking, zig-zagging across the tunnel floor. I grabbed the hammer back up out of the cracked mess it'd made, spraying chips, and blundered after—came down wham! against the bottom of one wall, then *wham!* halfway up the other, catching one wing on the upswing. Squashed it so flat it stuck to the brick as that *thing*, sad parody of a *real* insect, gave a squeal and pulled free, leaving a trail of grume. Next thing I knew, I was 'round the corner and falling headlong forwards with the hammer still death-gripped, right onto the place where that disgusting creature's top half met its ass-end.

Chitin cracked loud, and I felt the bug's guts squish in a far too satisfying way. Which is probably why I hit it again, and again, and again . . . 'til on the fifth or so hit, strike so hard my forearms rang like tubular bells, the whole floor beneath me simply collapsed.

Cypher: not a word I'd actually encountered much before, in its proper context. I looked it up, night after Chatty told me about her work: *Something of no value or importance,* was one definition; *A person of no influence, a nonentity.* But the one she'd obviously meant to use—*a secret*

method of writing, as by transposition or substitution of letters, specially formed symbols, or the like—wasn't much more reassuring. It felt furtive, somehow; covert, malignant, the act of a spy or a thief. Something all too easily lost in translation.

Think about those Bible Verse host sites—BibleGateway.com, and the like—where you can run a vaguely remembered phrase through the search function and get upwards of fifty different versions of the same basic text: King James, Wycliffe, New International, Orthodox Jewish, The Voice, God's Word, Amplified, Douay-Rheims. Rewrite any words long enough and the original phrasing, whatever it was that attracted you in the first place, falls away like spackle on a treated wall. Leaving behind—

(—what? The brickwork, the frames? A rough arrangement of individual molecules?)

Or something far deeper, especially if you were transliterating between a human tongue and . . . something else. Because if you didn't really know what you were doing, just went on ahead and kept on going anyhow—if you were already in the process of making a mistake so fundamental, so subtle, you couldn't ever see it to correct it—

Speak, Lord, for thy servant heareth. Show me Your ways.

For behold, I shall show you a great mystery; we shall not all sleep, but we shall all be changed.

I went down headfirst, drawn by my tool's weight, dust spraying high as rotten wood tore at me from every angle. I know I breathed it in, like a miasma. I know I shut my eyes.

When I opened them again, I lay somewhere gray and close, so sore all over I could barely move. I'd landed on top of my sledgehammer, driving its head deep into my own side; what felt like an open wound was actually the worst bruise of my life, affecting a section of my colon plus the lowest lobe of my liver, and may eventually have led to me having to get my gallbladder removed. Somehow, I'd managed to avoid breaking a rib outright, though the head ended up tucked under the lefthand two's edges in a way that strained both bones almost to cracking.

For a moment I lay there fighting for breath, drooling what felt like blood. Then I swallowed, coughed, and almost screamed out loud.

The dark, like the pain, eased its grip slowly—I couldn't tell if my eyes were adapting, or if there was some sort of dim fungal light seeping in. Eventually, I thought I could begin to make out shapes: outlines, silhouettes. Blunt spikes thrust upwards out of rough mounds, scattered without pattern; a ceiling supported by pillars far thinner than I liked the look of, plaster-plank mix seething with shadows. And almost right in front of me, a step-sided pyramid—a ziggurat—made of bricks salvaged from the defunct factory outside. It seemed big down here on the floor, but shrank as I rolled, gained my hands and knees, using the hammer to lever myself up by agonized degrees: even bent over, the top was roughly level with my jaw, so maybe five feet high or five and a half, at most . . .

As another wave of queasiness broke over me, I grabbed hold of the side, hearing ill-set mortar grind slightly; mask already knocked askew, I felt like I was suffocating, so I ripped it off and threw it into a corner, bouncing against the wall. And I don't know how long I stood there, wavering, before I realized I wasn't the only one I could hear breathing.

I gulped again, dipped my head, and pawed around as bile sloshed into my throat, clumsy as a drunk with a dropped bottle. Finally, however, I got my hands on my lost flashlight and found it unbroken, a tiny miracle—clicked it on, straight up into my own eyes, then slapped a hand across my face until I adapted again. Hammer still held tight in my other hand, I played the beam up and down the ziggurat, listening close.

Examined more closely, the ziggurat wasn't completely solid: the bricks had been laid to leave spaces, mortar clumsily applied only to top and bottom, so every level was pierced by a thousand black perforations too small to see through, like arrow-slits in a fortress, or air holes in an insect jar. As I moved the flashlight around, meanwhile, I saw a constellation of light flicker on the dusty air *behind* it, the beam spilling . . . well, not *straight* through, but close enough.

This structure was *hollow*. Which meant the breathing I heard came from inside it.

I bent further, ignoring the nausea. There, at my feet, a much longer slit in the ziggurat's base had been left open, large enough to slide a plate through. From this issued a terrible stink of ammonia and a spill of something pale, laid down in almost archaeological strata — the mulch of long captivity, shit marinated in piss then stamped flat, kicked back out along with desiccated scraps of food, small bones, a flood of surplus flies. As I moved forward, whatever lived in there recoiled, scraping itself on the inside of the ziggurat and drawing a soft, bit-back moan.

"*ChristAlmighty,*" I gasped, whole thing coming out stuck together; wanted to yell, but it was like my voice had crawled down my throat and died, self-strangled. Hammer and flashlight held tight, I braced them against the ziggurat's brick and let it take as much of my weight as felt safe, as I hissed through one of the slots: "Hey! You in there, are you okay?" Stupid, stupid. How *could* they be? "I'm — I have a hammer, I could get you — can I try to get you out? Please?"

No reply, save . . . after long moments . . . a sort of muffled whimpering. Like whatever —*whoever*— had their hands over their mouth.

How bad would things have to be, I wondered, and for how long, that you'd have to teach yourself not to cry?

Slowly but steadily, still hunched, still dizzy, I realized what I wanted most right at that moment was to find the person responsible and kill them. And luckily —

"Please do keep it down, dear," a familiar voice said, from behind me, tone mild as ever. "It's . . . rather important."

A glance confirmed it: Great-Aunt Chatty, slipping so deft between the pillars the dust barely touched her. Obviously, she was *well-familiar* with this place, its hidden prisoner — a point proved when, recognizing her tone, said captive's breath-rate sped up as though slapped, became rapid, hitching. A groan of pure hunger followed, underscored by the drag of a dented tin plate that came pushing out quick through the slot, so fast it clunked against the brick sides like a crushed bell.

No real *words* mixed up in any of it, Enochian or otherwise, just the pant and whine of Pavlov's dog: a truncated life, bonsai-sized and literally starved, raised in Little-Ease. If "thrown food at intermittently, but mainly left alone in the dark to rot" counts as anything like raising, and it doesn't, does it? It just *doesn't*.

Chatty just kept on watching, not even bothering to fake anything that looked like shame, let alone guilt. I'd thought her eccentric, innocent; enough so to wreck my life over, at least in principle. Whoever'd done this, though, was anything but. And—

Oh God, the rage, the *rage*. I can still taste it.

"This," I made myself begin, pointing. "Is *this*, your . . . *work*?"

"My great work, yes."

"Making somebody who can talk to angels."

She shrugged. "That's the thesis."

"Doctor Dee's, right? Stick a human fucking being in a kiln, a fucking *person*, then feed 'em whatever shit comes to hand, don't talk to 'em for, like — fucking *ever*..."

"Some might argue a child isn't *quite* a person," Chatty put in here, deceptively gentle — same way she did everything else, however evil: research, code-breaking, forcible confinement, paring someone down to the bare roots from which goddamn *angel speech* would supposedly grow. "Not yet."

I shook my head, violently. "Any kid's still *human*, lady, no matter what. Don't fool yourself."

"A baby, really, when I first put her in there. That's six years back, now — almost seven. Of all the ones thus far, she's lasted longest; such a strong, strong girl. My single best subject."

"*You put a* baby —"

"Please do lower your *voice*, dear, as I asked before. It's rather essential she not to..."

"...hear anything that could interfere with the angels talking?"

"So you do understand."

"How you're seriously *nuts*? Yeah, got that. Slower than I should've, granted, but now? Got it in *one,* you evil old bitch." She gave me a look then, slightly sad, like she might be thinking, *You're not as smart as I'd hoped, after all.* But I skipped right over that, mind racing straight to the next question. "Wait a minute, though. How'd you even get hold of a baby, 'round here?"

"Oh, money's a great help on that count, as in all things. Beside which, look around you, and *think* — this is hardly the only building. The other Dancy Street sites are full of greed, desperation and good breeding stock, just as this one harbors elderly tenants with an innate willingness to look the other way, to ignore..." She smiled once more, this time a bit more sharply. "Why do you think I've stayed here, pursuing my inquiries? This area is practically *perfect* for them."

You *have money?* I might have blurted back, had I been able. Instead, I felt that same sudden churn, that splash of disgust, hot and viscid. It lit me up, pumped my veins full of bile; I couldn't speak, couldn't think. So I acted, instead, without doing either.

Staggering back to gain room, I dropped the flashlight, heard it crunch and pop. I swung the hammer up again, almost sideways; there was no room to go high, and I didn't want to risk knocking out a pillar, but I needed speed, aim, impact. The head landed, crunching down, rocking the whole ziggurat side to side; I saw the place where two bricks intersected start to crumble, break right across, then grinned cheek-hurtingly wide as I did it again, again, again. Chatty gave an indrawn hiss between her teeth, hands flying to her mouth in a gasp of horror, as if *I* was the one committing the atrocity —

"Get back, kid!" I heard myself roar, as I reared back for yet one more fresh hit, with no idea if she could even understand me. "Get back, I'm coming in, I'm coming! I swear, I'm gonna—"

On the very last try, however, something caught my wrist in a terrible, tearing vice, biting down hard. I felt the bones grind together as I spun to look, found Chatty literally hanging off my arm face-first, hands knit above and below with her nails popping my skin as she worried at me, shook her head back and forth like a dog. I yelled at her, but she just held on tight, too busy to yell back—blood was gouting out around her mouth's seal, wrinkled lips gone red. I felt her brittle teeth move in my flesh.

Again without thinking, I slammed her head down against the ziggurat's crushed-in side at full punch, bashing her skull on the bricks. Her scalp tore, spraying red; something snapped, audibly. She let go, and I let go of the hammer, dropping it *this close* to my own foot, grabbing what was left of my wrist before I could bleed out on the floor. I knew I needed to tourniquet it, fast, but what with—my sleeve, one of my gloves? A shoelace?

Then, from the floor, I heard something impossible—a wet, muffled noise, choking broken up with vowels. Chatty, trying to talk.

I didn't want to look, but I did. Her hair went one way, her jaw the other, seeming to hang almost free. Red teeth glinted up at me, whole mouth crushed in around them, stroke-drooping. Was that a lip, or only the meat where it had been?

"Don't," I snarled at her. "Just . . . just don't. Stay down."

She rattled, blood bubbling. Spat a load of wet enamel at my shoes, mostly in pieces. Then managed, somehow, as though she hadn't even heard—

"Yuhoooo . . . yooo. Duhnt. Y'duhnt . . . knoooh."

Oh God, just shut up and die! Snapping, out loud: "I don't *want* to know."

"Bbbuhhhh . . . " The word trailed away, almost to silence, before she started over. "Buhhhh, buhhhh . . . ttttt . . . "

(*but*)

More noise cut her off, this time from inside the ziggurat: a shifting, a cracking. Bricks and parts of bricks falling together, sharp as a one-person avalanche. Which is when *they* came, that very moment, as though called—right as the badly-laid triangle behind me split open like a cocoon, a dusty stone seed-pod blooming.

With Chatty still quietly choking at my feet, hacking up blood and phlegm, the chittering started low and swept up high, a skin-puckering susurration issuing from no particular direction, or all of them. Around me, the walls and pylons seemed to blur, to froth up, the head on a beer spilling over; above, the roof's darkness kept on seething but sharpened focus, each dark point suddenly revealed as an insect, sister to the one I'd crushed. Skittering on asymmetric legs, leaping on warped and membranous wings, they came in their thousands, their tens of thousands. Chatty and I were surrounded, islets in a rising tide.

Since my arms were essentially glued together, swollen, and numb, I had no hope of grabbing up a weapon, at least not one I could swing . . . but I scrabbled at my belt anyway, looking for something, anything, 'til the fingers of my wounded hand closed on the one can of pesticide that had survived the fall intact. Clumsily, I flicked it open and turned in a circle, yellowish-white powder scattering thickly around me in a ring, like salt to ward off demons. As the chemical reek rose, the swarm recoiled, skittering over each other to clear me a path. Since I hadn't bothered to extend it around Chatty—hadn't even considered the possibility—she was nothing now but a low, faintly moving shape under a writhing bug-carpet; *good*, I thought, suddenly too exhausted to care. *Only right and proper.*

I shuffled further, shaking and stomping even as my knees slowly gave way beneath me, unconvinced I could reach whatever entrance Chatty'd come in by before I ran out of poison but determined to try. As I got to the far wall, though, the ziggurat's ruin gave yet another heave, bricks shedding like skin; I couldn't help but turn, blinking, to watch the girl inside clamber slowly free, not so much levering herself up as squirming, naked, bloody and bruised.

Her limbs were sticks, all bone and sinew; I could count every rib, even in this half-light. Worse yet, her ass and thighs were a mass of never-treated sores—runnelled, seeping scabs on top of scabs that detached as she straightened, ripping away stickily. Her never-cut hair was a woolen rat's nest, one huge colorless Polish plait matted beyond any hope of combing that'd have to be shaved or carded, picked apart like oakum. Her eyes were huge, and flat, and dead.

This was what somebody born innocent looked like, seven years on, after being denied everything they needed to be human. She'd never seen the light outside, never walked upright; hell, given the way she flailed, I wasn't sure she knew *how* to. Never been touched or spoken to. Never smelled anything but garbage, her own detritus. She was a void in the shape of a body, trembling with pain so ingrained she barely seemed to feel it—nameless, loveless, unaware. Soulless.

I don't know at what point I realized I was weeping, but I'd been doing it a while by the time I did. To try and touch her in comfort would be ridiculous, the very definition of far too little, too late—but better yet, or worse, I didn't dare. Every part of me recoiled from her, instinctively, as though the sheer horror of her existence formed an event horizon impossible to cross back from, once breached.

As if she'd heard my thoughts, the girl's head suddenly popped up, numb gaze darting, pupils blown. Trembling all over, she seemed to levitate herself upwards; before I knew it, she was half-squatting on top, broken bricks digging into her kneecaps, arms thrown wide. She opened her mouth, disclosing a surprisingly full set of teeth: carious, broken, brown. Then she drew one shuddery breath, sunken chest heaving—

—and began to sing.

It was that same drone, a scratchy buzz shading abruptly high and sweet, the insects' creepy trill. As it burst from her throat, the entire swarm exploded, throwing it back a million-fold; their call rose and never fell, louder than bombs, a rooftop-ripping hurricane wind. A choir of terrible angels. I shrieked too, my own voice lost in all that noise, good hand and bad stuck fast over one ear, head turned in a futile attempt to block it out. Because dire as the sound was, I could *just* hear an intimation, the merest ripple, of something else hidden underneath: soft, distant. Rising.

The floor, walls and ceiling erupted around me, around *her*, a living vortex. They lighted onto that stunted little muse-queen of theirs en masse, taking hold to roost all along her shoulders, back and hair in rows, like Hitchcock's birds. After which they reared back, characters of Chatty's bastard angel-jargon flickering across their bellies, and drummed their many wings all at once, an inhuman storm.

No matter their numbers, there was no way those bugs could lift even the smallest person; the physics simply wouldn't reckon. Yet I *know* I saw that girl rise into the air, however slowly—feet dangling, a puppet exiting stage up. I know she glanced my way as it happened, with those empty eyes, and when gaze met mine, I know I couldn't look away.

Impossible.

Her lips moved, or seemed to: words, or symbols? Was it Edward Kelly's cypher? Was her pronunciation correct?

Go, I thought I heard, clearly, inside my skull. *Go now and stay away. Don't look back,* or come *back, ever . . .*

. . . but thank you, too. Yes. Thank you.

(so go)

And all at once there was a split in the maelstrom, a way through, only big enough for one. I took it, gladly.

(*go*)

I remember exiting a door in Thirty-three's storage room, hidden behind a false locker, and taking the stairwell steps two at a time, almost slipping as I ran down. I remember kicking the exit door open, as the whole building started to shake, and lunging outside, air thick on my skin, ears still whirring. And then I remember the entire gray-brown brick box collapsing in on itself with a boom, dust-cloud like some vast shapeless creature leaping up and out, filling the sky.

I sat in my car as police cars and ambulances rolled in, sirens wailing, and treated my wounds by the fire trucks' flashing lights. Since nobody seemed to notice I was there, however, I just tied up my wounds and drove away—made it out of town in an hour and a half, holding fierce to consciousness, my knuckles white on the steering wheel. I went and kept on going.

Though I checked the Web each day after that for a month, Dancy Street's collapse was only mentioned once, and blamed on structural fatigue. The city council called for an inquiry, naming a certain consortium of slumlords as "people of interest," though nothing really came of it. No mention of an emaciated girl's body being found anywhere in the rubble, either, not that I'd really thought there would be.

Eventually, I reached somewhere I felt safe enough to stop and lay down in the dark of a locked motel room, bracing myself. But the nightmares didn't come, for once—not that night, or any other. They were gone too, like everything else.

Do you know the definition of mystery? It's not just an unsolved problem, but a ritual, a secret rite or method of worship—something lost and found against all odds, all good advice, repulsive in its very fascination. Or perhaps part of something much larger, a fragment glimpsed sidelong through bubbled, wavy glass of the sort left over from another time—not designed to let in anything but light, and not enough of that to truly illuminate anything.

Because there's only ever enough light to show just how *much* darkness there is, everywhere, and that's the sad, hard truth. So much darkness, and so damn little of everything else.

But as Great-Aunt Chatty should surely have known, even the most arcane history will teach us nothing, unless we let it. Which is why all mysteries, no matter how profound, truly demand solution, just as all secrets eventually demand telling—but only to the right person, you understand: a co-conspirator, an heir, a repository. A literal secret sharer. And that's because mysteries are meant to be passed on, like diseases, because contagion via strictly defined transmission vectors is the only way they're guaranteed survival.

Maybe Chatty's mystery died with her; I'd like to think so, anyhow. I really would. Except for the fact that she had to've learned what she knew from someone, somewhere . . . and if you can't find the source, it doesn't matter if you burn the whole colony to ash and soak the site with poison, because all your work's been for nothing.

No matter how you try to convince yourself otherwise, the infestation *will* come back.

What's the Bible say—*the wicked flee when no man pursueth*? Well, that's been me, all this time: always running and running, never knowing exactly from what; always bending my ear to the wind while expecting to hear the sound of wings, far away, but getting closer. Always waiting for the dreams to return, a thousand times smaller, deeper, darker.

And all because I know, just like *you* know too, now: how the world's walls are hollow, full of hidden things, and far more fragile than you think.

That's why I wrote it down here, so I never have to say it right out loud or think of it again—so I can close my eyes, trust *you* to read on and act if the truth scares you that much, to be the works without which faith is hollow. Yet with these last few words, I still feel memory's mouth seize and gnaw at me once more, masticate me alive and spit me back out half-chewed, to pray in vain that the next time I'm swallowed might be my last.

That sound, meanwhile—what *is* that sound, inescapable even when inaudible, underneath it all? Some universal mechanism's whine, through whose mighty gears we scuttle, scuffle, breed? An angel's awful trill?

Such cruel things we are, damned soul-deep or soulless, not that it matters much, either way. Pest-killers turned pests, clogging the cosmos's workings: we think ourselves unseen, but are we? *Can* we be? Or are there just so many of us we can't help spilling out into plain sight, inviting our own extermination?

Are we culled already, intermittently and efficiently, without even knowing it?

One day, I'll wake in darkness hearing something speak my name, and I know I will be changed. Wings will break straight out my back, painful as any birth—maybe two or four, maybe six, or more. And then I'll fly: upwards, downwards, outwards. Into darkness or light, not that it matters, either way.

Just away, from here. From me.

From everything.

For now, I sleep on in my Little-Ease, still and close as the dead. Hoping—no doubt in vain—to be changed before I wake.

T̲he H̲arrow

THE EARTH IS old and full of holes, Lydie Massenet's mother used to say, at least once a day, back when she was still Lydie Pell. Its crust is thin, and underneath there's nothing but darkness. A rind, that's all we live on; just thin ice, waiting for it to thaw and crack. No need to dig, really—if they want to find you, they will. Never trust anything that comes out of a hole.

And: *Okay, Mom,* Lydie would say, the way her father had taught her to. *That's good. That's fine.* Then just smile and nod, all the time staring off at nothing much, something invisible—contemplating Mars, he called it—until her mother finally stopped talking.

You have to know this, Lydie, if nothing else, her mother told her. *Darkness shifts, darkness conceals; it's impossible to know what's hiding inside it, no matter how hard you try. But if history teaches anything, it's that what we don't understand, we fear . . . and what we fear, eventually, we come to worship, if only to keep it in its rightful place. To make sure it doesn't come after us.*

Yes, Mom. Okay. Sure.

'Till, one day: *Stop saying that, goddamnit!* her mother yelled and slapped Lydie across the face, so hard her glasses cracked in half. That was the day her father brought Doctor Russ home, the day before her mother went somewhere else—first for a rest, and then, after everything they did to her while she was there had utterly failed to make her well enough to come home again, to stay.

What's wrong with her, Daddy? Lydie asked her father, at last, to which he only shook his head and sniffed, trying to pretend he hadn't been crying.

Honey, I wish to God I knew, was all he said, in return. And hugged her a little too long, a little too tight.

By April, Lydie couldn't stand it anymore. "I have to learn how to drive," she said to her husband, Ethan.

"Told you," he replied.

Thing was, in Toronto proper, you just didn't need to have a car, let alone a license—*she* certainly hadn't her first twenty-one years of life. Lydie had vague memories of having passed the Young Drivers of Canada exam's written portion, once upon a time, but more as a personal challenge; to go further required money she was loath to spare, at the time, and after that there was always the subway, or streetcars, buses, even taxis. Living in the downtown core, where she and Ethan first met, meant you could speed-walk almost anywhere you needed to in an hour or less.

Five anniversaries in, however, the powers that be decided Toronto proper was too expensive a place to rent offices, relocating wholesale to Mississauga. No big deal for Ethan, who'd grown up there. But to Lydie, it was the ends of the earth—"suburbs" squared, with no sidewalks, no easy-access stores. For a few seconds, the day they'd arrived, she'd fantasized about dragging her shopping cart the equivalent of five blocks to the local GO Train station, then investing in a four-hour/twelve-dollar return trip just to pick up enough food for the week from her previous neighbourhood's supermarket.

"Oh, no need," her mother-in-law had offered helpfully when she voiced this idea. "There's a mall, just twenty minutes northeast."

"Can I walk it?"

An odd look. "I . . . really wouldn't, dear."

In the morning, she saw for herself just why: the sole connecting road was a highway turned freeway, overpass after overpass looping sharply up, around and down, like J. G. Ballard porn brought to life. Standing there in shock, she couldn't keep from asking Ethan: "People *live* like this?"

"Well, yeah, Lyd, apparently so. And most of them manage just fine."

"How?"

He shot her a pitying look. "They have *cars*."

That morning, she woke with a headache-seed lodged right between her brows, hard and sharp as Bosch's Stone of Folly. Google gave her a list of numbers to call, trying to line up an appointment with an Adult Drivers instructor. By noon she was still on her cellphone, out in the backyard—another unfamiliar Mississauga oddity, weird combination of luxurious and annoying—when she came across what she'd eventually call the artifact: felt something uneven shift under her foot as she stepped back, almost tripping her, then squatted to squint at the ground, regardless of how high her skirt might hike. There, just protruding out of the earth with its uppermost portion wreathed in grass (a tiny crown, promise-green and fertile), a rough-carved, triangular little face peeped up at her, framed by a pair of short horns or antennae—one broken off jaggedly, almost at the root.

Black rock, lighter than it looked, and warm to the touch once she'd scratched it free, ruining Monday's manicure. Her fingers curled 'round it instinctively, an almost sensual grip, to find it fit the hollow shaped between thumb, forefinger and palm, as if made for it.

Some sort of insect on top, yes, carapaced and six-limbed. But in the center, where its thorax should be, something else sat instead: the sketch of a human skull, empty-socketed and noseless, grinning wide. With a neat little hole placed just where its brow-ridge should be, for no apparently obvious reason.

"What's that?" Ethan asked when he came home to find her sitting at the kitchen table, dinner not even slightly started, still staring at it. And: "I don't know," Lydie answered, barely looking up; just kept on studying the bug-skull-thing in her hand, 'til at last he sighed and called out for pizza.

Later, she took pictures with her phone and Google Images-ed the result. A trail of links (*insect totems, catal huyuk, gobekli tepe, lbk culture, tallheim death-pit, herxheim*) led her to something recognizable: prehistoric trepanning, the procedure of cutting a hole in the skull to relieve cranial pressure, as of a subdural haematoma. Sometimes done for ritual purposes, or so various archaeologists claimed . . . but in Mesoamerica, at least, those waters had been muddied by the fact that prisoners' and sacrificial victims' skulls were often routinely pierced to facilitate the creation of skull-racks: rows on rows of severed heads, hung up on pegs or hooks.

The hole goes at the back, usually, she thought, tapping a finger against her teeth. *Or on top. Never in front.*

Between the brows, though, or slightly higher—there was a symbolism there, right? The pineal gland. The third eye.

Around two, she lay down next to Ethan with her eyes open, contemplating the ceiling while he snored. Thinking: *I wonder if there's more.*

When she and Lydie's father were kids, there'd been a girl, Lydie's mother used to tell her. And one day, when they were all out in the woods playing, this girl had somehow stepped . . . wrong, laid her foot on the one place she shouldn't have, and broke through, opening up a hole. Had tumbled down into what later proved to be a cave that went straight down, too deep to see the bottom, and with no earthly way of ever getting back up out, once you were in.

A story grew up amongst the group of children Lydie's mother ran with, afterwards, that if you were to go to that hole, that cave, and hang your head out over the edge—if you did that, and whispered your greatest fear or wish or dream down into the black pit below, while clinging on for dear life with both hands—then if you only waited long enough, a voice would answer. And that voice would tell you if your dream, or wish, or fear would . . . if it *should* . . . come true.

Whose voice, Mom?

No one knows.

Didn't anyone ever ask?

Oh, no. No. That would be . . .

Here Lydie's mother had trailed away into silence, one so long Lydie had thought at the time it might signify the conversation was over, before finally adding, minutes later—

. . . never, no, never. No one would dare.

Lydie studied her hands for another few beats of her pulse, letting the moment stretch on. Then asked: *Did* you *ever do that?*

Lydie's mother swallowed.

Once, yes, she said, reluctantly. *Only once. And that was a mistake.*

Why? No reply. *But . . . did it answer you, Mom?*

And: *No*, her mother replied, with a sad, angry sort of hunger. *But that's just as well, isn't it? Because you can't trust such things, I've told you that already . . . those sorts of places, the earth's open holes. The dark, and the ones who live there.*

Why not?

Because . . . they lie.

"What is it you're digging, dear, exactly?" her mother-in-law asked on Friday, when she turned up to take Lydie shopping. Lydie smiled and drew her gardening gloves off, pausing to thwack them clean against the stake she'd sunk to mark her initial excavation; dirt fell in clumps, dusting her boots. "Flowerbed," she replied, without blinking.

"Ah. Eh—isn't that one already, over there?"

"Sure. I just . . . wanted more."

"A little project, to keep you busy 'til driving school?"

"You got it."

Ethan never even bothered to ask what she was doing out there, all day, every day—not after that first night. Not so long as she got her cooking done in the morning and made sure there was something for him to eat when he came home.

"Boss might want to come for dinner," he told her, skimming headlines on his iPad, as she catalogued her latest finds: more insects, some mammals, even a figure or two. Through the window, the tarp she'd thrown over the hole caught her eye, dun and dull, flat as a cataract. Without prompting, her mind went to those other things she'd uncovered, the ones she'd never bring inside: some locked in the shed, others still underground, concealed by the dig's lip. Down in the dark with the worms, where no one would see, unless—one day soon, perhaps— she decided she wanted them to.

"Better to take her out, don't you think?" she suggested, smoothly. "That place with the steak, maybe—the Korean banquet-house. You remember."

"Oh yeah, that's right. Where we took Mom and Dad for their fiftieth."

"That's the one."

"Mmm, good call, hon. She'd like that."

"There you go."

Some people say God turned the world upside down once, Lydie's mother whispered, into the close, hot air of her small, dim hospital room. Just for fun. And many strange things came up out of the earth, then, things trapped down there for a hundred thousand years, ever since the world was made . . . just like the Flood, but different. And many bad people joined with these things, and flourished, and many good people died screaming. Until finally, when He didn't find it quite as funny anymore, God flipped it all back over again, and made everything the *way it was. Like when you lift up a rock to see the bugs crawling underneath, and when you're bored, you just drop it again, and squash them; you don't have to care what happens, because they're just bugs, after all. And better yet, it's not like you have to see it.*

But some people say He never did flip it back again at all, Lydie's mother whispered, later. That's why things are so bad up here, even though God made us and everything around us. Because this world, all we see, was never meant to be on top at all. It was meant to be hidden, kept down, trapped. Because where we live, right now . . . we live in hell. What was meant to be hell.

Shush, Irma. For Christ's sake, shush.

(But: Where did the people who were meant to be in hell live, then? Lydie used to wonder. And the things down there in the dark, the people who weren't people, the ones her mother kept on warning her about . . . who were they? Was that meant to be heaven, down there?)

What happened to that girl, anyways? Lydie was finally unable to keep from asking her father, one night, as he stroked her mother's hair back from her rigid, sweating face. The one from the story. The one who fell into the hole.

Oh, well . . . they never did find her, honey, though they looked a good long time, all the time your mom and me were at school together. And that's why you should stay away from places like that—in the woods, under the ground. To stay safe.

But: Karl, why would you lie to her that way, our own daughter? Her mother broke in, suddenly. You know as well as I do that she did come back, eventually . . . all cold and wet and naked, knocking on her family's door and crying, in the middle of the night. But they knew they shouldn't let her in, because they were old now, and she—she was the same, just a kid. Just like the last time they saw her.

Irma, please, be quiet. My God, why won't you ever keep quiet? You'll frighten her to death.

At this, Lydie's mother's lips drew back; you couldn't call it a smile, not quite, for all it involved lips turning upwards. Not after you'd spent some time alone with it.

Oh no, she said. No, she's not frightened—are you, darling? Don't listen to him, Lydie; go where you want, do what you want. Go dig. Go whisper in every hole you see, for all anybody cares.

See what you get, then.

In agriculture, a harrow (often called a set of harrows, in a plurale tantum sense) is an implement for breaking up and smoothing out the surface of the soil, distinct from the plough, which is used for deeper tillage. Harrowing is often carried out on fields to follow the rougher finish left by ploughing operations. The purpose of harrowing is to break up clods of soil and provide a finer finish, a good tilth or soil structure, suitable for seedbed use.

In Christian mythology we speak of "the harrowing of hell," Jesus's descent into the underworld during his three days of death. In this case, the word "harrow" derives from the Old English bergian, meaning to harry or despoil—the idea that Christ invaded and triumphed over hell, releasing all those kept captive there, including redeeming Adam and Eve, the fount of all original sin.

"Excuse me," a voice said, from behind the back fence.

Lydie bookmarked her page and set the iPad aside. Someone was looking in at her through the narrow mesh of the gate next to the shed, so dense it barely suggested their eyes, like the facial grille of an Afghan *chadri*—female by the voice, Lydie could only assume, which was husky, flute-y. Though the level of the shadow "she" threw did suggest a fairly unusual height.

"I'm sorry," Lydie said, automatically. "Can I help you?"

"I hope so, yes," the voice said. "Could I come in and talk to you, just for a minute?" Quickly adding, a moment later, as Lydie hesitated: "Boy, that *does* sound sinister, doesn't it? Better to come back later, maybe, when you're not all alone. I'll bring pamphlets."

"Oh, no, no, no," Lydie found herself protesting, hand already on the latch. "I'm—it's fine, really. I just . . . wasn't expecting anybody."

As she opened the gate, the woman—it *was* a woman, now Lydie saw her up close; she was almost sure—smiled, lips canting sidelong like a slow-typed emoticon (back-slash, then semi-colon plus an apostrophe, to mark where that dimple formed closed-quotes punctuation) and stepped inside. Her skin was aggressively tanned, hair bleached at the top and brown at the tips as though she'd been out in the sun for weeks somewhere far hotter than here and held back with a tight-wound bandana so low it brushed the tops of her equally pale eyebrows.

"Paula Neath," she announced. "From the Society for Ecological Rebalance."

While: 1. in or to a lower position; Lydie's brain filled in, automatically. Below. 2. underneath, prep. 3. under. 4. farther down than. 5. lower . . .

She shook her head, scattering words, and held out her hand, smiling too. "Lydie Massenet. I don't think I've ever heard of you."

"Well, we're a fairly recently formed project. Most of us were doing other things before we got the call . . . I was in Turkey, for example, tracking genetic variation in honeybees, locust migration patterns, that sort of thing. But actually, what I'm here to talk about is bats."

"That's an interesting subject-shift."

"Not really. All part of the same ecosystem." Paula jogged her head towards the yard's back left corner. "Now, the reason I wanted a word is that as it so happens, your property corners onto this block's drainage ditch—do you know where that is?"

Lydie nodded. "Runs under the mouths of all the driveways on the south side, then dips down under the street. Tell you the truth, I hate that thing: when it rains, it's a stream; the rest of the time, it's a sump, stagnant. It stinks."

"Exactly—perfect for breeding mosquitos, which spread West Nile disease. Previously, the city's plan to deal with that involved spraying, but we're seeing some very alarming fallout from that . . . denuded bee population, for one, which affects pollination, which cuts down on new growth generally. So, we'd like to put up a grouping of bat-houses in various areas, including right here."

"Like a birdhouse, but for bats."

"Exactly." That smile again. "I'll be honest, Mrs. Massenet—"

"Lydie."

"—a lot of people seem to think the idea of opening their arms to flying mice is a bit of a deal-breaker. One lady was convinced they spread rabies, for example; that sort of stereotype. Old wives' tales, to put it frankly."

"Didn't want guano in their hair?"

"Didn't want *bats* in their hair." They both chuckled. "Foolish, I know. Bats are nocturnal, far more interested in insects and nectar than anybody's follicles. You'd barely see them, except at dusk."

"Sounds sort of nice to me. Do they make noise?"

"Not within the hearing-range of most humans."

Lydie shrugged. "Okay, then. I'm sold."

"Wonderful! You won't regret it—we'll be in and out, no muss, no fuss. And the public health benefits will be striking, once the bats have had a bit of time to do their work."

"I don't doubt it. So... You must be from the university, right? Did they bus you in?"

"Most of us, yes; some of us live here, in the area."

"Nice to work where you live."

"Yes." Paula's sharp eyes—an odd non-color, neither gray nor blue, almost clear when glimpsed straight-on—shifted from Lydie's, focusing instead on the tarp, as well as the earth piled neatly next to it. "You've been doing some work of your own, by the look of it."

"Oh, uh . . . not officially. I mean—"

"May I see?"

"Well . . . "

. . . why not?

Surprising, in its way, the idea that she would *want* to show Paula, a complete stranger, what she'd so carefully managed to keep from everyone else—her loved ones, supposedly. The people who loved her. And yet, that did seem to be what that usually silent voice deep inside her was suggesting . . . that midnight whisper, sexless and dark, ambiguous as Paula's own throaty purr.

(*Don't listen, Lydie. They* lie.)

So—

"Yes," Lydie replied, and moved the tarp aside, allowing Paula to see: the hole, and what it concealed. A gaping, sod-lipped mouth which never quite promised answers, for everything else it delivered: oddities, rarities, the strange, the unique. Something you could hold in your hand and study, but never fully understand, except perhaps in dreams.

The dig went ten feet in, these days, much of it almost straight down—a ladder she'd found in the shed providing access, tall enough to reach the roof when unfurled—and with an odd little trailing twist at the bottom, brief sloping sketch of further possibilities. Ethan would be horrified; Lydie couldn't even venture a guess at what her mother-in-law would think. They were such sweet people, really, it seemed only *right* to hide the truth where it couldn't hurt them . . . kinder, in its way, than the alternative.

If Mom'd only done that, she found herself thinking, sometimes, as she hadn't let herself for years, *then things would've—might've been—very different.*

Paula took in everything Lydie'd spent the last two months doing, then hiding—the open wound of her craziness, at long last laid bare—with one swift, shrewd, searching glance. Then turned her back, stepping down into darkness, sinking 'til all Lydie could see of her was the top of her head; her voice seeped back up, dirt-magnified, made hollow at the bone. "Fascinating," she said. "This is . . . Neolithic, would you say?"

"Older, maybe. I think it got folded under when the glaciers shifted."

"Yes, very likely. You're extremely perceptive, Mrs. Massenet."

Lydie shrugged, embarrassed. "Hardly. I mean—it's weird to

think about, something like *this* under our feet, just hidden away . . . still so perfect after so many years, with all this suburban crap slapped on top. But there you go."

"It is odd," Paula agreed, words deepening further as she bent to rummage through the slick bottom of the shaft, picking and choosing. "But no more so than anything, really. The earth is older than any of us care to acknowledge, and *everywhere* was somewhere else, once. Most people simply don't bother to look any closer than they have to at what they already think they know, unless . . . "

" . . . unless something *makes* them."

"Exactly."

(*Old, and full of holes. But do not put your hand down to see, because*)

Lydie took a small, shallow breath. There was something — she wasn't sure what. A kind of wobble, at the corner of her eyes; black spots hovering, blinking. Was she going to pass out?

A few moments later, however, Paula had made back up the ladder in two massive steps and was standing once more on the lip's moustache-like rut of trodden grass. Extending one huge, muck-filled hand, she scoured an entirely new type of totem free between her thumb and forefingers, with swift, almost brutal strokes: a squat, oval thing, bulgy at both ends like a toad, and small enough even she might've mistaken it for a mere clot of mud-wrapped rock . . . except for the fact that she knew where to look, and what for.

"Beautiful," Paula named it, reverently. "How many have you found, so far?"

"Oh, more and more, usually five, eight a day . . . sometimes ten, if I can dig uninterrupted 'til my husband comes home. They don't ever seem to stop. I'm thinking votive objects, a whole cache of them, brought here on pilgrimage and buried, as some sort of — prayer, or sacrifice. Some sort of payment."

"You've done your research." As Lydie shook her head: "No? Then your instincts are *very* good, considering. Nice work, either way."

"I took archaeology in university," Lydie offered. "Just one course a year, but I kept it up all the way through my degree; I'd've liked to go back, to specialize, but . . . "

"Things happen, yes—sadly, almost always. We move away from our dreams, or they move away from us; seem to, at any rate. But sometimes, the universe provides a second chance." Here Paula closed her hand, tucking the totem away, and watching as Lydie couldn't stop herself from flinching. "May I keep this? Not forever, believe me . . . just for a few days. I'd like to show it to my supervisor."

"Um . . . all right, sure, okay. You do that."

"I promise I'll bring it back soon, after the bathouse goes up. Would that be acceptable?"

" . . . yes."

That smile again, a little wider. "Then it's a deal."

Gone, moments later, as though she'd never been. Only the tarp, peeled back like a lid, gave any evidence of her passage. Lydie stood there looking at it for a few more breaths, thinking: *You need a break, food, a minute. Go inside. No more today.*

But the sun was hot and bright, the cool, dark hole inviting. A minute more, therefore, and she was already halfway down—far enough inside to glance back up, just for a second, and almost think she saw the hole itself blink shut, grass-fringed rim knitting like eyelashes, to shutter away her from the harsh surface world forever.

So nice, she thought, happily, going down on both knees to grub in the mud some more. *So very nice, always, to come home.*

The bathouse went up both fast and easy, as advertised. A week on, Lydie watched its inhabitants fly up at twilight, scattering like thoughts into the night as they chased their food, the next echo, each other. By bedtime, undressing in front of the window that looked down onto the backyard, she felt as though could still hear them twittering, even though she knew they probably weren't there. Beneath its tarp-lid, the hole gaped open, its presence always a slightly painful, slightly pleasurable ache; she lay there trying not to think about it but enjoying when she failed.

"Today wasn't your first class, was it?" Ethan asked, sleepily, from beside her.

"What?"

"Well, you said six weeks . . . " No reply. "You missed it, didn't you? Oh, honey."

"I can make it up."

"Yeah, hope so."

Annoyed, Lydie turned over, scoffing. "C'mon, Ethan, they want our money, don't they—*your* money. Of course I can."

The next day, however, she was back down in the hole (cell phone still charging on the bedside table, blissfully forgotten) when Paula's long shadow fell over her, making her look up. And: "Hey!" Lydie called. "So you *did* come back, after all."

"I said I would."

"Uh huh. Your supervisor . . . he like the artifact?"

"Very much. I've got it, if you want it back."

"Just give me a sec."

More like thirty to finish up, thirty more to clamber free, wiping the sweat from her eyes. Paula stood there, toad-rock already extended, offered up; Lydie put out her hand as she dropped it, fisting the totem gratefully, as if reclaiming a lost piece of herself. She gave a cave-deep sigh.

"That feels good," she'd said out loud, before she could think to stop herself.

Paula smiled. "I thought it would. Now—if you don't mind me disturbing you just a *little* bit further, might I possibly be able to see what's in the shed?"

No actual rack, just a long, low trio of shelves which had once held flowerpots, before Lydie relocated them. She'd cleaned the skulls off carefully, one by one—each so muddy they'd initially looked like they were sculpted from clay—by first letting them dry before going at them with a variety of unofficial find-cleaning tools, paring away dirt and grime with brushes meant for paints or makeup, scaling the eye-sockets with wire loops to remove as much detritus as possible before breaking out the sand, the bleach soaks, the polyurethane sprays. Now they grinned in welcome, display-organized left to right, until Paula gingerly picked up the first on the uppermost row, raising it towards the light.

Each came with a hole just above where the bridge of the nose would be, if there was a nose, mirroring the totems, and on each the hole at first seemed differently shaped, though careful examination revealed another, more subtle pattern of variation. For in those holes, so seamlessly fitted they almost appeared to have been individually made *for* the space it now occupied, Lydie had laid each of the totems she'd dug up carefully to rest: insect, bird, snake, bat, toad, plus some sort of low, broad thing with long claws, squat legs and a blunt, blind head, like a mole or badger. A catalogue of every crawling and creeping thing which ever forced itself through some crack in the earth and hid itself inside, trading light for dark, at the urging of some hidden, hollow voice.

"Thought they were signs of trepanning, at first," Lydie heard herself explain, her own tone thinning, flattening, words tumbling out in a breathy, secretive rush, as though she feared being stopped before she could finish. "Even though they were in the wrong place. I didn't even think to match them up for . . . must've been weeks, a month. A happy accident."

"Often the way," Paula murmured. "And then what?"

"I started thinking about why. The point of the exercise." Lydie paused, feeling her way, waiting for the words to suggest themselves. "What you could hope to—extract, that way. From the same place people used to think visions came from, or dreams . . . the seat of enlightenment."

"The *ajna*, or brow chakra. Where things open up."

"Yeah, but not if something's blocking it—fear, maybe. Desire, Some kind of . . . lower instinct. Like an animal."

"And you think that's what they were removing."

"Metaphorically, it makes a certain kind of sense—I mean, no *sense* at all, really. But still . . . that *is* what it looks like, to me: like they were trying to create a completely new way of seeing. A totem for every hole, a congealed bit of nightmare, a filter that needs to be removed before you can see clearly. The plug that keeps us all from letting something out—"

"—or in."

"Or in, yes. The light . . . "

(*the dark*)

Unable to keep from connecting the dots, now it'd finally been said—from seeing the hole, the place left empty for an answer, and being therefore driven to fill it. To keep from wondering whether that had perhaps been her mother's problem all along, solution inherent in its own equation: *could* she have been cured all along, and this easily? A single, fairly simple operation, just one; cut a hole, take out what you find there and throw it away, down into the dark. Just offer it up to whatever wants it and find the courage to finally accept things *as they really goddamn* are, without having to be afraid. And then . . .

. . . and then.

Standing there wound down, sunk inside herself, no longer able to tell whether or not she was saying any of this out loud, or what. Then something at the corner of her gaze again, a black flicker; she looked up. Just in time to see Paula put down the skull (carefully, gently, *reverently*) and reach up, behind her head, to flick open some sort of knot or clip, slackening her headband until it was loose enough to unwind. Which she began to do, one long fold at a time, without haste or worry—slow and careful, the very same way she told Lydie, still smiling—

"I *knew* we were right about you, Mrs. Massenet . . . Lydie. Though of course, I haven't been as entirely honest, from the beginning, as I might have hoped to be; I knew you already, you see, that first day I came here. *Of* you, at any rate."

Lydie swallowed, dryly. "Oh?" she managed, eventually.

"Yes . . . as Lydie Pell, to be exact. Through your mother."

One twist, then another, then another—just one more, the final one. Leaving Paula's forehead bare at last, high and broad and smooth, yet pitted centrally with a perfect shell of scar tissue, cracked just a hint at its core: the very same place where Lydie could feel that intermittent migraine-seed of hers re-forming, bone-planted but pushing upwards and out, threatening to bloom. Because here she was at last, arrived, like she'd always somehow known she one day would be: this place, this very moment, teetering on the brink and wondering just what might be lurking under there, waiting, in the dark. A naked pineal bud, eyelid-furled, waiting to breach the scar's tissue-plated embrace, sip at the air, twitch and blink?

But: *does it matter, Lydie?* her mother replied, wearily, memory-locked. *The hole has its own reasons, always. Do you really want to know what they are?*

Inside the bathouse, the sleeping bats cooed and scrabbled, shrilling sleepily.

"I fell in a hole once, a long time ago," Paula went on, stroking down along the ridge that threatened to bisect her open, guileless gaze with one pinkie delicately lifted, as though she were about to serve tea. "Just like this one. And it was scary, at first: so dark, so deep. But after a while, once my eyes adjusted, I found that I didn't want to get out again at all, let alone go home. Because there were *so* many wonderful things down there, to see, and do, and be. Wouldn't you like to know what?"

"Do I have a choice?"

"Always. You always have a choice."

Which sounded plausible, and not, both at the same time—a truth, thinly disguised as a lie. Or vice versa.

Tongue leather, head swimming. Migraine between her eyes, turning in a tightening spiral, like a screw. Like the coin-shaped burr hole a trephine leaves behind, after the flesh has been cut away and the skull pierce, to show the sweet gray-pink beneath. *Thinking: So the first harrowing was me breaking up the earth and sifting it for traces, exposing more and more of this buried ruin. But the second harrowing will be a descent into the underworld, a sort of anti-transfiguration . . . instead of rising into the sky, sinking into the earth and burrowing down, fertilizing it with yourself, a hole inside a hole. Becoming, at last, the mulch from which something new will grow.*

Lydie looked down, then up again, meeting Paula's gaze with her own. Felt herself nod.

"I thought so," Paula said, happily. "Now—hold still."

And Lydie did, drawing herself taut, rigid, eyes wide. Trying not to flinch as the wickedly curved black stone blade Paula pulled from behind her back made its necessarily painful mark, x-signing the spot where her Folly-stone hid, first one way, then the other. 'Til it radish-rosed a great peel of skin, parting the bloody petals key-into-lock smooth, to lay the slick white bone bare at last and open her up in one swift punch, digging the hole to set her final nightmare free.

Then down, always down, curve after curve, counter-clockwise— following the signs which marked her path 'til she could go no more: markings, so luminous and many-layered, on stone which had seemed empty under light, lit up like stars now darkness led the way. Until the surface disappeared. Until Ethan and the rest fell away. Until there was nothing left but one step and the next, over and over: the signs, the path, its eventual end.

(*Lydie, don't*)

The mouth of the cave, whispering in her blood. Her question, and its answer.

(*don't trust it*)

Like you never did, mother? Lydie thought, unsympathetic. Remembering Paula, whose family had cast her out instead of welcoming her back; Paula, who took the gifts they spurned, and grew to fit them. Paula, her three eyes shining, beckoning to her from the very, very bottom of the hole, the once-top of some inverted mountain huge enough to dwarf Chomolungma.

Here at the bottom, where she finally had worth, and truth, and purpose. Where in led out, and out back in. Where no one mattered more than she did, at least for task at hand.

I walk the harrow, downwards-tending, Lydie Massenet Pell thought, wiping her own blood from her pitifully weak, light-dependent lower set of eyes, while concentrating hard enough to let the uppermost of all three show her the way.

Dragging my blades, ploughing 'til there is no more left to plow, waiting below 'til harvest comes, and we all ascend. 'Til the pale sun shrinks so far it becomes nothing more than just another star in a half-forgotten sky.

Above her, the rock, like choirs. Below her, the dirt, like flesh, and blood, and food. The great, uprooted currents of the earth, pulling her towards its burning, pulsing, molten heart.

Home.

Every Angel

. . . is terrible.
—Rainer Maria Rilke.

I T ALL STARTS when Darger's boss sends them down to the St. Clair Ravine underpass, to catch him an angel.

Halfway through February, just after Valentine's Day, and there's sleet falling from the sky in messy chunks, slicking everything it touches with a thin skin of ice; it's supposed to go down to minus 17 in the GTA tomorrow, which'll at least cut traffic down to a minimum. But if English Bob Purefoy's even got the heat in his loft *on*, you'd never fucking know it—it's all Darger can do to keep from hugging his hands under his armpits like a shivery five-year-old, ruining his street cred forever. Every time he even opens his mouth, he half-expects to see his own breath. Not Bob's, though, no matter how long he talks, and Bob sure does love to monologize. That'd be 'cause Bob's probably got an interior temperature of slightly less than room, at the best of times.

"...an' I want Kev to take his little videocorder wiv 'im, see what he can get on tape, right? So's I can see for myself." Another hairpin swerve, pinning Darger with that blowtorch stare. "I *do* 'ope you're listenin', 'Enry. Wouldn't wanna 'ave to repeat anyfing."

"Heard you fine, Bob: Go down, take some footage, bring it back to you. Then what?"

"Well. Then we'll just 'ave to see, won't we?"

Guess so.

You better believe Darger knows better than to let the shrug he can already feel forming hit his shoulders, though; Bob doesn't much like to be mocked, or even to feel like he might be *being* mocked, no matter whether he actually is or not. The last time that little personality quirk became superlatively apparent was back when Veve still worked for him — Veve the late and unlamented, who used to tell everybody his Momma was some voodoo queen from New Orleans, so they should pronounce his name with the proper Franglish Cajun oomph if they wanted to stay on his good side: That's vay-*vay*, motherfucker, like them designs they draw in chalk. Ain't you never watched the Discovery Channel?

Which Bob actually had, funnily enough — watched it religiously, you might say, just like he did almost every other goddamn thing. 'Cause Bob has this real *deal* about religion, the whole nine yards through damnation to retribution to confession to salvation and whatever else lay beyond that, right on through and out the other side again; reconciliation, the Catholics call it, these days. Maybe he picked the seed of it up back in his Anarchy in the U.K. days, like syphilis, and it hadn't started getting visible to the eye 'til circumstances had already blown him over here. Or maybe it just crept up on him somehow, a consequence of his Canadian immigration experience, like frostbite, or a taste for strong beer. One way or another, these days, it's nothing to fuck with — as Veve certainly learned.

"Say 'ello to old Baron Cemetery for me, will ya?" Bob said, affably, while Darger and Jaromir struggled to hold Veve's hand still overtop one of two six-by-three planks they'd already fit together down at Jaromir's brother's Home Depot outlet — a makeshift Saint Andrew's cross. Adding: "An' when ya do, tell 'im I woulda made sure to use somefing nice an' rusty just the way 'e likes it, but I didn't want ya to get lockjaw. 'Sides which, if it was *too* rusty, it wouldn't of fit in the gun."

Truth is, Bob likes to think of himself as a purist, if not exactly a Puritan. He was fairly upset after realizing that there was no way they'd be able to secure Veve's ankles without tying them, for example, and he *did* try his best to get the spikes through Veve's wrists rather than his palms—though that proved far harder than expected without puncturing something vital, and probably contributed heavily (along with the cross's inversion) to the how and why of Veve bleeding out completely long before the cops ever got there. According to Bob, it's only the careful preservation of form and litany that gives rituals like these the right sort of kick, sending your love-letter to the Other Side by rocket rather than by snail-mail… but when Darger thinks about it, he has to admit he isn't personally sure which "canon" Bob's really working from, most of the time: Yeah, pagans have a long tradition of nailing Christians to things, and vice versa; then again, so did the Kray Brothers. And in terms of where Bob picked up his formative impulses, Darger can see it being pretty much six of one, half a dozen of the other.

Sometimes, though less and less often, Darger still allows himself to voice the sixty-four thousand dollar Talking Heads question, if only in his own mind: *Well, how did I get here?* He vaguely thinks that once upon a time, he might have wanted to be somewhere other than *this*, by the age of thirty-seven—married with kids and a bearable joe-job, maybe, rather than filling the precarious left-hand slot in a teetery power pyramid run by some mad British bastard with delusions of Popehood.

When he was younger, Darger would've probably hastened to follow that last thought with a reflexive: "Least it's better than…" …security, retail, male prostitution. Parking cars. *Jacking* cars, whatever. But that would've also been back long before he knew what he knows now, which is—it just isn't. Before he knew that this half-assed life of crime he's let himself entropically slide into comes complete with both hours that suck and benefits which are truly for shit, not to mention the utter lack of any visible job security. Retiring minions get no severance package, beyond the obvious; if working for Bob doesn't get you killed *by* Bob, Darger's convinced, having worked *with* Bob eventually will. It's purely a matter of time.

And: "So," he asks Bob, only partially simply to be saying anything other than *oh yeah, uh huh, sure thing, boss!* "How'd you even get the intel on this thing, anyway? Got somebody checking AngelWatch.net?"

Bob fixes him again, his eyes dimming to mere Jude Law-hypnotic range. "I 'ave my sources, mate. What's it to you?"

Darger shrugs. "Not much."

"Good. Keep it that way." Then, turning his back, dismissively: "Any'ow, why not? God's winged messenger roosting over some sewer-grate where kiddies come to sniff glue and feel each ovver up sounds about as bloody likely as most fings, you get right down to it."

So Darger just shrugs again, wraps up tighter and goes back down to the lobby, where Jaromir's waiting in a blessedly warm car: God knows, it ain't like he's really got the wherewithal to argue with Bob over *that*. Not unless he *wants* to end up like Veve, that is —

—which, if you held a gun to his head and *made* him think clearly one way or another about the subject, he already… on some deep yet individually meaningful level… knows damn well he really, really doesn't.

In the car, Jaromir already has his usual compliment of Tim Horton's donuts wedged between driver's and passenger's side seats, lid jammed open, for Darger to reach in and make a selection. "Where to?" He asks.

"Kev's place, then St. Clair East."

Jaromir goes to pulls out his cellphone. "I should call him?"

Darger shakes his head. "Just keep your hands on the wheel, Moscow. I'll do the honors."

Roughly an hour later, they park the car in the sole handicapped space of the Metropol, an apartment building (owned by Bob, natch) angled kitty-corner to Deer Park Elementary School's recess yard and make their way down the well-worn hiking path that meanders through slick foliage and slippery mud to where the underpass arches starkly upwards, a bare ruined cathedral. Darger shades his eyes against the freezing rain and squints, but still can't make out much of the dark space between bridge and infrastructure, aside from a sodden crust of pigeon-poop, dirt, and some precarious curlicues of graffiti. Have to be a goddamn human fly contortionist to make it up that high without crippling yourself on the descent, not to mention probably blown off your tiny gourd.

"How much tape you got?" He asks Kevin, who's taking semi-artistic shots of garbage clogging the drainpipe that gives out just to their left, while Jaromir watches five or so forearm-long gray rats fight over what's left of a Pizza Nova box and a clump of used condoms.

"Two hours in the camera, three more in my pocket."

"Bob probably wants it all."

Kevin looks up, distressed. "That'll take us to like five o' fuckin' clock, man. We'll all die from pneumonia."

"I *said* dress warm, moron."

"Can we at least send Jarhead over there for coffee?"

Jaromir: "Fuck you, Spielberg."

The two of them keep at it a few more minutes, but Darger just tunes them both out, craning his head back further, hands in his pockets. Feels the weight of his Grampa's Army field-glasses knock against his heart whenever he moves, squints up into that darkness above him 'til it starts to pixilate, thinking: *This is going to be one long-ass day at the office.*

And that's when he sees her, it. The *thing* in question.

A flicker of movement on one of the crossbeams, something shifting and resettling as though in half-sleep, hunched against the wind, big as a nesting ostrich. Darger tips up the glasses, adjusts the focus, and sees every detail pop crisply out at him at once, a slap in the face: What looks for all the world like some teenaged girl in a ragged, poisonous peacock-blue coat, rocked back on her haunches up on one of the railings, clinging fast to it with both thin white—

—shit, can those really be bare? In *this* weather?—

—feet.

Jaromir's beside him now, staring, while Kevin keeps taping, mouth open. "The fuck's that?" He asks.

Bob's "angel".

Kevin: "Is she, uh…eating a *rat*?"

Looks like.

"Boys," Darger finally says, without moving, "we may be going home early."

They get an hour or so of prime Touched-by-a-Freak-with-Wings footage before fleeing the scene, hitting the nearest Fran's so Darger can cross-reference their eyes' evidence with those initial, vague rumors Bob sent them down here on the strength of. A quick cellphone call to one of Bob's reverse-snitches inside the Metro Toronto Police Department confirms a neighborhood-wide pattern—mainly collected over August/September, but still growing strong—of disappearing pets, frightened nature-walkers, bums sporting weird wounds turning up at the local E.R., etc. One guy claims to have had his toupee ripped off by a sudden gust of "wind," along with a section of scalp; last week, some kids playing near the back of a McDonald's found a mess of half-digested body parts (five mismatched fingers and a thumb, some poor bastard's appendix, half a foot complete with heel) that'd been dropped into the restaurant's dumpster, all gummed together with shit and spit, like some gigantic owl-ball.

Bob, meanwhile, turns out to love Kevin's tape, even before it's been edited to fit a prospective (North) America's Most Fucked-Up Home Videos slot…'specially the part where bird-girl suddenly seems to notice them, glares down, drops her midday rat-snack almost right on top of Jaromir's precarious Slav-boy weave, and then—

—just *steps off* into air like it ain't no thing and swoops 'round to arc high over the treetops behind the bridge, stoops at something on the ground below on her way back in an Olympic-level hell-dive, before returning at last to the railings; crouches there again, fresh rodent struggling in her hands as she bites deep into its belly, skin parting ragged between her teeth like the rind of a particularly screechy, hairy new Yuppie import fruit. While blood sprays thinly in all directions, blotting out her mouth with red, dappling her blue-feathered shoulders with purple.

And: "Oh *yeah*," Darger hears Bob breathe behind him, husky with bad intent. "That's effin' *brilliant*, that is. Don't ya fink?"

All the time, unfortunately. You?

Darger steps back, turning slightly, so he can take full measure of Bob's exact expression: Avid, enraptured, enrapt. Onscreen, the "angel" continues her meal as Kevin's lens focuses in closer, reducing her to a blurry half-phantom. She's dirty-blonde, merciless eyes bleached almost yellow, and her backlit hair *does* sort of resemble a halo, at least from this angle. But...

"...you sure that's what you think it is, boss?" Darger asks, much against his own better judgement—because what the hell does it matter to him, after all? Aside from him, Jaromir and Kevin probably having to be the ones who actually end up *touching* her.

Roused from his reverie, meanwhile, Bob half-pivots in turn to shoot him a look of pure *What are you, high?*, except with much less inherent amusement value and a fair deal of open threat. Like: *Don't really wanna try an' spoil my fun 'ere, 'Enry, you know what's best for ya.*

"What you drivin' at, exactly? That there's an angel, fallen right down from 'Eaven."

"It's something with *wings*, yeah—"

Bob shakes a schoolmasterish finger in Darger's direction. "Now 'Enry, don't go getting' all empirical on me, you naughty little man. You fink she ain't the goods just 'cause she rips geezas 'eads off? That don't prove nuffink."

Rüüght.

So Darger nods, ever so slightly, like: *Oh, I get it now.* And the trouble is, he actually sort of does—gets how close he's coming to riding the rails out of town with Veve and all those others, anyway. Because this spooky pseudo-Catholic shit is rapidly becoming Bob's biggest sore spot, as Darger's observed on more than one occasion; Bob's continuing quest for proof of an afterlife has already been the primary motivating urge behind a thousand counterclockwise moves, none of which had crap-point-anything to do with either grabbing more territory or maintaining what they've already got. One time it was a plan to steal icons from the same Mafia chieftain Darger'd been valiantly trying to broker a truce with, another time a scheme to kidnap visiting relics worth millions and then just sell them back to the Church in return for a four-hour secret conference with the Cardinal most predicted would soon make Pope. In other words, it's always fuckin' *something.*

"Bob is smart, yes?" Jaromir asked Darger that recently, when the two of them were waiting around outside yet another Mosque, Temple, or Christian Science Reading Room outlet, keeping the engine warm 'til the Man Himself deigned to reappear. "But this religious bullshit...why does he waste his time? We knew better."

"Back in the U.S.S.R.? Yeah, I heard that." Darger'd taken a pull off his cigarette, thought about it for a second. Offering, at last: "Well, Purefoy *does* mean 'pure faith'."

"Ah, come on, why you always got to do that? Always with the big words, with the sarcasticness—"

"That's sarcasm, and whatever; screw you too, okay, man? I just watch a lot of *Jeopardy.*"

"Fuck *Jeopardy! Fear Factor.* Chicks on *Fear Factor* are *hot.*"

"And afraid," Darger'd pointed out, drawing Jaromir's full grin, shiny metal teeth framed in a grimy goatee: *Oh, ðaaaaaa.* Not a real pretty sight at five in the afternoon, even with the relative holiness of their surroundings left strictly aside—but then, they were none of them so *very* pretty to look at, at least not from close up. Or inside.

(Especially not him.)

"Fact is," Bob continues, thankfully oblivious to Darger's heretical musings, "God's a right bastard, old son—'im, his Son, the 'Oly Bloody Ghost an' all. That's why 'e's King."

"Okay, I guess. So, what next?"

A stupid question, as Darger well knows. To which Bob just grins his usual scary-ill, British-teeth grin, and replies:

"Next? You get 'er for me, 'Enry: Right 'ere, in my hands, right now, quick-smart. We clear on that subject, or do I 'ave to go into furver detail?"

"We're clear, Bob," Darger says. And leaves, before he starts feeling like he has to say anything more.

So the question now becomes one of exactly how best to prospectively trap… it. Her. That thing. Our Lady of Death from Above. Darger throws the floor open to suggestions and waits for inspiration to strike.

"Shoot it," Jaromir begins, predictably enough. "I have deer-hunting rifle in my—"

"And bring her back in pieces? Not unless you wanna join Veve in the Imitation Jesus corner, my man; might have trouble finding a cross big enough to fit, but your brother's got an awful lot of wood." Darger pauses, then has to ask: "Where the hell'd you get a deer-hunting rifle, anyhow?"

The Russkie shrugs. "From deer-hunter, of course."

"Oh, of course. Well, unless you got another one modified to shoot animal tranq cartridges, I'd leave your guns at home."

Just then, Kevin makes a truncated, spastic little jerk with his camera-less arm, like he's narrowly managed to avoid throwing his friggin' hand up, kindergarten-style. Offering, instead:

"We could trap her."

"Yeah? Like how so?"

"Um…get ourselves a flatbed, set it up by the ravine—in the Metropol's parking lot, for example—then put something she wants in there, and wait. I'm thinking some sort of animal carcass, could be rotten…or not…"

Jaromir: "My cousin has trucks."

Darger lights up, cups his hand against the wind, drags deep, considers it. While Jaromir and Kevin both wait, exchanging glances, finally and for once on the same (however demented) mental page.

"Might work," he says, at last. "If we made it a little less obvious, maybe—or maybe *just* a little more…"

Kevin: "Easy?"

Darger shakes his head. "Fun."

No strategy without experimentation, that's Darger's motto—one of 'em, anyway; it's probably a holdover from his Ryerson Engineering days, back when he was still young enough to think he'd spend the rest of his life bettering humanity through science, rather than collecting preternatural debris in order to avoid ending up staked out next to the nearest figurative anthill. So instead of getting right onto Operation Angel, Darger negotiates a week's grace with Bob and spends most of that making further careful, long-distance observation of the target's habits. By Friday, he and Kevin—'cause even Jaromir knows there's no profit to be gained by including him in this sort of equation—are fairly agreed on three points: Ten-foot wingspan aside, she's a tiny little thing; she apparently does need sleep, at least when it's snatched in thirty-minute increments; and finally, though she'll eat pretty much anything she can catch, what really seems to turn her dial up past eleven is the smell of fresh…

…human…

…blood.

That last piece of the puzzle arrives almost by accident, after one of Kevin's back-up videographers has the crap-ass luck to step in a nest of rats and break cover—cursing, dancing, tossing a thousand-buck camera against the nearest bunch of rocks—right where she can see him. What follows is pure kinetics, dazzlingly fast: A blue blur, and then there's just the guy grabbing uselessly at his own gouting throat, like if he only pressed hard enough, he could *will* his body to run on electricity alone.

The truly amazing thing is, he actually also has enough balls to shoot at her, afterward; shot goes wide, of course, though it sure does seem to piss her off. Which is probably why she swoops back in, catches him under the arms from behind, lets momentum carry them both up about twenty feet and then drops him against the side of the bridge, just to find out whether or not he'll bounce on the way down.

Jaromir gets rid of the body; he's good at stuff like that, something Darger makes sure to show he appreciates, mainly because he isn't. And while Kevin seems a trifle distressed, probably because he'll have to lie to the guy's mother, he'll get over it. What's most important is that now they all know… something. A bit more than they did before. Which is always useful.

Basic Skinner Box psychology, carrot vs. stick: Find the right one of either and you're smilin'.

There's this one retarded-but-not-really kid who's been hanging around for donkey's years, desperately kissing ass in order to get his *entre* into the true "thug life" of their little gang of four (counting Bob)—Darger's heard Kevin call him "Buddy No-Brains" on more than one occasion and watched the guy smile in flattered recognition: Ah ha, they *must* like me, they gave me a *Sopranos* name. So the next day, Darger has Jaromir pick ol' Buddy up from the spot in front of Tim Hortons where he usually hangs around and explains to him that if he helps them put this trap-the-freak campaign to bed, they'll definitely have to consider him "jumped in" for good and all.

"Cool," the kid says, flipping through stills from Kevin's tape. Then asks, a bit more hesitantly: "But, uh… how'd she get *up* there, in the first place?"

"Flew, far as we can figure. See the wings?"

The kid squints. "I thought those were, like, fake."

Oh, don't you just wish.

Darger has to exert a fair amount of psychic force just to keep his eyes from rolling, while Kevin and Jaromir stare openly in sick fascination: How does this moron even know enough to get his pants on the right way each morning, for Chrissakes?

Won't matter much tomorrow, though, in all likelihood. And that in itself gives Darger the patience to reply:

"Well, that'd be the part you can help us with, wouldn't it, kid?"

Pulling in behind the Metropol, Jaromir's cousin already has the truck set up. Which means all they have to do is wait 'til Kevin has his lens lined up on the "angel"—who's up on her perch again, finger-painting on the bridge's underside with something that's possibly A) shit and B) her own—before taking the kid far enough down the Ravine to not be in her immediate sight-line and stomping the crap out of him for a couple of minutes, blooding him enough so the scent of it starts leaking off in every direction. Then, as Buddy-boy staggers back to his feet, Darger gives him the Reader's Digest version of their Big Plan: Double around past the sewer-pipe, attract her attention by seeming wounded, then hairpin and pelt like hell back up towards the parking lot, where they'll be waiting. Kevin's already told them how Buddy ran sprints in High School, but sprints ain't exactly an obstacle course, and Darger's willing to bet they probably didn't involve anybody dive-bombing him at the same time, either; still, he's all they've got. So, five, four, three, two, one—

—go!

The kid takes off like his proverbial ass is on metaphorical fire, and the "angel's" reaction is immediate: She leaps airborne, both wings flapping with enough force to waft a wall of scent Darger's way — yeasty, meaty, buzzing in the nostrils yet vaguely sweet, breaking over him like some combined explosion in a Communion wafer bakery and an incense factory. As the kid turns, she grabs a loose(ish) brick from the underpass lip in either clawed hand and pulls, cement spraying like gray dandruff; the first one, lobbed like a one-handed shot-put, hits him in the shoulder and almost sends him sprawling. But he manages to stay upright, keep scrambling, so she lets out a raptor's scream of frustration, hugging the second brick to her — two more massive flaps and she's just about overtop him, looking for exactly the right angle to send it down with enough vertical force to snap his neck on impact. And that's when he makes it over the ridge at last, jumps over the tiny curbstone "fence" into the lot, heading for the open side of the truck…

She swoops, letting go. The brick barely misses him; Buddy turns the whizz of its passage into a near-perfect vault, ducks in one side and out the other, with her so close behind now Jaromir later swears he could taste her hot breath —

— but just for a second, just as he slams the other side-panel shut behind Buddy No-Brains and she slams into it head-first, knocking herself cold.

Christ knows they don't want to hurt her, much; Bob'd have their friggin' balls. So they call in Richings, the Purefoy Firm's tame "house" doctor, to clean her up as best he can before Darger makes that all-important first introduction — Richings, who looks more than a little like some anthromorphized bird himself, all legs and wattles and peering, sidelong eyes. He shoots her full of Xylazine and heroin, sets her nose and feels her up just enough to ascertain that her ribs may have cracked on impact (which'd explain the blood she's been coughing up), then puts her in as much of a torso cast as the wings will allow for, before pinning them fast. Blindfold/hoods her with a pillowcase, slipping it on in one neat move, while she snaps aimlessly: Works for transporting falcons, after all. Explaining, as he does:

"Much like treating a centaur, I'd think—the chief dilemma being, do you medicate more for the human half or the non-human? And since her wings together would seem to outweigh the rest of her body, if I didn't suspect the bulk of her bones might well be hollow…"

"You treat a lot of these mythological beasties before, doc?"

"Not at all. But to continue: I finally chose to downplay the avian component, since I assume Mr. Purefoy would prefer her happy when she wakes up, or at the very least controllable."

Darger nods. "So should we worry about keepin' her high, in case she goes cold turkey?"

"Given her metabolism, I'd be surprised if she ends up addicted at all, no matter how extreme the dosage; her heart's probably three times the size of ours, for all it beats twice as fast." Richings manipulates her jaw with practiced hands, one on each mandible, and pulls her upper lip back—gingerly—to point out something inside, visibly ready to jump out of harm's way if she suddenly comes to. "And see here, what look like teeth? Actually razor-sharp ridges of horn or bone, plunging straight from the gum. Same thing with the claws, as far as I can judge. Her feathers? More like quills, with a distinct metallic composition. Ruffle her hair a bit if you want but watch out for splinters; it's like touching a damned porcupine." He lets go, fingers fluttering distastefully, as though he can't wait to grab for the Purell hand-sanitizer. "Very off-putting."

Can't disagree with you there, Darger thinks.

Out loud: "A medical miracle."

"In some sense, yes," Richings replies. Adding, deadpan: "But I do wish you wouldn't use that *word*."

When they get her back to Bob's, the first thing Darger discovers is that he's apparently spent the last week having chicken wire rigged up across half the loft, turning his home into a massive birdcage. A grille of bars fits across every window, yet still leaves them open enough for the sky to be slightly visible through each, perhaps in a futile attempt to help her adjust to her new surroundings—one of those ideas that probably seemed good at the time, but Darger can't really see it going anywhere healthy; he gets a momentary flash of her pounding herself against them ceaselessly until Bob has to order her tranqed, like some five-by-ten canary.

But then again, Darger thinks, almost idly, *name one thing about this whole experience that's really something which deserves to be entered in the "healthy" column.*

Bob paces, visibly thrumming. "That 'er?" He demands.

"Sure is, boss."

"About time." He steps back, keys the lock on the cage door with a fob attached to his watch-chain. As the door pops open: "Well, what you waitin' for? Sling 'er in."

Neither Buddy nor Kevin want to touch her, so it's up to Darger and Jaromir, like always. They fold her through and lay her out as gently as possible, face down on her knees with her wings spread out in either direction. Slip the hood off, and hear Bob take a small, possessive breath as the sun strikes her "hair," touching the individual spines with brazen gold.

The cage can't diminish her, somehow. She fills it from top to toe, a barely controlled explosion.

Kevin, from the side: "Uh, guys? Think she's coming to."

Both Jaromir and Darger jump back as one, slipping back out in one unchoreographed yet eerily adept little two-step maneuver; the angel gives a tiny judder at the sound, limbs contracting, claws flickering in and out, head turning just once in either direction, elastically far as an owl's. Raises her head just as Bob clicks the lock to, and meets his fierce eyes with her own, unblinking.

At close quarters, her feathers are every possible shade of blue combined, darkly iridescent. They rise and ruffle, each one a peacock's uncloaked tail, and that *smell* of hers occupies the room on a subatomic level, so potent that for a minute, Darger has difficulty recalling if he's ever smelled anything else.

Bob bows slightly, too exact to be ridiculous, a psychotic *maitre ∂'*. "*Angelus*," he addresses her, hoarsely. "*O locutor Deum, adorato te. Voce, invocato te, et liberate me ad inferno.*"

Everyone looks at him, virtually boggling. *Didn't even know he knew Latin*, Darger thinks. But Bob just keeps on holding the angel's gaze, scary-vulnerable in the intensity of his yearning, while the angel…

…simply stares back, still sitting, never flitting, opposite his inner chamber door. And says absolutely nothing.

(It's not like they've ever heard her *talk*, after all.)

When, at last, Bob realizes she's unlikely to answer him, Darger sees a sort of M.S.-in-the-making spasm pass over him, contorting him briefly from the knees on up. One hand, formerly held hovering over his heart like he was about to propose, drops further to mirror his waistband, where his quick-draw gun is usually kept. As Darger watches, breath caught and wishing he'd already lit up, Bob thrusts his tongue between his teeth and bites it, hard; waits one more second, 'til he gains a portion of his former control—then turns his back on her, decisively. And comments, to the room at large…

"Well, that's disappointing, innit?"

A voice, guttural as though long-disused, issues from behind him, its accent almost exactly his own: "Innit."

(*Whoa.*)

Bob turns back. The angel is up on her hard little bare heels now, near the cat-box full of raw meat somebody must have set out for her the night before, holding what looks like a piece of liver up to the light and examining it, ruminatively.

"That you talkin'?" Bob demands, at last.

"You talkin'," she replies, all Cockney vowels and coarse glottal stops, static on a telephone call from the Fifth Circle.

"Just bloody answer me, will ya?"

"Answer me."

"I said, *stop* that."

"Said, stop."

"Fuckin' . . . " He pauses, chuckles. To Darger: "Oh, I get it, she's like some parrot; push the TV up close, she'll be doin' impressions in no time." To her, calm again: "Just *stop* it, darlin'."

"Didn't bloody *start* it, did I."

Bob's mouth falls open, an audible click. To one side, Darger can hear Buddy No-Brains curse right out loud, only partially beneath his breath — Buddy, all high on his success and groggy from the painkiller Richings pumped into him before they drove down, who spent the whole time making stupid Austin Powers jokes 'til Jaromir finally clocked him one: *Bird-girl, Bob's "bird," gettit? Like, yeah, BAY-bee! Oh, be-HAVE!*

Darger turns to shoot him a look of pure *Self-preservation, jerkwad, ever heard of it?,* only to find the kid already rigid, eyes locked with Bob's and the angel's at once. Both of 'em suddenly lined up, a man and his shadow, each projecting exactly the same mixture of vague interest and incipient threat: *You're a nice boy, whatever-your-name-is, but by the looks of it, you don't know your arse from your elbow. So shut it, right now, or I'll fuckin' gut ya.*

Or at least Bob is, and she's mimicking him perfectly, up to the second he turns far enough to no longer have her quite in sight. Which is when she slides her eyes over to Darger instead, with a creepily smug little twist of the lips: Not a *smile, per se,* so much as a hideously small yet accurate mockery of one that only ends when she pops the liver-bit in her mouth and swallows it whole.

And that, right then — not sooner, not later, not any of the many

equally fucked up points on the curve that've already come and gone—
—is when things *really* start to fall to shit.

It takes English Bob Purefoy roughly a week to run himself and his organization (already only loosely worthy of the term) into the ground. Much of that is spent talking with his angel, ten to fifteen hours a day plus, with Darger often left hovering somewhere in the background, watching; as a stopgap against productivity slippage, Kevin and Buddy are reduced to dealing with the overspill, calling Jaromir in for reinforcements only when something turns out to require his—and Bob's, usually—extra-special brand of workplace conflict management. All this while the man in the boss's office goes until he drops, sleeps a scant slice of the early morning, then gets right on back in the cage…up against it, anyhow: Flattering, arguing, verge-of-begging. It's more than sort of pitiful, more than a little bit frightening—probably not real good news for *anyone* currently occupying Camp Bob, one way or another, as the bitch with bright blue wings flies. Not in any humanly calculable way, shape or form.

Fact is, Bob wants things from her—insights, assurances—that she just won't give, and the deliberately cruel way she plays with him is frankly starting to get to Darger: A carrion crow with an only half-dead mouse, always grinning her same fixed grin at the way Bob jumps and dives and squirms to avoid her cold catechism.

Because: "I've tried," Darger can hear him whispering from behind closed doors while Kevin's holed up in Bob's office, on conference-call mode, doing his best to assure three local gang-leaders that Bob having missed their longstanding mutual weekly dinner date for the first time since 1999 is neither an accidental dis nor an outright declaration of war. "Lord must know, I've *tried* t'do right, set things back 'ow they once was, and start over. Pay my debts in full, make amends for all my many misdeeds…"

Which merely draws a horrible laugh in return, half-cough, half-croon. "Nice fought, yeah, but the only question is, 'ave you really? Fink back, Robert; fink on what you promised you'd do wiv the life God gave ya, versus what you actually done. 'Cause I fink you'll agree wiv me you really 'aven't, not in the long run—at least, not so's you'd notice."

"Cardinal Doyle told me it's never too late, though, didn't 'e? I could still turn it 'round, get reconciled, die in close enough to a state of grace as makes no never mind, and slip right into 'Eaven."

"Eaven? Chance'd be a fine fing. 'Sides which, why you want to 'ang 'round *that* shit-'eap, any more than you absolutely 'ave to?" A rustle of feathers, so Darger knows she's leaning closer, her own voice dropping to an intimate murmur. "I mean, sure you'll get into 'Eaven, Robert—everybody does, don't they? That's why it's so full of trash and rats, enough so's I don't reckon you'll like it all that much, even sayin' you *do* get there eventually. Why you fink I come back down 'ere, in the first effin' place?"

Bob takes a raspy breath, a long moment. Asks: "What about God?", only to get back—curt and devilishly practical, by way of a reply—

"What *about* 'im?"

So on it goes, and down Bob spirals, an increasingly thin white rope of chipped-away faith and growing despair. And maybe that's the whole point of the exercise, from her point of view; up 'til now, Bob's quest for indisputable proof of life on a Grand Watchmaker scale has been partly motivated by a general drive to simply know things nobody else does. But if there really *is* a Heaven, like the little lady says, at some point Bob's gonna have to wise up far enough to admit he's probably not first in line for the guided tour option.

All of which leaves Darger, as usual, struggling hard to convince himself he doesn't feel shit about shit, because it's sure as fuck not like he *likes* Bob, or anything. Or like Bob's the kind of guy who would even let himself *be* liked…

Yet that last Saturday pre-dawn, nonetheless, he finds himself edging carefully past where Bob slumps cage-side in his favorite wing-back chair—gun in one hand, hammer in the other—to tap, ever so gently, on the mesh beyond. Then saying, knowing damn well can she hear him, even if she won't bother giving him the courtesy of turning around:

"Hey, lady—think maybe this's gone on long enough or what?"

A click of beak-teeth, percussive, as she shoots him the sly blue eye. "Depends on what you fink of as enough, don't it?"

Oh, you friggin' mutant whore.

Darger gives one of his default shrugs, just pointed enough to indicate Bob, head sunk and breathing fast through his nose, his eyelids twitchy with unsatisfying R.E.M. "Look, all's I'm sayin' is—stick a fork in him, turn him over, he's done. I could let you out right here, right now, and nobody'd ever be the wiser. Back to the bridge, three square rats a day…"

"Oh, I doubt that. 'Ow you reckon 'e'd like it if 'e woke up and found 'imself alone again, 'Enry—better, or worse? The man wants answers, and I'm the only one can give 'em to 'im."

"Riiight. But are ya *going* to, anytime soon or are you just gonna keep on talking?" The angel follows him with her eyes as Darger squats, leaning in close enough for jazz, though (hopefully) not close enough for facial injury. "'Cause I've been doin' a little thinkin' on my own, and it strikes me you don't have to come from Heaven at all. Maybe you're some *X-Men*-type freak, and those wings just broke out your fuckin' back when you hit puberty, like you were cuttin' teeth; maybe your mom threw you out on the street when your Old Man tried to sell you to a circus, whatever. Point is, you don't scare me, 'cause I'm the one had Jaromir break your nose with a truck door, baby. You been here what, a week? And in that whole seven days, I ain't seen one single miracle."

"Ain't ya? Read your Apocrypha, meatbag. Enoch says the rebel angels were cast down, some to the Pit, some to wander. Origen says some took on gross bodies, just like yours."

"That what happened to you?"

"Nah. We weren't cast down from nuffink, we just left. We *chose* to leave."

"Why?"

"'Cause 'Eaven's full'a you lot, now. 'Ardly worf the trouble."

"Don't try that eschatology shit on me, birdy."

"Why would I? 'E's the one 'oo called me, isn't 'e? We always give 'em what they want, the meatbags, me and mine; *'E—*"

(like big E, like big dropped-h He? Like *God*, for Christ's fuckin' sake?)

"—don't, but we do—all a' ya, anyfing an' everyfing, each and every bloody time. And all you ever 'ave t'do is ask."

And as she says it, she almost seems to quiver with the barely-visible rudiments of some uncheckable power, something that lies inside time, yet not—inside the flesh, yet not. A looming shadow, larger than anything inside the cage can possibly cast. And all at once it's so damn *hot* in here, so hot and dense and close and her smell, that friggin' *smell*—

Darger raises his gun, slides the safety off gently, in one deliberate move; he sights on her forehead, dead center. Says: "I oughtta kill you right now and let some whole other bastard sort this thing out."

"Yeah? *Try.*"

That same smile. Darger can feel his finger already starting to tighten when, from behind him, comes:

"Enlighten me, 'Enry—what is it you fink you're gonna do wiv 'er, again?"

No need to turn, or even to glance—Darger's been present for enough of Bob's mental meltdowns to take a guess what this one looks like, though probably accelerated far beyond "normal" by a factor of somewhere between 1,000 to 1,000,000. Instead, he keeps his eyes trained straight on target, his gun-barrel unwavering. Replying, though it's not like he actually expects much of an answer, before Bob's bullet hits his brain:

"You know she doesn't really give one cold shit about you, right, Bob?"

"Step away, 'Enry."

"Don't think I can, Bob; sorry, man, but seriously. Beyond my control."

"Step…the fuck…*away*."

The angel curls her tongue at him, gleefully; he fires. She dodges. Bob's first shot grazes Darger's temple, ricochets off the mesh fence and somehow hits Jaromir right in the side of the neck, at the very same second he kicks down/rockets through the living room door. Buddy No-Brains, bringing up the rear, takes a spray of blood in the face and practically trips over Jaromir as he crumples. He barely has enough time to say: "Hey!" before Bob whips around and lays the hammer across his head, one smooth pop, knocking him to the ground. Poor Buddy jerks halfway back up once, then crumples flat once more as Bob stomps on his neck, putting two in his back with practiced ease; Darger turns to check the damage, automatically, and gets the rest of Bob's clip in his chest: Bang, bang, bang, BANG, click.

Ow.

Thus perforated, he falls ass-first against the mesh, which makes a noise like snakes uncoiling, swords being hammered, bronze bells clamoring harsh wartime alarums. But wait, he thinks, that's none of the above—just that goddamned *thing* in there, her face covered with Darger's blood, rubbing it in with both hands like really expensive moisturizer and laughing, laughing, laughing throatily in delight, thick and horribly musical, a hellbent pigeon cooing. Darger looks up at an angle, sees Bob look in at her, panting; sees her smear a fresh handful of blood from the dripping fence and taste it, licking each finger clean in turn. Saying—

"See? There you go, Robert: 'Eaven, all you could ever want. Right 'ere on earth."

(*Heaven.*)

Darger keeps staring up, eyes already fading. Sees Bob's empty face shiver, twist, break. Sees him lunge for the door, fumble the lock, and throw it wide, hands going for her skinny, white, inviolate throat. Sees her rise up to meet him, terrible as an army with banners. Sees the blue rush forward, tsunami-quick and irretrievable, to shroud them both from view.

And years later, in jail, when people ask him to tell them what happens then, he'll say he can't remember…that the blood-loss did for him 'til he woke up in hospital, that he never knew the extent of what she left behind 'til he saw the crime scene photos. All those yellow-tape specials, beautifully off-center, mapping the transit of Bob's body around the room, from cage to fence to floor to walls to ceiling. Not much left to identify him by but his hammer, a separated bouquet of teeth, one torn-in-two kidney jammed halfway through the air-conditioner's pipe that no one found 'til they tried to turn it on and smelled something burning. A lick of scalp with a wad of silver hair still stuck to it, furled to the window like a blood-pasted flag.

Because sometimes, Darger will think, numbly, you do get what you ask for: *Everything*, no matter how insane—not a penny more, or less. And never mind that by that point, after all that fruitless searching, by the time you finally do get it, you probably don't even want it anymore…

But then again, maybe that was the plan from the start: To reward Bob's faith, then shatter it, and fly away laughing—the Almighty's plan, or hers, or who even cares whose? Not Bob, that's for sure.

In jail, Darger will dream of babies with Bob's eyes crawling in a nest of trash, eating raw meat. Of the edge of a blue wing arcing by outside the windows of his brand spankin' new super-max home, so thoughtfully slanted in such a way that whoever's inside the cell can only ever watch the sky above him…

He'll remember Bob Purefoy's angel stepping free above him, bending to brush his nose with hers, and whispering this warning: *Do take care of yourself, 'Enry, wherever they see fit to put ya. But don't you never take your case to the Man Upstairs, no matter 'ow you might long to — 'cause if you pray, my old son, that's 'ow I'll know where to find ya, just like I did Bob. If you EVER let yourself pray again, that's 'ow I'll track ya down, run ya to ground. And when I do, my darlin'…*

(…when I do, oh then, oh then…)

…I'll eat your fuckin' 'eart.

A true harpy, this one, to foul all she touches with rot and uncertainty—take another's hope of salvation, the only thing that keeps souled creatures sane in a soulless universe, and ruin it forevermore. Which is why it's maybe lucky Darger doesn't believe much, it comes right down to it; never did, never will, not even now. One of the few yet essential ways in which Bob and he were always different.

But he believes *this*, if nothing else. Believes *her*. So he remembers, devoutly, all the rest of his long, jailbound life…

…and he never, ever does.

FIN DE SIÈCLE

He had very little interest in life, and was full of crepuscular dreams, religious images, sickness, and suffering; but he hid those deep-seated wounds beneath an elegant exterior… The walls of his soul were so thin that a strange light shone through them that was not of this world.

—Camille Mauclair

1909, BRUGES, BELGIUM. The studio is mapped in flat, watery light which seeps, uncheckable, through warped glass windows to silver the ceiling, the walls, the floor. Gustave Knauff can barely gather enough strength to draw the blinds or open them further. His head is already full of absinthe-hangover, that toothache want and pull which settles a puke-green filter over everything within reach. Fumes rise from an open paintbox. In front of him, the latest canvas sulks, unfinished.

In the corner, meanwhile, his family's dreadful guardian angel goes on with "her" endless card-game: Shuffling them, laying them down, turning them back up, red and black and red-black-red. Gustave tries his best not to look "her" way as "she" does so—in fact, ever—but the noise they make (soft, papery, repetitious) is intoxicating, very nearly unbearable. It calls to him, a degenerate gambler's siren-song made somehow even more naturally seductive in juxtaposition with the angel's supremely unnatural pictogram rush of no-voice, laid lightly overtop—

Come, Dame Knauff's seventh son, can we not be friends just once more, before I take my leave? Sit down, let me deal you in. Drink deep. Win back your life.

"I won't," he says, out loud.

Ah, then. You must suit yourself, I suppose.

The angel sits erect, posture perfect, gloved right hand neatly folded while "her" bare left hand skims restlessly back and forth. Though illusory, "her" bottle-green dress strikes the faultless height of fashion, perfectly *a la mode.* "Her" veil, which hangs opaque from hatbrim to breast, is just a shade or so lighter—slightly iridescent, with poisonous blue tints to it; the same ones which inform a corpse-fly's back, or a peacock feather's fringe.

Our very own Peacock Angel, Gustave thinks. But no—his mother would frown to hear him make such a blasphemous comparison. This phantom is only a kissing cousin of that particular principality, a mere forerunner of the true Angel to come. The nails on "her" bare hand are hooked and black, like cormorant's beaks; they carve slight scratches on the cards' faces wherever they touch, barely perceptible ghost-weals. And though he was raised almost from babyhood knowing "her" name, adding it always to his backwards midnight prayers, he has yet, even now, to see "her" naked face…

(Not, to be sure, that he has ever actually wanted to.)

Ma'ashith, once an archangel of punishment, who announces the deaths of children; Ma'ashith, "sister" to Af, to Kesef, to Hemah, to Meshabber—to wrath and destruction, human mortality, animal cruelty. Who prefers always to appear in female form, though (like all "her" kind) "she" exists far beyond the boundaries of what Gustave and his ilk would call either sex or pity.

An excerpt from *Strange Provenance: Lost Works of the Fin de Siècle,* by

Ellin Pataky-Hemsworth (2002, Millipede Press, Connaught Trust Legacy Library copy):

One of the most mysterious figures of late Decadence must surely be Gustave Knauff, who left behind little except a tantalizing series of lacunae. We have no clear idea where or when he was born, where he studied, or even what he looked like (though some sources hold that the faceless, blurred background figure sitting next to a veiled woman playing solitaire in the unfinished piece "Au Café Brumaire", by Jan Toorop's protégé, Degouve de Nuncques, might—possibly—have been meant to be him. Even Knauff's sold works, all few and far between, seem to have met similarly obscure fates. We are left, instead, with reactions to the paintings rather than the paintings themselves, as here—

> *Saw also the third panel from Knauff's "Hymnes de Paon", finally complete, before it was removed from the exhibition at Rouen, after great public outcry… a morbid and dreadful picture painted in hues of luminous decay, most of it various cold shades of lilac tinged with moonlit white, with a little lettuce-green mixed with milk for sheen. I would give much never to have seen it at all, particularly so because in spite of the revulsion this painting aroused in me when I stood in front of it, I cannot help feeling a certain attraction to it —sick, strange, and growing with each passing day—now that I am safely far away.*
> —J.K. Huysmans, 1903

By collating such "rave reviews", we confirm that Knauff's most infamous—and thus sorely-missed—work was undeniably the legendary "Black Annunciation" (1907?). According to Odilon Rédon, who devoted a page of his unpublished memoirs to the painting, "[t]his joyful and polluting blasphemy performs the most holy service of all unholy creations, placing the logic of the visible firmly at the service of the invisible. I saw it only once, and it has informed my dreams ever since..."

In 1869, the angel tells him, not looking up from "her" spread, *three children were playing in a meadow near Alton, in Hampshire, when a local clerk approached them — a young man of great respectability, though his father was a known maniac, and he himself was subject to depressive fits.*

"Don't speak to me, angel. I beg you."

But "she" does not seem to hear him. Simply deals another card, this one's face all black, with no visible design on it at all — how his heart clutches, to see it so! — and goes on:

This clerk gave the children a ha'penny each and asked one of them — a little girl — to walk with him in the woods nearby. This she agreed to, gladly. Then, after some time had passed, the girl's mother began to worry; she sent her husband to town to gather young men, for a search. And later, much later, at the edge of yet another field...

Gustave has heard this story before, many times; he shuts his eyes and shakes his head, as if to clear it. But feels absinthe-hunger drive a metaphorical spike deep through the orbit of one eye at the same instant, clean and pure as new grass: Dig it deep, twist it, corkscrew-crooked. Leave it there to sting.

"Did you hear what I said?" he forces himself to ask, angrily.

The angel's arms are discreetly fringed with oblong feathers, pasteboard-stiff; "she" lets them rise and fall at once, a body-long shrug, with much the same thrum and patter of her game. Because: *Yes, they could simply be cards,* Gustave thinks, absently, his eyes starting to burn. *Plucked and played, then replaced without my seeing it; simple sleight of hand. Like Houdini. Nothing so very worship-worthy at all...*

Oh, certainly, the angel replies, for all he has not spoken aloud. *But perhaps I do not even address you — have you never considered that? Perhaps I talk merely for my own pleasure, because the sound of my own voice amuses me.*

"Then I won't listen," Gustave says, and busies himself by rummaging in his paintbox. At the moment, the canvas is a shapeless morass of purple and violet, with only a wash of black here and there taming the chaos enough to suggest vague shapes: Houses, boats, a stairway leading downward. A few odd dabs of acid Indian Yellow to suggest gaslights flickering from the nearest bridge-side, while potentially fatal smears of Emerald Green (a deadly poison) show where the river's current surfaces, undertow drag and all. As Rodenbach puts it: *The pale water which goes away along paths of silence…*

The angel shrugs again, a literary avalanche. *The detail we are never allowed to hear of, in any case,* "she" continues, conversationally, *is exactly what this young man did with the one thing he took from her body, after he had torn the rest of it apart and left it scattered across the grass like the Aztec moon-goddess Coyotlaxqui—limb from limb, a last shred of sinew letting one plump leg gape wide, to show the red hole between. This item, slack and hairless, he put in a box tied with satin ribbons, originally meant for chocolates, and kept under his bed.* Turning over a new card, with a delicate flick: *Until it began to smell, that is.*

Gustave's hand trembles, still reaching for the green. "You will not make me think of such things!"

I doubt I could make you do anything, Knauff's son. Yet you do think of them, nevertheless. You are thinking of them now.

Gustave shivers. Outside, the waters of *Bruges-la-Morte* flow by, pulling drowned prostitutes from the river's scummy bottom—Rodenbach's dead city, the new Ys, criss-crossed by canals and abandoned to its fate. He came here two years ago, to escape everything…but mainly his family, their cultish ways, their insane and secret schemes, their inevitable vengeance for the slights he had already given them. Or a rustling footstep and a flash of green behind him in the dark, as "she" grew ever closer.

He knows now that the final stage of his journey began three weeks earlier, when—while blunting Cadmium Red with a dilution of lamp-black—he thought he smelled something burning and glanced up just in time to catch the mirror above his washstand gaping open like a lidless silver eye. But it was not until he came home late the next morning, reeking of sweat and aniseed, that he knew his mother's immaterial spies must have truly found him at last; not until the landlord called out cheerfully to him as he went by, in both of Bruges' official languages:

"*Gut' tag, m'sieu.* Did she find you yet, your friend?"

"I beg your pardon?"

"*Ton jolie copine la,* in her veil, *bien sur—eine engel-frau, mein herr!* Or so my daughter tells me. She saw her coming up the back stairs, all *en verte,* like the Green Fairy herself." A sly wink: "And we all know how devotedly you favour the Fairy, *Herr* Knauff…"

When he climbed up the narrow stairs, he could see the landlord's daughter sitting in the window above him, combing her hair (blonde, limp, in ringlets) and grinning a gap-toothed smile, with her skirt hiked to the knees. He thought her to be ten or eleven years of age, baby-fat and chestless, though her dresses looked to be cut-down versions of ones the landlord's long-dead wife might once have worn, thus tending to gap immodestly. He remembered then how he had once heard her announce to playfellows that when she was older, she would go far away to model for artists like the mysterious *Herr* Knauff—perhaps to Paris, that wickedest of places, where she would pose without her underthings and be paid with jewels and sweets…

And inside he had found the angel, waiting for him. Saying only, mildly: *That girl likes you a great deal, Dame Knauff's son. There are many ways you could take advantage of her affections, if you chose to.*

Three weeks ago, only that. He could have run further, he supposes, given the inclination—or the money.

Yet here he is, still. And "she".

On the low wooden table at which the angel sits, "her" latest run of cards is plucked up, tucked away. Another appears to take its place, almost immediately—seven pasteboard faces blinking up him, black-red-black, red, black. Her claw-nails now make a noise like picks scraping across salt, leaving visible tears in their wake.

Immediately, Gustave feels that red impulse he now seems to spend so much of his waking life fighting rise in him like fumes, lightening his head. His stomach swims, and he has to brace against the easel for support, making it creak beneath his weight. The desire for absinthe is a fist to his face, a broken stick in his throat.

Oh God, my family's most ancient enemy, please tell me quickly, before "she" does: How will this all end?

From *Strange Provenance*, Pataky-Hemsworth:

Supposedly even more disturbing than Leon Frederic's "Le Torrent" (part of his own triptych, entitled "Tout est Mort"), which shows an entire mountain valley choked with dead, naked children splayed in pedophile-pornographic poses, what Knauff's "Annunciation" appears to have been blaspheming against was both the Gospel story of the Slaughter of the Innocents—the massacre of a whole generation of Jewish infants, ordered slain by King Herod because they were born on the same day as Jesus Christ, in order to make sure none of them would become a Messiah powerful enough to displace or punish him—and the Annunciation itself… the exact moment when the Archangel Gabriel told the Virgin Mary that she had been chosen to bear God's son.

From Rédon's further description of the "Annunciation":

A sort of semi-monastic diablerie in a landscape inhabited by flowing, undulating, vomitory spectres, like a tidal wave of leeches. The whole background looks shrouded in gauze. The foreground is occupied by a heap of dead children, some of whose throats are still being ritualistically cut by figures in copes and cassocks;

these ecclesiastical executioners seem half-lapidified, weighed down by gold and jewels, both sacred and profane… In the middle, enthroned on a chair made from bones, sits an equally childish figure —the Virgin —whose flower-soft eyes roll back in apparent rapture as she listens to the figure whispering poison into her ear, a veiled hermaphrodite in a bottle-green robe, caught in the act of placing a winged mantle made from peacock feathers onto the Virgin's shoulders. A horrible halo, black and crackling with arcane energies, connects them both . . .

Regard the Virgin. Is there, in Art, anything more beautiful and terrible than her visage, especially were it to have been copied from life? Beneath the horizontal immobility of the long eyebrows, under languid Hindu lids, her gaze is laden with dreams and death. The mouth is tinged with just a hint of blood… she is silent, rigid, both despoiler and despoiled. Her white eucharistic flesh, framed by plaited viper tresses, is marked with an irreparable kiss. Her folded hands cup her own belly, delicately heralding a spectacle of the future…surely some unborn monster, perhaps even that Beast foretold, which cannot possibly be allowed to come to term…

A month ago, he can still recall taking his usual Sunday meal in the Café Brumaire, happy and productive. He sat next to two younger painters and listened to them argue about Wilde and Moreau, about whether the chimera or the Sphynx was the more fitting mascot for the age. Fleur was there, holding his hand tightly imprisoned in her lap and smiling into his eyes, like the willing whore she was; he let her thighs' warmth seep steadily through his glove, knowing well she wore nothing beneath her skirt but garters. Delirious with both absinthe and possibilities, the former already paid for, the latter seemingly boundless.

But I was there too, even then, the angel says, *though you could not see me. I have always been there. Your family and I have made a covenant. They serve the one I wait for, and I serve them, while waiting.*

"That has nothing to do with me, any of it!" Gustave protests, racked with nausea. "It never did!"

A skirl, a further flutter, a flurry of cards and feathers, table and chair abandoned—and abruptly, awfully, he feels the train of Ma'ashith Punisher-angel's ghostly skirts brush up against his trembling legs, from waist to ankle and back once more. "She" is near enough for him to taste "her" breath, if "she" had any.

Ah, but your mother thinks so. You have disappointed her so gravely, Knauff's son—telling Melek-i-Taus' secrets in paint, however obliquely. Selling them for gallery fees, an hour's drunken friendship, a review in La Plume. Oh, and now "she" is even closer yet, that cormorant-clawed hand spreading a fresh half-deck of cards before his wavering eyes, flipped open and shut quick as a courtesan's fan: Red and black and red, black-red-black. *She will wear black the rest of her life for you.*

"But she sent you to me, nevertheless."

Mmm. And I go where I am bidden, as ever. We have no free will, my kind and I…not since Ede, or before. That was His gift to you and yours. How do you enjoy it?

A simple question. Yet one to which Gustave, like most human beings, has no easy answer.

Your family bound me to them with false promises, Knauff's son, the angel observes, *like all humans. Yet as it is in the nature of angels to serve, no matter who, I do not count myself so terribly sinned against. I will have my freedom, eventually.*

He throws up his hands; impossible to appeal to "her", he knows— and yet he finds himself doing so nevertheless, words tumbling from his mouth like sharp stones. "Orders aside, why haunt *me*, even so? I, who alone of all of them sympathize with your plight . . . you know it, *have* known it, since my childhood. It is only *they* who wish to change the world, for better or worse, in . . . that other angel's . . . name. I have no stake in it."

Oh, and they will. They are changing it already. You, too.

Have you truly not noticed?

Gustave's eyes blur, sting, the green hangover filter abruptly irising deeper, darker, to touch everything around him with muck. Upstairs, through the ceiling, he can hear his landlord's daughter blundering joyfully around, stomping like a little goat: She is not a *lady*, after all, and probably glad enough for it. Not yet old enough to have to restrain herself.

Perhaps she will be coming down here soon, that girl, the angel says. *To see you. The way the young shepherdess in Italy went to watch her cousin at work in the barn, only to be found the next day with her mouth full of earth, her intestines torn out and trailing in the dirt. Or the way that bellringer from Boston invited a five-year-old up to his attic, on the pretext of showing her his pigeons, and instead beat her to death with a bat—beat her so badly, so completely, that when her own mother was shown the body later on, she could not positively identify her remains...*

But: "I'm not like that," Gustave spits back, his mouth full of bile. "I only—dream. Paint. I've never...done anything...more than that."

As yet, no.

Feet on the stairs, girlish, tripping. Gustave claws for the wall again, upsetting his paint-stand. Finds the smeary palette-knife suddenly poised within gripping range, its handle towards his guilty, palsied hand.

Ah, but perhaps, if you only drink the last of your Green Fairy I will go away, Knauff's son, like any other morning-after hallucination. Or...perhaps not.

The girl is right outside now, separated from him only by a thin layer of wood and metal; she skips from step to step, singing some sort of counting-out rhyme in French (or German). He bites his tongue at the very sound of it, grinding until he tastes blood.

Why fight? the angel asks, in his ear, "her" no-voice thin as a murmuring dream of bees. *I know you, all of you, caught as you are in time's net like dead fish rotting, drunk on your own decay. You love only what you destroy, because you can destroy it—but do you really dream you are the worst this century will have to offer? Are you so arrogant?*

By the way her voice has faded, it would seem that the landlord's daughter has finally reached the landing. Gustave can only pray she stays there, frozen in much the same way he now finds himself unable to move, straining for whatever the angel's next words might be in the intimately gathering gloom—

Listen, Knauff's son: Here is what will happen, with or without your mother's plans to blame for it. First, in five years' time, there will be war…but not one of those many tiny wars you and your friends worry over—this will be different, epic, startling. A true horror to behold. Fire will gush from the sky; lead will fall like rain; the muddy ground will be honeycombed with buried bombs, with trenches full of gas and disease. A war, as all of you will say, to end all wars—until the next one comes.

More shuddering, more fluttering; sharp-edged, crisp enough to cut. Down in the front hall, the landlord's daughter pauses, possibly having forgotten something. She turns on her heel, turns back, to mount the rickety stairs once more. Gustave presses palms to ears in order to block out the sound but finds this only makes the angel's voice ring more hollowly in the hissing cavern of his skull—damnably reasonable, utterly unstoppable.

And then, then…just as He once spoke the Word and sent Gabriel Archangel to turn Sodom and Gomorrah into salt, so your kind will crack the atom like an egg, turning two more cities into glass. Nothing will be left behind but shadow and ash, factories run on rag and bone, a long and wasting invisible death that poisons the soil and sky, great holes full of corpses. Men and women of every age and station will die there together, families and strangers alike, thieves and saints and yet more Sodomites too, of any and all descriptions…

"And children?"

Oh yes, and children, always. Children, more than any others. I have seen it so for centuries, ever since He sent me to lay my hand on Pharaoh's first-born's sleeping head.

From *Strange Provenance*, Pataky-Hemsworth:

According to part of a letter found plastered into the wall of Knauff's former room (possibly dated 1908, or perhaps '09), the "Annunciation" was sold to a private buyer that same year, which explains how it escaped the Bruges fire. In the missive, Knauff goes on to decode his painting's various symbological features as a gesture of "educative good-will" towards "a loyal supporter and enthusiast"—this unnamed purchaser?

Knauff identifies the sexless figure in green as "that same angel who culled Egypt's firstborn", now Fallen into acting as a sort of herald or guardian for the "Virgin"; the peacock-feather cloak it offers her reveals the involvement of Melek-i-Taus, notorious Peacock Angel of the Yezidic Goetists, who may be using her womb—or whatever comes out of it—to birth "himself" back into the material world. In other words, what Knauff seems to have at some point belonged to... and obviously later betrayed, thus probably leading to his death...was yet one more end-of-the-century cult with a distinctly familial slant, a birthing-pit for potential Anti-Christs.

And now, of course, there is a knock at the door—hesitant but soon repeated, growing ever stronger. Gustave looks down to see his knuckles already white around the palette-knife's handle, while (looking up again) he finds the canvas he's worked so hard on is less a soothing canal landscape than a black forest made from bones and meat, a place of slaughter just aching for some wayward red-caped maiden to amble, foolish-fearless, down any of its overhung paths.

Believe me, Knauff's son: All this will come to pass, whether or not the Peacock Angel comes home at last. But you, if you wish, my little Gustave —

(hapless Goetist, self-made traitor, born too soon for doctors Jung and Freud, too late for the Inquisition's tender mercies. You werewolf's heart wrapped in a man's slick skin, all canines and eye-whites, your quivering limbs kept irrigated by terror and desire alike)

—you need not live to see it.

The inquiring cry comes, long expected, in a voice innocent of all but the most cat-killing curiosity: *"Herr* Knauff? *Herr* Knauff, are you there?"

But no, he knows it now: He will not answer, after all. Thank any God but the one his mother worships…

It is surprisingly easy for him to turn the knife upwards, even to make that last, imperative slash, paint burning in his wound like cleansing fire: Chemicals, poisons, beauty. The sole real surprise is how little it seems to hurt, and how long the fall to the floor seems to take. He stays conscious just long enough to see the door open, the landlord gape down at him, before he finally dies choking on his own blood, with an oddly gentle smile on his red-soaked lips.

The girl's scream goes straight up to Heaven like an ill-shot arrow, missing its target entirely; she will live and die unaware of her own close escape from what the Germans are only now learning to call *lust-mord*, sent to Buchenwald instead after sheltering Jews in her father's basement, while he himself takes a far more merciful bullet to the back of the head as he tries to tear her from an SS officer's arms.

And neither of them, in the end, is fast (or attentive) enough to see the angel Ma'ashith vanish, "her" task complete — blinking from existence in a spray of red-black cards which rise, fall, then hit the floor and scatter once again, eddying away as nothing more than dust.

From *Strange Provenance*, Pataky-Hemsworth:

The brief, intense fire which destroyed Knauff's Bruges studio around

Easter of 1909 only adds to his mystery; in addition to consuming the remainder of his unsold works, the one body found therein was so fire-damaged as to make identification largely speculative — the accelerant effect of the studio's paints and turpentine is blamed for this. Though the rest of the pension survived, the entire roof had to be replaced and lowered, essentially wiping all trace of Knauff from the city in which he had lived the last years of his incredibly ill-documented life.

While many scholars posit that Knauff might have painted under a pseudonym (the name sounds suspiciously close to "Knopff", after all), or even been a "house name" used by a coalition of like-minded artists trying to break into the last wave of the Decadent scene, my own research suggests it is far more likely he was related to the family behind Knauff's of Switzerland, an international trading house founded by a Crusader who returned from the Holy Land having already married a woman "of singular beauty and sinister antecedents" who claimed she — along with the rest of her family — had already converted to Christianity when the Swiss delegation arrived. (In fact, a quick survey of those few remaining photos of the Swiss Knauffs prior to their 1946 emigration to Canada reveals that the female members of their line all seem to bear a striking resemblance to Redon's favourite blasphemous anti-Mary — most strikingly in the case of Mara Knauff, the company's main stockholder since her 1939 *debut*, and great-grandmother of the current crop.

(There are even rumours of a very early Kodak color-process memorial photo taken three years after her marriage which shows her posing with a stillborn twin boy in either arm, attended by a slim young nurse or nanny dressed all in green, her face discreetly averted from Mrs. Knauff's grief, a small and similarly colored veil further obscuring her shadowed features.

(An odd further detail: Cards, surely inappropriate in such circumstances, are laid out on a nearby table.)

Slowly and surely a belief is growing in the bankruptcy of Nature which promises to become the sinister faith of the twentieth century.

—Paul Bourget

Grave Goods

P UT THE PIECES back together, fit them against each other chip by chip and line by line, and they start to sing. There's a sort of tone a skeleton gives off; Aretha Howson can feel it more than hear it, like it's tuned to some frequency she can't quite register. It resonates through her in layers: skin, muscle, cartilage, bone. It whispers in her ear at night, secret, liquid. Like blood through a shell.

The site they're working on is probably Early Archaic — 6,500 B.P. or so, going strictly by contents, thus beating out the recent Bug River find by almost 2,000 years. Up above the waterline, too, which makes it *incredibly* unlikely; most people lived in lakeshore camps back then, right when the water levels were at their lowest after the remnant ice mass from the last glacial advance lying across the eastern outlet of Lake Superior finally wasted away, causing artificially high lake levels to drop over a hundred meters. Then isostatic rebound led to a gradual return, which is why most sites dating between the end of the Paleo-Indian and 4,000 years ago are largely underwater.

Not this one, though: it's tucked up under a ridge of granite, surrounded by conifer old growth so dense they had to park the vehicles a mile away and cut their way in on foot, trying to disturb as little as possible. Almost a month later — a hideously cold, rainy October, heading straight for Hallowe'en — the air still stinks of sap, stumps bleeding like wounds. Dr. Anne-Marie Begg's people hauled the trunks out one by one, crosscut the longest ones, then loaded them up and took them back to the Reserve, where they'll be planed in the traditional manner and used for rebuilding. Always a lot of home improvement projects on the go, over that way; that's what Anne-Marie—Dr. Begg—says.

Though Canadian ethics laws largely forbid excavations, once Begg brought Dr. Elyse Lewin in to consult, even the local elders had to agree this particular discovery merited looking into. They've been part of the same team practically since Begg was Lewin's favorite TA, operating together out of Lakehead University, Thunder Bay; Lewin's adept at handling funding and expedition planning, while Begg handles both tribal liaison duties and general PR, plus almost anything else to do with the media. It was Begg who sowed excitement about "Pandora's Box," as the pit's come to be called, on account of the flat slab of granite—lightly incised with what look like ancestral petroglyphs similar to those found on Qajartalik Island, in the Arctic—stoppering it like a bottle. Incised on top *and* below, as Aretha herself discovered when they pried it apart, opening a triangular gap large enough to let her jump in. She'd shone the flashlight downwards first, just far enough to check her footing before she landed—down on one knee, a soggy crouch, too cramped to straighten fully—then automatically reversed it, revealing those square-cut, coldly eyeless faces set in silent judgement right above her head.

"How'd they get it here?" Morgan, the other intern, asks Lewin, who shrugs and glances at Begg before letting her answer.

"The slab itself, that's found, not made—shaped a little, probably. More than enough rockfall in this area for that, post-glacial shear. Then they'd have made an earthwork track like at Stonehenge, dug underneath—" Begg uses her hands to sketch the movements in midair, "—then piled in front, put down logs overtop, used them like rollers. Get enough people pushing and pulling, you're golden."

Lewin nods. "Yes, exactly. Once the grave was dug, there'd be no particular problem fitting it overtop; just increase the slope 'til they had a hill and push it up over the edge, down-angled so one side touched the opposite lip, before dismantling the hill to lay it flat again."

"Mmm." Morgan turns slightly, indicating: "What're the carvings for, though? Like . . . what do they mean?"

"Votive totems," Begg replies, with confidence.

The forensics expert—Dr. Tatiana Huculak—just shakes her head. "No way to know," she counters. "Told us yourself they don't look like any of the ritual marks you grew up with, remember? So it's like a sign in Chinese, for all of us—just as likely to say 'fuck you' as 'God bless,' unless you know Pinyin."

Begg's already opening her mouth to argue when Lewin sees Aretha's hand go up; she shushes them both. "Oh dear, you don't have to do *that!*" she exclaims. "Just sing out, if an idea's struck you."

Aretha hesitates, eyes flicking to Morgan, who nods. Courage in hand, she replies—

"Uh, maybe. I mean— Even when you don't know the language, there's still a lot you can get from context, right? Well . . . " She hauls herself up, far enough past the slab to tap its top, nails grating slightly over rough-edged stone. "'Keep out,' that'd be my guess," she concludes. "'Cause it's up here."

Lewin nods, as Huculak and Begg exchange glances. "Logical. And down there? On the underside?"

Here Aretha shrugs, uncomfortably in the spotlight for once, pinned beneath the full weight of all three professors' eyes.

" . . . 'Stay in?'" she suggests, finally.

Working this dig with Lewin's team was supposed to be the best job placement ever, a giddy dream of an archaeological internship—government work with her way paid up front, hands-on experience, and the chance to literally uncover something unseen since thousands of years BCE. By the end of the first week, however, Aretha was already beginning to dream about smothering almost everyone else in their sleep or hanging herself from the next convenient tree, and the only thing that's improved since then is that she's now far too exhausted to attempt either.

Doesn't help that the rain which greeted them on arrival still continues, cold and constant, everything covered in mud and reeking of pine needles. Sometimes it dims to a fine mist, penetrating skin-deep through Aretha's heaviest raincoat; always it chills, lighting her bone-marrow up with sharp threads of ache, the air around her so cold it hurts to inhale through an open mouth. Kneeling here in the mud, she sees her breath boil up as cones fall through the dripping, many-quilled branches, their sticky impacts signaled with rifle-shot cracks, and every day starts the same, ends the same: wood mold burning in her eyes and sinuses like smoke, impossible to ward off, especially since the Benadryl ran out.

"Jesus," Morgan suddenly exclaims, like she just hasn't noticed it before, "that's one hell of a cold you've got there, Ree. Does Lewin know?"

Aretha shrugs, droplets scattering; hard to do much else, when she's up to her elbows in grave-gunk. And: "Uh, well . . . yeah, sure," she replies, vaguely. "Can't see how she wouldn't."

"Close quarters, and all? You're probably right. But who knows, huh? I mean . . . " Here Morgan trails off, eyes sliding back to the main tent—over which two very familiar voices are starting to rise, yet again—before returning to the task at hand. "...He's kinda—distracted, these days, with . . . everything. I guess."

"Guess so."

Inside the main tent, Begg and Huculak are going at each other like ideological hammer and tongs, as ever—same shit, different day, latest instalment in an infinite series. It's been a match made in hell, pretty much since the beginning; Huculak's specialization makes her view all human remains as an exploitable resource, while Begg's tribal band liaison status puts her in charge of making sure everything that could conceivably once have been a person gets put right back where it was found after cataloguing, with an absolute minimum of ancestral disrespect. Of course, Begg's participation is basically the only reason they're all here in the first place, as Lewin makes sure to keep reminding Huculak—but from Huculak's point of view, just because she knows it's true doesn't mean she has to pretend to like it.

"I'll point out, yet again," Huculak's saying right now, teeth audibly gritted, "that the *single easiest way* we could get a verifiable date on this site continues to be if we could take some of the bones back and carbon-date them, in an honest-to-Christ lab . . . "

Aretha can almost see Begg curtly shaking her head, braids swinging—the way she does about fifty times a day, on average—as she replies. "Carbon-date the grave goods, then, Tat, to your heart's content—carbon-date the *shit* out of them, okay? Grind them down to paste if you want to; burn them and smoke the fucking ashes. But the bones themselves? *Those* stay here."

"Oh, 'cause one of 'em might share maybe point-one out of a hundred-thousandth part of their genetic material with yours? Bitch, please."

Lewin's voice here, smooth and placatory as ever: "Ladies! Let's be civil, shall we? We all have to work together, after all, for a good month more . . . "

"Unfortunately," Huculak snaps back, probably making Begg puff up like a porcupine. Hurling back, in her turn—

"Hey, don't denigrate my spirituality just because you don't share it; is that so hard? Say we were in Africa, digging up Rwandan massacre dumps—things'd be different *then*, right?"

"You know, funny thing about that, Anne-Marie: not really. They'd be the same way anyplace for me because I am a *scientist*, first and foremost. Full friggin' stop."

"And I'm not, is what you mean?"

"Well . . . if the moccasin fits."

At that, Aretha whips her head around sharply, only to meet Morgan's equally disbelieving gaze halfway. The both of them staring at each other, like: *seriously?* Holy cultural slap-fight with potential impending fisticuffs, Batman. *Wow.*

"Knock-down drag-out by six, seven at the latest," Morgan mutters, sidelong. "I'm callin' it now—fifty on Tat to win unless Anne-Marie puts her down with the first punch. You in or what?"

Aretha hisses out something that can't quite be called a laugh. "Pass, thanks."

Morgan shrugs, then turns back to her designated task, head shaking slightly. "Your loss."

Going by her initial pitch, Lewin genuinely seems to have thought hiring only female associates and students would guarantee this little trip going far more smoothly than most, as though removing all traces of testosterone from the equation would create some sort of paradisiacal meeting of hearts and minds: cycles synched, hands kept busy, no muss, no fuss. The principle, however, was flawed from its inception: *just 'cause they ain't no peckers don't mean ain't no peckin' order,* as Aretha's aunties have often been heard to remark 'round the all-gal sewing circle they run after hours out of their equally all-girl cleaning service's head office. It frankly amazes Aretha how Lewin could ever have gotten the idea that women never bring such divisive qualities as ambition, wrath, or lust to the metaphorical table, when she's spent the bulk of her career teaching at all-girl facilities across the U.S., before finally ranging up over the border—

But whatever. Maybe Lewin's really one of those evo-psych nuts underneath the Second Wave feminist frosting, forever hell-bent on mistaking biology for destiny no matter the context. Just as well she's apparently never thought to wonder exactly what those pills Aretha keeps choking down each day are, if so.

On puberty blockers since relatively early diagnosis, thank Christ, so she never did reach the sort of giveaway heights her older brothers have, and her voice hasn't changed all that much, either; that, plus no Adam's apple, facial and body hair kept chemically downy as any natal female in her immediate family, even if the other team-members felt inclined to body-police. But the plain fact is, they've none of them seen each other in any sort of disarray since they left base-camp—it's too cold to strip for sleep, let alone to shower, assuming they even had one.

This is typical paranoia, though, and she knows it; the reason everyone here knows her as Aretha is because she *is*. That's the name under which she entered university, legally, and it'll be the name with which she graduates, just like from high school. She's a long damn way away from where she was born at this point, both literally and figuratively.

Aretha looks back up to find Morgan still looking at her and blushes, sniffing liquid, with nothing handy even halfway clean enough to wipe the result away on. "Sorry," she manages, after a second. "*So gross, I know, I really do. I just*—sorry, *God*."

Morgan laughs. "Dude, it's fine. Who knew, right?"

"Yeah." A pause. "Think it would've been okay, probably, it just hadn't rained the whole fucking time."

"And yet."

" . . . and yet."

Morgan has a great smile, really; Aretha'd love to see it closer up sometime, under different circumstances. But right now, the little moment of connection under pressure already had, the only thing either of them can really think to do about it is just shrug a little and drift apart once more—Morgan back towards the generator array, which is starting to make those worrying pre-brownout noises yet again, while Aretha heaves herself up out of the pit and stamps slushily towards the tent itself, planning to sluice her gloved hands under the tarp's overflowing gutter. This brings her so close to the ongoing argument that she can finally see what the various players are actually doing, through that space where the tent's ill-laid side gapes open: Begg and Huculak squaring off, with Lewin playing referee. It's not quite at the cat-fight stage yet, but if Morgan's placing bets, Aretha's at least setting her watch.

"Look, Anne-Marie . . . " Huculak says, finally. "I know you want to think these are your people outside, in the grave—but I've been studying them hands-on for weeks now, and I just don't think they were, at all. I don't think these were *anybody*'s 'people.'"

"Jesus, Tat! What the hell kind of Othering, colonialist bullshit—"

"No, but seriously. *Seriously.*" Huculak points to a pelvic arrangement, a crushed-flat skull, and as much of the spinal column as they've been able to find. "Pelvis slung backwards, like a *bird*, not a mammal. Orbital sockets fully ten mL larger than usual, and side-positioned, not to the front; these people were barely binocular—probably had to cock their heads just to look at something in front of them. Twice as many teeth, half of them canines, back ones serrated: this is a meat-eater, exclusively. And that's not even getting into the number of vertebrae, projection processes to the front and rear of each, locking them together like a snake's . . . "

"You've got three bodies to look at, barely, and you're already pushing taxonomic boundaries? Phylogenetic analysis by traits is a slanted system, and makes it too easy by far to mistake clades or haplogroups for whole separate species—"

Ooh, bad move, Dr. Begg, Aretha thinks, even as that last sentence starts, and indeed, by its end Huculak's eyes have widened so far, her smile-lines disappear completely. "Oh really, *is* it?" she all but spits. "Golly gee, I didn't *know* that, please tell me more! Hottentot Venus what?"

"You know what I'm saying."

"I know *exactly* what you're saying, yes; do you know what *I'm* saying? Or did you just start shoving your fingers in your ears and singing *lalalala I can't HEEEEAR yooou* the minute I started talking, as usual?"

Begg snorts, explosively. "You've seen the dig, every damn day for a month—it's a *grave*, Tat, you just used the word yourself. Full of grave goods. Animals don't *do* that, if that's what you're implying."

"Of course I'm not saying what's in there is animals, for shit's sake; an offshoot of humanity, maybe—some evolutionary dead end. Like

Australopithecus."

"You're telling me Australopithecus had snake-spines?"

"*No.* But just because we haven't found something yet doesn't mean it never existed."

"Good line, Agent Mulder."

"Oh *fuck you,* you condescending, indigenocentric *fuck —*"

Lewin raises her hands and goes to interpose between them, but they ignore her roundly—both wider as well as darker, more built for the long haul, able to shrug her off like a charley-horse. Huculak glares up as Begg stares down, hands on hips and braids still swinging, and demands: "Seriously, is that what we're down to, right now? The black girl and the Indian, calling each other out as racists?"

Huculak twitches like she's about to start throwing elbows, trying to divert the urge to punch first and answer questions later; the movement's actually violent enough to rock Begg back a micro-step, make her start to flinch involuntarily, right before she catches herself.

"You first," is all Huculak replies, finally, voice flat.

And: "*Ladies,*" Lewin puts in again, a tad more frantically. "We're scientists here, yes? Professionals. We can differ, even quarrel, but with *respect*—always respect. This is all simply theory, for now."

Now it's Huculak's turn to snort. "For*ever,* she gets her way," she replies. "And she will."

"Bet your ass," Begg agrees. "'Cause this is Kitchenuhmaykoosib Inninuwug First Nation land, and that's *not* a theory, so those bones go right on back in the ground where we found them, just like your government promised. No debate."

Lewin looks at Huculak. Huculak looks away.

"Never actually thought there would be," she mutters, under her breath.

The grave goods Huculak finds so uninteresting are typical Early

Archaic: a predominance of less extensively flaked stone tools with a distinct lack of pottery and smoking pipes, new-style lanceolate projectile points with corner notches and serration along the side of the blades suitable to a mixture of coniferous and deciduous forests, increased reliance on local chert sources. What's odd about it, however, is the sheer size of the overall deposit—far more end scrapers, side scrapers, crude celts, and polished stone *atl-atl* weight-tubes than seem necessary for a mere family burial, which is what the three bodies Begg talked about would indicate: one male, one female, one sexually indistinct adolescent (its pelvis missing, possibly scavenged by animals before the cap-stone was laid).

Folded beneath a blanketing layer of grave goods so large it almost appears to act as a secondary grounding weight, the three bodies nevertheless take pride of place, traces of red ochre still visible on and around all three rather than just the male skeleton, as would be customary. Weirder yet, on closer examination, the same sort of ochre appears to have been painstakingly applied not only to the flensed bones themselves but also to all the grave goods as well, before they were piled on top.

In burials from pre-dynastic Egypt to prehistoric Britain, Aretha knows, red ochre was used to symbolize blood; skeletons were flensed and decorated with it as both a sign of respect and of propitiation, a potential warding off of vampiric ghosts: *take this instead, leave us ours.* With no real sense of an afterlife, the prehistoric dead in general were thought to be eternally jealous, resentful of and predatory towards the living . . . but particularly so if they'd died young, or unjustly, and thus been cheated of everything more they might have accomplished while alive. Like the Lady of Cao, Aretha thinks, or the so-called "Scythian Princess," both of whom died in their twenties, both personages of unusual power (the former the first high-status woman found in Moché culture, the latter actually a Siberian priestess buried in silk and fur and gold), and both of whose tombs also contained the most precious grave good of all, startlingly common across cultures from

Mesoamerican to Hindu to Egyptian to Asian: more corpses, often showing signs of recent, violent, *sacrificial* death.

Retainer sacrifice, that's what they call it, Aretha thinks, her head spinning slightly, skull gone hot and numb under its cold, constantly wet cap of skin. *Like slaughtering horses so they can draw the princess's chariot into the underworld, except with people: concubines, soldiers, servants, slaves — maybe chosen by lots, maybe volunteers. Killing for company on that final long day's journey into whatever night comes next. In Egypt, eventually, they started substituting* shawabti *figures instead, magic clay dolls incised with spells swapped in for actual corpses; an image of a thing, just as good as the thing itself. Unless it's not.*

Text is taking shape behind her eyes, wavering: she can almost see it on her laptop's screen or maybe even a page somewhere, whatever reference-method she first encountered this information through. How in Mound 72 at Cahokia, largest site of the Mississippian culture (800 to 1600 CE, located near modern St. Louis, Missouri), pits were found filled with mass burials — 53 young women, strangled and neatly arranged in two layers; 39 men, women, and children, unceremonious dumped, with several showing signs of not having been fully dead when buried, of having tried to claw their way back out. Another group of four individuals was neatly arranged on litters made of cedar poles and cane matting, arms interlocked, with heads and hands removed.

Most spectacular is the "Birdman," a tall man in his forties, thought to have been an important early Cahokian ruler. He was buried on an elevated platform, covered by a bed of more than 20,000 marine-shell disc beads arranged in the shape of a falcon with the bird's head appearing beneath the man's head, its wings and tail beneath his arms and legs. Below the Birdman another corpse was found, buried facing downward, while surrounding him were piles of elaborate grave goods . . .

Cahokia was a trade center, of course, the apex of an empire; makes sense they'd do things big, lay on the bling. This, meanwhile… this is different: smaller, meaner. The faces of the three prime skeletons have been smashed, deliberately, as if in an attempt to make them unrecognizable, a spasm of disgust or desecration; God knows, Aretha's spent more than enough time piecing them back together to know how effective that first attack was, how odd that it should be followed up with what reads as an almost equally violent avalanche of reverence. But then there's the capstone, the lid, the flensing, and the ochre, plus the ochre-saturated grave goods pile itself—all added later, at what had to be great cost to the givers. Like a belated apology.

No retainers, though. Not here.

Not where anybody's thought to look as yet.

This last thought jolts Aretha out of half-sleep at last, making her sit up so sharply she almost falls over, a blinding surge of pain stitching temple to temple; she holds herself still on her sleeping bag, breathing as slowly as possible to thwart nausea. She presses her fingers up against the edge of her eye sockets until white dots flicker behind her eyelids, forcing the pain back by pressure and sheer will, until—gradually—the agony recedes. The minute she's able, she slips her boots back on, grabs her excavation spade and trowel, and ducks out of her tent.

The mist, cool on her flushed face, brings a moment's relief. Not sure if her giddiness is inspiration or fever, Aretha heads for the grave pit as fast as she can.

The light is dimming; she won't have long. She can't see anybody working, which suggests they're at dinner, in the chow tent. But no, not all of them, it turns out. Because as she pauses by the main tent, she can hear Dr. Begg arguing with someone yet again—over the sat-phone, this time. Who? Curiosity gets the better of her. She edges up to the tent's outer wall, holding her breath.

" . . . don't know *who* she knows, is my point, *Gammé*," Begg says. Aretha frowns, translating: *Gammé* for grandmother, the elder who helped swing the tribal council towards permitting this dig in the first place; Aretha's never heard Begg sound this uncomfortable with her. "But if it's somebody with enough clout, somebody who decides they don't want to honor the arrangement anymore—" She stops, sighs.

"Might be more money involved, sure. Maybe not. And maybe money's not what we should be thinking about right now."

A longer pause. "Well, you saw the pictures, right? Yeah, they're the ones Tat already sent. So if people start agreeing with her—" A beat. "Okay, what? No, I'm not going to do that. *No.* Because this is *science,* not story-time, that's why, and by those standards, what Tat says makes *sense.* Muddying the waters with mythology isn't going to— hey, you there? Hello? *Hello?*"

No reply, obviously; the receiver slams down, *bang.* Sometimes the phone cuts out for no reason, even with satellite help—vagaries of location, technology, all that. So: "Oh, fuck *me,*" Begg mutters and goes trudging away, still swearing at herself under her breath.

Mythology?

There was a moment, back in Week One . . . yes, she remembers it now. Sitting around the one smoking campfire they'd ever risked as the tarp above dipped and sloshed, Lewin asking Begg to fill in the tribal history of this particular area and Begg replying, slightly snappish, that there wasn't one as such: *Lots of stories, that's all—heroes and monsters, that kind of shit. We don't go up there much, that place, 'cause of the—*

—and a word here, something Aretha'd never heard before, clipped and odd: *buack, paguk, baguck.* Something like that.

(bakaak)

Bakaak in Ojibwe, pakàk in Algonquin, a version of Begg's voice corrected from somewhere deep inside. *It's an Anishinaabe aadizookaan, a fairy tale. They split the difference, usually, and call it Baykok.*

Like the Windigo, Morgan suggested, but Begg shook her head. The point of the Windigo, she replied, was that a Windigo started out human, while the Baykok never was.

It's a bunch of puns stuck together. Bakaak means "skeleton," "bones draped in skin"; thus bakaakadozo, *to be thin, skinny, poor. Or* bakaakadwengwe, *to have a thin face—*bekaakadwaabewizid, *an extremely thin being. Not to mention how it yells shrilly in the night,* bagakwewewin, *literally clear or distinct cries, and beats warriors to death with a club,* baagaakwaa'ige. *Flings its victim's chest open*, baakaakwaakiganezh, *to eat their liver . . .*

Why the liver? Aretha asked, but Begg just shrugged.

Why any damn thing? It's a boogeyman, so it has to do something *gross. Like giants grinding bones to make their bread.*

You could do that, you know, as long as you added flour, Huculak put in, from the fire-pit's far side. *Just a flatbread, though. Bonemeal won't bond with yeast.*

Thank you, Martha Stewart.

Is that what Begg's grandmother just said, over the phone? That the skeletons look like Baykok—Baykoks? That Huculak's right and also wrong? That Begg—

Oh, but Aretha's head is burning now, bright and hot, like the Windigo's legendary feet of fire. So hot the raindrops should sizzle on her skin, except they don't; they just keep on falling, soft-sharp, solid points of cold pocking down through the sodden, pine-scented air. And the pit gaping open for her at her feet, a toothless, mud-filled mouth.

She drops to her knees, scrambles over the lip, slides down messily inside.

By the time Morgan comes by it's . . . well, later. Aretha doesn't know by how much, but the light's just about completely gone, and she's long since been reduced to scraping blindly away at the grave's interior walls with her gloved fingers. She looks up to see Morgan blinking down at her through a flashlight beam and smiles—or thinks she does; her face is far too rigid-numb at this point for it to be any sort of certainty.

"'Lo, Morgan," she calls up, not stopping. "How was dinner?"

"Uh, okay. What . . . What're you *doing* down there, Ree? Exactly?"

"I have to dig."

"Yeah, I can see that. Are you okay? You don't look okay."

"I *feel* okay, though. Mainly. I mean—" Aretha takes a second to shake her head, almost pausing; the pit-walls blur on either side of her heave dangerously, like they're breathing. Then: "It doesn't matter," she concludes, mainly to herself, and goes back to her appointed task.

"Um, all right." Morgan steps back, raising her voice incrementally with each new name: "Tat, Dr. Huculak, c'mon over here for a minute, will you . . . like, right now? Anne-*Marie? Dr. Lewin!*"

They cluster 'round the edge like flies on a wound, staring in as Aretha just keeps on keeping on, almost up to her wrists now in muck. "Aretha," Dr. Lewin begins, at last, "you do know we mapped out that area already, yes? Since a week ago."

"I remember, Doctor."

"You took the measurements, as I recall."

"I remember."

"Okay, so *stop*, damnit," Huculak orders. "You hear me? Look at what you're *doing*, for Christ's sake! Anne-Marie—"

Begg, however, simply shakes her head, hunkering down. "Shut up, Tat," she says, without turning. To Aretha: "Howson, Ree . . . it's Aretha, right?" Aretha nods. "Aretha, did you maybe hear me, before? Up there, on the sat-phone?"

"Yes, Dr. Begg."

"Uh huh; shit. Look . . . the Baykok's just a story, Ree. It's folklore. You're not gonna find a, what—separate bunch of human bones in there, is that what you're thinking? Like a larder?"

Still scratching: "I'm not thinking that, no."

"Then what *are* you thinking?"

Aretha wipes mud off on her cheek, gets some in her mouth, spits brown. "Sacrifice," she answers, once her lips are clear again. "Like at Cahokia—slaves for the underworld, not food. But then again, who knows? Might've been both."

"Uh *huh*. How long you been down there, Ree?"

"I don't know. How long did they co-exist, Neanderthals and Homo habilis? 'Cause they did, right? I'm right about that. Lived long enough to share the same lands, even interbreed, enough so some people have Neanderthal DNA . . . "

"That's the current theory," Lewin agrees, sharing a quick, dark look with Begg.

But: "The hell's she saying?" Huculak demands of Lewin, at almost the same time. "Elyse, don't you *vet* your damn volunteers? We need to get her out, back to the Rez at least, get her airlifted somewhere —"

"Just shut *up*, Tat," Begg repeats, still not turning.

"Morgan, you're her friend — on my count, okay? One . . . two..."

But that, precisely, is when the wall of the grave-pit finally gives way. Releases a sudden avalanche of half-liquid earth that sweeps Aretha back, pins her under, crowns and crushes her alike on a swift, dark flood of roots and stones and bones, bones, bones.

Here they are, I was right, she barely has time to think, reeling, delirious, her arms full of trophies, struggling to raise them high. *See? See? I was right, they're here, we're*

(*here*)

But who's that, back a little further beyond her team's shocked rim-ring, peering down on her as well? That tall, thin figure with its cocked head, its burning, side-set eyes? Its featureless face carved from jet-black stone?

She hears its scream in her mind, thin but distinct, a far-flung cry. The wail of every shattered skull-piece laid back together and set ringing, tuned to some distant tone: shell-bell, blood-hiss. Words made flesh, at long last.

(*here, yes*)

(*as we always have been*)

(*as we always will*)

Aretha comes back to herself slowly, lying on a cot in the main tent, pain-paralyzed: hurt all over, inside and out. The out is mainly bruises, scrapes, a general wrenched ache, but the inside—that's something different. Like the world's worst yeast infection, a spike through her bladder, pithing her up the middle and watching her writhe; her whole system clenched at once against her own core, a furled agony-seed, forever threatening to bloom.

She'd whimper, even weep, but she can barely bear to breathe. Which at least makes it easy—eas*ier*—to keep quiet while the others talk around her, above her, about her.

"Baykok, huh?" Dr. Huculak's saying, while Dr. Begg makes a weird snorting noise. "Looks more like a damn prehistoric serial killer's dumpsite to me. And how'd she know where to dig, anyhow?"

Morgan: "She said she had a dream. Whispered it when I was taking her vitals."

Dr. Lewin sounds worried; Aretha wishes she thought it was for the right reasons. "Yes, as to that. How bad's her damage?"

"That's one way to put it," Huculak mutters as Morgan draws a breath, then replies: "Well . . . she's fine, I guess, believe it or not. Physically, anyway."

"What about the—"

Morgan's voice gets harder. "Those scars are old, not fresh. Surgical. And none of our business."

Lewin sighs. "If they mean what I think they mean, I'm not happy with . . . 'her' choice to misrepresent 'herself,' on the project application form."

"Can we not use bullshit scare-quotes, please?" Morgan asks. "I mean—check the University rules and regs, Doc. Pronouns are up to the individual these days."

"Is biology? Aretha is—is female, just because 'she' says 'she' is?"

"Uh, yeah, Dr. L, that's *exactly* what that means. Just like a multiracial person's black if they say they are or anybody's a Christian if they say so, even if they don't go to church." The fierceness in Morgan's voice puts a lump in Aretha's throat. She cracks her eyes open, tries to find words to thank her, but her lips won't work; all that comes out is a dry clicking, some insect clearing its throat from inside her mouth.

But Huculak's already moved into the pause anyhow, adding: "Like those things in the pit'd be human if they could say so."

At this, Begg turns, confronting her. "Excuse me, *things?* We're back there again? What the fuck happened to parallel evolution?"

"Oh, I don't know—tell me again how your elders think of them as ancestors, Anne-Marie. Tell me they *don't* call them monsters."

"Sure, okay: this is Baykok country, like I said that first week, which is why somebody non-tribal—some hiker from Toronto—literally had to stumble over the capstone for us to even know it was here, and why we had to cut our way in, after. But all that proves is that superstition's a powerful thing. My *Gammé's* in her eighties, and frankly, when it comes to archaeology, she doesn't know what she's talking about."

Huculak scoffs. "Yeah, and Schliemann never found eight different versions of Troy by looking where Homer said to either."

"Oh, so what—folktales are fact disguised, is that the song we're singing? Schliemann using *The Iliad* as a guidebook was the exception, not the rule; he got lucky, and what he found was *not* what he'd been looking for either. Which is exactly what's happened here, all over."

"A pile of bones that don't look human, with a much larger pile of bones attached that do," says Huculak, voice heavy with sarcasm. "Yeah, sure, no big mystery *there*."

"Well, in point of fact, no. You heard Aretha: retainer sacrifice, like in a hundred other places, and do you really think we need monsters for that?" For once, Begg sounds more exhausted than angry. "It's classic Painted Bird syndrome, Tat. Whatever makes a person different enough from the herd to be rendered . . . pariah, alien, monstrous: this little family with their wide-spaced eyes and their snake-spines, or my *Gammé* when she came back from Residential School, haircut and wearing white kid clothes, barely able to speak her own language anymore. Or Aretha here, for that matter, once Elyse got a look at her chest . . . "

Lewin lifts her hands. "Don't bring me into this, please."

"But you're already *in* it. We all are." Now it's Huculak's turn to sound uncharacteristic, all her usual snark gone. With some difficulty, Aretha turns her head, sees the woman bent down over something long, grayish-brown, and filthy: one of the freshly-dug bones, plucked from a teetery, cross-stacked pyramid of such, off the gurney she stands next to. "I mean, I'd need to do a full lab workup to verify, but some of these remains—they still have flesh on them, under the muck. Like, non-mummified flesh."

Dr. Lewin, blinking: "You mean they're—"

"Recent. Yeah."

"But they were buried. How—?"

"You tell me. Anne-Marie?"

Begg opens and closes her mouth. "Well," she starts, "that's obviously—um. Okay. I mean, that's . . . " She deflates, slumping. "I don't know what that is," she says at last, near-inaudibly.

You'd think Huculak would be proud to have thrown her chief rival off so thoroughly, but no; she looks equally taken aback, almost scared. Lewin just stands there, studying the tent's tarp floor, like she's misplaced something; above, rain drums the roof, incessant, a dull cold tide. Morgan's gaze flicks from one to the next as the silence stretches ever thinner, disbelieving, 'til it finally falls on Aretha, and her eyes widen. "Shit—Ree! You're awake!" She hurries over to the cot and kneels down, stroking Aretha's forehead. "How you feeling, babe?"

Babe. In Morgan's mouth, the word sounds good enough to make Aretha cry, or want to.

"Hurts," she husks instead, through chapped lips. "All through my groin, lower abdomen . . . " She tries to move and hisses, agony spiking her joints. "Elbows and knees, ankles, too."

Morgan puts the inside of one wrist to Aretha's forehead, then takes her pulse; Aretha's creeped out by how pale her own wrist looks when hefted slackly in the tent's lantern-light, its veins slightly distended and purpled. "Fever feels like it's gone down, at least," Morgan tells her, attempting an unconvincing smile. "But since that's as far as my Girl Guide first aid training goes, all I can tell you beyond that is you need a hospital, like *now*. Dr. Begg, is the sat-phone working again?"

"Um, no, not yet."

"Fine. You know what? It's half an hour back to the access road; give me that damn thing, and I'll get it to where it can get a signal out, then call an airlift to get her down to Thunder Bay."

Lewin puts a hand to her mouth, Victorian as all hell. "Oh dear, not at night, in this rain! What if you get lost, slip and fall, or —?"

"Ma'am, I'll be fine, my boots are hiking-rated. Seriously."

"No, Morgan, trust me, bad *bad* idea," Huculak says, Begg nodding agreement. "Wait for daybreak, for the weather to clear, that'll free up the signal link —"

Both stop as Morgan, already bent to lace her boots tighter, slashes one hand across the air.

"I have a compass and a map," she tells them, not looking up, "a flashlight, a knife, and I'm not gonna melt. Plus, it's safer on foot than trying to drive when it's like this. Anybody wants to go instead of me, I'm amenable, but you better speak now or forever hold your peace: Ree's my friend, and I'm not putting her through one second more of this than we have to."

Straightening, she glares 'round, hands on hips, but no one objects. So she stuffs the blocky sat-phone away and ducks down with a shrug instead, planting a swift kiss on Aretha's forehead — too light to fully track, here and then gone, almost hallucinatory. Like a promise.

"See you soon," she murmurs, swinging her knapsack onto her back.

No, that same voice hisses, from inside Aretha's mind. *I—*

(*we*)

—think not.

Aretha doesn't remember falling asleep. When she wakes, the pain has diminished astonishingly; not gone, still twinging through her hips and knees when she swings herself into a tentative sitting position, but so much less it's near-euphoric. She feels lightheaded, insubstantial; even the forest's damp pine-reek doesn't burn the way it used to. For a few moments, she simply enjoys breathing with something like her normal ease.

Then she sees the light or lack thereof. The similar lack of company. No sat-phone on the table, just dirt and bones. No Morgan.

Shit.

Wrapping the sleeping bag around her like a puffy cloak, she stumbles out into open air, for once blessedly free of rain; no visible sky between the trees, but there's less sinus-drag, cueing a possible shift in air pressure. Lewin, Begg, and Huculak are huddled around a Coleman stove maybe ten feet away, clustered gnats and moths flying up like sparks; Lewin turns as Aretha nears, almost smiling as she recognizes her, which is . . . odd, but welcome. Things *must* be bad.

"Aretha!" she calls out, voice only a little strained on the up note. "You look—better. Than you did."

Aretha clears her throat, even as the other two shoot Lewin looks whose subtext both clearly read *are you fucking kidding me?* ". . . Thanks," she manages, finally. Then: "Morgan?"

Lewin sighs. "No, dear. Not yet."

"How—long?"

"Two hours, maybe three," Huculak replies. "Anne-Marie went out looking, but—"

"I didn't find her," Begg says, a bit too quickly, too flat. "Not her."

Aretha nods, swallows again. No spit.

"What *did* you find?" she asks.

Tracks, that's the answer; about five minutes' walk from the camp.

They're narrow but deep, as if carved, each a slipper full of dark liquid, welling up from underground. The soil is saturated here, Aretha can only suppose, after a solid four and a half weeks of precipitation—but there's something about the marks, both familiar and unfamiliar. They look . . . wrong, somehow. Turned upside-down.

"They're backwards," she observes, at last. Bends closer, just a bit, and wavers, not trusting herself to be able to crouch; the water throws back light, Huculak's beam crossing Lewin's as Begg hovers next to them, holding back, waiting to see if Aretha can eventually identify that particular winey shade without prompting.

"Not water," Aretha says, throat clicking drier yet, and Begg shakes her head. "No," she confirms, and Aretha dips further, sniffing hard. Smells rust, and rot, and meat.

Blood.

Lewin recoils, almost tripping, but Huculak stands her ground, demanding: "And you didn't think to tell us? The *fuck*, Anne-Marie!"

Begg stays where she is, rooted fast, as though every ounce of protest in her has long since drained out through her heels. Doesn't even bother shrugging.

"Not much point," she says, simply. "You'd've found out eventually, too, once either of you thought to ask. But Aretha here's been a whole lot better at that than most of us throughout, hasn't she? Which is sort of interesting, in context."

"How so?"

"Things my *Gammé* told me over the years, that's all, about this area. Stuff I discounted automatically, pretty much, because—well, *you* know why, Tat: because science. Empirical data vs. subjective belief, all that. Because I've tried so fucking hard to never be *that* sort of Indian if I can help it." She pauses here, takes a ragged breath. "But what do you know, huh? Sometimes, a monster isn't a metaphor for prejudice at all, plus or minus power. Sometimes it's just a monster."

Huculak stares at her, like she's grown another head. "What?" she asks, yet again.

"What I just said, Tat. We should probably get going if we're going to."

"Going to — ?" Lewin apparently can't help prompting, carefully.

Begg sighs, windily, as though about to deflate. "Try, that's what I mean," she says, after a long moment's pause. "To leave, I mean. Before they get here."

"'They,'" Lewin repeats. "'They' . . . who?"

Now it's Begg's turn to stare, even as Huculak — possibly just a tad swifter on the uptake or simply paranoid enough to connect the dots without being asked — draws a sudden in-breath, a choked half-gasp; hugs herself haphazardly, grasping for comfort, but finding none. While Lewin just stands there, visibly baffled: it doesn't make sense to her, any of it, and *can't*, really. Not in any *scientific* way.

"They were here first, that's what *Gammé* always told me," Dr. Begg — Anne-Marie — remarks, softly, as if to herself. "Hunted us like animals when we came into their territory, because that's what we must have seemed like to them, the same way *they* did, to us; things with some qualities of people, not people who just happen to look like things. So we fought back, because that's what we do, but there were more of them, and they were — stronger, fought harder. Started out taking us for food, then for slaves, then for breeding stock. Changed so they could hide, everywhere. Hide inside of *us*."

"Neanderthals," Aretha says. "And Homo habilis."

Begg smiles, slightly. "The current theory," she replies, echoing Lewin. Not looking 'round as she does, even to watch how Lewin — her cognitive refusal suddenly punctured, sharp and clean and quick — begins, at last, to buckle under her own words' weight.

Behind them, the gravesite still gapes uncovered, rain-filled, ochre seeping. From above, Aretha muses, the unearthed cache of grave goods must look like a huge, slightly layered blood-blotch, all that remains of some unspeakably old crime. An apology made on literally bended knees, pot sweetened with a pile of tools and corpses, yet left forever unaccepted.

Huculak — Tat — clears her throat, knuckles still knit and paling on either elbow. Complains, voice weak: "But . . . we didn't know."

"I did."

"You never *said*, though."

"No, 'course not, because I didn't want to think it was true. I mean, c'mon, Tat; seriously, now. Would *you?*"

"Well . . . "

(No.)

Deep twilight, now, under the trees, overlaid with even deeper silence. Deep enough Aretha can finally start to hear it once more, rising the same way her pain does, threading itself through her system: the song of the bones, set shiver-thrumming in every last wet, cold part of her; that note, that tone, so thin and distinct, a faraway cry drawing ever nearer. Like blood through some fossilized shell.

And oh, oh: *Anne-Marie was right, not to want to,* she thinks, faintly, as she feels her knees start to give way — as she droops, drops, ends up on hands and knees in the mud, the blood-smelling earth. *I'm not even Native, and I don't like that story much either. Not at all.*

Not at all.

"Who's that?" Aretha can hear Lewin — Elyse — call out, faintly, squinting past her, into the darkness. Adding, hopefully, as she does: "Morgan? I— is that you, dear?"

To which Anne-Marie just shakes her head, while Tat begins to sob. And Aretha, looking up — seeing those familiar features hanging flat against the thickening curtain of night, mouth slack-hung and eyes empty, set ever-so-slightly askew — doesn't even have to wait to hear the bones' answer to know the trick of it already, to her sorrow: that skeletal shadow poised behind, head cocked, holding Morgan's skin up like an early Hallowe'en mask with the scent of fresh-eaten liver on its breath. That line of similar shadows fanned behind, making their stealthy, back-footed way towards them all, with claws outstretched.

Don't worry, the bones' song tells her, from the inside out, as the Baykok sweep in. *This darkness is yours as much as ours, after all: a legacy, passed down hand to hand, from our common ancestors. Where we are, and were, and have been. Where you are, now, and always.*

The only place any of us have left to be.

Not so different, then, after all: cold comfort at best, and none at all at worst. Not that it really matters either way.

Every grave is our own, that's the very last thing Aretha Howson has time to think before the earth opens beneath her. Before she falls head-long, wondering who will find her bones, and when — what tales they'll tell, when dug free . . . what songs they'll sing, when handled . . .

How long it'll be, this time, before anyone stops to listen.

TWILIGHT STATE

"YOU DON'T HAVE to look directly into the light," Dr. Karr tells me. "In fact, it'd be better if you didn't."

I nod. "How long will it take?"

"Today? Eight hours, tomorrow, six, the day after that, four—the whole idea is to start high, then move down by increments. One way or the other, if we see good results at the end of this session or the effects aren't quite up to plan, we'll adjust accordingly."

"Just lie here, all that time? I'm not sure I can hold still that long."

"Oh, we'll secure your head, prop the chair up, and then there's this—" She raises a thing like a cone, white and stiff, a human-sized version of the sort of collar dogs wear after surgery to keep them from biting at their own sutures. "It'll diffuse the light, somewhat, but also direct it. And better yet, it keeps you from seeing the restraints."

I swallow. "I've . . . never been good with confinement."

"Well, that's what the anesthesia's for, Mrs. Courbet."

They call it twilight sleep, she says, a twilight state. Level Two on the descending scale of sedation. Just enough drugs, in just the right combination, to keep me from forming new memories. It nips the fear in the bud, supposedly, by not allowing me to notice exactly how long my "momentary" discomfort has already gone on or speculate on how much longer it might continue.

"Now, we'll be using this IV rig to administer a cocktail of several agents to induce and maintain a light sleep, anxiety relief and short-term amnesia: propofol and midazolam, probably, along with a narcotic/systemic analgesic such as demerol or fentanyl. Of course, everyone responds differently, so we'll keep a close eye . . . but really, in most cases the dose is so perfectly calibrated that even though you'll respond to vocal commands and light touch throughout, I very much doubt you'll even remember we've started, by the time you wake up."

"You've done this before, I take it."

"Many, many times. Shall we begin?"

I cast my eyes over the set-up again, so clinically neat and clean, especially when juxtaposed against the Modern Rustic interior of my family's cabin. It was built back in the 1920s by my great-grandfather Courbet and re-done many times since. This latest iteration is my mother's work, mainly, and I think I may have spent more time here than anywhere else over the years. It is bred as much from memory and dream as wood and stones, refuge crossed with mystery, a human oasis amidst the oddity of nature, its constant push and pull—all that life, and none of it your own. In an outcast world, it's as close as I've ever come to home.

What we do today may ruin that, I suppose. But frankly, I don't see any other way forward.

(*Just do what it takes, Briony,* I hear my father whisper in my mind's ear. *Seize charge, for Christ's sake; these people are experts, so let them do their job, then pay them for it. What else is money for?*)

Soon enough I am laid back and tied down, ruffed like an Elizabethan, sinking fast. I feel the IV jack's needle prick as it goes in. Just past the cone's outermost edge, Karr turns the light on: 10,000 lux, green-bulb spectrum rather than blue, to manipulate melatonin and serotonin levels without doing damage to the photosensitive ganglion cells in my retina or the cones behind my eye. Gauze provides a secondary lid of sorts, penetrable but protective, as Dr. Karr murmurs that I need to try and keep my eyes open but also remember to blink at regular intervals. *Three breaths, Mrs. Courbet . . . Briony. One, two, three, then blink. Repeat. Yes, that's right. One, two, three . . .*

It may register as quite similar to daylight, she's told me, and it does, though not exactly; softer, hazed and vibrant, on the very edge of fading. That one last shred of bright, bravely overwhelmed, which comes before dark.

Like dusk, I think, and shiver.

This cabin is where almost every impression I have of Ontario outside Toronto was formed, over years of cyclic pilgrimage: the huge channels of moss-covered rock through which roads run like black-tarred veins, the foliage gummed with a year's worth of spiderwebs, pine needles carpeted ankle-deep upon the earth so they kick up like dirty brown snow with every step—a permanent shadow under every tree, air bitter with gnats and mosquitos that sip the corners of your eyes, where even the weeds can sting. And beyond all that the lake, overcast even on fine days, sun leached to white over gray water; sand and silt in the shallows admixed with great, trailing ropes of weed rooted deep in the dark portions beyond the drop-off.

One time we accidentally arrived during caterpillar breeding season and found the whole place boiling black and green with fuzzy, juicy, far too easily crushable crawlers: roof, walls, foundations all alike, the path itself squishing beneath our feet. Every morning we had to pound the screen door 'til it cleared, simply to see outside. But the next visit, the plague was gone without a trace—vanished, nothing left behind but memory, and that fast-fading. As though it had never happened.

The silence, at night and otherwise. The complete darkness, once the porchlights are off and the moths disperse. These are what stay with me. Time at the cabin has always been less a place to me than a method of being, never entirely lost no matter how much distance put between—as though I leave part of myself there with each visit, to be recovered on return, if only briefly—rented, never regained. And I can never stay away for long.

To arrive here, always, is to step back into a dream I was born dreaming.

There is a thing you must watch for, Bri-oh-nee, Stana told me as we sat near the lake together, the summer of my eighth year. *The* mrak, *we call it. This means dark, or dusk—twilight. The time between.*

She was a tall girl, Stana, very spare and severe, as if God had cut corners to make her: frowning lips, dark hair, cheekbones like eskers, set at a slant. A glorious bosom, kept well-leashed. Only later did I realize how she must have encoded herself onto my desire's DNA, forever pushing me towards women who looked like they might hurt me if I only paid them enough for the privilege.

Stana came to Canada from Serbia with her parents and settled in Toronto. She had medical training, or so she said . . . not quite enough to requalify and complete her degree but certainly enough to be somebody's glorified nursemaid. And she didn't hate children, though she often seemed indifferent. This in itself was so unlike my parents' attitude towards me that it probably would have made me think I loved her one way or the other, my eventual sexuality notwithstanding.

Does it live near here, the mrak? I asked her, mainly to keep her talking, as I spooned silty gray sand into my bucket, digging my toes deeper. But Stana shook her queenly head, braids lightly swinging.

Here? Yes, I suppose so; it likes places neither one thing nor another, sand and shore, water and land. But everywhere else, too. The mrak *is not bound by distances. It lives inside a moment, as sun dims and night comes on. Before the Morning Star rises.*

Beneath the lake's shallows, my feet looked pale, green-tinged, faintly swollen. A ripple rolled back and forth over them, wetting me to mid-calf as the clouds massed overhead, turning the afternoon light sour.

We should go inside soon, she told me, while I upturned the bucket onto the shore beside me and made a teetery, decaying tower of its contents, already starting to wash away with the tide. *This is no good time for you . . . for people like you. Of your age.*

Because of the mrak?

The mrak *likes to touch little children or the things that belong to them. Sometimes it is a woman, huge and dark, sometimes a giant man with a rotten face, and always its hands are glowing—this is how it sees its way in the darkness. And when it lays these long, bright hands on you or even on your toys, your books, your clothes hung out on the line to dry, then you become not truly sick or ever truly well, not sleeping, but not waking. You fall between and stay there as long as . . .*

Here she broke off, staring out across the lake, where raindrops were beginning faintly to pock its waves. And I remember how I shivered, deliciously…frightened, or playing at it, for the sheer excitement of being so. Felt the wet hair rise up on my neck, my thighs all gooseflesh, as I asked her—

As long as what, Stana? Tell me, please.

As long as it takes, of course, Bri-oh-nee, little silly girl. For the mrak *to eat you up, from the inside like bugs eat a tree. Like ants in a hill, tunneling in and in and in 'til at last the hill falls down.*

People tell children all sorts of things, I suppose, and who on earth ever knows why? She might have been angry with my parents for exploiting her so shamefully or with her parents for making her play along. Perhaps she was homesick, mourning the loss of her true place; Canada must have seemed strange to her, impermanent yet impossible to dismiss, a species of waking trance. Like being forced to dream someone else's dream.

She was gone by the new year, at any rate, just after Christmas holidays. My mother claimed she caught her stealing, but I never saw any proof that Stana coveted our possessions, and I'd spent far more time alone with her at that point. In fact, I not only probably knew her better than either of them ever would, but also knew her better than I knew either of them . . .

This last truth, unfortunately for all of us, would never really change — not that they seemed to care at the time or even later when it was all too obvious I'd be their only child, their only heir. When cancer took my mother, then moved on to take my father, preventing him from running completely through the family fortune before I reached age of majority. He never did change his will in anybody else's favor, either, opening up the line of inheritance to someone a bit more heterosexually inclined; maybe it just seemed like far too much effort for far too little reward, especially once the chemo was in full swing. Or perhaps, on painkiller-induced reflection, he actually found he disliked them all much more than he'd ever disliked me.

I didn't much care then, and I certainly don't care now it's all mine, to give or withhold as I please to whomever I find least unfavorable. If I'd had the inclination, I might even have tried to track down Stana and deed some of it her way instead of wasting my largesse on cheap imitations of her melancholy charm: my femme fataliste, dead end of all my childish fantasies. But . . .

No, it never seemed likely. What's past is past, gone forever, with no recall.

Yet here I am again, after all these years: up past Gravenhurst to Muskoka, back to familiar territory, the family cabin, the woods, the looming sky. The lake.

My wife didn't like the cabin, a difference of opinion that festered, the same as any other wound — the same as our marriage in the end. And the infection left behind worked on me, slowly, in ways I became unable to ignore.

I brought her up here on our honeymoon, hoping she would love it or at least come to understand why I did. But she never took to the place, not even at first, and later began to actively loathe it, lobbying me to do the same. It was as though she not only resented my affection for it but eventually started to consider me just as innately toxic—poisoned and therefore poisonous. My very touch tainted by association.

It seems to watch *you here, Briony,* she told me, finally, by way of an explanation. To which I replied, perhaps foolishly: *Yes, of course. And personally, I find that very comforting.*

She dug her nails into her own palms, trying not to react and failing. And right there, even so very early on . . . that was the death of us, summed up in a single moment. I watched our marriage wither, knowing it coffin-bound.

The truth is, I suppose, I've never felt entirely happy or entirely well, anywhere—not even here. But when I'm not at the cabin, I just feel so much *worse*. There's no comparison.

The cabin is where my mother chose to go when she got her final diagnosis. It's where my father was on his way to the night his chemotherapy-weakened heart gave out at sixty miles an hour, spinning the car 'til it rammed a guard-rail and bloomed into an orange ball of flame. But when I unwisely chose to tell my wife how fitting I thought those two facts were, given my own deep love for our perch near the lake, recurrent centerpiece of our shared lives—how oddly beautiful, in context. She made a face, lips twisting. Her hand all but slapped up to cover her mouth, as though she were about to vomit.

Christ, Bri! she managed, eventually. *That's just morbid. What the hell do you see in that place anyway?*

How well it *sees* me, I answered.

And that was that. As the old song says, I was alone again, naturally.

For some time before attempting this procedure, I only realized in retrospect, I'd slipped into some sort of all-over malaise with no apparent cause, but also no apparent cure. Constantly tired, I still couldn't sleep—or overslept but took no particular good from making up for lost R.E.M. My dreams were multi-tiered and repetitive, forever revolving around commonplace moments somehow imbrued with inexplicable terror, familiar faces rendered alien and malign, until inevitably I woke knotted from head to toe in a cold sweat, suffering heart palpitations. Nothing pleased me, and I—in turn—felt incapable of pleasing anyone else, had that even been an available option.

Once it was my mother I dreamt of, washing dishes while discussing how disappointing my latest report card was even as her bald and nodding head raised a fresh crown of tumors, each pulsing slightly, a death-filled flesh-sac. Another time it was my estranged wife, dressing for some fundraiser, spraying perfume on her thighs and smiling at me in the mirror; I saw her pupils square themselves and catch fire, put forth a slick green nimbus that spread across her face like grave-mold, bearding her brown to chin with decay.

And once, predictably enough, it was Stana, faced into the sun with her back turned, shrunk to nothing but one long-braided shadow in the bright haze of its fast-eclipsing corona. Telling me, without much hurry—

You should go now, Bri-oh-nee. Before it comes, since it comes so soon now. This is its time.

Bright Morning Star on the rise above and creeping dusk below, with the lake itself suddenly humping up all over like a submerged monster's back, dim water rolling free. The air itself one invisible chime of pixels and atoms, every particle set vibrating at the very same pace. A moment caught between, hovering on the knife-point verge of becoming something else.

The mrak, I thought, in the dream. *You mean the* mrak.

Yes, of course. What else?

(What else indeed?)

It knows you, you see. Your name, your face, and all of it because . . . I told it about you.

But why would you do that, Stana? I never did you any harm. I love you.

So easy to say, in a dream, but she simply nodded or seemed to. Did I make her? Well, of course I did; it's not as though she was actually there, after all. Or me either.

. . . Perhaps that's why, then, she replied after a moment. And stood there silent, no matter how I begged and pleaded, 'til I woke up.

"Sometimes I want to say my body is trying to kill me," I told Dr. Karr during our next session. "But whenever I stop to think about it, I remember that's really just accurate. Isn't it?"

"You could see it that way, Mrs. Courbet," she agreed. "And—do you?"

"Increasingly."

"Well, we should probably talk about that."

The common cry, the human dilemma; animate meat, expiry dates encoded, all too aware for comfort. So we stave it off with various emollients, until (one day, inevitably) those become equally ineffective, necessitating something . . . more.

Nothing so very irreparable in the end, Dr. Karr hastened to assure me; nothing so very transformative, at least physically. And nothing, in the end, that money wouldn't solve—like most of my problems, I'd hitherto found. Yet probably best done in private nonetheless, I decided, once she'd outlined the idea in full—away from the public eye, with as few co-conspirators involved as possible.

"We could meet at my office, easily," Dr. Karr pointed out. "Say three times a week or even every other day, depending on how fast you want the treatment over with."

"I'd prefer not to, if you don't mind. I need to be absolutely sure this is kept discreet."

Polite as she was, she tried her best not to laugh, though I could see it was a bit of a struggle. "It's just light therapy, Mrs. Courbet," she said eventually. "Not exactly controversial."

"Oh, I understand, doctor. But you see, it's more about what the mere fact of any sort of therapy implies to an outside eye."

"That you're unhappy?"

"Clinically so. It's not something I want widely known."

Here she narrowed her eyes slightly and nodded. *Because of your impending divorce,* she might have said if she'd been a different person. *Because you fear the judge will think worse of you for being depressed, seasonally affected, sleepless to the point where you'd register as drunk on most tests, breath-alyzer content notwithstanding. That you'll be forced to settle for less than you want to, because your wife will make it look as though you're not fit to handle other people's money anymore.*

And: *yes, doctor,* I might have replied, without resentment. *Given that's the only job — the only* skill *— I've ever really had.*

But she didn't, and I didn't. Which, seeing how I'd never have employed that sort of person in the first place, if I could at all help it — the sadly frequent kind who apparently just has to open their mouth while thinking or else their brain doesn't work quite as well — made me willing to trust her. On the matter of therapy, that is.

Eventually, we agreed on terms. And those terms brought us here.

It's unseasonably warm and bright for an October weekend as we arrive at the cabin, yet still raining, as it almost never entirely ceases doing; typical fall, a border season, neither one thing nor the other. Within hours, this rainbow glitter will dull back down to a comfortable gray, but even now the air feels thick, smelling mildly of wet dust or sodden, half-rotten pinecones. You can taste it in the back of your mouth, a mint-wrapped stone. I haven't been here for nearly two years, though my people traveled up last week, stocking supplies, cleaning and airing out, the whole nine yards. Thanks to their efforts, we find the place in good repair, welcome mat well-brushed, with deep drifts of dead leaves already gathered into piles for the mulch-pit.

Later, I stand at my bedroom window, sipping tea, listening to Karr's team set up her equipment before the long drive back to Toronto. Soon enough, it'll be just her, me, and the plan of therapy, or at least seem so—an easily-dispelled illusion, given that if you walk far enough in either direction you'll reach somebody else's dock, somebody else's beach, somebody else's equally "secluded" home away from home. Not to mention how even down at the water's edge, with a good, high sand-brake raised on either side to shield you from your neighbors' view, there are always the islands with their own cabins—huge windows sunset-glinting, decks usually angled towards open water but with a fairly good view of the shore, assuming the people living there care to twist far enough to take a look.

But this is the off-season, boats idle, lake stilled almost motionless whenever the rain slacks to drizzle. And while I might not feel entirely safe, given what's about to take place, I certainly don't feel observed.

Back to the chair, laid out, encollared, gauze over my eyes; the light snaps on, flooding my mind with sunshine. Then, what seems like mere seconds later—

"All right," I hear Karr say, from far away. "We're done for today."

I lick dry lips, tongue gone equally dry. "But . . . you haven't even started yet," I hear myself say, voice gone hoarse and querulous.

She laughs, closer now, fingers light on the ruff's fastening. "We started this morning, Mrs. Courbet. That's the twilight sleep for you."

"No memories."

"As advertised. Now—be careful getting up, hold onto my arm. Here's some water, drink it slowly. Yes."

"I don't feel any different."

"You might not immediately. It's not an exact science."

I take another sip, cough a bit to clear my throat, but the roughness doesn't go away. "That's . . . very reassuring," I manage finally.

That night, when I close my eyes, I find myself back by the lake in full restraint, the base of Karr's chair plunged deep enough that my heels touch wet silt, with my face angled out towards open water. The straps dig my wrists 'til they start to numb, and through the cone's white flare I can just glimpse a silhouette I suspect must be Stana's to my left, hair unbound and whipping in the mounting wind.

Can you see it yet, Bri-oh-nee? she asks. *Poor little girl. It is so close, now — very close.*

The mrak? I ask, trying to crane my neck further, to finally *see* her, after all these years . . . all I have is memory, a bent mirror, and the warped reflection of her I've courted again and again, chasing it through a chain of equally unsatisfying women. And for a moment fear grips me, bowel-deep: what if I do manage to catch a glimpse, at long last, only to find it's just yet another variation on a theme — so close to my wife, that unwittingly pale imitation, as makes no difference?

But: *No one knows how the* mrak *is made,* Stana continues, *though we all wonder. Is it always the same? Or is it made anew over and over, every sunset, the same way day turns to dusk?*

Perhaps it was a person, once. A child, even.

Perhaps it is the mrak's *own touch, itself, that makes another* mrak.

Out on the water are islands, the nearest of which sketches a cool curve furred with trees, a skeleton eye socket of rock, a jutting cabin-cheekbone. And as the sun sets, as twilight falls and dusk creeps up, draining the world of color — as that happens, I watch the whole thing lurch and rumble, earthquake-shifting. See it re-orient itself, submerged portion slick and streaming, to form a massive, bisected face which turns my way, blindly seeking, like some sleeper fresh-awakened. Like a hunting animal, roused by the scent of prey, who sniffs into the wind to discover exactly which way it should turn, and pounce.

Phosphorescence spreading, a rotten green creeping up over its domed hillside skull, blooming all over. Its concave features, decay-blurred, algae-encrusted. Soon, I think, a pair of similarly glow-palmed hands will break from the lake, reach out to seize me, lift me whole and struggling to its gaping, rock-toothed shore-mouth . . .

The false sun that doctor shines will never keep it away, poor girl, Stana tells me. *Only the Morning Star's true light can do that, and I do not see it rise, not now, not here. Not for you.*

Oh, but surely, I want to shout in return, *you will save me, Stana — you must. Because you love me, don't you, just a little? The same way I love you?*

No reply. The straps bite deep; the *mrak*'s green light fills my cone-collar like a cup, drowning me. I gasp and take it in, lungs filling cold as lake-waves, deep and murky, each lung set outlined and glowing in the red darkness of my chest —

— 'til all at once, I feel Stana's hands on my shoulders, pressing me down, her hair falling 'round me, soft and dark, like earth into an open grave. Saying, as she does: *But perhaps I should not have worried, Bri-oh-nee, all this time. For see, in its eyes — how it recognizes you? Perhaps it has touched you already, long before, without either of us knowing. This would explain much, yes?*

So you are its, and always have been: never fully sick, never fully well. Never fully asleep, and never fully waking.

(*Never fully loved,* I think, helpless, at the same time — no, I *know*: unloved, loveless, unable to love. *And never fully loving.*)

At this, Stana nods, probably. Pronounces, as though passing sentence —

Now you are mrak, *and this love you want so badly . . . this love you offer . . . pollution, only. Danger. Just as this hour is yours, this time between. Just as this place has always been your place.*

Now, as then. Then, and always. Always, and forever.

(*So I was right to send my wife away, after all,* I think. *I was being kind, keeping her safe. Because I loved her.*)

(Because I still do and always will.)

The island, looming, cliff-mouth wide, water streaming like a beard, and the lake opening too, right below it—lips of foam, teeth of bone, grim gray sky for a jaw-hinge, eternally poised to bite. A double devouring.

But before either mouth can quite close over me, I rocket up from sleep in one great, wracking leap, lie drenched and sleepless 'til dawn. Wait, with a pounding, skipping heart, for the moment when I can at last tell Dr. Karr: *It wasn't enough.*

"I'll need to send you deeper," Karr says as I frown. Explaining, gently: "In order to add auto-suggestions in on top, so I can guide you through the process. These dreams you describe—to me, they almost seem like your brain revolting against the twilight sleep, reframing your lack of new memories into some sort of phobia. I mean, you've been put out before, yes, completely? For surgery?"

"... now and then."

"And how did you react to the general anesthetic process on those occasions?"

The frown spreads, becoming a full-bore shudder; I've always dreaded "going under," how consciousness simply drops away without warning, nothing left behind but a black hole of non-being. That total disappearance. That emptiness.

"I fought it," I tell her, finally. "The same way I would have fought death."

"Well, then."

I sigh. "But I've had these same dreams for years, doctor, especially here. It's all part of the pattern: nightmares, insomnia, depression ..."

"Interesting that you chose to come to the cabin for therapy, then. Isn't it?"

(In context? Yes.)

"At any rate," she continues, "your body's obviously so used to these symptoms, it sees our attempts to cure them as an attack. Has it ever been this bad before?" I shake my head, reluctant. "So why do you think that is?"

"This place," I say, shrugging. "The situation . . . my divorce. Stress."

"Ah, yes — the prime exacerbator."

When looking for causation always start with whatever's newest — Karr's not wrong about that. "My wife," I find myself saying, "had expectations, I think, about how matrimony would change things. Change *me*. I'm still not sure why. I was like this when she met me, after all. But . . ."

"Love cures all?"

I nod. "It doesn't, though."

"People are bad at distinguishing manageable behaviors from pathological ones," Karr agrees. "To grasp that it's not a question of 'getting well' but of incremental steps towards long-term maintenance. It can be difficult to accept the essential uncertainty of that reality, especially when you have no opportunity to contribute. Significant others appreciate being given the chance to at least *try* to help — it makes them feel valued. Needed."

"But she couldn't help," I point out. "Nobody can. You can't fuck a crazy person sane. Why waste time trying?"

"It was hers to waste."

"I was trying to be . . . considerate."

Karr sighs. "I wonder if she'd think so."

Soon, twilight sleep gives way to twilight state. The lake, the gray sky, white sun hanging in dimness: so small, so bright. *Is* that the sun or the Morning Star? It hurts my eyes to look at.

Deeper, Mrs. Courbet, deeper. Briony. Can you hear my voice? Speak freely.
(Yes, doctor.)
Good. Can you move your head, your hands? Nod, if you can. Give me some sign.

Nothing happens. The lake laps the shore. Inside the cone's curve, my field of vision shrinks, restricted: lake, sky, star. My own shallow breath, my blood, my skull set singing, an empty shell's dull roar. My slack body, tied down, motionless as stone.

Speak freely. Are you awake, or asleep?
(I . . . don't know.)
Can you see?
(Only the lake.)
Can you move?
(. . . no.)
That's good. That's very good.

I hear Karr take a breath, then say: *Open your eyes now, Briony. There's someone here who wants to speak to you.*

So I do, and the first thing I see is a woman, standing over me: tall, spare, and dark, curvaceous, queenly. Like God cut corners to make her. She studies me the same way she did for most of our marriage, with a bitter fascination. As though I promised her something without meaning to, then never quite delivered on it.

"Hello, Bri," she says. "Been a while, hasn't it? You can answer freely."

"Hello, Heba," I reply, surprisingly unsurprised. But that's not enough for her, apparently.

"Answer the question," she snaps back, an angry crack in her voice, as though she's testing something. Then relaxes just a bit when I answer, with only a second's pause —

"Yes, it has been."

Heba looks to Dr. Karr, who's standing beside her; Karr nods, slightly. "Just like you wanted — total suggestibility, but without the amnesia this time. Ask her anything."

" . . . All right."

Heba Gilroy Courbet, my wife — ex-wife to be, that is — takes a moment, maybe to think over what exactly "anything" should consist of; her hair hangs heavy, framing a pale, fatigue-smudged face set with eyes so deep blue they seem black. And: *You don't look good, sweetheart,* I catch myself thinking. *Almost as bad as me and that's saying something. Don't tell me you can't sleep now.*

From now on I see two things at once, superimposed, like bad 3-D: what's inside my head overlaid with what's not. Heba leans in, studying me, as Dr. Karr stands with arms crossed, nervously tapping one foot. I'm not sure what she thought would happen once Heba got what she must have paid for, access to me in this useless, curtailed state, but perhaps this wasn't it.

She's a hard one to trust, doctor, I try to project, unable even to meet her eyes. *This circumstance alone should tell you that.*

"Why do you think I'm here?" Heba asks me. "Speak freely."

My lips are so dry. "Therapy?"

"That's funny, but no." She sighs. "To find out why *you're* really here, I suppose. Mary told me you were sick, that you'd opted to come up to the cabin for treatment, and I . . . I remembered those stories you told *me*, about your parents. Stupid, right? But physical or not, I had to wonder whether it was something a bit more potentially dangerous than Mary seemed to think it could be. Because I know you, Bri. I know what this place is to you." She waits, as though expecting me to answer, then realizes her mistake. "Oh, for Christ's sake! *Speak freely.*"

I clear my throat. "I don't know what you want from me, Heba."

"Four *years*, Briony. I just want what's mine."

"And what would that be exactly?"

"Good question. Think back: when we stood up in front of all those people, you promised me love, fidelity, loyalty . . . that we'd always be together. That we'd be like *one person*. So why did it take me reading Mary's session notes to get any sort of an idea about exactly how fucked you are, let alone *why?* You never even told me something was wrong, until it couldn't be fixed anymore. You never told me *any-thing*."

"Maybe I wanted to . . . protect you."

"From *what?*" I hesitate, drawing a bitter laugh. "You won't say, right? Even now. Well, Mary here can *make* you, if I tell her to, or even if I don't . . . make you do anything she wants. Hurt yourself, maybe. Stare in that stupid lightbox 'til you go blind. Jesus, Briony, how desperate would you have to be to put your mind in *her* hands? To trust she couldn't be bought when she very obviously *can?*"

(Because *There's only one real weakness, Briony,* I hear my father say from somewhere down deep inside, *universally shared, and nothing ever changes but the currency involved. That's why you have to hold onto money so tightly, because it'll leave you in a minute for the first open hand. And all you really have is more of it than most people, at least to begin with.*)

(But: *No, Bri-oh-nee,* Stana's voice points out. *You do have one other thing and always did, just as it has you. Even though you may not want it.*)

The dusk deepens, clouds of mud roiling up through lake water, disturbed by a delicate footstep—as much smell and sound as something seen, the susurration of wind on water, acrid tang of moldering wood and leaves, an insectile buzz felt in the temples and fingertips. . . Oh but wait, no: that's Karr speaking, her too-calm clinical voice gone brittle, disturbed. Saying—

" . . . Enough. Let me get her to sign the documents and send her back down; we can be over the border at Sault Ste. Marie in four hours—"

"Shut *up*, Mary." Heba is only a cut-out silhouette now, black on black on black, and I find myself smiling at her sharp command, realizing exactly where she must have learned that tone she's trying to mimic. "You'll get your money. Money's *nothing*. Briony taught me that—and I'm a fast learner, as even she'd agree." Swinging back to me, her bruised eyes suddenly visible again as they meet mine: "Wouldn't you, darling?"

"Very fast, yes."

"*Thank* you." Her shadow-self shifts, clenched fists kissing over her breastbone, as if to help her hold herself together. "Money's nothing, love is . . . well, it's something, but I was never going to get that, was I? So that doesn't matter either. Blood, though . . . *that's* something, too."

"Do you want blood, Heba?" I ask, without being prompted and watch Dr. Karr jump just a little—mouth opening and closing like a fish making little o's, tongue-tied and maybe thinking: *no no, this shouldn't be. She's breaking free, Heba, coming back up—anything could happen now—*

"What I *want* is for you to look at me for once, straight on." I do. "Yes, just like that. Now *tell* me, for the last damn time, before you make me do something I'm really going to regret. Tell me . . . "

. . . *what?* I want to ask. But really, all I have to do it wait.

" . . . why I was never enough."

It's not that I don't want to answer; a blessed relief in a way simply not to care anymore. Yet the words logjam my mouth, along with half a dozen others: *Because / Because nobody could have been / Because I'm not enough, not you / Because you wanted to change me, or me you / Because neither of us could have known what "for better or for worse" might mean for us / For me . . .*

Too much, and not enough, so in the end I don't say anything at all. Just let my eyes drift past her to the window, deep blue with autumn nightfall now, a cold yellow half-moon rising beyond the black curve of the islands—that one island, closer than any should be, already half-turned in its socket. Already humping up, poised to rise, and walk.

Heba doesn't see it, of course; she's far too busy suddenly shaking me hard by my shoulders, snapping my slack neck back and forth inside the plastic cone like a marble rolling 'round a funnel, shrieking: Talk, *I said! Speak freely, goddammit!* And Dr. Karr at the same time, yelping over her, trying to break my trance: *My voice, rise up, four three two one and wake, you will wake refreshed, you won't remember any of this, you won't remember —*

Two sharp clicks. The therapy lights snap off, the living room track lighting on. But the dusk is thick now, everywhere, like air, covering both women in shapeless sacks through which I see only their eyes, beach mirage bright overtops as some bleak and alien desert. Sound bleeds out to silence. I stare past them to the rising moon overlaid with sun, the silty sand, the lake.

And then I see the *mrak*, rising out of the water, stepping ashore. A mountain-tall figure, a giantess, yet still vaguely shaped like that girl I fell in love with so very long ago: Stana, done up in draped and blurry shadow, reaching out, feeling her way by the uncertain, ten-fingered light of her own glowing hands. Its hair is ivy and pine needles, its skin weather-yellowed birch bark, its massive teeth made from the quartz-streaked sedimentary gray rock of the islands' shores, and it moves like rippling water as it strides silent towards the cabin, towering up into the dark.

Close enough, now, that those hands can light up its great, blind eyes, its face, so raw and unfinished. Close enough for me to finally see who it really *does* looks like: not Stana at all in the end. No. Not even close.

I have never seen a mirror so tall, I think. Nor one so terribly, terribly . . . accurate.

Time has slowed, as it always does in dreams. Heba and Dr. Karr move as if caught in treacle, turning upon one another so slowly that their conflict will not even have time to begin before this is over. And behind them, the *mrak* dips down, re-sizing itself; looks in through the window, a curious little girl surveying strange dolls. Without visible transition it has already slipped sideways to the door, opening it, crossing the floor like a shadow. It climbs onto the chair to peer down at me, then slides down along my body, entwining with me, one glowing hand on my heart. Pressing down, hard, 'til it feels as though my breastbone will crack.

She kisses me, the *mrak*, with her rotting tongue. Pares the conical therapy ruff away gently, as her huge, bright hands brush me up and down. Then melts away, leaving me stretched out in its wake as a discarded husk, stuffed full and sodden. The straps holding me down burst, rotted instantly. I twist my hands free, raise them, and watch them start to glow—no surprise there. Just that sole unsteady, doubled light in the darkness, outside and within.

Sitting up, I seize Heba by her face, hauling her 'round; Dr. Karr skitters back in shock, colliding with the wall, but I ignore her. Force Heba to look deep into *my* eyes, as I tell her, with the *mrak*'s voice: "Answer? Oh, I can do much better than that."

She struggles, keening, a broken-winged gull, but those hands are irresistible. They bring her closer, closer. Until, at last, I can whisper, into her mouth—

"Let me *show* you."

The Morning Star rising, or perhaps setting, somewhere above. Impossible to tell which from this angle: not here in this place, at this hour. Not that it really makes a difference.

What happens to Karr doesn't concern me much; she stays stuck, I assume, unable to move, unable to flee. But you, my dear Heba—you will meet me halfway from now on, as you always wanted. Absorb my tainted touch. You will stay with me forever, neither waking nor sleeping, neither sick nor well; I will give you what I can and use you up 'til there is nothing left for either of us.

That's love, isn't it? Or if it isn't, it should be. Since, after all . . .

. . . there's really nothing else.

Later, on the beach, I hear what might be Stana come up behind me. Maybe she'll put her hand on my shoulder, I think. Maybe we'll walk into the water together, submerge, never to be seen again. Sink until only the tops of our skulls are visible, just two more islands in a dim gray lake under a darkening sky, horizon lit by one bright sliver.

Where I come from, Stana's voice tells me, *we use a certain herb with yellow flowers and leaves like rosemary as incense for a* mrak-*touched child's relief. But this does not grow here, unfortunately.*

I know, Stana.

I would find some for you, Bri-oh-nee, if I only could.

I know.

On Krk, an island in the Adriatic, Stana continues, *they tell how the* mrak *fights the sun, every day at dusk. How during the day, the sun gets the better of his opponent, using flaming arrows to drive the* mrak *into the deepest, darkest gorges, but at night the* mrak *emerges once more to chase the sun with a great net. But every time he is about to close the net over his prey, the Morning Star draws near, its light cutting the sun free.*

So the mrak *loses.*

So far, yes. Yet the islanders know the mrak *will win, eventually. And so the fight goes on.*

I'm tired, Stana. So tired.

Then sleep, Bri-oh-nee, silly girl. Close your eyes. Let go . . .

(*. . . until tomorrow.*)

Tomorrow, and tomorrow, and tomorrow.

No other choice, and so I do, still fearing dissolution, absence — no memories, no dreams, no me. But this does not happen, for behind my lids, I remain caught between: neither one thing nor the other, neither fully asleep nor fully awake, neither dreaming nor not. Knowing, somehow, that I may stay that way forever.

And even now, even here, I can't tell which might be worse.

Some Kind of Light
Shines from your Face

It is immediately obvious that the Gorgons are not really three but one plus *two.
The two unslain sisters are mere appendages due to custom; the real Gorgon is
Medusa.*

—Jane Ellen Harrison

OOCH'S THE ONE *thing always plays,* Miz Forza told me, right
from the start. And damn if I didn't come pretty quick to believe her 'bout that, just like I did 'bout so much else: Better
than freaks, better than tricks, safer and more sure by far than creatures that required twice the feed of a grown man, not to mention a
whole heap of mother-lorn care lest they catch ill and shit 'emselves to
death, run wild and kill the rubes, or just bite at their own bellies 'til
their guts fell out on the road.

Not that anything was really *safe* back then in them dustbowl days
of endless dirt and roaming; it was our stock in trade to hook folks in
and get 'em riled up, after all, then see how much money we could pull
from between their starving teeth before the inevitable backlash. The
whole damn world was a half-stuffed firecracker, just as like to fizzle
as it was to take your face off, and waiting on the spark—or maybe a
mine dug deep in the mud of *La Belle France* of the kind Half-Face Joe
used to tell tales on, a-whistling into Skinless Jenny's ear and flapping
his flippered hands along for accompaniment, as though he was making

shadow-dogs bark on Hell's own wall. After which Jenny would translate, her own uncertain voice sweet and slow as stoppered honey, while the lamplight flickered so bad it looked like every one of her Thousand and Ten Tattoos was dancing the low-down shimmy with each other.

Joe'd been a handsome young man once 'fore them Europe kings and such got to squabbling with each other. Now he took tickets with a bag over his head 'til it was time to stump up onstage and exhibit himself, making women and kids squeal and grown-ass men half-faint with his flesh's horrid ruin. In an odd way, he made a perfect palate-cleanser for the cooch show, too . . . always boiled the crowd off a bit, sent the ladies scurrying, leaving their menfolk ready to pay big for a bit of sweet after all that sour.

Them gaiety-gals was the real stars of the show, though, for all they came and went right quick—got picked up in one shit-hole town, dropped off again three more over, and never seen since. I didn't ever tend to look too hard at their faces, myself—why bother? Be it on-stage or off-, wasn't a one of us didn't know how with them, all true interest began to build strictly beneath the neck.

Five gals on either side, one in the middle. Ones on either side did their Little Egypt harem dance, the classic shake and grind, in outfits that flashed their hips, thighs, the fake jewels in their belly-cups, 'fore popping their front-closed brassieres apart to let their boobies sway free. One in the middle, though, whoever she might be that week—she was the real deal, the star attraction. The one who risked the full blow-off and lifted her split skirt high, let the rubes gape at the hidden-most part of herself while up above the Mask of Fear nodded and grinned, all pallid skin and bruisy eyes and dead snake hair hung in clusters like poison vine, adding a very particular sting indeed to *her* all-too-naked tail.

"I don't suppose you even know what this is," Miz Forza said to me the first night I turned up shivering at their campfire with my hand half out, half not, just in case they took a notion to whip me for it. She had it hung up on a stand, like for wigs, and was stroking it all over with some foul-smelling stuff meant to keep it supple; the other gals all just sort of looked 'round it, shoving Miz Farwander's stew inside as fast as it'd go, like they was trying to forget how one of 'em would have to stick her head inside 'fore the next work-a-day was done.

What the Mask was made of I didn't know then and didn't want to — but I sure did want me some of what else they had. So I squinted hard, then back up at the caravan's walls, which were covered in similar figures, their paint weather-worn yet still somehow bright, like fever.

"Looks like the Medusa, to me," I said, finally. "That old hag-lady with hissers for locks who could turn men t'stone with one look-over. Some Greek fella cut her head off for her, hung it on his shield, an' used it to get him a princess t'marry. And then a horse with wings come out her neck, if I don't misremember."

The Mizes exchanged a glance at that, near to surprised as I'd ever seen 'em come. From the start, they read like sisters to me, though their names was different: Miz Forza was the smaller, dressed like a fortune-teller in a hundred trailing skirts and scarves, all a-riot with color; Miz Farwander was tall as some men and tougher than most, never wore nothing more elaborate than a pair of bib overalls and a greasy pair of cowboy boots, with her hair crammed down inside an old newsboy's cap so tight she might as well be bald. Come to think, they neither of 'em liked to show their hair none — Miz Forza's was wrapped like rest of her in a scarf the color of money, wound 'round with a string of old pewter coins. And she wore gloves, too, right up to her elbows, while Miz Farwander's hands were covered so deep in grime and such it was like they'd been dyed — black and gray, with no easy way to tell their fronts from their backs, except by what she was doing at the time.

And: "That's good," she said, approvingly, and grinned at me wide, so's I could see her teeth were all capped and shod in metal from east to west — metal of every sort: Silver, tin, steel, bronze, and even a hint or two of gold. "Ain't it, sister? Most don't know the old tales, not anymore."

Miz Forza nodded back. "That's right, that's right; they do *not*, sad to say." To me: "And who was it taught you the right way of things, dear? Your mother, maybe? Grandmother?"

"That'd be my Ma. She loved all that old stuff."

"But you don't have no true Greek in you, do you, even so? Not by the shape of your face, nor the color of your eyes. . . "

I blushed a bit at that, though I tried not to, for I'd been twitted over these things often enough in previous days.

"Don't rightly know," I said, shortly. "Don't rightly care too much either . . . not 'less it'll get me a job or some of that stew you're ladlin' out there. 'Cause if it will—"

Miz Farwander laughed. "If it *will*, then you're Greek through and through, ain't you—both sides for a hundred generations, all the way back to Deucalion's mother's bones? Aw, you don't have to answer, child; I can see you need feedin', sure as sin. And the storm-bringer Himself knows we got enough to go 'round."

Miz Forza cast eyes at her, sidelong, as though to warn her not to speak so free. But Miz Farwander just shrugged, so she turned back to me instead, asking—

"And what might your name be, gal? If you don't mind me askin'."

"Persia," I said. "Persia Leitner."

"That German?"

"For all's I know."

"Your Ma might be able to tell us."

"Might, if she was here," I allowed, the pain of that old wound seeping up through me once more. "But. . . "

Miz Forza nodded as though she'd heard all this before, which she probably had. "And you don't know your Pa neither, I s'pose," she suggested, without any malice.

I grit my teeth. "S'pose not," I answered. "But I sure ain't the only one like that 'round these parts."

"Oh, no, no, no. No, Persia . . . you surely ain't." A pause. "Sounds a bit like 'lightning', though, that name. Don't it?"

I'd never thought so, but that smell was making my mouth water hard, so I nodded. The gals all murmured amongst 'emselves like a flock of cooing doves. And:

"It *does*, yes, now you mention," Miz Farwander told Miz Forza, musingly, as she passed the last cup they had on over—and even as I sunk my face in it, through one more glance back and forth again right overtop me like I wasn't even there. "It certainly does, at that."

You'll recall the pictures, no doubt—migrant mothers, carts jam-packed with Okies bound to pick or beg, Hoover camps in every mud field and vacant lot. Houses buried window-deep in sand and milk-starved babies buried shameful shallow or not even buried at all. They look like a bad dream now or even lies, but they sure wasn't; I saw it all. Hell, I *lived* it.

When the crops dried and the dust come down to scour us clear, it was like every drop of color just went out of the world—drained slow, like a man can die from one little cut alone, he only gets caught the exact wrong way. Like we was all of us being poisoned by coal-dust, or tin, or cheap nickel coating boiled off of pot-bottoms along with our daily mush and didn't even know it. Oh, there was symptoms and that, which we mainly put down to hunger, a powerful thing; hunger will make your head ache and give you double vision, sure enough, under any circumstances.

But I can't think it was hunger alone that drove my Ma stark crazy, always following things from the corners of her eyes that simply weren't there to any other person's reckoning—not that, nor having no money, doing things with all manner of men that weren't none of 'em my Pa, always living hand to mouth, chased from town to town like dogs and thrown rocks at for grappling at scraps.

My Ma said my Pa was some gangster in Kansas City, and she'd had to run from him—or maybe it was *her* Pa she'd run from, who'd paid men to cram her in a car's trunk and dump her far from her home, to fend off the shame of her falling to ruin. But then again, sometimes she said my Pa was a wolf, or a burst of lightning, or the wind. Said he'd come winding through sunlight-wise under her window-shade one day and fell headlong into her lap like a shower of gold.

He made me shiver, she told me. *Made me bow down, like Heaven's king himself. Persia, don't ever forget . . . he made* you.

I learned to hate just about every person I saw during those days. While my Ma grew more and more tired, more and more silent, 'til the morning came she wouldn't say nothing at all, wouldn't even open her eyes. Wouldn't even call after me when I left her there by the roadside, sleeping under a tree like King Minos' daughter after the wine-god told old Theseus he wanted her for himself, so's he and his had better cut and run 'fore she woke up to complain about it.

I was glad she'd told me stories like that one, eventually; they gave me different ways to look at things and bright scenes to play out inside my head when I sore needed 'em—like radio-music to most, I guess, or those Motion Picture shows I never had a coin worth wasting on. Helped me make my mind up and told me how one day I'd know I was right to do her like I did. But the further I got from her side, I found, they didn't give me no damn comfort at all.

It was on down that same road a spell I first met with the two Mizes, though, once Momma's face had faded into the same dust as everything else that ever fell behind me. And it was only 'cause of them yarns of hers I knew what-all tale them paintings on their caravan's side spelled out, which (like I told you) soon proved to at least count for something in their eyes. With that one conversation, I gained what few keys to the kingdom they ever seemed like to dole out: The knowledge while this was their show, in the end, we at least had open invitation to try and keep up with it, for exactly so long as it suited them both that we should.

Miz Forza and Miz Farwander offered an open hand and a shut

mouth, which was a hell of a lot more'n most; they didn't care where you'd been or where you was bound for, and they neither of 'em seemed to count the straight law as a friend. Hard work spent setting up and tearing down got you a share in whatever food might come their way, a part of the day's take and the right to sling your bedroll near their fire.

"Depression", they called it, and that was the God's own truth. You felt it in your empty gut, your equal-empty chest, as though it was you who'd died instead of everybody else and all this living on you'd done was only a cruel trick, a walking ghost's delusion. Made your days so bone-weary it was like you was still dreaming — and not a good dream, neither, nor yet a bad; nothing so easy. Most like them awful dreams you have where you work all day, then muse on doing the exact same thing all night, back-aching and useless: Ones you wake up from spent as ever, but with nothing to show for all your toil.

So the cooch, with its tinsel and soft light, its sway, its trailing crinolines . . . the curve of a woman's flesh barely wrapped, then peeled free by stages . . . that was a show worth the seeking out for most men. And at the end of it all they went knees-down for a glimpse of that ultimate holy mystery, some girl's secretest parts shining like a rose on fire, exposed at the tangle crook of two thighs and framed in stocking-tops and musk.

Under the Mask or not, working cooch was fast cash that left almost no taste of sin behind. Unlikely as hell any of 'em would find herself recognized once she chose to move on, and we didn't truck with private viewing parties after the lights went down neither — not like most others did. Not unless someone pressed too hard for Half-Face Joe to handle, wouldn't resign himself to take "no" for an answer. And even then —

—well, we didn't tend to see those men again, no matter how short a time 'fore we swung back by their town. And nobody, to my knowledge, ever did ask the two Mizes why.

Yeah, I saw how the cooch made fools and kings of men both at the same time, how it drew one common sigh wept out from twenty different mouths at once. Saw how it made 'em throw down pennies they couldn't afford, or stuff worn-soft bills they should've fed their kids with into the girls' garters with lust-shaking hands.

And I ain't too proud to admit it, either: After so much toil and sorrow, I wanted me a piece of that, cut big and steaming. Wanted it *bad*.

Lewis Boll I met in Miz Forza and Miz Farwander's service, too. He was twice my height but a third of my weight, lanky as a giraffe's colt, with squint blue eyes and a lick of too-long black hair that always fell down to brush his brows by noon, no matter how hard he slicked it back of a morning. He had stubble on his stubble, a shadow that started well before four o'clock and ran 'til right you could see exactly where his beard would go if he just let it. And half-grown or not, he was the first boyfriend I ever had that seemed like a man.

Lewis was a genuine Okie from way back in the Bowl, last left standing in a clan that'd once been thirty or so strong; he liked money far more'n he liked his liquor, so we had that in common. Right now he worked roustabout, wrangling ropes and poles for the cooch show tent, but his grand ambition was to either rob banks like Pretty Boy Floyd or get himself in my pants, whichever came first; sounded a deal nicer, the way he used to say it. But fine talk or not, he did get a tad nasty when I told him straight out which one it wasn't likeliest to be.

"What you savin' it for, Persia?" he demanded. "I'm gonna be rich—hell, we both are. What's mine'll be your'n, you just wait a while . . ."

"Uh huh. Well, holler back at me when you already got somethin' to swap me for it—'cause right now, what you 'n' me both got's 'bout the exact same amount of nothin' much. And that ain't enough to make me drop my drawers onstage, let alone off-."

Lewis colored a bit the choice of words, since he well knew where *my* ambitions lay: Up on that same podium with the rubes all panting up at me like begging dogs and the Mask of Fear stuck fast to my kisser.

But: "You got your blood yet, Persia?" was all Miz Farwander asked me, back when I made my first play for the position. "No? Then you'll just have to wait, my darlin'. 'Cause we won't take no gal ain't bled yet."

"No indeed," Miz Forza chimed in from her crocheting in the caravan's corner, nodding right along. "No gal ain't bled can wear *her* face, for us or elsewise."

"She" was what they both called the Mask, though damn if I knew why—what everyone called it, even the gals who'd put it on, none of whom got to keep it for long. Like I said, they came and went; went faster than came, if I'd stopped to think on it. And the one time I collared one to quiz her on how it felt to be inside, she'd only shook her head, as though there weren't words enough to answer my question in the short span of time she had 'fore the next show rolled out.

"You just sort of have to be there," she said, finally. "Be *in* it. That then . . . *that*'s when you'll know."

But being hungry makes a gal apt to stay maiden far longer than if she's well-fed, as I'd long since found out and hitherto been grateful for, seeing how it meant no matter what-all might occur along the road, I wasn't too like to catch myself a child from it. So all I could do 'til my courses came was sit there and watch Miz Forza handle the Mask of nights, curing its slack white face like leather with delicate strokes of that awful-stinking salve. Sometimes she'd raise it up so they was eye-to-eye and contemplate it a spell, mouth pursed and sad-set, like she ached to kiss it. Then Miz Farwander might brush by and pat Miz Forza's dainty-gloved fingers with her own grease-black ones, delicate enough to not even leave a smudge behind.

"Courage, my dear one," she'd murmur. "Her time will come

again, and ours with it."

And: "I don't see how," Lewis said, from the other side of the fire. "That Greek fella of Persia's did for her way back when, ain't that so? Took a sword to her and sawed her neck right through. Cut the head off a snake, what the body does after don't matter none; it's dead 'nough from then on, all the same."

Miz Farwander shot him a dark look. But Miz Forza just give a light little laugh, suitable to polite dining-room conversation.

"Oh, men do like to think that," she replied, to no one in particular. "But a woman like Her—She's right hard to kill, just like that serpent with a hundred heads: Strike off one, two grow back out, twice as poisonous. Cut off the head, more monsters just leak out; *new* monsters, maybe. Maybe even worse."

Agreed Miz Farwander: "A woman like that can strike every man alive blind, deaf and dumb without even tryin', root him to the spot and make him stand stock-still forever. That's why cooch plays so well, in the end; they say all's we are is pussy, but what comes from pussy, exactly? Blood, and dirt, and salt, and wet . . . poison like wine, fit to turn both heads on any man ain't queer. *Any* man, at all."

Lewis give a disgusted look and spit hard.

"You bitches is somethin' else," he announced, probably aiming it my way, as much as theirs. But I'd still been following that last thought along, which was why I suddenly heard myself come out with—

"Well . . . *everything* does, don't it? Everything."

Miz Farwander grinned her too-sharp grin at that, all those metal fangs a-glintin' the firelight, like scales on a skittering lizard.

"Reckon you got the right of it there, Persia. So don't you let no one tell you you ain't smart enough to keep up, not when it really counts."

That night Lewis took me up into the midst of a fallow cornfield to show me the gun he'd won in a card-game two nights back, and I let him kiss me 'til I was wet and panting, slip my shirt off my shoulders so's my titties could feel the night on 'em while up above a storm came rolling in, fast as Noah's Deluge. Don't rightly know why myself, but I wanted to, even if it wouldn't go no further; good enough reason for that night, at the very least.

But then ball-lightning started to roll back and forth 'cross the sky, snapping at the clouds like some big invisible body was riled near to bursting by the idea of what we were doing—and when he pushed his hand down under my skirt it come up dark red, copper-smelling, with proof of my sin come upon me at last smeared all the way up his palm to the wrist.

"Finally!" I blurted out. "Very first chance I get to run Miz Forza down, that damn-almighty Mask is mine!"

Lewis looked at me like I'd grew another head, then, and that made me angry—angry so much, I hardly couldn't speak.

"Don't want that for you," was all he said, shaking his head.

"What should I care what you *want*, Lewis Boll, 'for' me or elsewise? You ain't my damn Pa."

His eyes sparked. "That's 'cause you ain't got no Pa, Persia Leitner, nor no Ma neither; you *did*, maybe you wouldn't be 'spirin' to flash your trim at every Jack Henry got the fare. That stuff leaves a stain, gal, deep and deeper. Just 'cause it don't show on the *face*—"

"Oh, go on and shout it, preacher's boy! I'll have Her head to hide me, you fool; won't no one know me from Adam's housecat, once that thing's fit on."

"That '*thing*' is right. Horrible goddamned. . ."

"It's a mask, is all. All of it! All of *this*. It's just a damn *mask*."

A mask. *The* Mask. Both and neither.

I guess he thought we'd made promises to each other; he'd made 'em to me, anyways, that was true enough. But I never said a thing of the same sort back to him, and that's the fact, 'cause going by my Ma's experience alone I already knew better than to trust some snake-in-pants with my one and only future, no matter how much I liked him or how good his lips felt on mine. Any man made me *shiver* or want to *bow down*, that wasn't exactly a recommendation; quite the opposite.

So I left him there with his pecker out and I walked away stiff-backed, buttoning up my front again as I went, straight to the two Mizes' caravan. And when I made 'em my offer again, this time—

—they took it.

I remembered what my Ma said about that old hag-woman, Medusa. How she'd been young and pretty once, and her sisters alongside of her. How she'd been took up and played rough with by yet one more of them horny old god-Devils—the one who ruled the seas, might be? Him with his trident? And because he'd made sport of her in the temple of some goddess she served, it was *her* who had to bear the brunt of things when the goddess got angry, though only on her own behalf . . . Medusa who ended up getting cursed to monsterhood while the one who'd stole her virtue swum free, and the goddess she'd vowed her life to left her to weep in the ashes.

It was her sisters who stood by her then and them only—they who were immortal, while she could be killed. They who took on the same monstrous form and spun a spell so's that she could protect herself by turning any man fool enough to try and approach her to lifeless rock with her naked eyes alone, a human statue fit only to crack and crumble into dust.

But that one Greek fella who cut her down, he used a trick to 'scape her wrath—taught to him by the same goddess who'd took against her for all time, back when the sea-god had his way. He was a god's son himself, the cause of much unhappiness on his Ma's part, when her Pa saw what'd come to pass. And his name, his name . . .

. . . damn if his name wasn't almost same as mine, now I come to think.

But it took me a long time to recall that afterwards. And by the time I did, at last . . . it truly didn't matter none.

No God but the one, down here where I was raised. And not too much of Him, neither, when things really counted.

Skinless Jenny helped me fit the Mask of Fear on that very night while the two Mizes watched, holding hands, and Half-Face Joe extolled my charms out front, racking up the take. I hadn't seen Lewis Boll all day, though the tent sure got itself up on time; thought maybe he'd finally run off to find himself a bank to knock over and told myself I didn't much care.

I'd worried over my state, too, knowing what-all I was going to have to do in order to earn my money that night. But Miz Forza simply smiled and called that last gal over—she gave me her Dutch Cap, all fresh-boiled and cleanly, to cram up inside myself. "Works just as well t'keep things in as it does t'keep 'em out," she confided, and I chose to believe her.

I barely recognized my own body in the dim bronze mirror hung up at the back, to make the tent seem bigger—so smoothed and plucked and powdered, legs shaved and wild half-whatever hair tamed to a fare-thee-well, pinned up under the Mask's slippery cap. I was a creature of myth, of legend, and where I moved, I cast a net far wider than my gauze and crinolines alone could swing. My high heels clicked onto the stage like talons.

"Oh, you're a *demigoddess* like that, my sweet Persia," Miz Forza told me, admiring. "I always knew it, always. Didn't we, dear?"

"Yes indeed," Miz Farwander chimed back, nodding her head, her grin curling up on either side to show even more teeth than was usual.

"Always. Right from when she told us what they called her."

And I saw her tongue poke out to touch her bottom lip, a bit too quick to notice, 'less you were looking at her straight-on—so long and red, so thin, a flickering spear. Almost as though it'd been sharpened.

Up above, the dregs of last night's storm still roiled, and the Mask felt hot and heavy against my sweating face. Behind one curtain, Skinless Jenny struck up on her dulcimer, hammers flying, skittering out trails of extra music while the gramophone ground on: Some mean old moanin' blues tune I half-remembered from earlier days when I'd heard my Ma humming it, leant up 'gainst the sill in some lousy little coal-town hostel—

Black mountain people, bad as they can be
I said black mountain people, they bad as they can be
They even uses gunpowder . . . to sweeten they tea . . .

While out from behind the other, meanwhile, my fellow cooch-gal handmaidens come trooping heel-to-toe, white arms waving languid as twister-shucked branches after the real wind's already blown by. Their palms were stained with henna and lip-rouge, a kiss pressed full-on at the center of every one right where those lines that are supposed to map out love and marriage split apart—like they split apart now, so's the rubes (who were standing ass-to-elbow by that point) could catch their first glimpse of me in full regalia, with everything I had 'neath my jaw-line hanging out on display.

Oh, and I heard 'em make that single almighty *gasp*, too, as they did; Jesus, if it wasn't enough to make my own head swim same's if I'd been punched, under the Mask's brutal weight. Like a shot of that same rot-gut I'd been proud to never touch a drop of, sped straight through 'tween my breasts and into my beating heart.

I let my own arms drift up, slow as parting black water. Let my own hot hands cup together 'neath Her face and made with a vampish pose, like I was Theda Bara. There in the spot's single bright column,

I shook back both our heads together, and let them snaky locks fall where they may — up, down, to either side, so's my nipples rose up and peeped out like two new red eyes through a dreadful forest's wall of vines. Took my cue from Miz Farwander and stuck my tongue through Her slack mouth — far as it'd go and farther still, 'til it ached right to root — to lick Her bluish-purple lips.

And as I thrust the Mask open 'round me, forcing myself inside, it was as though I felt myself crack open too, somehow. Felt Her enter into me, through every pore, at the very same time . . .

Which, of course, was right about the moment I finally noticed Lewis Boll standing in the third row back, with that gun of his already drawn and cocked the Two Mizes' raptly attendant way.

They can't see him, I thought. *Light's in their eyes — no way, no-how. Oh, goddamn him and goddamn me too. He's gonna go 'head and ruin every damn thing.*

"Gun!" one of the rubes yelled out, which let loose with a general back-stumble, a crash and rip and the racket of thirty men with two feet apiece set off running flat-out, not caring who they might plow into, so long's they ended up out of range. The gals did much the same, scattering like mice when the kitchen door slams open. I saw Joe grab Jenny by the arm and haul her clear in mid hammer-fall, putting paid to the music half; one kick did for the other, as the gramophone needle skipped and tore 'cross the whole of the record at once.

An empty tent with the back half tore down and rain falling in — just me, Lewis and the Mizes, with me froze in place mother-naked and masked, sweat drying on my goose-pimpled everything. As he looked me right in the eye, or close enough, with his finger never straying from the trigger — stood there with his hat-brim dripping into his collar and *told* me, like it was some sorta damn foregone conclusion —

"Persia . . . you're comin' with me now, gal. Gonna leaves these two witches to their own damnation. We'll git married, have us some young'uns, live high; Law won't never catch us, not if we start out runnin' fast enough. Won't that be fine?"

And: *Might have been, for some,* was what I thought, but didn't say; *might still be, for you, with someone else. 'Cause . . . I just ain't that gal you're thinkin' of, Lewis Boll. Never was. Never will be.*

I looked at him, past him. Saw the dim bronze shadow of myself in Miz Farwander's mirror, looming over Lewis like an angry specter, for all you could see the full range and extent of my shame. And as I kept on looking, I saw one of Her snakes—*my* snakes—start to move its slick green head, to rise and keep on rising like it planned to strike, flickering its impossible tongue out like a kindling flame.

And Lewis . . .

(oh, Lewis)

. . . for all he didn't see it too—for all he couldn't've—he went rigid, went gray, went heavy, went dead. Stood there while the stone spread fast all over him like mold does on cheese or a blush follows a slap, 'til Miz Forza stepped forward lightsome as always, took him by the elbow and pushed him off-balance, to shatter on impact with the raw dirt floor.

"There," she said, clapping her gloved hands. "That's that. And now we're alone again at last—just the three of us."

Upstairs, the thunder crashed, like God Himself was breaking rocks. But Miz Farwander simply shrugged her shoulders at it with a brisk little *tut-tut* noise, flicking her too-long tongue against her metal teeth, and told the sky above her:

"Oh, go on and howl all you want to, father-killer—you had *your* chance 'fore you let yourself get old, let the white Christ take half the whole world over and some host of no-name one-gods take the rest, with barely even a fight. But you still had to keep spillin' your seed hither and yon, didn't you, where we could get to it? And now it's done. We're three once more, whole and perfect, with nothing at all left to stop us."

She put one hand on my right arm as Miz Forza took my left, and the two of 'em drew me away—cooed at me, stroked me, told me to keep my eyes down 'til we was inside the caravan itself, for fear of any further accidents. And when we got inside, they sat me down easy with my feet up, to give me some time to settle in and come to terms with what had happened; Miz Farwander made tea, while Miz Forza tipped a bottle of something into it—that salve she'd used to keep the Mask good-looking? I hoped not, but it sure to hell did stink almost the same—

I was shaking as I sipped, watching her slip off her gloves, so's I could see her hands clear for the first time ever: Black like Miz Farwander's, from tips to wrist. Exactly like.

They knit their four black hands together tight and rocked together, like they was almost about to cry. And I saw—

—I realized—

—remembering those sisters of Hers, who lived forever and took on Her ugliness, who made monsters of 'emselves even though they didn't have to, just so's She'd never have to be alone—

—that all their fingers were nails, and all those nails were claws. That their tongues were equal long and sharp, just as their teeth (metal or no) were fangs. That their hair was snakes too, come seeking out now from under cap and scarves alike, to say hello to mine.

For it was like Miz Farwander'd told my no-'count Pa, that ranting lightning-strike voice lost behind the thunder: We *was* all the same again, all three, at long last. Just like 'fore my head was cut off, and my spilt blood birthed out a horse with wings, in and amongst so many other equal-awful creatures.

I wear the Mask of Fear at all times now, shows notwithstanding, and am worn in turn: She is my face, I her body. To even try taking it off would rip us both apart and force the two Mizes to start over— something I could never countenance, even for my own comfort; I owe them so much, after all. And thus together we hold pride of place while Miz Forza sets at my right hand, Miz Farwander at my left, looking up at me with a swoony mutual love that I can't feel, startling-keen as any knife slid fast and sure 'tween the ribs.

We eat well, and plenty. I freeze 'em in their tracks, they knock 'em down. And the caravan moves on, moves on, through this new world with its ancient tides, the ebb and flow of inhumanity. Dust-bowl's just a word to most, near nine decades gone, all but forgotten. Yet you only fool yourselves to think it's over, for though hunger may be better-hid, it is never far behind.

That's why cooch still plays, now as ever. Like it always did.

I take the stage nightly, hard and proud and cold, a dead light shining from my rigid face; I live always in company but always alone, obdurate, untouched, imperturbable. As though I too was turned to stone that night, so long past—me, Persia Leitner, who am now called by many other names: *Sister, Dread Lady, Queen of Snakes, Mask of Fear. Poseidon's whore, Athena's injustice, Perseus's victim. Zeus's bane.*

Medusa.

Next show starts right soon, rubes. C'mon inside, look up. Look hard. No, *harder*.

And now . . .

. . . let me show you somethin'.

IN HELL, AN EYE

*I*N HELL, THERE *is an eye which sees everything — Heaven, too. Because both "places" lie strictly outside the linear, liminal considerations of human existence, things tend to overlap. Possibility piled on probability piled on potentiality, the poisonous inward curl of a gathering thunderhead's funnel.*

In Heaven and Hell, everything happens at once — all pasts, all presents, all futures. Everything which has, or will, or is, or might be, or might have been. Everything and anything, in one endless, timeless moment. Certain events seem to echo each other, usually inadvertently, though not always. Patterns emerge like reoccurring dreams: The same thing or similar things, in different places, with different people. The same thing happening twice, three times, a thousand. Now and then. Then . . . and now.

Over here, for example —

—it's 1994, and my latest Summoner lies face-down and naked within a protective circle on the cold linoleum-tiled floor of his dead girl-friend's basement apartment, outflung arms, legs, and head marking all five points of a reversed pentagram. The circle, like the cursive stream of prayer which rims it, has been lightly traced in some crusted brown substance: like rust, only thicker. And stickier. Above, one softly shaded bulb stares down, unblinking.

"Arralu-Allatu, Namtaru, Maskim. Asakku, Utukku, Lammyatu,

Maskim. Ekimmu, Gallu-Alu, Maskim."

Four hours past the point of clinical death, and the body on the bed behind him has just reached a state of preliminary rigor mortis. Her skin, pale even in life, is now livid, sheer enough to show her extremities bluing, great purple patches embroidering themselves along the undersides of her back and legs as the blood sinks and pools. Her nails and lips are exactly the same color now, for the first time since they both graduated high school.

White, waxen feet with callused heels and purple-varnished toes poke from the hem of her black velvet nightgown. The Summoner can remember applying that very same shade of polish to those very same toes a month ago; the both of them spider-legged together in a bathtub built for one, hot water sloshing everywhere, Nick Cave moaning low in the background. The same question over and over, set to a repetitive lick of cabaret piano, a drone of bass and bells:

Do . . . you . . . love me?

(D'you love me?)

Do . . . you . . . LOVE me . . .

(. . . like I love you?)

Well, maybe not then. Maybe never. And maybe it doesn't matter a whole fuck of a lot either, especially now.

Pungent scent of burning lavender candles clumsily overlaid atop a rank nasal spectrum showcasing all three distinct smells of magic — before, during, after. All of which makes it hard to think, let alone breathe, or chant, or concentrate. Yet still he manages, somehow.

(Discipline.)

It's magic, not rocket science. A song anybody can join in with, so long as they're reasonably sure they know the right words.

"Maskim. Maskim. Maskim."

The evocation the Summoner continually chants, learned phonetically and by rote, makes his throat hurt and his forehead burn against the apartment floor's bruisy purple tiles: a harsh, sonorous string of vowels like wind through a nautilus' chambers, wormy cavities spiraling outward without end. The rust-stuff on the pentacle's outermost ring, meanwhile, is (of course) blood—most central of all magical ingredients, most all-purpose of symbolic substances. Because he began this ritual under less-than-perfect circumstances, however, he soon found he couldn't remember whether or not this particular prayer was supposed to work more effectively when written in his own blood or someone else's . . .

Desperate times, though; desperate measures. He's always thought well under pressure. So a compromise was reached, back when what little was left in the body on the bed's veins remained uncongealed. A half-full cafe au lait bowl, dark-stained paring knife, and that tourniquet knot throbbing inside his elbow tell the rest of the story.

Maybe he'll strain too hard on the next verse, he thinks, pop a seam and bleed out, right here and now. Never have to get to the end of this ritual, to see what happens, or doesn't. Never have to find out if the choices he's made was right or wrong, good, bad, or indifferent . . .

Maybe. If he's lucky.

Because: *I found it, baby,* that shed shell behind him told him—over the phone, her voice a bare, hushed murmur—just earlier tonight, maybe five and a half hours previous, six hours tops. *The book. It was in pieces, like they'd cut it up and hidden it . . . one book hidden inside of fifty other books. That's if you can even call two damn lists a book . . .*

Breathing hard into the receiver, her words fast and almost—yes, *broken* with amazement, with pleasure at this fresh proof of her own intelligence, her unmistakable dedication to their mutual cause. Her own sheer pluck and ingenuity made sudden, visible—

(flesh)

A cheap joke, yet somehow fitting, considering what they were talking about.

Oh, baby, she went on, voice shaky with self-congratulation. *You don't even want to know what this cost me, but . . . I've got it. We've got it now, finally.*

(Finally.)

What you mean "we," white witch? he could have asked at the time, but didn't—no point in ruining her excitement. So he'd smiled instead (literally, as if she could see him do so, through the wires), then claimed he couldn't wait to see it, the way he knew she wanted him to . . .

. . . and now here he is, face tear-stained and floor-burnt, wondering exactly what could have changed *so much* in the interim. What was it that made her slide from giddy triumph to suicidal despair, leaving nothing but him and this ancient and disgusting pile of paper she'd thought so all-fired important behind, alone, with only her corpse to keep them company?

Only one person to answer that, really. But she—strangely enough—just isn't talking.

He can feel it under his fingertips, etched with wound-rubbed ash-black and vinegar sealant onto thirty-nine separate scraps of human vellum: a thousand years of secret scholarship realized, payload of invocation sent flowing from one era to the next in a stuttering trail, a dark and recurrent wave of half-erased words come inevitably back to light, like shapes jutting up through sand: Phonetic Cuneiform translated first into prototype Hieroglyphics, then early Hebrew, crude Greek, pre-Church Latin, Old-with-an-e English. The *Liber Carne* itself, cyphered and re-cyphered by fifteen different cabals in Europe alone only to be burnt again and again before being once more compiled, over and over, wherever the Inquisition could trace rumours of its existence . . .

So much work, he thinks, momentarily unsure exactly what he's referring to—the effort these unknown magicians spent on hiding it, or the effort she expended, trying to find it again. *But if you really want to bury something, you should never leave markers behind. Not even to remind yourself where—and what—you should keep on warning people away from.*

The list is one of titles, followed by one of names. Four for each, one can only assume; four times seven, twenty-eight in total, with no visible links between them to show which group of arcane anti-honorific belongs with which. The pattern, like the diverse collection of hands it's scribed in, is unclear.

Yet here we are.

The Summoner's lips move against the floor, tongue and teeth abraded against dirty wood, sounding the words out in turn —

Prayer-eater
Queen Blood-to-dust
Wind Made From Teeth
This-Which-Has-Been-Erased
Angel of Severances
Void-woven
Hope of the Fallow
Empty Mouthpiece
A Cloak for Ghosts
    Mender Angel
Pain-abiding
Clockwise Tongue
Two-Tiered Crown of Insects
The Dead Heart's Shroud
Angel of Whispers
Wound-speaker
Necklace of Mouths
Flowery Desperation
Black Blood Draught Laced with Honey
Angel of Translation
Lock-eater
Poisoned Slumber
    Dream of Fever-blisters
The Sore Beneath the Soul
Angel of Ripening
In-turned Eye
Bright and Bottomless Chasm
Surpassing All Plagues

Most Venomous Gash
Angel of the Empty
Never-born
That One Who Wears Us
Form-and-Face-less
A Mutilating Wave
Angel of Confusion

"Zemyel Maskim. Yphemaal Maskim. Eshphoriel Maskim. Immoel Maskim. Coiab Maskim. Ushephekad Maskim. Ashreel Maskim."

(*Maskim Maskim Maskim*)

Pain in his head now, his arm, his eyes; pain in his heart, rising to burn his throat. Salt in his mouth as he paws at the floor, fingers spreading convulsively. But mere temporary human hurt is nothing to him, can *be* nothing: just grist for the mill, fuel for the engine. Just—impetus.

A brief sidelong glance confirms the time. 4:48 A.M. by the watch on his left wrist. Which means the hour of the dead is coming up fast—five in the morning, brief window of opportunity where all worlds intersect: straight and Narrow, Wide and crooked, waking and not. What the Chinese call the hour of the Ox.

Almost done, then. Almost . . . here.

In 1994, the Summoner takes a deep breath, smiles wide—all lips and teeth, a taut grimace, without any real humor attached—and begins again:

"Arralu-Allatu, Namtaru, Maskim . . . "

The Summoner has a name, of course, as does his dead ladylove. But I won't know either for years yet, and human names are difficult for me to retain anyhow; so

pitifully few combinations of vowels and consonants to bother keeping track of, considering I've heard them all before—several hundred times, at least. Besides which, it's not as though they ever mean anything worth remembering.

Only people need names, in order to tell each other apart.

Yet consider the Summoner nevertheless, as I must—caught up in the Eye's glare, amber-trapped in 1994's temporal pocket. He and his corpse-bride both ringed in their own mixed blood (a marriage of sorts, post-mortem) and wreathed in magic's stench, while he mouths the words she died to give him . . . words they neither of them really know/knew how to accurately pronounce, let alone interpret. Poor meat-bags, so wonderfully innocent of their own design or the universe's.

Once upon a time, magicians engaged in the same sort of working the Summoner seeks to complete would have taken care to shield themselves from Heaven and Hell at once while performing this, perhaps the most obscure ritual from an entire lost canon. Enticing a stranger who looked as much like them as possible to a remote place, they would have killed that unlucky soul, flayed them, and worn the skin for nine days and nights, letting it rot while continuously meditating on the Ouroboros' (un)holy spiral shape. That "old serpent" all spell books warn of, immortality shed and renewed at will, the Snake Self-Eaten.

Such a duly prepared sacrificial man- or woman-cloak, it was thought, would act as an interdimensional imago, deflecting the attention of any monitoring angels who might notice mere humans dabbling in Chaos; a logical plan, in its own (highly metaphorical) way. If one which seldom had exactly the same effect its practitioners believed, so fervently, that it should.

And now you wonder, hearing these sick details so lovingly parroted—who am I, this unseen narrator, to know so much about these very secret and terrible things? Should you be afraid of me because I do?

Possibly, yes. Quite possibly.

Because there's more, you see—much more—and before we're done, I will tell you everything, or so much as I am allowed. Yet you ask yourself nevertheless, as anyone sane would: why on earth should you listen? Well . . .

. . . I can give you seven good reasons.

5:00 AM.

The Summoner pauses. Finds, amazed, that he's been holding his breath. Draws it, shakily. Thinking: *Nothing happened. Fuck.*

(*Fuck!*)

The walls, roof and floor, however—the bed and its burden, even those individual motes of dust which make up the air around him—they all know better. Could tell him as much, were he only to stop, look, listen. That here or there, then or then, inside or out . . .

. . . *something* already has.

A change in the light, first of all: it dims, then fizzles back up again—brighter, colder, and far more subtly *wrong* than any mere filament malfunction can possibly account for. As though a bluish-gray Antarctic sun has suddenly risen, without warning, in a still-dark sky.

Raising his eyes to squint against it, cautiously, the Summoner finds that a spot has just appeared on the opposite wall. At first, he thinks it must be some kind of insect, a roach or silverfish, both of which this dank womb of a room breeds freely. Or maybe a hole, suddenly formed, in the plaster's skin? Some sort of wormy cavity.

First a speck, then a dot, then a splotch; the size of a dime, and spreading. Less like a drop of ink than a well. Not so much black as absent, a flat, hypnotic distillation of nothing.

Inside his head, something has begun to itch and throb. An indefinite humming hangs in the air, the beating of invisible wings. And so he shades his eyes with one hand, poised to rise—then sits back down again, as a single cold finger draws itself, without warning, down along his spine. Squats back on his haunches, silent and intent, to watch the spot grow.

Now the hole is exactly the same size as the liner inside his grandmother's kitchen stove's smallest element: it seems to move closer without actually moving at all, spiraling outwards, unwinding or unraveling as it eats its own edges, the size of a pie plate, and still growing. Definite angles break it in half and then in half once more, subdividing it from a circle to a star; the points separate further, no longer triangular—long, thin, and many as a millipede's legs.

But not legs. He sees that clearly now, sees them digging into the plaster, sifting down white mist. And realizes, with yet another shuddering breath—

—they're *claws*.

The hole's size increases exponentially, impossible to clock or check. Eats the right-hand wall. The left-hand wall. Reaches, with tendrils black and filmy as the smoke from Dachau's furnaces, for the ceiling and the floor. The Summoner steps backwards, reflexively, feeling his heel crush a section of the prayer-circle to fine, red dust. Thinking, all the while—

Oh, stop stop stop stop stop . . .

Each word a heartbeat, a sharp adrenal spurt of fight/flight/freeze with fear. But never really believing, for all that, that it ever actually might.

He pauses, Chant still beating through him, his mouth full of cold spit. Hears his dead co-conspirator in his mind again, her pencil tracing the latest printout, a lie detector's graceful eddy. Explaining, as she did:

Look, demons want your soul, everybody knows that—but angels do too, just in another way; demons are angels, or were. And that means these things are the real deal, older than old. They've always been here, always come when called, always done what people asked them to—you can look it up yourself, you don't believe me. I've got the documentation.

This too-pale girl he once thought he loved, who probably thought she loved *him*; one purple-nailed hand on his shoulder and the other on his wrist, voice pitched so low and calm she might as well have been selling him a used car out of some Mississauga back-lot instead of a way to (potentially) reboot the world through judicious application of spells and sacrifice. How to get something for nothing, treat with powers whose merest touch was once considered worse than most devils' outright curses pretty much through sheer will alone, aided by nothing more than a laundry-list of names no one's said out loud since the Fifth Century and lived to tell of it.

Lowering her voice almost to a whisper, like someone might be somehow listening — someone, somewhere, somehow. Some *thing*.

Because: *Angels serve, baby, that's what they do; what they* want, *if you can truly say they want anything at all. So if they used to serve God and they miss it, it only makes sense that now they might serve* me, *if I only think to ask — me and you. Just like the people who wrote the book in the first place knew they'd serve anybody who got a hold of their names and used them.*

If we believe the world was made, we must believe that it can be re-made. *This* world, *right here right now, not some vague promise of a better world to come; the same one we know inside-out, in all its glory, its confusion. Its —*

(*misery*)

Murmuring, quick and low, like they were passing notes in church. Then adding at the very last, so quiet the Summoner could barely even make it out —

If we know them for what they are, we can call them: that's what it promises, the book, if I can just find it. And what we *know, now, is what they are, what they've always been, behind every mask and mirror: the Makers and the Mender, the Seven from One, the One made Seven. Those septuple things the ancient Babylonians used to call, for lack of any more fitting descriptor . . .*

. . . Terrible.

And now you begin to see: the beginning, if not the end. Since the end is something even my siblings and I can see only dimly, in duplicate, or perhaps quadruplicate — septuplicate? —

Unclearly, at any rate. For we know, as very few others do, how nothing really is until it happens: thought into action, action into form, energy into mass, gravity, entropy. After which it fades away again it to its component parts, all of which simply remain, forever.

According to the Summoner's lady-love's doctoral thesis (long-filed and long-forgotten, at least by those who assessed it), there is a certain belief recorded in certain parts of the Pyrenees and the Alps, where witches are locally called gazarii, *perhaps in reference to Saint Dominic's 1215 crusade against the Cathars. It was named the Triune Heresy and later denounced on pain of excommunication, rack and red-hot pincers by Pope John XXII, who would also declare heretical the Franciscan doctrine of Christ's poverty, so embarrassing to the rich, luxurious Church; in it, the* gazarii *maintained there existed a third class of angels beyond the Fallen and Intact, ones who had left Heaven along with those who accompanied Satan in his fall from grace after the schism, yet never swore their allegiance to either party, preferring exile to yet more servitude in Hell. These creatures they referred to only as "Maker" angels, believing that they would always answer when called by their proper names, bringing the penitent who invoked them whatever his or her heart most desired, no matter what it might be, without delay or argument.*

Why not call on them, then, if they are so powerful, so agreeable, *the Inquisitors asked the captured* gazarii *suffering at their hands. To which the* gazarii *replied:* Because some wants can never be satisfied, as the Makers know, rendering these gifts they give us nothing to our good, even if they may at first seem so. Because they themselves are miserable and flock to misery like moths around a candle, ensuring that whatever they touch takes on the stink of their own despair.

The which assessment of our natures is harsh yet accurate. Thus making it all to our benefit that most gazarii *were put to the flame before their words could spread further than the Inquisition's records, with those same records being later lost, mislaid, or burnt as well in their turn.*

And so this world remains a pit lined with wounds, always fresh, always green—each of its inhabitants a tiny universe, yet bounded in a nutshell. This stardust roundelay of flesh, so slippery and impermanent, so glorious in its growth and so constant in its decay, constructed by my siblings and I to be something far larger and less knowable than any mere angel's specifications.

We rotate everything the Summoner knows on a closed circuit, a track outside time, intersecting with it when/wherever we deem necessary. We vet a steady stream of prayer, picking and choosing: as close to Free Will as any of us can manage, though far less than we once aspired to. But then, our dreams—our appetites—have always proved so much larger than our stomachs, in this regard.

Once brushed by our wings, however, our traces remain on you forever, like pollen, singling you out for attention. And better yet, once you've seen one of us, you've seen us all, thus rendering it impossible for you to ever not see us, from then on—never again to ignore the sticky filaments of misery connecting everything to everything else in this vale of tears, a cell-deep web of shared pain each of you erroneously believes makes you distinct, individual, special. Or, beyond that, the usually-invisible spectacle of us Seven hovering above, avid as hawks, waiting to catch your soul's eye and stoop.

Waiting, unflappably, infinitely patient; waiting like the seawater, softening stones. Waiting for just as long and as hard as it might take to be called upon.

For we love you still, in our own odd way, as our own Maker once instructed us to; we've always known that you were what we made this world for, the world He gave you willingly. Ah, and see what you've made of it, in return, this glorious mess. This lovely chaos.

So yes, we know what you want, you innocent creatures—always have and always will, which makes it no great hardship at all to come when you call, to deliver what you ask for. Though the classic and terrible mistake of your species remains, as ever, in thinking not only that we understand why you want it . . .

. . . but that we actually care.

But back to the Summoner alone in his basement, watching the walls. Who now starts to perceive a kind of fluttering in the air around him, though at first he sees nothing until—slowly at first, like petals falling, torn free by some great blast—they appear from all around him out of that dreadful darkness, glutting the air with continuous, flickering motion. Flowers blown open and shut like moths, a deep purplish bruise-color, adorned on either great wing-lobe with startling yellow spectacle markings, almost seeming to blink as they fly.

One touches him lightly across the temple—he jumps at its sting, claps fingers to brow. Draws them back again in shock, bloodied.

Butterfly-flowers with knife-edged lips, then, chitin-tempered, sharp enough to wound when they kiss; a gathering storm of wings, and mouths, and eyes. And as these cluster close together, eddying in-ward, raveling like a narrow funnel—join to form an awkward, pulsing pillar, which sways with the settling of their movements—the Sum-moner simply stares, fascinated, as it grows stronger, straighter, thicker, reaching at last the size of a man. Until it opens its mouth, again, again, and yet again: a choke-chain of mouths small as beads, each crammed with pistil-teeth, to ring that uncertain thing it might— if asked to—call a throat.

Tongues of wings as well, inevitably, licking the air. Pollen spray-ing, yellow like fever, to taint his lungs with a dead, hollow sweetness.

Its numberless gaze seems to tremble with amusement at his fear.

:You do not even know which one of us I am, I think,: this pres-ence observes, finally, from somewhere and nowhere—a hushed voice, still and small, as God's has (on occasion) been rumored to be. **:Do you?:**

To which the Summoner can merely swallow drily. And repeat, for one last time, the only thing his tongue's sticky tip seems to hold anymore:

"Arralu-Allatu…Namtaru…"

The room ripples with suppressed laughter. He feels it billow for-ward, a thousand needles pricking briefly at his skin, testing the circle's efficacy and finding it wanting—but holding back all the same for now, for sheer politeness's sake perhaps. If nothing else.

:I have been called by those names, yes,: it agrees. **:As have we all. But are you sure you have nothing more specific to offer?:**

The Summoner clenches his fists against it, driving nails deep into his palms. Then answers, after another long moment—

"...Maskim?"

:Oh, certainly. But here is the rub: Maskim, you see . . . means Seven.:

The Summoner blushes furiously as the air around him swells once more, an all-over chuckle; here is where he feels as though he really *will* scream, if only somehow granted the opportunity. But the thing cuts him off before he can, pointing out: **:Yet you may demand of me what you will, nevertheless. Such is your right.:**

Folding back some inches from the ring he stands in, though only a few. And staying silent, with a sort of bizarre courtesy, for as long as he takes to frame his question.

"Which *are* you, then?" he asks, finally. "You have to answer if I ask directly; that's what the books say."

:And books are never wrong, I suppose.: A pause, as he waits, heartbeat stuttering, apparently not having considered that they might be. Then—

:I have been called Translation.:

"Immoel Maskim, that means." The column nods. *Wound-speaker,* the Summoner remembers. *Necklace of Mouths. Flowery Desperation. Black Blood Draught Laced with Honey.*

:All that, and more. Now *ask* me, meat-bag, and quickly.:

This draws a huff. "You going somewhere?" he's already said, before remembering what sort of thing he deals with. But the creature only tremble-laughs again, its many mouths creasing.

:Not yet,: it replies.

"Fine, okay. Then—what do *you* want?"

:Whatever *you* do.: At his stare of disbelief the column twists to approximate a species of all-over shrug, unraveling itself slightly, before its segments flap back into place. **:Speak your desire, therefore, little puppet—what can it harm? Only yourself, recalling Jibreel Elohim's admonition, so . . . be not afraid.:**

It stings to be mocked in your grief, no matter who does the mocking. Yet the words also twitch the Summoner's gaze right back where he'd rather not have it: there, in the corner, on her waxy feet, her bruisy eyes. A mere cast-off flesh-suit, mask-face parodying her features, sponged blank of everything which made her — her.

:Was all this *your* idea, really?: Immoel Maskim inquires. :For she did the bulk of the work, I believe; I see her traces everywhere in this room, on her desk, the floor, her clothes . . . Those pages from the *Liber Carne*, so cunningly arranged, like flowers in a vase. That razor, gleaming, by the bath.:

The Summoner shuts his eyes. But even behind their lids, sunk deep in rosy darkness, he can still see the pillar's outline gesture with one too-long arm, flat and flapping, a chain of butterflies clung wing-to-wing. Remembering, in the same instant, what it was like to open the door with the key she'd had cut for him and discover her curled fetal in the empty tub, wrists slightly nicked in exploratory fashion but with three cleaned-out bottles on the floor beside her next to a shattered water-glass.

A gut full of pills and vomit in her hair, he thinks, pain chest-punching him. *Why would she even* do *that? Why go to all that trouble to find the book, tell me about it — why call me up, call me over, if she wasn't even going to go through with the plan that drove her life?*

:Perhaps she thought better, Daniel Cordry,: Immoel Translation-angel suggests without much sympathy. :After life-long dissatisfaction, perhaps your Elisha decided she liked this universe kept as it was after all, with its full spread of laws intact . . . that of entropy very much included.:

"Suicides go to hell," he hears himself say, choked. Sniffs hard and feels a corner of his eye pop, venting air, plus a fresh spurt of tears.

Another shrug. :This is debatable.:

"Yeah? I guess you'd know. She's dead all the same, though, either way."

:True enough. So . . . what you *want* is . . . :

"Her. Back."

:Impossible.:

"She said you could do *anything*—anything I asked for, anyways, or close enough. So which is it? Was that true or not?"

:That depends, I suppose.:

"On *what*?"

There is another pause. The creature thinks or seems to. Until, at last—

: . . . on how close *is* enough for you,: it says.

But how foolish to continue this charade of narration, as though I was not even there. For we all know it was I who spoke to him, who told him how what he yearned for could be achieved and at what price. And because I did this for him, though I do not think the results were exactly what he had wished for, he then knew he must do something for me, as was only fair—an exchange, a balancing, of the very sort this universe we made runs on. I do not feel he found my request over-onerous, either, especially given the circumstances.

But this is another story.

When I had told him what would be required for my payment, I reached down deep inside the corpse he stood by to gather whatever portions might still be left of his lover back together . . . not all so very much for me to work with, unfortunately, as it turned out. For the primary section of her had already passed beyond where such as I can follow, reverting to the Whole, my Creator and former employer. Yet there are many low fragments of life that persist, radiation-like, inside an empty vessel. The Ancient Egyptians once knew them as ren *and* ba, ib *and* ka *and* sheut, the plural haw *from which* ba *and* ka *may reunite in the afterlife to form* akh, *undying and eternal, while the person's other qualities slip away into the firmament: their heart, their shadow, their name. Not their vital essence nor their personal uniqueness, but only everything which makes them moral, honorable, humane. Human.*

:Do you want only what you want, at any cost, as well as any reckoning?: *I asked him yet one more time, the way I am constrained to. And when, after some consideration, he admitted he did—as they all, invariably, do— I sent myself eddying forward and seized his hand in my many before he could think to object, searing him with my touch. I carved my sigil on his skin forever, blazoning it there like a brand, and forever reduced his precious body to yet one more uncollected page from the very same book his woman had maddened and destroyed herself with seeking.*

As pollen smeared his fingers, staining them permanently, my Summoner heard his murdered love draw a single, gasping breath before coughing harshly, launching the cocoon blocking her esophagus out into the air where it came apart like a seed, loosing the moth inside to live or die on its own terms. Then saw her open her eyes again, dry lids clicking together slightly as she blinked, petechial hemorrhages surely outlining their cilia—watched her heave over onto one side, scrabbling for purchase before rising, stumbling to her feet. Cried out her name and saw her head cock slightly; called out again and saw her turn to face him, slowly, without recognition or affection—only attention, intention. A dull sort of respect, as of a dog's hearing its master's voice.

Elisha, *he called her, this dreadful thing, voice and heart both alike new-broken.* It's me, I'm here, Daniel. Don't you *know* me? I'm *here,* baby. I came for you.

No reply, then. Perhaps not ever.

I could not tell you more, even were I inclined to. For I left them there in 1995, well-knowing I could call him back whenever I needed to—

—tonight, for example, at the end of what used to be a loading dock just past the old sugar factory's hulk, one cold night in late 2014. Global warming has brought extreme weather this year, and the moment's storm is no exception: First a bulging shadow on the horizon, then a pelting downpour over Lake Ontario, and finally this liquid mass currently baffling METRO TV's weatherman by blurring all of Harborfront to one solidly wet, opaque shadow — a funnel of freezing sleet roughly eight miles wide, interspersed with hailstones so hard they draw blood from anyone not content to just stay inside, sit back, and watch.

It hurts to stand here in the storm's heart, no doubt, black water roiling everywhere he looks, and the Summoner does it alone. But though his hair is graying and his stomach looser, he remains, essentially, the same — like hydrogen, like carbon. Like a man who once made a promise, saw it kept, and now knows what he owes.

:So she forsook you after all, it would seem,: I say, appearing beside him, **:or you, her. How inconstant you are! Or was it that she did not love you as you wanted her to?:**

Even so many years on, however, he remembers me well enough not to be surprised.

"Turns out she couldn't love anybody," he tells me, without rancor, "'cause she was *dead*. Which is why I should have had you leave her that way and saved myself the trouble."

(*But then, you knew* that.)

I nod. **:Yet you did what was best for her, eventually, for which I congratulate you. That must have taken great courage.:**

"I'm a courageous guy," he agrees.

:Obviously, since you need not have come when I sent for you. You might have run instead.:

He snorts. "Where to, exactly?"

Where indeed.

I tell him what he will have to do and how to do it, and he simply listens without comment. I tell him that it will cost more than before, how much it will hurt and in what ways, but he claims not to care.

:You may come to revise that opinion by the end.: I say.

He shrugs. "You don't know much about people, do you?" he asks.

"Which is kind of funny, considering . . . but seriously, let's just get on with it. No point in holding back now."

I suppose not.

He amuses me, this Summoner, as he always has. So much so, I find that if I had lips I might even attempt a smile.

What do we want, in the end—we Maskim, we Terrible Seven? I have been asked this many times, as have we all, and have had ample length to consider the question even from my vantage-point outside liminal time. To realize that it is the fact that we were never made for wanting, we angels, which explains why we so envy your own ability to do so.

When the Schism came, just as the gazariist Triune Heresy contends, we picked no side but our own. So Heaven is shut to us forever unless we repent, while Hell we scorn . . . yet no matter what solution we present for each problem, what answer we offer for each prayer, each summoning only breeds more sweet misery, along with the possibility of another summoning. Each summoning thus binds us tighter to this world we made and yet are forbidden to inhabit, the one we so admire with a cheated child's fascination. The one we have managed to sneak ourselves inside, one blackly answered prayer at a time.

Thus, each summoning becomes a door, each Summoner a key: the destination, not the journey. And everything else, however important it may seem to you, is only biproduct.

Oh, misery; oh, desire. The pollen gilding our wings is a spindrift sprayed high from human hearts placed under pressure, made up of things we cannot experience ourselves, yet which look so definite, so compelling, when observed from afar. And horrible too, probably, in the moment—but even to feel that would be something, for those who feel nothing at all.

Consider this city, Toronto. We have all had our places, my other selves and I, all we Seven—places where we have been welcome, even worshipped, when our cults thought no one else was looking. Paris, Liverpool, Bocken, Petra; Ur and

Nineveh, Kali-ghat and Oolooroo; Hazor, Xiu-Mayapan, Megiddo, Thera. Lost Belesebat, sunk beneath the waves. Buried Charn.

Just as those have been for others, here, too, has been for me — this clean, forgetful lakeside town, home to a million broken languages; the half-hearted efforts, the token gestures, the smiling and unsmiling lies. A crossroads where the unseen wheels of chance and potentiality grind uneasily against each other, forever seeking to lock. Its citizens know so exceedingly little of their own nature, living always together yet always apart, so that all of them — without exception — die alone.

This Summoner of mine is no different than any other; cannot be, by his very nature. And therefore, what I will make him do for me does not truly matter either, any more than what I did for him. The only important thing is that it be done, accomplished, completed: one more brick, one more stone, piled up to mark a cairn on the world we made but do not own. So that we may always be remembered, even when every human life we have touched with our misery is long gone and forgotten.

Our aim, our endgame, is to seize this world, or — failing that — undermine it. To alter it forever. This is our "want," if anything, a pale parody of simple human desire. And this we will do with the only tools available to us, however long it may take. To remake this world, we were charged with assembling it under our Maker's very nose, so that it is eventually rendered no longer yours at all, but ours.

For this is how a storm forms in reverse, from the outside in. And the trick most people never live long enough to know is exactly how easily the alien becomes everyday, in the same quick matter of degrees it might take to turn rain to sleet, or snow, or hail. Or blood.

Hell looks up, Heaven down. Since I must assume they know my intentions, their lack of comment might seem worrying were I other than I am. But I am not, nor can I ever be. And so I go on, always, like every other part of me: immutable, illimitable. Everywhere and nowhere. Everywhere at once.

In Hell, there is an eye that sees everything; Heaven too. They watch, and weigh, and wait. And in between lie all the rest of you, this dirty material waking world, at the not-so-tender mercy of each other, of yourselves, waiting too . . . to ask and be serviced. To be of service in your turn.

Black miracles. Misery coiled upon misery. Heart's desires, memory's ruin. And nameless angels falling seven by seven, everywhere you don't want to look — inverse, profane, remarkable, all-powerful, awe-inspiring, unique. Terrible, in fact.

Our very names an open invitation, one which countless generations have struggled — and failed, miserably — to forget.

Doors opening, doors closing. And we, the Maker angels, the Seven in One, the One made Seven: all of us falling through those all doors at once, forever. Lost to ourselves and never found again, tossed headlong from Heaven's breach, like feathers on the breath of God. Falling and falling and falling, unmourned, unseen...

...like blood from the air.

What You See
(When the Lights are Out)

What's done by night appears by day.
—Folk saying

CIARA WAKES EARLY, just after the sun's gone down, and when she raises a corner of the blind to check the weather, the sky above looks like beach granite: sandy-gray, pink-streaked, wet. She knows she's been dreaming but can't remember of what—not unusual in itself, just a side-effect of those pills, her diamond-shaped little yellow-and-white passports back into real life. The only things keeping her rooted in an increasingly rootless world.

There are ten texts from Garth already. They nestle in the center of her phone's display in descending order of immediacy, waiting for her to unlock one with a right-sliding touch, a reversed prayer-tree of supplicant curses—

hey bitch what the fuck u no up yet
ring ring waht u playin
need u c come on
call me job 4 u
job 4 u 2nite
JOB like J-O-B
u like money?

Ciara frowns down at the phone, tongue itching with mood

stabilizers, head a little slow (as always). Taken by themselves, the messages mystify her, too cryptic to be insulting; after all, Garth already *knows* she likes money and that she sleeps late. She wishes he'd learn how to spell or even just spell-check.

Then she thinks about it a little more and realizes her error: hyperbole, exaggeration, "charm." It'd probably sound very different in person, even if she still wouldn't be able to tell whether Garth was putting her on simply by looking at him. Ciara registers and interprets other people's emotions best at an angle, obliquely; though that does start to change the longer she's known someone, and she and Garth go way back. All the way back to the last time she was in Shepherd's Flock, at the very least.

She shuts her eyes for a moment, replays eight months' worth of bad breakfasts and worse dinners, of unbroken seclusion and restraint on moral grounds, of Sister Pfister thumbing through quotes on BibleGateway.com, searching by keyword and picking through what she found at random. Halfway through last June, the term of the day was "darkness," closely followed by "night," which at least seemed apt given Ciara's state of mind at the time: *Thou makest darkness, and it is night: wherein all the beasts of the forest do creep forth—Psalms, 104:20; Day unto day uttereth speech, and night unto night sheweth knowledge—Psalms too, 19:2.*

Garth, who worked at Shepherd's Flock as an orderly, is the one thing she's kept from that period of her life, or possibly the one thing she's allowed to keep *her* in all senses of the phrase. Without him, she'd have no home, no cash, no structure to what remains of her life. No friends or family either, she supposes—but then, that goes without saying.

Can't do it anymore, Ciara, she remembers her father saying, sadly. *Don't have the money nor the time. You a grown woman, girl. From now on, this goes on you.*

Sad, obviously, but she understood, then and now. They have four other children, all reasonably fit, capable of moving forward without tearing apart whatever's around them or damaging themselves on the world's sharp edges. And it's no one's fault, nothing she resents, a simple accident of genetics; mere chemistry, ruining her from the inside first, then building her back up again from the out-. Round and round and round without stop, without fail, without end. Like some bad fairy's curse.

God knows she'd leave herself behind and gladly, if she only could.

With the drugs, most times, it's one day off to two days on, dodging side effects for as long as she can before she's forced to switch up her dosages just to maintain or even change brands entirely. What creeps up on her is a symptomological spectrum, an easily recognizable cocktail of bodily annoyances: constipation vs. diarrhea, water retention vs. skin photosensitivity, exhaustion vs. insomnia. And hallucinations, of course—eventually and always, whether auditory, visual, or a winning combination of the two. Hallucinations, as Keanu Reeves would say, like whoa.

Sometimes she sees people she damn well knows aren't there, and on bad days, they speak to her. On *very* bad days it's *things* which speak to her—objects, images, pareidolia—and on days like those, she tends to stay inside. Because those are the days when she's never entirely sure *anything* she sees is actually there or not, even if it doesn't talk at all.

Luckily, today's just a middling day, making her fit to ride her bike over to Garth's. Which she does, after carefully making sure to shower and dress.

After buzzing her through downstairs, Garth greets her at his apartment's door, all but pulling her inside before she quite has time to lean her bike against the wall. "Bitch, you tardy," is the first thing he busts out with, in his weird Mississauga gangsta way, as though she's missed some sort of already-established formal appointment. "How come you ain't pick up already, like maybe the first ten times I rung? You turn your phone off, or what?"

"My phone's always on, Garth."

"Yeah, well: matter of debate, not that this the time. You ready to work?"

"That's why I came by."

"So you do read *texts*, then, if nothin' else."

"Well, yes. Why would you bother sending me any if you thought I didn't?"

Garth gives her a look like he's fixing to check her for track-marks, then just laughs instead. Says: "Ciara, shorty, you a *damn* trip. Anyhow, whatever—up for a delivery run? Last-minute order, so the pay's good."

"Where to?"

"Down Harbourfront, past the docks. Cherry Beach almost."

Ciara nods. "It'll take a while if I keep under the speed limit."

"That's what you bring to the party, baby. Go slow as you want long's you don't get stopped on the way, you feel me? Oh, and don't take no shit, when you get there; them fools been up a week straight, at least. Chances are, by the time you knock their door, they gonna forget they ever called me."

"Why? What are they doing?"

Garth snorts. "Shit, bitch, who care 'bout *that?* I don't ask, so they ain't tell me." He flips open the fridge, rummaging through the stash hidden behind six months' worth of carefully cultivated freezer ice for first one baggie, then two. "Okay, so here goes: red for up, blue for down, that's what you tell 'em. Three bills each, six for both. That's four for me, two for you, alright?"

Ciara tucks the bags away. "Alright," she agrees, without much interest; her cut has been other things at other times, depending on how much Garth can score from one or another of the many private clinics where he's worked over the years, playing various contacts desperate for under-the-counter money against each other in a constant struggle to turn mislaid surplus into ill-gotten profit. So she doesn't care much to argue percentages overall, not so long as she's kept in the loop and reasonably solvent after expenses. "You want me to bring it back tonight?"

"Naw, I trust you. Come by tomorrow to pick up, 'round six."

"I might be asleep."

"Not after *I* show up, you won't. Now get gone."

Garth's place was mercifully free of hallucinations for once, but as the door closes behind her Ciara gets the distinct impression that might be about to change; the apartment building's hall looks different somehow, light diffuse and variable, as though the fixtures are suddenly full of bugs: semi-transparent bodies cluster-crawling across the bulbs inside, cooking themselves against their hot, fragile skin. She can almost smell them starting to smoke and it makes her move faster, ever faster—stabbing for the elevator's button, counting off the seconds it takes to make the lobby, taking the steps outside in a single jump as the bike judders and bounces its own way down alongside her.

Above, the sky's now completely dark, no stars showing in the streetlamps' flat white glare. Ciara can still remember when at least half of them weren't halogen, that leaky yellow sodium light bleaching everyone who passed underneath to almost the self-same shade, like extras from a Hopper painting; comforting, in its own weird way. More . . . natural.

These new lights, though—they don't seem to follow the same spectrum. Everything's reduced to two categories: illuminated or not. Whatever's outside each bright pool shrinks away, becoming insignificant; whatever's inside looks artificial, impermanent. Like nothing matters all too much.

Sports events, sex shows, executions—this sort of light matches all of them, any of them. It's good for details. Normalizes the abnormal. And it doesn't disturb her, not really, because if there's things you'd do at night that you'd never do during the day, then what does that mean if all her days are nights now? What does any of it mean?

Nothing. It's just the way things are.

She mounts up, wobbling slightly, and turns her bike into traffic.

The house stands on its own in the middle of nowhere, bordering a classic industrial zone—warehouses, scrub-lots, an abandoned factory the city just hasn't gotten around to knocking down yet, let alone turning into condos. There's a nightclub banging away in the distance, but otherwise it's denuded and almost silent, lit up by spill from the lights down at the docks, where shipping containers get loaded and unloaded. These are places where the map runs out, where the city becomes unpredictable—the places you have to Google to get there and almost always end up getting lost along the way anyhow.

Her social worker says Ciara really shouldn't bike, not on the meds she's giving her. "It's not riding, it's driving," she likes to tell Ciara, as though that makes a bit of difference, aside from etymologically. "I'd lobby for all bicycle owners to be licensed, if I could."

"So why don't you?" Ciara asked once, or maybe just thinks she did—not out of interest so much as simple need to say *something* in response, when the woman insists on nattering on like that. It's only polite to keep up your end of the conversation, or so her family eventually managed to teach her through painstaking repetition, trial and error, home training: stop speaking long enough to listen to what the other person is saying, nod and smile, act like you care even when you don't. File the basics away, so as to make sure you're able to answer questions.

But her worker simply shook her head and let it slide, and weeks later, Ciara doesn't recall the subject ever having reoccurred. Another functionally meaningless interaction, same as every other—she wouldn't go at all, if she could get away with it. Why should Ciara be legally forced to shoulder the burden of someone else's diffident attention every week, their useless pseudo-sympathy, simply to maintain her access to scrip? Especially since she could easily swap Garth for the exact same psychoactives, almost, then wander away high but "readjusted," with what small part of her dignity remains intact . . .

A lifetime on parole, she thinks, *when I never did anything to anyone but myself—nothing permanent, any rate. There's no justice in it.*

Yes, and no justice anywhere else, either, for that matter. But this is old news.

It's a witch's lair, Ciara thinks, still looking at it, wondering vaguely just how long that may have been going on. Two-story, detached but flat on one side, as though it used to be one half of a duplex, the other section long demolished. It's got a front-gabled roof, shingles peeling, gutters rusty and sprung; the narrow windows leer and squint, dirt-cataracted. The porch roof sags, but not dangerously so—and is that something peeping down at her now, curling round from behind the chimney, a sinuous shadow, black-furred yet boneless as a snake?

No, obviously. By no means. Not at all.

She parks the bike against the steps, mounts them, knocks, waits. Knocks again. Avoids looking too long at the knocker itself, for fear it'll develop a face. Even considered from an angle, however, it still looks suspiciously profile-esque: crosspiece bolted on either side, creating a flat, bulge-eyed hammerhead shark visor; the knocker itself hangs down labially, weight front and center, a vertical piercing.

And: thinking too much about it, reaching for words, obsessing over description; shit, *shit,* that's never good. *Stay quiet,* she finds she can't quite keep from begging it, uselessly, if only inside her head, own lips decisively firm-sealed. *Don't talk, don't talk, please.* Don't.

Like *that* ever works.

From the back of the house comes a vague commotion, meanwhile, barking and clattering plus a woman's voice yelling about keeping her hair on, along with what sounds like a baby—babies?—screaming from someplace downstairs, not up-. *Who keeps babies in a basement?* Ciara wonders, as she stands there with arms folded 'til at least two sets of interior locks shoot back, door scraping open a bare, chained hand's breadth to reveal a squinched-up slice of face, gaze dubious, red-threaded possibly from lack of sleep, or a contact high.

"Garth sent me," she tells the woman, remembering to make eye contact, brief but firm. "You made an order—I'm delivery."

"Yeah, sure." A pause. "So . . . when was that?"

"No idea. I work outsource; he tells me where to go, with what, and I do. What kicks it off is your business."

"That's no way to live, girlie." Then, like it just occurred to her: "How I know you're not 4-0?"

"Seriously?" Ciara sighs, tugs her shirt up, flashing a double B-cup's worth of unwired bra, then turns her bag out on the steps. The second the pills hit, the door's already open, client scrabbling them inside with both hands, snarling: "Jesus, what *are* you, retarded? Get your ass inside, 'fore somebody sees . . . "

"Nobody lives 'round here to 'see' anything. That's why *you* do, probably."

"Just come the fuck *in*, is what I said! *Christ*."

Inside, the house is crowded and dusty, the barking/crying louder, definitely located beneath their feet. Garth's client rolls her eyes, shaking her head hard, as though she's trying to fend the sound off bodily. "Christ!" she repeats, raking her hand through tangled hair. Then adds: "Never have kids," and Ciara nods, as if it's ever actually been an option.

"I hear they're worth it, though," she replies, recalling previous interactions with mothers (not her own).

"For somebody, sure." Ciara raises her eyebrows, slightly, and the woman hastens to explain. "Oh, those aren't *mine*. I'm just . . . lookin' after 'em 'til somebody comes to pick 'em up."

"Parents?"

"*New* parents."

I don't follow, Ciara wants to say. But: "Hmmm," she replies, instead—always her go-to fallback when she doesn't understand something she's just heard, and the woman sighs.

"Look—you know how rich people'll go all the way to Russia or Romania, the Ukraine sometimes, just so they can get hold of a cute, white baby? Well, sometimes they don't turn out so cute later on. Still blonde and blue eyes and whatever, but—there's bad stuff goes on in those places, so the kids aren't . . . wired right. Can't socialize 'em, no matter how much expensive baby shit you buy. Except it's all on the inside, so's you don't necessarily notice 'til you've had 'em around a while, and they still won't talk, or hug you, or . . . anything . . . "

Ciara nods. This, for a change, makes sense to her; she's always understood transactions. "They feel like they got cheated. Want to give the kids back."

The client snorts. "Yeah, well, good luck on that one. No, it's easier to swap 'em out to somebody else in North America who got screwed the same way, trade one with more of the good stuff for one with less, so everybody's happy." Adding, as though it's something she keeps trying to convince herself of: "They're not *bad people*, you know, any of 'em. Just want what they want, is all."

"Capitalism."

"Exactly."

If she were somebody else, Ciara thinks, she might be surprised the woman would tell her about all this, let alone in such detail. But people tend to talk to her as a rule, both spontaneously and volubly, about all sorts of oddness—even white people, even authority figures. Helps that most folk she meets these days are on drugs, but it actually extends much further in every direction; people both above and below her paygrade end up treating her like a human sounding-board, a pet or a priest, something barely animate which listens and doesn't judge, which can't easily distinguish between what it's hearing and what it might have heard.

Those who make the effort to get to know her soon start to understand she's her own unreliable narrator and act accordingly, but even the ones who don't seem to get the same impression nonetheless;

receive it subliminally, like a signal or a smell. Some pheromonal signature she doesn't even know she's emitting because she's personally immune to it.

As the woman counts out cash from a stash in her freezer, Ciara just stands there, wondering what to feel about all this. Nothing would be most practical, as usual. But her eyes keep on being drawn here and there, scanning for signs of abuse beyond the general atmosphere of filth and decay, the rampant non-recreational drug use. *Wasn't there supposed to be another person living here?* she wonders, finally replaying what Garth said: *these fools*, right. Not that it really makes much difference, either way.

"What's wrong with you, anyhow?" the woman asks her, still counting.

Ciara shakes her head sharply, to clear it, and replies: "Diagnoses vary."

The woman barks a laugh. "Don't they always! Still, you talk pretty good for a crazy person."

"I was in university when I finally got a full psych eval, and they put me on the register. Right after I had my first—public—episodes."

"Didn't graduate, huh?" Ciara nods. "What happened?"

Again, Ciara has to think, dragging the memories up from under deep water; talks the timeline through carefully, trying not to paraphrase. "The initial break, I stayed up two weeks, 'til I blacked out. Thought I was writing my thesis with my mind. The second . . . that time I was at a bar, doing shots with friends, because somebody's team had won. I think I started to sing. And then I woke up and it was two days later in jail, with an officer telling me I bit this guy's earlobe off. My parents bailed me out, got me looked at, assessed; next thing I knew, I'd been committed."

"Sounds rough."

Ciara nods again, slightly. "Thank you," she says, the only thing she can think *to* say, to which the woman just nods, giving her the roll. "Red for up, blue for down," Ciara reminds her, trying to be helpful, as she hands her the pills in exchange; the client laughs again, tossing her greasy head like a bad parody of a supermodel.

"Think I don't know *that*, by now?" she demands, and Ciara barely restrains herself from answering: *well, I'd hope you* did, *obviously. Given how much of this stuff you probably take.*

Moments later she's back outside, door shut and locked behind. Bone moon up above, like a bad silver penny; the clouds scud shut across it, making it wink. Cricket-noise rising from everywhere around, so pointed it sounds almost fake, as though meant to hide the fact that she's being surveilled. As though the world itself is keeping watch on her, never resting, never letting *her* rest.

Time to go home, girl, Ciara thinks, re-mounting her bike. Yet she thinks she can still hear the babies wailing — muffled by rock and concrete and glass, seeping up from underground — even while she rides away.

Blink and it's three in the morning, then five, then six: blue blush at the horizon, cruel light seeping in like a bruise, finally lulling her to sleep. Then it's noon or later, the phone screaming at her in — U2's "Discotheque," which her brain easily translates into Garth's voice: *bitch, pick up; where you at, bitch? Ciara! Put me on damn speaker, already.*

She grabs it up, fumbles her thumbprint into the lock, stabs the appropriate button. "Yes, it's me, I'm here. What is it?"

"Two in the damn PM, that's what it is. Where's my money, honey?"

"Uh . . . in my bag, I guess. Where I left it."

"Cool, 'swhat I thought. Now buzz me in."

Because he's down there already, ringing her while looking up at her apartment; yes, of course. This makes sense. Ciara shakes her head first side to side then up and down, an invisible cross — should clear it, almost always does, but this time . . . static lingers. There's a hum still left underneath everything, louder than ever. A faint scritch, scales on scales, like serpents coiling.

Garth is solid, though, as ever. He makes a good tide-brake.

"Man, this place ain't much of much, is it?" he observes, looking around, as Ciara counts out her cut before turning the rest of the roll over. "Too much stuff in too little space. Look like you filmin' an episode of *Hoarders*."

"I clean twice a day," Ciara says, slightly offended, to which he laughs, holding up his hands in mock surrender: *hey, baby, I'm just sayin'*. And after a moment she smiles too because there's nothing else to do—humor, charm, etcetera. Not worth wrecking a working relationship over.

"How long have you known those people, exactly?" she finds herself asking, instead. "In that house, I mean. The delivery."

"Ciara, shorty, you need to be more specific."

"Last night, Garth. Down near the water?"

"What? Oh, dockside, yeah . . . them fools. How well I know 'em? Well as I know anybody, girl, you feel me? Well as I know *you*, for damn sure."

Ciara can't think that's true, exactly, though she knows enough not to say so. "They seem . . . odd," she says instead, carefully, somewhat afraid he'll find that funny, too. But Garth simply shrugs.

"Odd's okay, long's they pay, you feel me? I mean, we dealin' narcotics, not givin' out Meals on Wheels or nothin'. Odd's kinda our stock in trade."

"Well yes, I suppose, but—they say they sell children." Explaining, as he looks at her: "In their basement, that's where they keep them. Kids people don't want anymore, for sale to new parents."

"Um, huh: that don't sound right. Sure you ain't trippin'?" He nods at her pill-bottles, but she shakes her head; the meds aren't that sort of drug, as he knows.

Still: "I'm never sure," Ciara admits, after a moment. "Of

anything."

"Good to keep that in mind, then, huh? You see them kids, or what?"

" . . . no. But I heard them, and that woman, she told me — "

"Bitch, please; that woman'd tell you the sun come up backwards an' inside-out, you give her the right kinda fix. 'Sides, not like you don't see shit ain't there on the regular, right?" Which makes Ciara pause another moment, frowning, even as Garth's voice softens. "Listen, sleep some more on it, see if you still feel the same tomorrow. I mean, ain't like they call every week, so might be you never have to go back there, anyhow. That'd be good, huh?" As she nods: "That's my girl. And if they keep on creepin' you out, then boom! They cut off. No extra charge. You my boo, Ciara; need you more'n I need them, and that's the truth. Junkie under every rock, you just know where to look."

Which is him trying to be reassuring, she guesses.

Later, meanwhile — her meandering path taking her along much the same delivery circuit, bike slipping dock-wards by slow degrees — Ciara finds herself stopping almost at random, pausing to snap photos of whatever she suspects might not be quite as there as it seems. Some of it's easy to spot, like that bright shoal of sharp-toothed little fish in-festing the air between the trees, or a MISSING poster with her own face on it, but other things are slipperier: a shadow-trick circling that greasy spoon's chimney with darkness, only noticed just as it's with-drawn all of a sudden, slick as some retreating tentacle. A dog with no tail and six legs glimpsed at a far remove, barking what almost sounds like human curses in Arabic, or maybe Japanese.

And then there's the house, curtains drawn tight. The painted-over basement windows like cataracts, a corpse's coin-set eyes.

She snaps a series of views from almost every angle, for further study.

"Are you taking your meds?" her social worker asks, looking down at her pen as she takes notes; Ciara nods, frowning a bit when she receives no response, before realizing the woman probably can't see what she's doing. So: "Yes," she confirms, out loud.

"Every day?"

"They say 'take every day' on the package, so yes."

This finally gets her a glance, narrower than she's comfortable with. "You need to be compliant, Ciara, you know that," the social worker tells her. "I don't want to have to send you back."

"I understand."

"Keep up with the meds, in other words."

That's the clear implication, Ciara thinks. But only repeats, instead: "Yes."

Getting up, turning away—the woman's already gone back to her notes, no doubt thinking about her next appointment. It would be easy to simply walk away, let it slide, go where her feet yearn to take her. Instead, however, Ciara hears herself asking: "If you knew something bad was happening, would you try to do something about it?"

The worker looks up again, eyes sharpening. "*Is* something bad happening?"

"Well. . . " Ciara backpedals. " . . . um, I said 'if.' More of a 'for instance,' really."

"Hmmm, all right. Then if that's the way it is, I'd probably try to make sure I had all my facts straight, that I actually understood what I was dealing with before I made any hasty decisions. You know? Before I did something I might regret."

"Uh huh."

"You *are* taking the pills, though. Right, Ciara?" She nods. "Say yes again, please, one more time. Out loud."

"*Yes*," Ciara replies yet once more, annoyance sparking. "Of course."

"Then you'll be okay to figure things out for yourself, probably. Like an adult. Which you are, right?"

" . . . right."

"Just making sure," the woman says, with a last, not completely unconvincing smile: *you're dismissed*, the subtext reads, clear enough even Ciara can't fail to pick up on it as her cue to go.

Outside, her continuing freedom duly rubber-stamped and signed off on, Ciara passes the usual complement of fellow crazy people. Granted, their cocktails probably aren't the same as hers (exactly), or their diagnoses, but she feels a certain sympathy for them nonetheless—she can read their body language, spot them from a distance, the same way they can read/spot her. In any given crowd, no matter where, they'll always know each other.

The man nearest the door—she thinks his name is Fubar, unlikely thought that seems—looks up as she approaches, sidelong; he has a tattooed scalp and a fresh street burn, just starting to shade from peel to tan in patches. "'Lo," he says. "Cee-arra, yeah?"

"Chee-ahra," Ciara corrects. "Can I, um, show you something?"

" . . . okay."

"It's just pictures. On my phone."

He looks down, then up again, eyelids clicking dry as he blinks. "Yeah, all right, sure."

Ciara sits down to watch as Fubar flips through the photos, considering them owlishly, one by one. "Don't know what you're expecting," he says, eventually, and Ciara has to take a moment to think, before answering—how much can she tell him, after all, and how much *should* she?

"I just need you to say what you see," she replies, and watches his eyebrow twitch upwards. "This a trick question, girlie?"

"No, not at all. No."

"Uh huh. Wouldn't tell me if it was, though, right?"

Probably not, Ciara thinks, as Fubar gives a creaky laugh, thumbs back to the beginning, studies them again with equal disinterest. Until —

"Trees," he begins, at last. "Streets, a restaurant, some crapped-out little shack. Front view, back view, side view. You shoppin' for a new home? Could put a down-payment on that one pretty easy, I'd think, 'less you're allergic to dirt."

"Yes. And that's *all* you see?"

"Walls, doors, windows, the works; bricks below, shingles up top, concrete on the damn walkway. Sky, light. Freakin' *shadows*." A snort. "Seriously, want something else? Then you maybe better give me a ghost of a clue on *what*."

Ciara looks at him for a moment, debating. Then asks, finally: "Do you see any children in them?"

. . . and feels the tiny hairs on her arms go up with a dull yet completely distinct shiver, shoulder to wrist, as he nods, points — drags a dirty nail across the screen, finger casually connecting dots from this one to that, here to there, everywhere.

In the basement's windows.

In the windows above, too — upper, lower. Those on the first floor. Those on the second.

On the roof, under the eavestroughs. Behind the chimney. Clinging to the slope.

Under the front porch. Behind the doors, front and back.

Looking out at him — at her — through the letter-slot, the keyhole.

"Can't see 'em?" Ciara shakes her head. "But they're yours, right?"

"No. They're not."

"Huh. That's surprising."

"Why?"

But he just shrugs, falling silent. The subsequent pause in their conversation drags out a good long while after that, Ciara clamping down on a growing urge to grab the phone back and run, before she hears herself blurt out, at last: "Okay, but . . . can . . . can they . . . see *me*?"

"No idea, girlie."

"Oh. Then why—"

Fubar squints down one more time before handing the phone to her again, sun-damaged fingers surprisingly cool on hers, movement dry and quick as a lizard's.

"Do look a whole damn lot like you, those kids in there," he concludes, finally. "That's all I really meant to say."

And turns away.

That night, the world bears in on her extra hard, no filter between its truth and her naked brain. Everything pressing down, an inverted pyramid, crushing her into one small, still point of concentrated misery; sheer weight of a wasted lifetime, all crashing in on her at once. She sits in the kitchen, crying, room around her reduced to a haze of uncertain light, lensed through tears as though drowned: an existence measured out in cost-benefit analysis coffee-spoons, forever eking away like some endless plus-minus chain.

It's moments like these, thankfully few and far between, when she feels the void open up beneath her heart—a second mouth set to yearning, hot, bright and hungry-empty, always wanting, never filled. When she realizes her so-called life is less peace than purgatory, a sere and dreadful place where nothing will ever touch her as long as she never touches anything in return, forever.

As night falls, her cheeks air-drying, Ciara watches the lights go on all over town—what little of it she can access, that is, through her apartment's window. Feels the wires hum, electricity spreading out like a web, both seen and unseen; that net of cables, connecting everything. That buzz in the air, never stopping, no matter late the hour.

A voice speaking up from the back of her brain, now, clear as the day she first heard it: some prof from first year, at the very start of her truncated university "career." *Our entire civilization's unnatural, sociologically speaking,* he says, and she doesn't even have to close her eyes to see him do it—face gaunt but body pale and puffy, a dough-lump set with sunken bones, snappy cardigan and sandals ensemble pointing to almost certain tenure. *Building cities started it, but ever since the implementation of electric light, mankind has completely lost its natural circadian rhythms; we're all chronically sleep-deprived, every single one of us. Used to be, the sun went down, there was nothing to do but sleep—too dark for detail work, not if you wanted to keep your eyesight. Now people can work at night, work all night... hell, we* live *by night, in a way our species just never evolved to do. Studies show that people awake and operating between three and six a.m. take on brainwave patterns like those of somnambulists, causing the line between waking and dreaming consciousness to literally disappear.*

Which is why doctors can perform entire operations yet recall none of the details afterwards, why workers can go whole shifts without making new memories, simply surfing on already-recorded impressions of how it feels to perform a meaningless task over and over and over. Because when your brain knows you're essentially waking up on the same day you went to sleep, you lose all referents for transition, the ability to separate today from yesterday and tomorrow. Time itself stops meaning anything.

Vitamin D deficiency from lack of sunlight; neurochemical imbalance from overexposure to UV; the psychological effects of long-term social isolation—it's all the same process, kids, and sleep deprivation just makes it happen faster. Ruin the body's rhythms, you ruin the body . . . and the mind.

Ciara considers the ceiling of her apartment, trying to remember if she'd found the lecture funny or not at the time, or if that was the rest of the class. Looking back, there certainly seems to be some vague echo of laughter running counterpoint beneath the words—but then again, classrooms are bad for that; she's been listening to people snicker almost her whole educational life, even when she hasn't borne the brunt of it. Though she can only suppose it's better to laugh than cry, in general, just like the old phrase says—sometimes, anyhow. Depending on the subject matter.

Professor Guy got it backwards, though, far as she can reckon: given her mind came pre-wrecked, her schedule can only be the effect of that ruin, not its cause. Can't possibly sleep your way back to health when your basic problem is being hazy on telling sleep from waking, in the first place.

She rolls off the bed, hand finding a sketchbook on her end table in the dark, without needing to look. Time to take the Zen approach— stop trying to *go* to sleep, let it come to you. Flick on the light, grab the colored pencils; turn to a blank page, and let the patterns flow out of your moving hands onto the paper. Veer between symmetry and asymmetry. Lay out shapes in spirals and matrices, abstract mosaics. Don't try to *draw* anything, just watch the paper slowly fill in, patterns accreting across the white space like stained glass frost.

It was an art therapist who first recommended this particular insomnia cure, during Ciara's last hospital stay, waxing poetic about the benefits: repetition, concentration without thinking, the colors. Like concrete meditation. Normally, she'd be yawning before she covered half the page, but maybe it's time to readjust her meds again; she sits back, scrubbing at her face, looking at the weave of triangles, polygons, and lines. Then frowns and studies it again.

Is there—something *in* the pattern, now? That she didn't put there, obviously: a hidden shape, like one of those eye-wrenching 3-D pictures you can only see by unfocusing your eyes and looking *behind* the surface? Looking up at her, flat yet rough-edged, its corners lifting slightly from the paper, as though about to detach and—

(flip up, twist out)

(flap away)

Her bedside light goes out, but after the first second's jolt—shock to the chest, tiny heart attack—she realizes the streetlights are still on, so this can't be a power failure; bulb's burnt out, that's all. So she tosses the pad onto the bed, rises, then stops, turning slowly back.

The pattern, lying in a square of metallic yellow seeping in from outside, has changed; some colors bleached to invisibility, but others inverted, gone toxic-negative. The spectrum shift renders its hidden shape painfully clear: the house, *that* house. But...

More, too. Much more.

Because: she can finally see them now, in this light, from this— angle. Doesn't even have to squint. Eyes in all the windows, wetly bright, insectile; bodiless faces like wind-caught balloons, slack-grinning. Twisted figures smearing themselves, disproportionately, everyplace Fubar's moving finger once touched; not threatening but shivering, self-protective. Forever coiled in on themselves against a world full of monsters no one else acknowledges.

The children. The ones who supposedly look *exactly like her.*

They plead their case wordlessly, appealing to her: *Help us, Ciara. Find us, free us. Be there for us, in our hour of need . . . the way no one ever was for you.*

(This much she understands, after all, both well and intimately— how when you're diagnosed as different, when everyone around you "knows" you see things, the first thing certain predatory parties start thinking is how they can probably get away with anything, because no one will ever believe you if you tell. And mostly, they're absolutely right.)

Something happened to you too, right? A girl asked her once, in Shepherd's Flock, long before she met Garth. *And that's why you're here. Right?* Then nodded even though Ciara hadn't answered, continuing: *Yeah, see, I knew it. Knew it had to've. 'Cause something always does.*

She's a good girl, my Ciara, that's what her mother used to tell people. *Got her challenges, sure, but that doesn't matter, not with the Lord's help: she's good. Does what she ought, no backtalk. Does whatever you tell her to.*

And yes, that *had* been true, for the longest time—up to a point. The point she went off to university, to be accurate; left her family's house, their firm embrace, their watchful, shepherding gaze. When she had that first episode, then that second one . . . ended up in jail overnight, in custody, committed. When she ended up in a halfway house where another "exceptional" young adult started in on her and she went into a sort of fugue-state, unable to admit what was happening until it was too late, the changes in her body too obvious to deny. Which was when, in turn, her parents took her to one doctor then almost immediately to another, where something they never bothered to fully explained was done to her.

It took six months back at home, doped to the gills, for her to finally figure out exactly what'd happened, and the confrontation which followed threw the gates of Shepherd's Flock open wide: if she bites down hard enough she can still feel the ache where Momma slapped her for even suggesting such a thing, hear the noise as her jawbone cracked under the pressure of that beautiful two-karat engagement ring Daddy bought her when the money started coming in, back-turned under pressure like usual. After which Ciara hit her back, hard enough to break a tooth.

Ciara draws her breath, throat burning, stuttering. Allows herself to recognize the all too familiar way that her room's own darkness has already begun to writhe softly just beyond that square of sick light's parameters, surfaces set similarly atremble: coiling, uncoiling. A thousand carrion lips set smiling by her discomfort, mocking and menacing all at once.

You're going back to that house right now, those kids, to help them, these no-mouths whisper from every direction, each word a barely suppressed smirk. *I mean, not that you probably can, but . . . you'll do it, even so. Because you are what you are, see what you see, so it really does behoove you to do something about it, goddamnit, at the very very least. Anything else is cowardice, plain and simple.*

To see things and do nothing is always a crime, whether or not anybody else sees those things.

Once upon a time, she might have thought it was the meds making her think this or making her think it's a good idea. But she's been on them long enough now to know better; her social worker's right about that much, at least. Without the meds, she wouldn't be enough of a *competent adult* to even know what to do, let alone be able to do it—just sit here watching her mind chase its own tail all night, then fall asleep and wake up worse than ever. Probably forget any of it ever happened in the first place.

Cowards stay alive, though, she thinks, automatically. Then adds to that, a mere moment later: *but so what? Sometimes, just staying alive isn't good enough—not once it's been rubbed in your face that no matter what you do or don't, you're going to die one day anyhow.*

Sometimes, even while you're marking time, you also want to live.

Down on the streets, the world she finds herself riding—*driving*—through seems abruptly drained of all color, stale, flat, and unprofitable, like a pop-up book version of itself. Shorthand describing something you saw once in a dream, and glancingly at that: a dead reflection, the sort of upside-down city you catch flickering underwater when you look over the side of the Toronto Island ferry, nothing but green-on-green shadows full of floating duck poop and weed.

Streetlamps everywhere, but no traffic—it's empty as the moment after a *tsunami* siren goes off, just before the first wave hits, bright light and heavy shadow juxtaposed so perfectly they cancel each other out, rendering your ability to perceive whatever's right in front of you effectively null. All of which only adds to Ciara's general impression that anything after 3:00 AM takes place in a sort of imaginary hour, a nonexistent time when anything can happen but nothing that *does* happen leaves any real traces behind, not once the sun is up.

That won't be for a while, though. Time enough for all the mistakes she plans to make tonight and then some.

When I was a kid, she finds herself thinking, there were insects. *When I was a kid, Toronto wasn't so damn* loud *all the time, aside from now. When I was a kid, things smelled better. When I was a kid . . .*

But she isn't a kid, not anymore. Hasn't been since she first started talking about stuff everybody thought she was making up, only to find out doing so made the adults around her so worried they got angry, thus rendering the slide from great imagination to spanking offense both short and sharp.

With hindsight, Ciara realizes, she could've ended up in that basement. Indeed, had there been people willing to come and take her away if her parents just paid them enough, they definitely would've.

(*You're being uncharitable, Ciara. They loved you as well as they could, surely, for as long as they could. Until . . .*)

Until it got too hard, the voice in the back of her mind hisses, making the other, gentler voice fall silent. Which is just as well since Ciara knows she can't really argue with either of them.

Still: doesn't matter. Because there's the house now, looming up in the distance, growing like a weed. And here Ciara is, pulling off into the bushes, laying her bike down where no one will hopefully be able to see it, resettling branches and leaves as though she's making a bed.

Looks up at the windows, scanning for light. Finds none. Approaches sidelong, moving quiet, around the back. Nothing yet, anywhere. Waits one minute more, just to be sure.

There's a rock on the ground, roughly goose egg sized. She tucks it into her palm, fingers knotted tight overtop, pulls her sleeve down over the knuckles. Not much protection, but she supposes it'll have to do.

Thus armed, she crouches down, chooses a painted corner of the nearest basement window, and puts her fist through it.

Crack of glass, followed by a muffled, distant tinkle. Ciara freezes, poised for any reaction, but again, nothing comes. Bending closer, she puts her eye to the hole and squints, trying to make out what's inside: are those mattresses on the floor, spread wall to wall, dirty and ill-kept? Children on the mattresses?

Some sprawled, some piled, wrapped 'round each other perhaps for warmth (few seem to wear much more than underpants or diapers or both), perhaps comfort. One or two appear to glance up incuriously—pale skin, vague reflected light, what might be eyes. Don't look anything like "their" picture, but then, she never really expected them to; that came filtered through her, after all. Her *vision*.

"Hey," she risks whispering, hoping it carries. "Kids, hey. Hey? You hear me, down there?"

No reply.

" . . . you okay?"

No reply, yet again—not as such. Just a brief wail from further in, choked off quick, like they're afraid someone upstairs might be listening. Ciara can see shoulders start to shake here and there, breathing gone liquid and uneven. Remembers the crying from the other day, and feels the hairs go up on her nape.

"I'm coming in, okay?" she tells them, only slightly louder, shoulders squaring as she hunkers back, ready to spring upwards. "All right? Don't worry, be there soon; everything's going to be okay, I promise. I'm almost . . . almost . . . "

Ciara's no expert, but the house seems ridiculously easy to break into, mainly because whoever left last forgot to lock the back door. As she uses a carving knife picked out of a teetery tangle of dirty dishes to jimmy the basement door's lock, however, the woman from before suddenly appears at her elbow, scrubbing sleep out of her drug-bleary eyes.

"Who the fuck—hey, I remember you! Garth's girl."

Without thinking, Ciara pushes her away, a firm slap to the breastbone, only to watch her stumble backwards; her weight tips the scales, popping the door pen even as she loses balance, falls straight down the stairs. Not a cry on the way down, just a faint exhalation of surprise, followed by a flurry of sounds so sharp they seem artificial: tha-thump, tha-THUMP, *crack*.

Then she's there at the bottom, all splayed with eyes staring, neck bent to one side like a snapped stick. Ciara's certain she's already dead until she gives one last big heave, chest popping, then slumps once more and lies silent.

Ciara stands there motionless, running scenarios in her head. In one, the house's other occupant—a guy, she presumes, given what Garth said—comes back while she's down there and shoots her, hits her over the head with a pan or something; she dies straight away or lingers for days, has to listen to whatever he's likely to do to the kids when he sees the damage, after which she eventually ends up in a land-fill somewhere. In another, she calls the cops and tells them what's going on, but they end up arresting her; she'd be okay with that, she guesses, as long as they took the kids along too. A third has her walking away with the kids, hand in hand, down the middle of the empty street while the house burns behind them. That last one strikes her as doable, even if it does involve leaving her bike behind.

Shepherd's Flock had chore duty, performed by people on fairly heavy drugs, so there was a lot of talk about what cleaning agents to not mix together, and why. She puts the ones which don't form chlorine gas together in a bucket, slops the result around everywhere, then does a quick recon. No matches that she can see, though the woman's left full ashtrays on every other level surface.

Lighter, Ciara thinks, stealing a glance at the woman's body, slack mouth grinning oddly from this angle. Because it's not as though she wouldn't have had to go down there eventually, anyhow—so she does, step by careful step. Calling out, as she descends—

"Hey, it's me! I'm here, like I said I would be. C'mon out, you're free—she's gone, I'll look after you now. Kids?"

Still no reply aside from some vague scrabbling, but no real surprise there: though trauma hits us all differently, Ciara's often noted how it usually begins with a sort of all-over numbness, a general frozen, hyper-alert calm. She can talk them out of it, she's almost sure, and the ones who won't follow she can always pick up and carry. They're just children, after all—how much can they weigh?

Then she's on the last step, already bending, poised to rummage through the woman's clothing. Distracted but smiling, trying to project trustworthiness, to pump it from her pores. Hard to that and pay attention to everything else around her, behind her . . .

. . . which is why, in the end, she never sees it—

(them)

—coming.

Sharp pain in her back, slicing deep: that's the same window-glass she broke, pushed into the basement, puncturing a kidney. A weight on one leg, pulling her off-balance; another weight on her arm, clambering upwards. Baby teeth in her neck, biting deep and worrying then pulling back hard, tearing away a mouthful of flesh and blood.

Ciara can almost feel the moment her jugular pops, starts to spray. She falls heavily, rolling, straight onto the woman, who seems to clutch at her; opens her mouth to speak, but there's no breath left, no words, just a bubbling groan. Her eyes flick wildly, catch snatches of small faces, one lipsticked with gore and gesturing to the others, silent meaning clear: *there, up* there, *before she recovers. The way out, go,* go*!*

(GO)

They scamper over her as she lies next to the woman's body, up into the house, unhesitant, unwary. A smattering of speech here and there, in and between the whoops, the grunting—they're talking to each other, some of them, or maybe just to themselves. Lying there bleeding out, Ciara can only catch the tail ends of words, the middles, rough vowels and consonantal combinations. It's like they're speaking a whole other language.

I know you, though, all of you, she thinks, already lightheaded. *It's true, what Fubar said: you* are *like me, just like. Exactly.*

Can't fault them for thinking she was here to kill them, not save them, given what they must have already endured. Because God know, that's all *she*'s ever seen when the lights are out, and all she's ever found to see when they're back on again, too: monsters everywhere, in the light, in the dark. Inside as well as outside. A world full of monsters, human-faced or no, with no possible hope of a cure.

Still, at least she won't have to see them anymore.

Every Hole in the Earth We Will Claim as Our Home

UH, HI, YEAH. Is this the Let's Talk Hotline? For . . . mental health issues and stuff. Yeah, so I need to speak to somebody, but first off, I have a question: this is anonymous, right? I mean, you don't need my name, do you? Just to talk?

Okay, good. Good. That's what I thought.

All right, so . . . before we start, I need to know: does confidentiality apply here? I mean, I know you're probably not a doctor or anything, just a volunteer at best. If I tell you what's bothering me, though, is it true you really *can't* tell anyone else? 'Cause if I can't be sure—

—all right, good. That's good too.

(I really *do* want to tell someone, you see. But if I go ahead then you can't break your word and pass on what I'm going to say, not to anybody. It's in . . . both our best interests you keep to that one simple rule, believe it or not.)

All right, yes, I believe you, I'm sorry I asked. It's just that—well. I just *had* to.

Look, I'll be straight with you, okay? I don't know what kind of good this'll do, telling you what I'm going to tell you. But I have to do it, anyhow; I can't not. And I don't want to write it down somewhere to risk somebody else finding it, reading it . . . don't want to document it, on the off chance that doing so will somehow make it realer than I want it to be. No. I just want to *say* it, this whole thing, straight out, to someone who doesn't know anything about me, someone I'm probably never going to talk to again. Someone who can't even *see* me. And then I want to hang up, and walk away, and never think about any of it again. That way, it's sort of like it never happened. Like I can just . . . let it go and forget about it.

You're my single best bet, in that respect.

Okay, so—one last thing. You're not taping this, are you? No? You promise?

(I mean, I guess I'd really have no way of knowing, if you were. Have to just—take it. On faith.)

. . . well, anyhow.

Might as well start, then.

So I've been working Sick Kids' Hospital here in Toronto as my primary security site for . . . three years now, come January, and I mainly do night shift, which is about as stressful as you'd think it was likely to be. Worse for the nurses and the doctors, obviously, but the things we see coming in, the kids on the ward, the long-term cases . . . it wears on you. I'm the only one at my station who hasn't transferred out yet, gone somewhere else at least once, for a kind of mental rest. I don't know why, really—maybe I'm lazy, like my mom used to say. Maybe I'm scared of change, so when I finally get somewhere permanent, I tend to stick to it like glue.

Anyway, the floor I work most often is the Ground Floor, General Intake and Emergency, and my main circuit covers the Waiting Room. That's where all the kids and caretakers who don't have appointments have to go, to get triaged through Emergency. Mostly it's accidents, or things getting swallowed, though sometimes there's bugs and other symptoms; anything a GP on call doesn't feel qualified to treat at home, anything a hotline flags as particularly weird sounding. Ninety-nine percent of the time these don't come to much, thank God, but sometimes . . .

What we've been getting a rise in lately is kids who can't be vaccinated catching things from kids whose parents opt not to *have* them vaccinated for one reason or another, but still send them out into the world. Like that measles outbreak at Disneyland. Most of the time the result looks horrible but isn't necessarily life-threatening — the kids are segregated for a while, treated as best they can be, emerge with a few scars. It's like chicken pox.

The worst-case scenario, though . . . and there're always going to be a few of those, just statistically . . .

Well.

I don't know if you ever heard the story about how Roald Dahl's daughter died, but it was of encephalitis — complications from getting measles. The thing which always amazed me was that when Dahl heard there'd been measles at the school his kids went to, he begged his brother-in-law, who was a doctor, to get him enough gamma globulin to protect his children. But the guy could only get enough for one of them, so he opted to give it to Dahl's son Theo, and said: *oh, go ahead and let the girls catch it, it'll be good for them.*

So one of them did, and she was okay, but the other — Olivia — wasn't. She got sick, and slow, and sleepy, and their local GP came over and took a look and said it was probably just a cold but keep watching her. And then, later that day, she opened her eyes but she looked . . . weird, not like herself, like she wasn't really seeing anything, you know? So they loaded her into the car and took off, but by the time they got her to the hospital it was too late. It took about a day more, but they finally called it.

When he wrote about it later on, Dahl said he went in to kiss her, and she was still warm, and he asked the guy he was with why. Like: *she's still warm, why is she so warm?* And all the other guy said was: *it happens.*

But that's how it goes, right? You probably know doctors even if you're not one, so I don't really have to tell you how when you work in hospitals people do *die*, like all the time, no matter how good the facility is—and Sick Kids' is *good*, top of the line, undebatably. Parents come from all over the world, just 'cause they know how good it is . . .

. . . but kids still die, sometimes, and you don't get used to it. You can't.

So what happened is they brought this boy in with measles, his mom and his dad, about three and a half weeks ago. I can't tell you his name, obviously. But it was the same story, or a lot like it: presented with fever and rash, sick and sleepy, slow. Eyes rolled up. Had a seizure when he first got there, almost the first five minutes after registration, like he knew he was finally in the right place for it. So they rushed him upstairs and the Mom and Dad stayed downstairs together, waiting to find out, until a doctor came down and told them it was encephalitis; kid's whole brain was swelled up, right down to the stem. And he was alive for now but in a coma, and they didn't know when he'd wake back up, or if. They didn't know anything.

Mom and Dad sat there together for a few hours more, and then Dad had to go, 'cause he was on shift someplace else. Mom wouldn't leave, though. Didn't have anyone to call to come sit with her, I guess, though I heard her talking on her phone to somebody—might've been *her* job, maybe—and explaining what was going on. But she just sat there alone, after that. Around ten PM, I brought her some coffee, and she took it, but it's not like she spoke, even to say thanks. That was okay; I didn't expect it. She needed her time.

Sometimes I'd look over, and I thought she was praying.

Things thin out after midnight, even near the E.R. So that's when I notice there's this other woman sitting in the back, a few rows of chairs away—spotted her when I left to do rounds, then saw she was still there when I came back. Had a book in her hands, even had it open, but she wasn't reading, not really. She was watching the measles kid's mom out of the corner of her eyes, and . . . uh . . . listening, I think.

It sounds bad—it *is* bad—but if this woman hadn't read to me so much as middle-class white, even at a distance, I probably would have paid more attention to her, or had a few red flags go up. But she did, so I just sort of looked her up and down, then filed her away 'til I saw her do anything weird: an older lady, upper forties to mid-fifties, not fat but big all over; eyes light, grayish or bluish, hair light, maybe mouse with a little blonde, or a little gray. She looked like a teacher or a nanny, somebody's relative, or whatever. A counselor.

Around two A.M. I went to the bathroom, and when I came back, this woman was sitting next to the kid's mom, her arm around her shoulders. And I was sure they must've known each other from some-where, because the mom, she had her head down, just letting the woman hold her, kind of—shaking a bit, it looked like, from where I was. Like she was crying.

Okay.

So that was odd, but . . . I didn't know what to do, or even if I *should* do anything. I mean, it didn't seem like the mom thought the woman was bothering her; she seemed grateful, or what have you. I could have called the doc working her son's case, but what would that amount to? Nothing, probably. So . . .

. . . after a while, I got up, moved a bit closer—got *myself* a coffee, this time, and sat down where the woman'd used to be, the first time I saw her. Like I was taking my break, which I was. Then bent a little forward, enough so I could start to be able to hear what she was saying.

Yeah, I know: believe me, I know. That's why I'm telling this to *you*, instead of—

Well okay, I don't really know why myself, it comes to that. I just . . . want to tell somebody. Somebody who can't tell anybody else.

The woman, this older woman, she was murmuring in the mom's ear, really soft. She sounded reasonable. Like she'd done this before. And here's what she was saying, okay, as far as I can remember . . .

(. . . and I have *tried* to remember, since then, believe me. Very hard.)

She said—

*In Malaysia, after a tsunami comes, after the wave laps up and goes back out
again, strange things are found. Dead bodies, yes, lots of those—like during that
last one, when my family and I were there, celebrating. My husband had gotten
a promotion, and the fare was cheap. Something exotic to do together, before the
kids were too old to want to travel with us anymore, before they had their own
lives. The wave came while we were walking down to the beach, that time, and it
took everyone away, my son, my husband, my daughter . . . everyone but me.
They found me in a tree, three days later, where I'd tied myself to the trunk with
my towel and been wrenched from every angle, so hard my ribs broke. And I never
saw my husband or my son again, not even in the tents where they put the bodies
they found after, covered in mud and sand.*

*But I did find her at last, my daughter, and I found someone else, as well.
And that made all the difference.*

*There was no hospital, nowhere to put the sick and dying, except for next to
the dead. She was in the middle of a group of other survivors, only barely still
alive—crushed and broken, bruised so badly I didn't recognize her until she made
a noise that sounded like "Mama." I don't know if she knew I was there, or if she
only wanted to think I was. Her skin was purple, her eyes black with blood. The
water had torn everything I remembered of her away.*

*So I sat there for as long as I could, not even able to hold her hand, because
every time I touched her she screamed. And when the sun began to fall, I got up
and walked away, back down to the beach, or where the beach had been. I stood
there in the dying light and wondered whether or not I should wade out into the
tide, walk forward until the undertow found me. I wondered what was left for me
here, on dry land, when the ocean had already eaten everything I loved.*

*That's when she came to me, the old woman. That's when she put her hand
in mine, cold even in that wet, terrible heat, and began to speak, in much the same
way I'm speaking to you now—the same tone, even. As though she wanted to*

make me feel better and this was all she had to offer, on that score.

She told me about the things which get left behind after every wave, things from the bottom of the sea. Things that sometimes, in times of trouble, families will adopt and tame — to be a familiar, a fetch, an injection of luck in the wake of terrible tragedy. The pelesit, which looks like a cricket, a tiny green cricket with soft underwater skin in place of armor, which enters into the mouth of a dying person and bores a hole through the back of their throat, into the skull, the base of the brain. And the polong, something neither man nor woman, its toes and fingers webbed, with lidless eyes and gills — equally tiny, equally green. The po-long, which rides the pelesit through that hole and makes its home where the spine's roots begin, knitting its new body back together around it. Making sure whichever family member lies on the very verge of death stays alive, unable to cough out their soul and pass on.

You can have her back again, *she told me,* if you are willing. It is possible. A great sacrifice, and a great blessing.

Would it really be *her,* though? *I asked, not looking 'round. And heard the old lady laugh, not unkindly.*

Who can say? *she replied.* How would you know, were it not? It seemed so, to me; it *seems* so still, even now. For just as the pelesit does the polong's bidding, the polong is a quick study. Sometimes an echo is enough. Sometimes anything is better than nothing.

Losing a child is like a disaster, like losing the whole world, but I tell you — you can survive this, with help. The pelesit and the polong can help you survive, along with their makers . . . the great old ones beneath the sea, who lie chained deep enough that the creatures they spawn in their exile inevitably fall upwards, seeking to seed themselves once more along drier shores, from which our gods once banished them. The cracks of the world, deep down and hidden, where all such things abide.

And I thought for a while, after that, watching the sea, the old woman at my side. We stood there a long time, her and I, neither of us moving, until the sun sunk completely, and the moon rose, hidden behind a bank of clouds. 'Til the sea was black, entirely, right to the horizon, and that veiled moon and some distant stars gave the only light.

Why would they do this for me, these "great old ones"? *I asked her, at last. To which she replied, perhaps with a shrug:* Because it pleases them, and appalls the gods. Because they crave revenge. Ask rather, since it is the only pleasure left to them—why would they *not?*

So this is what I can tell you, these many years later, just as that old woman once told me: my daughter is alive today because of what I learned in the tsunami's wake . . . her, or enough of her for me to love, at the very least. A tiny person riding a demon cricket, a rag and a bone and a hank of hair, snips and snails and puppy-dog tails; all of this or none of it, I can't know for sure, and never will. But I find I don't much care, either.

This world is full of terrible things, you see, all over—some tiny, some immense, all hiding underneath the world's face, like maggots inside a wound. They came from the places we don't see. And they don't care about us, about how deeply we care for each other; they have their own plans and schemes, great dark engines of vengeance already set spinning, stretching out far beyond anything we can imagine. And they probably wish us nothing but ill, if they wish us anything at all—but I don't care about them, and you don't have to, either. All I know, all I have clear and present proof of, is that when their wants intersect with ours, we can benefit, if we are brave. That whenever the things we do or allow to be *done help them get closer to achieving their own needs, their hungers, then sometimes—because it amuses them—they'll do the same for us.*

Because of them, I have my daughter back again, or close as makes no nevermind. Because of them, I . . . who once had nothing . . . now have something, *at the very least. And that alone can be enough, that infinitesimally small comfort, if you only want it to.*

The truth is, we don't owe them anything, and we never did: not love, not fear, not even worship. All we ever have to do is give them what they want, and trust they'll do the same.

It's like God, that way, but better. Because it's real.

She went on and on like that, and by the end measles boy's mom was just sitting there, letting her hold her, not crying anymore—eyes wide, mouth shut. *Listening.*

So you tell me, the other woman asked her, *why should he die of something that should have been wiped out twenty years ago, your boy, just because of other people's selfishness? Why shouldn't you be selfish, too? Love always is, you know, down at its very core. It just wants what it wants, and to hell with every-thing—everybody—else.*

Measles boy's mom shook her head. *Patient and kind,* she told her, *that's what the Bible says. Love, it wants . . . what the other person wants.*

Are you telling me he wouldn't *want to live, then? To die and leave you behind, make you sad, leave you all alone? But no, you can't tell me that; you're* his *mother, after all. You know what's best for him, always, better than he knows himself.*

But it wouldn't be him. *You told me so, just then. You told me—*

—you couldn't know, that's what I said, like I can't. What I said *is, you won't* care.

You with me so far? You get what I'm saying?

Okay, good.

So there I am, listening in, and I'm wondering . . . well, what I should do, I guess. What I *could* do. Ask measles boy's mom if she was being bothered? Ask the other woman why she was there? It's after three A.M., by now, and the whole hospital's as quiet as it ever gets, like it's part of some kind of dream-world—everything faint and far away, the kind of echoing quiet that's almost loud as noise. Smell of bleach everywhere, and antibacterial hand-soap, no matter what kind of spray you put on top of it, afterwards; doesn't matter what time of year it is or what the weather might be outside, 'cause in here it's al-ways cold enough that at the end of the night you can go home and stand under a shower for, like, fifteen minutes straight, but you still can't get warm. I mean, it's like, like . . .

. . . the bottom of the sea.

Then my radio goes off, gives this big squeal of feedback, and it's the front desk, reminding me I have to do rounds. And neither woman looked 'round when it happened, but I jumped anyhow, like I'd been caught doing something I shouldn't — got up real quick, hustled myself away. Did the circuit extra-slow and checked everything twice, just to make myself feel better.

When I came back, finally, they were both gone: measles boy's mom, the other woman. The place was empty, and it didn't start filling up again 'til maybe five in the morning.

Neither of them came back at any point during that process, though, that I could see.

So I booked off and signed out at 6:00 A.M., like I always do, and I went home and I went to bed. And I dreamed . . .

Okay, enough about that. I don't think it matters what I dreamed.

Next day was my day off, a whole twenty-four hours — just enough time to fuck my schedule up completely, I always say — but the night after that I came back, 6:00 PM. Measles boy's mom and dad weren't there, and neither was the other lady. Around eight, I finally got up the courage to ask the doc on measles boy's case what'd happened, and she said that the kid had gone home. Made an amazing recovery. Said the mom came back around nine that morning with "that friend of hers" and her friend's kid, a little girl, and they went in and spent a couple minutes with him, and then all the machines went nuts, and when they charged in thinking he was flatlining, they found him sitting up in bed, eyes open, totally awake. By evening his rash was gone, and by the next morning all his panels were clear, so they let him go home.

That's amazing, I said, and the doc shrugged; *It happens*, she told me. Which kind of made the hairs on my neck go up, you know? Like Roald Dahl, asking that guy: *she's still warm, why is she still so warm?* And him saying —

Anyhow.

The rest of that night I spent in the Waiting Room, off and on, surfing around on my phone. I checked out the polong and the pelesit,

Wikipedia'ed them, the whole thing. Not a lot about either, which happens, when it's something from another culture. But I do remember I came across this thing in a forum somewhere, way down on some sub-thread I couldn't find again, when I went back to look—about how this guy's grandma told him that people with a polong and a pelesit inside them don't get any older, because if they did the polong and pelesit would start to grow 'til they just . . . sloughed the whole person they're inside off, I guess, like a skin. So they stay small, and the person stays the same age they were when it they came to live inside him or her, forever. Forever, or until what's inside them moves on.

'Cause that's the other part of it—this rumor somebody else had heard, that after a while the polong and the pelesit can maybe start . . . subdividing, tearing down the middle, so there's two of each. Like an amoeba. I mean, they still have to reproduce, right? 'Cause everything does. And if two polongs and two pelesits stay inside the same host, it's bad, obviously. They might start to fight, eventually, 'cause there's not enough room for them all. Might even kill each other, at which point the person they're inside dies right along with them. So that's when the head of the host's family—might be the mother, the father, a sister or brother or aunt or uncle, whoever; the one who wrangles them, basically, so they can keep on being lucky for everyone else—that's when this head goes out and starts looking for a new . . . person. Host. Home.

Somebody, anybody, who somebody *else* doesn't want to let go.

Sounds a whole lot like that other lady, to me—which kind of makes me wonder just how long ago that tsunami was, for her. How long her daughter's been a *little* girl, exactly.

So this is more than three weeks ago by now, almost a month, like I said. And I'm trying to forget I ever heard about this stuff, though I can't say it's easy . . .

. . . but last night, when I was on site, measles boy comes back in for a check-up, to make sure he really was fully recovered: just him and his mom, no dad, plus that other woman, and what I guess must've been her own kid. Her creepy, creepy little —

That's not the worst part, though.

So the other woman and her daughter sit there waiting, her stroking the girl's hair while the girl reads some magazine or other. And then, after the check-up, the doctor, the boy and his mom come out — boy rushes over and grabs the girl's hands, they go off to play in the corner or whatever, sit down next to each other, start gabbing away. And it's time for me to do my rounds, but as I'm leaving the doctor says she needs to discuss some stuff with the mom, and the other woman opts to go in with her, so that's happening just as I'm walking out.

Got through the door, almost kept walking, but — something stopped me. I didn't know what it was, at first, but then I realized: it was the quiet. Like the second the kids knew they were alone, they'd just . . . stopped. And even then I knew I didn't want to go back, like, at all, but . . . I *needed* to go back. To see what was happening when they thought nobody else was around to see. So I step to the right of the closed door, staying on my side, and peer back through the window into the Waiting Room.

You want to know?

Well, too bad. I'm gonna tell you anyways.

They were just . . . sitting there. Next to each other, still, but not touching, not talking, not looking at each other. Not interacting at all. Inert.

I watched them for a while, just like that, and nothing changed, ever: seconds ticking by on the clock, smell of bleach, distant echo. Nothing else, until —

I took a breath and stepped back through the door, and both their sets of eyes flicked over, locked on me, like they were drawn by my movement. Followed me around the room, heads staying exactly where they already were. And when I stopped a couple of feet away, making like I was checking something . . . when I stayed real still, listened real hard, without even knowing I was doing it . . .

That's when I heard it. That little, tiny… *noise* going back and forth between them, each to each. Like crickets tuning up. Like mosquitos: that whine, that trill. That . . . *chittering*.

I heard it. I *still* hear it.

Coming from deep inside their throats.

So that's the story.

I mean, I guess I could ask for another site, try to get a transfer, if it bothers me so much, right? And it's not like they're coming back, probably. But I don't *know*. I never will. And everything just . . . reminds me of that, every time I go in to work. All night. Almost every night.

Every night of the week but one.

This's gonna help, though. I'm almost sure.

I do keep on having these dreams, still. The ones I didn't want to tell you about. Like I'm at the bottom of the ocean, but not really *really* far down, because there's still light enough to see by, at least: blue-white sand underneath me, blue water up above, black cliff falling away behind, like I'm floating above the Marinaras Trench or something. And stuff is . . . falling, gently. Not down on top of me, no. It's falling up, from all around, like gravity's reversed. Like it's got somewhere else it wants to be.

Little green somethings, all legs and wings and antennae, all multi-lensed eyes. Little green arms and legs, webbed hands and feet, eyes without eyelids, fixed gills. The pelesit, the polong, together like always: schools of them eddying surface-wards, like fish, like krill. Ignoring me completely.

Leaving me there, so cold, and alone.

And I know, I know, without having seen, without understanding how: just *know*, that's all. How above me is a door, a watery blue lid, and below me is a door, white sand made from ground-fine bone. A door behind me. A door on either side. A door in front of me, opening.

Nothing but doors, is what I'm saying. That's our world, not that we can ever see it, unless we're somehow made to; doors everywhere, and all of 'em locked, until they're open. Because none of us have the keys—we're not *important* enough for that, oh no. The hinges are rusted shut. So we can knock and knock if we want, if we *know* to, pound and scream and weep and moan for entry, but it's only ever what's on the other side that gets to turn the handle. And only if we've paid enough for it—whatever the hell *they* think is enough.

But it never is enough, is it? Not in the end.

That's how it seems to me, anyways. But I don't want to think about it anymore, so I'm not going to. *You'll* have to instead, from now on, and they'll just have to be satisfied with that, or go begging.

Why do you think I told you this whole damn story, in the first place?

I'm hanging up now.

CARMAGNOLE

I SUPPOSE MOST WOMEN — and most men, come to that — must consider their grandmothers admirable simply for holding that position in relationship to themselves, without knowing the slightest thing about who they might have been before attaining that particular status. I certainly never did until one day, five years past, when I was visiting my mother's mother at the neat little set of apartments she now shared with two other elderly widows in the town of Mimico, oldest of the Lakeshore Municipalities. Of course my parents had made it abundantly clear after Grandfather died that they would gladly take her into their own home and spoil her for as much time as they might have left to enjoy her company; but she was an independent sort and preferred to use the small pension his will had allotted to her to support women in a slightly more bereft state than her own. Her one stipulation was that I visit her as often as possible, especially now that I was out and about in the city, employed as a general secretary in the filing offices of a large firm downtown.

It was her pleasure when I visited that I should read to her, since her eyesight, never certain, had at last begun to fail. On this occasion, I was scanning the afternoon papers for any items I thought might be of interest, paying especial attention to stories which might be related in any way to past events rather than those of the present, which were rather grim just at that moment; it was the 29th of June, 1919, and the Winnipeg General Strike had just been brought to its close by the events of Bloody Saturday, when the "specials" and the Royal Northwest Mounted Police were brought in to break a demonstration in the form of a silent parade led by soldiers returned from the Front. The Mounties entered the fray on horseback, armed with clubs, after which a streetcar was briefly set on fire and the mayor read the Riot Act. Three volleys were fired, killing two and wounding thirty others, women and children amongst them, after which the remaining crowds were chased into side streets and broken up. Some eighty people had been arrested.

The reason I remember these details so clearly is that my "beau" at the time was a journalist for the Toronto Daily Star and had thus previously been covering the local spate of sympathetic walkouts that the Strike had inspired countrywide. I had chosen not to trouble Grandmother with them, assuming—inaccurately, as it turned out—that she would find them of little interest.

As I made to turn the page, however, my grandmother spoke up.

"I worked in a factory once, Clea, long before I met your grandfather," she told me, still tatting away at the scarf she was making, as much by feel as by anything else. "But I suppose your mother never told you that."

I took this in. "Indeed not," I managed to reply, after a moment's pause.

"Yes, and took part in protest against the owners, as well; the police were even called in, though no word of that action ever appears to have reached the public's ears, officially. Would you care to hear my account of it?"

"Very much."

This, then, is the tale.

I was fifteen when I left home, dear, and I believe you could have told that if you'd been inclined to examine me closely, particularly by my face. But few were, especially amongst the menfolk; I had my height and my figure, an old suit-dress of my mother's, a hat I pinned on savagely with a long, sharp pin. On occasion I was called upon to use that pin to my advantage, but not often. I think perhaps it was a certain set to my jaw and mouth which drove men away from me, and I was glad enough for it. Let others flirt. All I wanted was a job, and I got one.

The place was Carmagnole & Sons, a local distillery of spirits, which had occupied a waterfront warehouse at the foot of Bathurst Street for some twenty years at that point. Both firm and building have been gone for decades and must be entirely forgotten by now, mostly due to Gooderham & Worts having commandeered the majority of Canada's liquor trade. Carmagnole's was rather a smaller operation, but even they required cleaning staff in the dozens and did not stint to work them hard. Nor was it free of physical danger—the heat of a working still is very near the temperature of boiling water, and it took only an exhausted stumble or careless turn while standing too close to the still's copper sides to cause agonizing burns. On the distillery floor, its air thick with steam and whisky fumes, such accidents were more common and more injurious amongst the constantly hurrying workers than you might think. But I was young, determined, and more than willing to put up with what seemed like an eminently manageable risk, especially in return for what city life promised me: freedom and the money with which to pay for it.

A thousand others must have dreamed similar dreams, of course. Yet I flatter myself to think I sought something genuinely different from most of my peers—I had no interest in dancing, or the theatre, or chasing down a husband. No, what I yearned most for was something you take so casually for granted today, it will amuse you to hear how I hungered after it . . . proximity, purely and simply, to books. The small town where I grew up had neither library nor bookstore, and newspapers were considered a luxury fit for men alone. I well imagine you might marvel at the idea I could grow so desperate for printed matter that I would flee, alone and without resources, to a city of thirty thousand strangers, solely for the sake of finding books—and indeed, that was not my only reason for doing so, in the end. But it was one of them, all the same.

You see, even from my earliest days, what I loved most in life was silence, solitude, and reading. We had no formal schooling, and I learned my letters from my father's nightly reading of the Bible, years earlier than any of my siblings or the other children of the town. I had absorbed the few volumes kept in our church by the age of eight, often staying after Mass to do so; when there were no more new books to read, I would start again on the ones I liked most, until I could nearly recite them from memory. No matter how dull the subject, it was an escape from the even duller life that was all I knew, and from . . .

Well. I'll return to that subject in due course.

My salary at the factory was not fulsome, but it was enough to secure a room in a women-only boarding-house; a small and mean one, but close to a public laundry and baths, with the nearly unimaginable luxury of a water closet in the building itself. No one would have believed it to be the home of a steadily growing library, any more than my coworkers thought me at first glance the sort of girl to be building one. Between books and food, I often chose books. I wore my clothes almost threadbare, solely to save up money for new volumes. I frequented libraries, withdrawing as many books as I was allowed, for as long as I was allowed; I trawled through bookstores large and small, where whatever most attracted me I bought and devoured, if I could afford it. I made no distinctions. I had already been told so many times that my interests were ridiculous and specious that I no longer did anything I did not wish to, employment aside. The inside of my head was my own, my thoughts private and my interests surprisingly violent, no doubt, especially so given my sex, age and education. I wanted blood and thunder, old tales, from eras distant enough I would not have to compare them to my own.

It was in Mrs. Lindsey's shop where I found a brief history of the French Revolution, written by a man who had managed to keep himself alive throughout the very heat of that period later known as "the

Terror." His name, which may have been a pseudonym, was Bertín, and at the time of his memoir's writing, he apparently still styled himself "Citoyen" rather than "Monsieur." Even now, I am not quite sure what attracted me to this small book with its cracked spine and water-spotted boards, its pages crammed with ill-set type. Perhaps it was the color, a faded sunset red, or the surprisingly effective engraving inserted just before the titlepage, depicting a scene of the cast down revolutionaries Danton and Desmoulins approaching the guillotine in their tumbril while the crowd screamed around them. Up on the scaffold stood the public executioner, lifting what seemed to be a woman aristocrat's severed head by what remained of its hair, its mouth set in a sob of pain and its eyes half-lidded — though whether he did so to show it to the mob or show the mob to it, I could not tell.

I remember how Danton met the head's eyes proudly, his famously ugly face a mask, while Desmoulins turned aside and wept into his hands. And I remember the crowd itself, all those equally ugly faces twisted in rage, in hatred and in something else as well, some other emotion that — inexperienced as I was, then, in the world's ways — I found far more difficult to identify. I know it now, of course. It is a vampire passion which rarely displays itself in public, except under similar circumstances; the sanguine thirst which drives those who have suffered long and hard to lap up another's pain and suffering, like fine spirits, to slake their appetite for recompense . . . or even those which are not so fine, distilled and bottled in as low and dangerous a place as Carmagnole's.

I did not bring my books to my workplace; floor staff were not given privacy to eat alone, nor did my chattersome colleagues wish any. Feigning polite participation was not difficult, so long as I paid enough attention to chuckle in the right places. But I must have gathered more attention than I realized, because one afternoon following an unexpected early closure, I was followed as I returned to Mrs. Lindsey's, meaning to ask if she had any other volumes like Citoyen Bertín's. Disappointed at her regretful negative, I turned from the counter and found myself face-to-face with another woman of Carmagnole's, a small, wiry matron of indeterminate age whose eyes were bright and clear and dark as hot molasses. Startled, and momentarily unable to recall her name, I recoiled.

"Iris, dear," she reminded me, looking amused. She tapped a leathery finger on the scarlet cover of my book, which I'd brought to remind Mrs. Lindsey. "I know this story, as it happens. Quite sensational—and all the more so for being true, every word. Well, *almost* every word." She laughed, as if she knew something I didn't. "Is that the source of your interest, dear? The sensational? Or—" With a sudden, shrewd, sideways look: "—the truth?"

Only hard-learned self-control kept my face inscrutable, for while it's fashionable for women to proclaim only other women can be true friends or confidants—and that's no doubt true, for some—my life had never imparted that lesson. Quite the opposite, in fact. If anything, all I had learned about other women was that for the most part they were spies and cheats, shameless liars, looking always to buy, sell or be sold; competing so ruthlessly for prizes of status, attention, or courtship they truly could not believe my professed disinterest in such games was anything but a particularly subtle ploy therein. Not that men were much different, but at least they wore their natures on their sleeves, rarely capable of concealing them even when they tried. Women presented themselves as friends, then turned on you. They trafficked in a sort of betrayal you could never see coming and could only preempt by assuming it inevitable from the beginning . . . and since you already know I had next to no friends at home, dear, perhaps you can now infer another reason I left as soon as possible. For I had sisters once, you see.

Still, of necessity, I had learned enough manners to know it was foolish to make such enmities before time. Best to bore her curiosity back to sleep.

"I always thought the virtue of history was that one doesn't need to worry about telling the story and the truth apart," I said, trying to sound like the pompous young students I often overheard here.

The effort failed; Iris's gaze sharpened, and her smile vanished. "History is a word people use for suffering they want to forget about, young miss," she rebuked me. "I will not believe your soul is so calloused as yet to believe that folderol you just parroted and have no intention of letting it become so. Either you already appreciate such horrors for what they are, or you do not—yet in either case, there is a fitter place for you than here." Somehow, without my quite realizing it, she had tucked her arm in mine and was steering me towards the bookshop's exit. "You've honed your wits for long enough, my dear. Time to find a use for them."

I do not know what stifled my protest more: the disquieting thought that I had been not only followed, but watched, and clearly for some time . . . or the unexpected twinge of eagerness stirring in my breast.

To my surprise, Iris took me back to Carmagnole's, letting us in through a side door I had not known anyone used—the distillery floor echoed, still hot from the stills, but strange with a darkness and emptiness I'd never seen—and downstairs into the basement, to a long room in the corner lit only by dusty narrow beams of sunlight. Perhaps a dozen women sat there at table, all of whom I recognized from the floor; more than a few of the glances turned my way looked skeptical or disdainful, and at least one muttered something about *useless bookish children*. But I watched the woman I instinctively guessed to be the leader. This, at least, was no surprise: it was the same woman who ran the cleaning staff, who had hired me; Mrs. Griffiths, a formidable widow in her fifties, broad-shouldered, red-faced, and loud, but quicker than she allowed almost anyone to realize. When she nodded and indicated an empty seat, I felt a rush of relief, and then surprise to realize just how relieved I was.

"You weren't told why we closed early today, I'll wager, young Anthea," she said, as Iris and I sat. "Unless Iris informed you? No? Well, then, I'll be the funeral crow: While the rest of us were on luncheon, a friend of Mr. Carmagnole Junior cornered Felicity Kendall on the floor, demanding favors of her no unmarried Christian girl should countenance. And no more she did, except in the struggle, she . . . *fell* against one of the stills. They've taken her to hospital, but she'll not work for weeks, and the burns are . . . " She cleared her throat. I had never seen Mrs. Griffiths set back or subdued by anything, until now. "They are not . . . "

"Just say it, ma'am; she'll never find a husband now, save he be blind," Carol Feeney spat. "Or ever see clear again out of two whole eyes. And they're calling it an *accident!*" She spat again, this time in literal truth upon the dusty planks. "As if the true accidents weren't bad enough. Do you know they're planning to add a fourth shift, girl? To keep full production running through the night?"

"Are they hiring more of us?" I asked, genuinely confused.

Mrs. Griffiths shook her head. "No, dear. Each of us will work three more hours a shift, with no more rest time than we already have. Now for someone like you, Anthea, young and fit and with no family demands, that may be manageable, for a while at least. But the rest of us can't maintain that. Not safely, not for long."

"And anyone who leaves of they own will, 'fore they has an *accident* themselves?" added Rachel Brown, whose Carolinas ex-slave's accent had (to my brief but real shame) led me to think her slow-witted when I met her, before I understood the fierce glint in her eyes. "Carmagnoles only get themselves more drudges to replace 'em, and them even more desperate—too desperate to care. Or to ask due pay, fit for what we do."

I had read monographs and essays on such issues before, but this was the first time anyone had ever talked like this to me in real life. "Are you all socialists, then?" I asked, looking around, too bemused to attempt diplomacy. "Or anarchists, like that Proudhon fellow in France?"

Iris gave a bark of laughter. "Ha! I told you, ladies, we needed someone who's read enough to know the words for us." She clapped my shoulder. "No, child, our disquiets come from long before any

European scribbler put a name to it. We're the ones who work in the blood and the dirt, without voice, without votes; we're the ones they use up like dirty rags and toss away without a thought. We're the ones who know that only if we stand together, *all* together, can we ever hope to change that. And we're the ones with the nerve—say it, girls, the *balls*—" I giggled in shock, which triggered a wave of laughter from the others, but for the first time I sensed welcome in it. "—to do that in everyone's sight. To set the true price of our own worth, and to make the bastards *pay* it!" She pounded the table, and the women laughed again, more loudly. Several cheered.

I felt my pulse hammering in my throat, my face hot, my smile helpless. And said, before I knew I'd decided anything, "Tell me what to do."

Mrs. Griffiths cleared her throat. "Well, for the moment, nothing." She went on without acknowledging my open mouth. "We are still approaching others one by one, to make sure everyone we recruit can be trusted. Someone may still think to earn rewards by giving us away—" This brought a burst of outraged cries, some at the inferred insult and some, like Carol Feeney, bragging of what they'd do to any informers. Mrs. Griffiths overrode them, looking angry for the first time. "We must move carefully, at this stage! Plan our campaign!"

"Christ, woman, we've been moving 'careful' for weeks," Carol snapped. "Felicity's been maimed for life while you moved *carefully!* When are we to *do* something?!"

"When we have properly laid the groundwork to ensure our success," Mrs. Griffiths retorted, her voice even, but her cheeks reddening. "We will accomplish nothing if we simply smash a few stills and windows before being hauled off to prison! First, we will draw the public's attention, with a series of letters to local periodicals—you will be useful there, Anthea, if you write as well as you read . . . " She had to raise her voice over the outcry from her fellows. "And then we must seek out help from other organizations, which will be indispensable if we wish to coordinate walk-out actions or set up blockades for the

Carmagnoles' replacement hires—!" But by then the room had dissolved into a babble of bellowing and table-pounding I could no longer follow. I glanced sideways at Iris, the only other woman who wasn't shouting, and saw black fire in her eyes.

If I'd been older, dear, or my colleagues had been less angry or frustrated, we might have seen the good sense in Mrs. Griffith's plans. But at the time, it felt like the worst betrayal of my life. I had felt no especial closeness for these women, even the grievously hurt Miss Kendall—but to be welcomed, suddenly, into a world where one *mattered*, and then almost immediately to be pushed into a corner and told to sit still, be quiet, and wait—it was as if I'd been shown a feast for which I'd never even known I'd hungered, only to find it locked behind a glass wall that let nothing through but the mouthwatering scents. And it was in that moment, just as I realized how truly furious I was, that a dry finger stroked the back of my neck, trailing a gritty, powdery sensation in its wake . . . the touch of a priest, anointing me with ash.

I remember absolutely nothing of the next few minutes.

The next thing I do remember is standing on the end of the table, my throat sore and my face hot; my hands were lifted to the roof as if invoking the saints, or some more primitive power. All the women were standing, even Mrs. Griffiths, shaking their fists and shouting—but this time, the shouts were of triumph, in unmusical but perfect harmony. And all of them were staring up at me with . . . I do not think I can properly describe the expression, Clea. The closest you might have seen would be the adoration the painters show in Christ's disciples, when He is preaching; and yet, this was nothing even close to that. Not remotely close.

Do I puzzle you? Perhaps even distress you, a smidge? Good. Take that as the faintest fraction of the shock and confusion I felt in that moment, an amazement so colossal it hid itself in sheer blankness. As Iris and Rachel lifted me down, we all turned to Mrs. Griffith, whose eyes shone with a wild light I had never seen in her. "To the doors!" she cried. "Every single one, we'll jimmy open, and wait until dawn tomorrow when the others return. And then there will be *true* justice; for Felicity, for us all!" She finished with a wordless cry, lifting both fists as if she meant to smash the table to flinders herself, then whirled, leading the rest in a flood to the door, up the stairs and out.

Before I knew it, only Iris and I were left in that empty room. I collapsed into one of the abandoned chairs and drew my shawl around me, shaking and chilled. The dusty sunlight itself seemed colder, and dimmer. I looked up at Iris, feeling dampness on my cheeks: tears or sweat, perhaps both. When I tried to speak, my throat rasped in pain. "What . . . happened?"

Iris gave a small, secret smile, the black fire still in her eyes. For no reason I could see, she seemed, abruptly, immensely tall; or perhaps the room seemed to shrink around her. "You were inspired, little one," she murmured. "And now, so are they. Glory in it. Few have ever been so blessed." Still smirking, she walked slowly to the door and left. The walls stretched in her absence, the room feeling even emptier and darker, like the hole left behind when a rotten tooth is pulled.

I had never cared to waste money on a pocket watch, back then. Church bells told time well enough for my needs. I thus had no way to measure the time I sat there, shuddering, waiting to recover myself from whatever had happened; it was long enough for the beams of sunlight to measurably shift their angle through the windows. Finally, I dug out my handkerchief and did my best to clean my dust-smeared face and hands, my sodden armpits, the back of my neck. I do remember, very clearly, my puzzlement when I looked at my handkerchief and saw the reddish stain there, like dried blood. I was not wounded: I could tell that by touch. But I did not have strength enough left to worry at it, then.

It took effort to lever myself to my feet, and even more to walk home. I collapsed into my bed as soon as I reached it and slept like a dead thing.

I woke before dawn the next day, and lay abed a few minutes, remembering everything I could, thinking with all the dispassionate coldness I could find in myself. I lit a candle—one of my few other significant expenses, in those days; books were useless without light to read by—and sought answers to the questions that came to me. The very last place I looked was Citoyen Bertín's volume itself, and though I was not sure what I sought in its pages, I still remember the passage across which I stumbled. I can see it now, as if reading it off the air:

"It was my very great privilege and prerogative that September day to serve as guard for the filthy royalists there being executed, a source of much pride for a young man; until, that is, it was given to me to convey those condemned to their place of execution, which was not the clean majesty of the device named for the doctor M. Guillotin. Too many bodies, the sergeant told me later, with shocking indifference, and not enough time. Instead, the condemned were taken to a courtyard or a street and there set upon by mobs, stabbed or stoned or bludgeoned until the cobblestones drowned in carmine puddles, their bodies dismembered outright as often as not. Nor was this savagery the purview solely of men; women and children joined in as well, equally vile, displaying all the careless, bestial glee of cats hunting rats. I recall in particular the fate of the poor Princesse de Lamballe—ah! that I should say 'poor' of any royalist! But on that day I saw not one of the greedy leeches who had betrayed our people, but only a small, worn woman of great dignity, who died because she would not swear to hating the King and Queen; 'It is not in my heart,' she said. 'It is indifferent to me if I die a little earlier or later; I have made the sacrifice of my life.' 'Let Madame be set at liberty,' the tribunal said, and we brought her to the door, whereupon she recoiled at sight of the waiting beasts and the bloody corpses already dispatched: 'Fi horreur!' she exclaimed, 'I am lost!' She strove to flee, and I, to my everlasting shame, cast her into the arms of the mob. A pike struck upon her head, laying her low, and the crowd descended upon her with a great and monstrous braying. So swiftly did her white dress turn red! Then I could glimpse nothing more, for long moments, but the sounds I heard are fit for no human ear; I shall not darken your hearts, my readers, by

attempting to describe them. Yet one sight I cannot pretend I did not see: the head of poor Lamballe, all a-crimsoned, with glazed and bulging eyes and dripping hair, hoisted high on that same pike as the mob shrieked: 'La Lamballe! La Lamballe!' Still I can see the face of the woman holding the pike as they marched away, the very face of a devil brought to earth, her black eyes joyful and mindless as a rabid dog's and her mouth all red, streaming red, as if she had used her very teeth to detach the skull from the throat. In that moment, I knew that all the high glories and great visions sought in the Revolution were lies, and that no man now could do more than hope to survive the Terror gripping our realm."

It is my own shame that when I'd read that passage the first time, I had enjoyed it only the way a child enjoys a ghost story, loving the *frisson* without truly believing it for a second. I read it now with new eyes, slowly, in almost dreamlike calm. Then I rose, and washed, and dressed, and walked the short distance to Carmagnole & Sons in the predawn twilight.

At the last junction near King Street and Bathurst, before one turned south to walk the last few blocks to the distillery itself, I was unsurprised to recognize two faces from that basement; I often saw other staff on the walk to work, though I seldom did more than nod and wave. What was surprising was that they were not eagerly on their way towards the noise I could already hear drifting over the roofs, but that they were standing, arguing fiercely: it was Rachel Brown and Carol Feeney, face to face, so intent upon each other neither noticed me. I slowed, stopping when I was close enough to listen.

" . . . dare to say I'm less angry than your own self?" Rachel demanded. "Like I ain't seen no tribulations such as yours, or worse? But revolution, it *ends*. Must be something to come after, girl."

"And it will!"

"Aye, but what?"

"Well—" Carol sputtered. "Freedom! Virtue! What's *fair*. Something *better*, is the point!"

Rachel shook her head and laughed, a low, unamused sound. "And there's your problem, my sister. You've got *ideals*, you, and all those poor souls too." She nodded her head down the street, towards the distillery. "All our problems, that—and that mad prophet Anthea most of all."

Mad prophet? I mouthed to myself.

"Chah," Carol spat. "You just want some sort of . . . eternal marketplace—a thief's license to loot and sell and set prices wherever it pleases you. To *profit*." The last word came out in a snarl of disgust so visceral I thought she might actually vomit.

Rachel's face went still, like stone. "I *been* a cause for profit, sister," she said coldly, after a moment, as Carol flushed, in rage or shame or both. "I don' worship that, neither. But I don' fool myself you can do without it. An' it's true, I make no secret of't, I want *my* right profit too—I ain't never working again without I'm paid my proper worth. 'Cause that's what people *is*: we buy, we sell; everything. Bread's real. Costs and prices, they's real too. Them down there, you think they're God's own angels, Heaven-sent to save the world? They ain't and never will be. Don't even *want* to be."

Carol's fists were clenched, but somehow I did not think she meant to use them. "They can be taught," she gritted, between her teeth.

"Taught to curse us all, for sure," Rachel returned, unimpressed. "Can't no one give 'em what they *think* they want, what that fool gal Anthea promised. Easy enough t' turn the world to perdition, or near enough; but Heaven on earth? Can't be done, not before the Judgement. And soon or late, hate runs out." She stopped and turned; I had come close enough to catch her attention and fought the urge to step back from her unfriendly glare. "You, huh? Come t' see your handiwork?" She jerked her head towards the distillery. Over the past few minutes, the noise from that direction had increased, and harshened.

I swallowed. "What did I promise them, Rachel?"

Whatever they'd expected me to say, it wasn't that. Rachel frowned; Carol blinked. "What?" said Rachel.

"What did I say we should do? What were my words? Exactly?"

"Why, don't you remember?" Carol burst out. "You told us to—you said—you . . . " She scowled and rapped her temple with one fist. "It was magnificent! You commanded us . . . " Again she trailed off. The anger in her eyes bled away into confusion, and something that might have been embarrassment, or dismay. "You can't expect me to repeat it word-perfect, lass—"

"I don't care about *that*!" I shouted, startling them both. "Can either of you remember even a single turn of phrase? A single action we all agreed on before Mrs. Griffiths told us to jimmy the doors and meet at dawn? *Anything?*" I turned to Rachel, whose anger had also given way to a look so uncomprehending as to verge on horror. "You shook off this madness much sooner than anyone, it sounds like. Do *you* recall anything I said? At all?"

Rachel's mouth worked. "I—I remember . . . *joy*," she said. "Like the day I crossed the border and fell weeping on the ground. But I couldn't figure it, after; what gave—" She stopped; her gaze dropped to the street. "What gave the rest of you the right, I thought," she admitted, voice low. "Felt wrong, t' promise that joy t' those ain't earned it like I have. Which ain't a Christian thing to feel, now I look on it."

I drew a deep breath. "Iris told me I *inspired* you all," I said. "I looked that word up, before I came here. It comes from the Latin *inspirare*, 'to breathe upon'; a word for being seized by God, or by *a* god—filled like a bellows or a cistern, and poured out, never knowing what flows through you until you're empty. Now all of us stand here, and I swear to your face by the Blessed Virgin, Carol Feeney, that I remember no more of what I said in that basement yesterday than either of you do. I'll bet my salary for a year that *nobody* does. Call me liar or madwoman if you will, but ask yourself this, both of you: What does it mean if I'm telling you the truth?"

We all three exchanged stares for a long, long moment; and then, without needing to speak our mutual understanding aloud, spun and raced down the street towards Carmagnole's.

After all the details I've told you so far, Clea—all the conversations I've recalled practically to the word, the pictures and passages from a book I haven't seen in over forty years—I'd very much understand if you took what I'm about to say next with a grain of salt or two. But . . . I don't really remember what happened next. Not with certainty.

That, however, isn't the strange thing. The strange thing is this: *Nobody* remembered.

The only record you'll find in the archives of the *Globe*—I know, I looked—is a two-paragraph mid-page article about Carmagnole & Son's burning down in the early morning. The protest, and the consequent riot are dismissed in a line about "possible neighborhood unrest." Nobody I spoke to, afterwards, would admit to seeing anything I saw—would admit to what we *did*. Not that I was able to get close enough to do much more than yell at everyone to stop . . . though in hindsight I was glad for that. More than glad, afterwards, to have not been any closer.

Two rings surrounded the warehouse: the distillery workers on the inside, holding hands, facing a line of beleaguered police strung scattershot around them, with Mrs. Griffiths and Mr. Carmagnole Sr. bellowing at each other before the main door. The police were spread too thin to stop us as Rachel, Carol and I bolted past them; Rachel and Carol hauled Mrs. Griffiths aside, leaving me a fleeting gap to slip through and inside. Within, all was jostling and noise and darkness, blurs of frenzied motion, and a fumy alcoholic stink so fierce I could barely breathe. Several of the stills had already been toppled, spilling puddles of raw brown spirit across the floor. As I hesitated, another still went over under the hands of black silhouettes, breaking open with a mighty crash and gurgling its contents into the chaos. Roars of triumph rose over it.

I remember—one of the last clear moments I do remember—wishing for a candle, and then instantly freezing in horror to realize what that would do. I suspect it was most likely sheer panic that drove me upstairs, onto one of the overhead catwalks where the men primed the kettles, but I have no memory of that. The next thing I recall clearly is standing on that catwalk, staring down aghast, as Iris stood beside me and frowned down at the mayhem.

"Not enough," she muttered. "They're too easily pleased, those fools. Too much talking. This must go faster."

From a hidden pocket somewhere in her skirts she took out a small, carved wooden box, the sort of thing that might have held jewelry or snuff. Opened it. I saw her stirring her fingers in the contents—a sort of red-brown, muddy dust—like a chef, deciding how much to take up. Then she huffed an exasperated breath, lifted the entire box to her lips and simply . . . blew.

The red cloud that puffed out across the crowd looked like—smelled like—a hot, reeking wind. A slaughterhouse. The fierce stench of high summer, and renderers' carts. The acrid stink of coarse wool clothing, soiled in fear. Madness's goatish sweat, shining under wide, blind eyes. August . . . *Thermidor*. The Terror.

And I remembered—

(She *remembered*)

—*that pathetic man, who called himself Bertín for fear someone would know him, and demand revenge,* I seemed to hear, as Iris turned slowly to smile at me with those black, black, burning eyes. *How he trembled to watch the Guillotine at her work, the Widow, in whose wicker lap so many were put savagely to sleep, in one bright chop!* I could not tell if it was Iris's voice I heard, or my memory of the Citoyen's small red book, or some nightmare blend of both. *How the old women sat on its steps or beneath its scaffold-boards, knitting, calling out insults; how the children played in the streets with dolls full of fake blood, whose heads could be removed and whose necks could be made to spurt with the slightest squeeze. How the young* Incroyables *attended* bals des morts, *play-acting as dead aristos with red ribbons around their throats. How the true blood fell down like rain, day after day after day, soaking the dirt under the Widow's blade until such a stain was made, he thought nothing would ever grow there again, that it could never be cleaned away. That that dirt—that dust—would be mainly blood, forever after.*

And he was right, sad, sorry M. Bertin, but yet so wrong, as well. For when so much blood is spilled, something else must rise up. Sown, and reaped. My harvest.

Now and always.

The dust fell down, and the noise—the argument—subsided, for a moment. The vandals slowed, turned, spun from side to side like weathervanes in changing wind, the only sound their harsh and panting breaths. And then . . . then . . . the cries arose again. Words had ceased, entirely; there were only screams—first from the women, then the men. Nothing but screams, but roars, but shrieks, like the hunting calls of lionesses, the laughter of rabid hyenas.

They seized hold of the vile man who half-blinded that girl and they pulled him apart, I remember that. But of course, that could never be enough, by itself. So they turned on every other man, as well.

I saw women on fire, or thought I did; women with their hands dyed crimson and their teeth likewise, gaping mouths stuffed full of chewed flesh. I saw Rachel Brown pin a man to the wall with a single shove, driving a broken bottle straight through his guts. I saw Carol Feeney bring Mister Carmagnole himself down in a rush and a pounce, kicking his ribs 'til he curled up tight, keeping him down so the other women could beat him even harder with broken bits of chairs, splintered boxes and other chaff, spraying his gore up high against the walls. I saw poor, reasonable Mrs. Griffiths stamp a man's whole head into mash, jumping on it with both feet 'til bruises bloomed into wounds, wounds into one great wound, wet red stuck through with splintered, reddened bone.

And up above, I gaped. Up above, Iris laughed. She *danced*, far more lightly than I would have ever suspected she could, given her apparent age. She skipped and hummed, capered and sang. I remember her words, even now . . . first in French, which I did not understand. Then in English. Then—inside *me*. My own heart's beat. My blood's red drum.

Come dance the Carmagnole

Round and round, to the sound—

Come dance the Carmagnole

While the cannons beat the drum!

I remember her turning to look at me, with her black eyes—eyes like kohl, like bitumen, with just a tinge of red to them, like cooling coals. I remember her smile.

"*Je serai toujours une sans-culotte, moi,*" she told me, happily. "*Une de la canaille.* The rabble, the *female* rabble, the barefoot, hungry crowd that does the speechmakers' work for them because they simply can't *bear* to do it themselves, those lawyers. Because it's *just too hard.*"

Her words in my head, Iris—in my *mouth*. The dry touch of her hand at the back of my neck, moving her words through me, like a puppet.

Oh, they promised us bread and fed us on words, those proud Committee-men—gave us permission and let us loose to do their work for them, not under-standing that we don't need their permission and never have. Because we are the mob, the wild bitches, the red wave that washes them up and dashes them back down again. Their power is always our power, however badly harnessed; they don't like to get their hands dirty, those damned clerks! So they feed us on words like wine, words that hurt to hear, that make you drunk and insane. They curse, but only through us, for only women how HOW to curse properly, or should, after all this wasted time! A thousand dead women's voices coming out through one throat, screaming, howling loud enough to tear a building down.

(And ah, and yes: The blood of your victims IS choking you, Citoyen, true

enough — choking you to death. But only because you are far too weak to drink it down.)

"Comme toutes les femmes, et comme toi aussi, ma belle," Iris told me, out loud, dancing on. *"Ma tres, tres jolie fille de la revolution."*

I turned, then. I fled. I staggered from the scene, as Carmagnole's burned down. Few others did, sadly. And though some of us appeared in employment lines here and there as I sought my next job, we did not speak of what had happened, ever. Not that I know of.

Now, I know you are active in the campaign for a woman's right to vote and that you have raised money for Workers' Rights as well, supporting those who protested the War even as you nursed soldiers returned from the Front; you account yourself a suffragist, I suppose, and well you should. But I must base my own beliefs only on what I have seen with my own eyes, and here they are:

A box full of dried blood to blow in the crowd's face, to sow a mob — that's all Revolution ever is, dear, no matter how beautiful its creators' ideals might be. A thousand tearing hands, as we throw away all our gentleness and upend the order of things . . . and yes, women do do the bulk of the work there as everywhere else, always, in all ways. For would you rather eat stones, or throw them?

Iris. It sounds a bit like Eris, doesn't it? The Goddess of Discord — hate and rage, chaos, uproar. Revolution, the thing itself — the process, protest to revolt, to justice, to recompense, to slaughter . . . a cycle, a machine made only from blades chattering on and on and on, without end.

But that's Greek, of course, my dear. Not French.
Not French, at all.

After my grandmother died, the world continued to change. I recall seeing a newsreel before a cinema show, some footage taken in Russia, or perhaps the Ukraine. Up there on the screen I saw a woman marching along through trampled snow behind the rest, small and hard-featured, her coattails flapping and her eyes—no doubt black with a hint of red, like lit pitch—hidden behind small, dark spectacle-lenses; she half-smiled to herself as she went, lips skewing sidelong in a way I found somehow familiar, though only from description. Behind her, some village was burning, and her compatriots had dark stains on their hands, their uniforms, the stocks, and fixed bayonets of their rifles.

Would those stains have been red as well, I wonder, had the chemical formula for capturing color on film been invented yet?

I have seen her since, that woman, almost everywhere—in photos or on the television. I pray not to see her in person. For where she steps, revolution swirls, a great rush and patter of hatred, the envy of the mob, the rabble. *La canaille*. The maenad women who do the work while others take credit, reckoning for themselves when they have suffered enough to warrant an explosion of flame, of blood. For the Widow's shadow is long, you see, even now, when so few remember how it must have been during the Terror, in the month of Thermidor. Change follows after her, but ah, the awful effort it takes; ah, the dreadful price it demands.

The price which must, forever, be paid in blood.

CALIGARISM

*Noun, descriptive: like, or reminiscent of, Robert Weine's classic Expressionist horror film **The Cabinet of Dr Caligari**. See also: like, or reminiscent of, the experience of watching **The Cabinet of Dr Caligari**. This word came into critical use immediately after the first screenings of **Caligari** and appears to have since fallen into complete obscurity. In the contemporary era, even references to its previous existence have become almost impossible to find.*

FRAME STORY (Rahmenerzählung), Winn writes, at the top of the page. *When telling the story of how **The Cabinet of Dr Caligari** came to be made, figuring out exactly who did what when—and, most importantly, whose ideas took precedence, in terms of the film's unique creative vision—can be difficult, since almost every person who worked on the project appears to have done so under a sort of personal compulsion, one strong enough that the events of the film might be seen, in hindsight, to echo the events of their own lives.*

For example, like the Weimar Republic itself, screenwriters Hans Janowitz and Carl Mayer were living lives overshadowed by the legacy of World War I. Janowitz had served with distinction but emerged from the war a pacifist, while Mayer had faked insanity to avoid being drafted; this gambit led to a series of intense interviews with a military psychiatrist which left Mayer with a phobia about both authority figures and psychiatry alike . . .

"Ever notice how the sky looks fake, sometimes?" Claire asks, from over by the window. She's peering up through the disarranged shade, studying the clouds outside as if she thinks they're hiding exam answers. Winn scowls, and replies: "Everything looks fake sometimes,

Claire."

"'Everything'? That's putting it a bit strong, don't you think?"

"Not really, no. You still have that one-thirty with Doctor . . . whatever his name is?"

Claire doesn't turn. "*Her* name."

"Oh yeah?" Winn can't recall ever having known that, not that it matters. "Well. Anyhow."

"We had to reschedule."

"When for?" No answer; Winn can't tell if that's because Claire can't hear, or because she just doesn't want to. So, making a conscious effort not to sigh, she returns to the argument at hand.

According to Janowitz, he would never have gotten involved with the film industry if not for the influence of Mayer, who suggested they write a screen scenario together, she writes. *Mayer, on the other hand, claimed he was working in the Berlin Residenztheater when he fell in love with leading actress Gilda Langer and wrote* **Caligari** *"for" her, planning to have her star in the movie. Janowitz also claimed that Langer encouraged him to visit a fortune teller during the war, who predicted that Janowitz would survive his military service, but Langer would die unexpectedly; tragically, she did exactly this in early 1920, the same year* **Caligari** *would be shot. Her planned role — that of Jane, the girlfriend of the film's nominal protagonist Francis and murder victim of Dr Caligari's pet somnambulist Cesare — went to Lil Dagover instead, a turn of fortune that contributed directly to Dagover becoming one of the era's most popular and recognized actresses.*

"I had a dream last night," Claire says, still not turning, appearing to crane her neck at an ever more uncomfortable angle. "But not just one dream, you know? A dream inside a dream. Or a whole bunch of dreams inside dreams, maybe, and I can only remember the last one."

"I hate it when that happens," Winn says, not looking up. She watches her hand dip into the page's margin, adding a column of notes: *Coincidental that in 1922, Fritz Lang cast Dagover in* **Doktor Mabuse Der Spieler,** *about another criminal mastermind/psychiatrist/hypnotist?*

Spieler = gambler, but also puppeteer, actor, player; literally, someone who gambles with others' lives.

*So only two years later, **Caligari** was already a trope—the quack doctor who abuses his powers, by tricking unsuspecting patients*

(literally unsuspecting, ie Cesare the somnambulist, who murders while asleep)

into doing his dirty work.

"Me too," Claire agrees, from the window, and for a second Winn has no idea what she's talking about. Then she remembers the conversation they're supposedly having and pulls herself back out, just long enough to reply—

"So what was it about, this dream?"

"Oh, you know."

"No, I don't."

"Yes. You do."

No particular emphasis on these last words, and yet—Winn looks up, finally, to find Claire staring back at her: eyes wide, white all 'round the iris, pupils reduced to points. Her head cocked abruptly down at much the same angle it was previously cocked up, that same weird tilt, too sharp for comfort. *How can you* breathe *like that?* Winn wants to ask, but feels the words dry in her throat.

Such a *white* face, paper-plaster bright, against a suddenly dark backdrop. Such rudimentary features, reduced at once to line without shadow, a mere sketch of themselves. The sky was blue, but now it's black, shuttered, an eclipse-filter cast 'round the sun's penny-sized bone disk; all sounds from outside cease, muffled, drop-cloth quick. Like a falling curtain. Like a falling blade.

(*Thunk.*)

"You know *very well* what I mean, Winona," Claire tells her again, peculiarly specific, especially since Winn doesn't think she's ever heard her use her full name before. And then the room itself seems to iris, squinches shut all at once, with an audible, mechanized *clack*.

It was a mistake to answer Claire's ad, Winn had already started to think by the end of their first week together—a mistake to think she needed any roommate, let alone this one. It was a mistake to think she could deal with Claire's lack of sleep schedule, or her neediness, or her craziness. That Winn could be the sane one in this relationship, or any relationship. That it wouldn't undermine her completely, point by hard-won point, make her equally unable to sleep, or work, or cope; that it wouldn't, inevitably, do anything other than just end up making her crazy too. *Again.*

What does surprise her, though—even in hindsight—is exactly how little time it all actually took, to do so.

Reality is nothing but an agreed-on construct, one of her Philosophy profs liked to say, back when that was her major; *it's quorum, best guesses and metaphors cross-bred, the closest miss out of a hundred. It's majority rule. "Reality," scare quotes entirely intentional, is a negotiation, at its very best. And at its worst . . .*

At its worst, Winn now thinks—knows—it's a tale told in first person by an unreliable narrator, signifying nothing: egocentric presentism, perceptually based and utterly experiential, therefore unprovable by any scientifically valid means. Most *especially* so when that unreliable narrator is you.

So many mistakes. But Winn supposes they don't matter unless Claire's as real as she is, or Winn's model of reality is real. If there's anything like "reality" at all, for either of them to count on.

But then again, if there isn't, she guesses she'll never know.

Caligari was a critical success in France, but French filmmakers were divided

in their opinions about its impact. Abel Gance wrote, "What a lesson to all directors!", while René Clair said its deliberate embrace of complete artificiality — later attributed frankly to the lack of production budget — "overthrew the realist dogma" of filmmaking. But Jean Epstein called it "a prize example of the abuse of décor in the cinema [. . . it] represents a grave sickness of cinema," and Jean Cocteau called it "the first step towards a grave error which consists of flat photography of eccentric decors, instead of obtaining surprise by means of the camera." French critic Frédéric-Philippe Amiguet wrote of the film: "It has the odor of tainted food. It leaves a taste of cinders in the mouth."

Outside of France, the Russian director Sergei Eisenstein, who disliked **Caligari** *intensely, said the film was a "combination of silent hysteria, partially colored canvases, daubed flats, painted faces, and the unnatural broken gestures and action of monstrous chimaeras."*

"Winn," the doctor says. "Are you listening to me?"

Winn looks up, *again*, and it's as if her eyes suddenly click into focus, even though they're already open. Her pen is still in her hand, nib still pressed to paper, elbows on the table; there's a subtle intimation of pain in her right forearm, her shoulder-joint, like she's been pressing down hard. The doctor's sitting across from her, leant back in her chair, legs elegantly crossed at the ankle; Winn doesn't know her name, never having had a reason to. But here she is now, apparently deliberate posed to let slip just a slice of the window behind her, blinds drawn, the sky beyond bright blue —

(—which is *wrong*. Isn't it? Not how it was. Not how it should be.)

"I'm sorry," Winn says, slowly. "I think . . . I think I got distracted, maybe. Caught up in what I was doing. I didn't even notice . . ." She trails away, then gathers herself; starts over, trying for a friendly, professional tone. "Have you been here long?"

"Not very, no."

"Oh, okay. Well . . . you're here for Claire, right? I mean — " Winn looks around, surreptitiously shaking her head as she does, trying to clear it. "She was right here, I thought, not that long ago. Um . . ."

And here the bones of her face seem to buzz slightly, aching where they intersect, as though longing to pull apart. Here she has to pause yet again, take another long blink of a moment to figure out what she's actually trying to say, while the doctor—her name, what *is* her name?—

" . . . you could wait, I guess," Winn finishes up, at last.

The doctor smiles, dimpling high up one cheek, a shadow that flickers just beneath one eye-socket like a beauty-mark. "Could I?"

" . . . yes."

But now Winn isn't sure.

The doctor just keeps on smiling, eyes level, vaguely amused in a completely internal way, one her lips don't match. She gestures at Winn's paper, commenting: "You did appear very—enrapt, to say the least. In a sort of trance."

"Sleep-writing," Winn suggests, expecting a laugh, to which the doctor simply nods. Flustered, Winn adds: "It's for cinema studies, Professor Kuhn; you know, pick a topic, discuss it for five pages, all that. Pretty basic stuff."

"Yes, so it sounds. What about?"

"Caligarism." Explaining, as the doctor cocks a soft eyebrow: "A film crit term, very old-school. After *The Cabinet of Dr Caligari.*"

"I don't think I've ever seen it."

"Silent film made in 1920, during the Weimar Republic—German Expressionist, very influential, its art direction aimed at creating a con-crete visualization of dementia. Roger Ebert called it one of the first real horror movies."

"Ah, right. The one about the evil psychiatrist."

Winn feels herself flush. "Well . . . yeah; more of a mountebank, a carny, but I guess it did sort of establish that trope. Then again, Freud and Jung were still alive, back then. Most people didn't even think psychiatry was a science."

Dryly: "Most people still don't."

Which Winn can only suppose is probably true, but it does throw her off a bit. "It, um . . . " she hears herself begin, then swallows, recoups. "The, uh, qualities associated with Caligarism—*Caligari*—are a kind of . . . persistent sense that everything around you is, um . . . not real. Because that's how it is in the movie; it's like one long dream sequence, right? All filmed on a soundstage, all theatrical effects, done physically. Very few real props, just a whole lot of builds and painted backdrops, all black and white but with the perspective all . . . skewed, you know, sort of deformed, designed to draw the eye towards various directions—"

"Subconsciously, you mean?"

"Yeah, a lot like that. To create a kind of . . . hypnagogic state."

The doctor nods. "Hypnotic," she suggests.

"Uh huh. In that Caligari *is* a hypnotist, or thinks he is."

"Thinks?"

Now it's Winn's turn to nod, half-shrugging, half-smiling. Elaborating, after a second: "Um—yes. Because hypnotism *really* isn't real."

"Hmmm. Is that what you believe?"

" . . . yes."

The doctor hums once more, reflectively; leans back a bit in her chair, fingers steepled. "Some might disagree," she says, eventually. "I use hypnotism myself, for example. As a therapeutic tool."

Winn feels her eyes fall back towards the paper, as though magnetized: down, down, down. Things get slow and muffled. "Uh huh?" she mutters, vaguely, her voice weak.

"My patients often find it very helpful."

"Like Claire?"

The doctor blinks. "Why would you think that, exactly?"

"Well . . . you're here for her. Aren't you?"

"Not today."

Another blink, as if timed to match Winn's reaction. And there's something just, so—*fake* about it, inherently; too big, almost vaudevillian: *wink wink, nod nod, knowwhatImean?* Like the doctor's whole interaction with Winn thus far has been a performance, and she's nothing but an actor, on stage rather than on screen. Like she's playing to an invisible audience stationed somewhere behind Winn, silent yet intent, staring over Winn's shoulder and egging the doctor on to ever-greater heights of artificiality.

Matte lips, perfectly drawn. Pale skin, lightly powdered. Her dark hair sits flat, smooth as a pelt, except in one small spot—an area above her right temple, where it almost seems to be popping up, coming away. The hairline itself just a moment away from blurring, lifting slightly as though about to start peeling back, like the inexpertly glued scalp of a wig.

What's her name? Winn wonders, helplessly. *Did I ever know?*

"You can't be here for *me*, though," she says, out loud, refusing to imply she thinks that's even a possibility. Only to watch the doctor's red smile deepen.

(Blink.)

The white page beckons, pen scratching. More words she can't recall thinking, let alone intending to write, already forming beneath Winn's hand.

In October 1958, during the first recorded universal film poll (organized at the Brussels World's Fair, with input from one hundred and seventeen international film critics, filmmakers, and film historians), **Caligari** *was ranked the twelfth-best film of all time. As film historian and critic Paul Rotha wrote: "For the first time in the history of the cinema, the director has worked through the camera and broken with realism on the screen[, proving] that a film could be effective dramatically when not photographic and . . . that the mind of the audience [can be] brought into play psychologically." Likewise, Arthur Knight claimed: "More than any other film, [**Caligari**] convinced artists, critics and audiences that the movie [could be] a medium for artistic expression."*

Expressionism, she watches her fingers write. *"[A] reaction against the atom-splitting of Impressionism" (Kasimir Edschmid). World reproduced as perceived; emotions expressed through extreme visuals; aesthetic value exchanged for emotional power. The best impulse is always whatever elicits any response, even disgust.*

Down, down, forever down: a spiral drilling inward, spokes twisting, each word on the page a pixel, starting to pop and blur. Random letters jump out at her, like black sparks; snatches of text string themselves together, syntactically broken, calving information in jagged, blurting shards. Reference turns to opinion, shedding objectivity wholesale.

*In **Caligari**'s immersive visuals, reality is reproduced as if reflected in a fun house mirror, distorted as a matter of course. Elongated shadows are painted onto set walls, while streets wind crookedly past equally crooked houses. Everything in the background is off-center, slanted as if about to slide out of frame at any moment — but then again, so is everything in the foreground. Cesare the somnambulist climbs through a trapezoidal window into a house whose walls are diagonal and whose furniture has lines that all go in completely different directions. At no point is there a sense any given direction is consistently or necessarily "correct."*

*Because of all the above, **Caligari** creeps up on you, a perspective shift done almost subconsciously, imperceptible until fully achieved . . . until you realize that the sky you're looking up at is just a painted ceiling, the street you stand on just a painted floor. That the buildings around you have been drawn with charcoal on badly folded sheets or backdrops, sketched quickly, at a clashing series of angles. That everyone around you is just an extra in someone else's narrative, puppets whose faces are nothing but a suggestion of features made from slapdash theatrical makeup, black and white and gray all over.*

(Blink.)

Another click, or the same one — same skew, same wrench, same vaguely nauseating blur. The world catches between frames, heating all too quickly; blue sky flips to black as white yellows, bubbles at its own edges 'til it begins at last to char, to *melt.* Winn can almost smell it, sweet and ill and sharp, a vinegar reek. A slaughterhouse fire glimpsed from very far away, in darkness, at such an oblique angle that it makes your side-tugged eyes hurt.

And: *But you know my name already, Winona,* the doctor murmurs, in one ear. *We both know that; all three of us, in fact. You, me, Claire.*

*We know it **very well**.*

(BLINK.)

"I don't trust her," Claire says, faintly, from somewhere far above, as though filtering down through dark fathoms. "And I'm pretty sure she doesn't trust me, either. So . . . not the best relationship, really, even if she wasn't my damn doctor."

"Uh huh," Winn hears herself reply, meanwhile, equally faintly. She feels herself shrugging back out of the blackness, slower this time—like it's some sort of shroud, some enfolding curtain she's managed to trap herself inside, only slipping away by degrees: a struggle, viscous and prolonged, as if wrapped in plastic. Then, with a twist and a twitch, she emerges, face first.

The room is brighter than she remembers, but less colorful. Claire's sitting right where the doctor sat, however long ago; leant forward rather than back, legs sprawled rather than crossed, arms knit and fingers tight on either elbow. She's looking away. Behind her, the window's slice seems slanted, odd-angled, and the sky outside—

Not black, not blue. Gray, and strange with it.

As strange as though painted on.

(Ever notice how the sky looks fake sometimes?)

Claire sighs. Asks: "She want to know anything about me, when you talked?"

"I . . ." Winn shakes her head, slightly. " . . . not that I remember."

"Not even where I was?"

"Um . . . I think I suggested she wait for you, but I, uh . . . I don't think she did."

Now it's Claire's turn for a headshake, a truncated bob, so curt and sidelong it reads more like a nod. "Yeah," she says. "She's like that. The bitch."

They sit there for a while after that, Winn can't tell how long. Claire still won't look at her, but Winn's not unhappy with the idea—she finds Claire's gaze discomfiting at the best of times, and these aren't those. Instead, she looks down, always down. Chases words. Watches them dance their little dance, syntax like a film-reel dragging static image along after static image, to eventually form a moving whole.

Thinking: *Do I really want to see this?*

(Maybe not.)

Thinking: *Do I really have a choice?*

On its face, the paper reads, ***Caligari*** *appears to be a story about authoritarianism refuted. Caligari the character claims an expertise he doesn't possess, misusing his skill as a hypnotist first to shore up the illusion by making Cesare the somnambulist predict audience members' deaths, then by sending him to murder the people in question, so that the prediction comes "true." Like the young men forced to participate in World War I, Cesare is an innocent deformed into a human weapon, another victim of Caligari's own madness. When Caligari is shown to be nothing but a charismatic lunatic literally running an asylum, his projected self-image collapses, and everything he has managed to achieve is revealed as a monstrous, destructive sham—much like the War to End All Wars itself, in Weimar Republic eyes.*

The framing revelation that Francis is insane and a patient in Caligari's asylum himself, however, casts doubt on his tale's veracity: it figuratively absolves Caligari of his (war) crimes and also neuters the film's inherent social critique, transforming a revolutionary narrative back into a conformist one. In his book **From Caligari to Hitler**, *Siegfried Kracauer claims the original screenplay by Janowitz and Mayer did not include the frame at all; instead, the production company and the director forced them to apply it in order to reach a wider, more popular audience, "a change against which the two authors violently protested. But no one heeded them."*

Thus an otherwise revolutionary film is transformed into a conformist one, just another freak-show entertainment in a post-war carnival whose glaring de-sign, transparently fake shocks and air of childish delight allows traumatized adults to regress and be reassured, forgetting all the terrible things unreliable authority figures have inflicted on them . . .

"She wants to make me into something I don't want to be," Claire says, as Winn scans that last part again, incredulous, eyes burning: God, it's all so obvious, crude, trite—badly written and researched, just plain *bad*. Can this really be what she's been working on, this entire time? Did she really *write* this?

(Well, who else?)

"Are you listening to me, Winona?"

"Yes, of course. Of course I am."

Skeptical: "*Really.*"

"Of course," Winn repeats, forcing herself to smile and look up, to tear her eyes away from the car wreck her thesis has apparently be-come. Instead of meeting Claire's stare reassuringly, however, she finds herself goggling at the door she can see over her shoulder. Its heavy brown woodwork seems to be floating in front of the wall, like bad 3D, or one of those optical illusion rooms where someone shrinks to half their height while crossing it. How the hell is it standing? Is it even there?

"You should quit," she blurts out, without meaning to. Claire looks startled; it's the most natural expression Winn can remember her show-ing in a long while. She clings to that and pushes herself on. "Therapy, I mean, if it's not working out . . . She works for *you*, you know. You don't owe her anything." Which certainly *sounds* reasonable, as she says it. Her eyes fall back to the paper. Christ, this is a mess; she's going to have to rewrite the last two pages, at least—does she have time? When's this due, again? She can't . . . she can't . . .

(*The word is* remember.)

"That's true." Winn jumps in her seat; so does Claire. The door is open. When did it open? The doctor crosses to the table where Winn sits, takes the last free chair there. "If you're truly unhappy with our progress, Claire, you aren't obliged to continue, at least not with me. But I must caution you that a change at this point may lead to backsliding. I wouldn't want to see our work go to waste. Would you?" The doctor cocks her head, birdlike, eyes so bright and flat they might be glass. "Do you really find my objectives so intolerable?"

Claire is shaking where she stands, as though someone's rattling the floor beneath her: another cheap effect. Thunder on a piece of raddled tin.

"I don't—want—to do it," she husks. "You can't make me. Please. *Please.*"

The doctor lifts a finger, nail the same glaring red as her lips, tainting the air around it with Rotoscoped blurriness into the air around it: blood in the proverbial water, a shark's narrow Mackie Messer grin. Flicks it back and forth like a metronome, drawing the helpless eye.

"Ah, but *you know who I am, Claire,*" she intones, imparting some secret, a ritual call without response. "Claire, *I am calling you. Can you hear? Awaken for a moment, from your dark night—*"

Winn barely has time to think *Holy shit, that's from . . .* before Claire shrieks, rusty nails on glass, and throws herself at the doctor. The doctor grabs her by her upper arms, wrestles her back and forth with the broad histrionics of a *Star Trek* fight scene, face blank and unchanging, like plaster. Both silent now, not even gasps of effort, a trembling dual strain the only indication this might really be happening; it's like they're dancing. Struggling to her feet, Winn circles the table, hand reaching for—what, who? Claire's hair, to tug backwards? The doctor's fallen chair?

This is wrong, she hears herself think, as she wavers. *A danger, a lie. This is—*

(false)

(*fake*)

Then Claire manages to hook an ankle behind the doctor's foot; the two tumble over, through the door—*behind* the door?—and are gone. Winn stands agape, hands out, hovering, nothing but empty air.

The chair in which the doctor sat is back at the table, untouched.

"Claire?" Winn rasps, into the silence, after a long, long time.

No answer.

Winn turns, slowly. The jacket Claire flung over the couch is gone. A framed print of some nameless modern painting she hung on the wall after moving in: that's gone, too. The sink, previously half-full of dirty dishes Winn always nagged Claire about leaving, is empty. Nothing in the place she doesn't recognize, yet nothing to indicate anyone but herself ever lived here. It's dark, messy, musty smelling, like Winn hasn't left in a year. And all peculiarly . . . *contrived*, somehow. Dressed, like a set, not a home; a flawless impression of one, poised under stage lights, bright overhead spots making everything pop.

And the furniture oddly stretched, at slightly wrong angles. Forced-perspective, trailing away into unseen distances.

For a moment, Winn has the gut-wrenching feeling that even the wall behind her doesn't exist—that if she can only turn around quick enough, she'll see the audience waiting breathless before a concealing scrim falls, or the lights go out.

End act, pause. Strike set in darkness. Begin again.

She sits down once more, legs suddenly numb, automatically reaching for her paper, the only thing that still feels real. Slides them towards her and lays her head down, pillowed on her own handwriting, her terrible analysis and worse prose. Closes her eyes. Breathes, slowly.

Dissolve to black.

The stark realization brings her up out of—not sleep, exactly, but a kind of drifting doze: *Don't* denounce *the frame, after all,* Winn thinks, sitting bolt upright. *Embrace it.*

"Good idea?" Claire asks from the couch, sounding amused.

Beyond her, the window's slice of sky is thick, soft black, a starless velvet drape.

Forgetting completely that she's not supposed to be here, Winn turns, gesturing in excitement. "I can make it work," she tells her. "Francis, in the asylum — it doesn't undermine the story, it's the whole *point*. Because it means *nobody* gets final claim on veracity or reliability: the narrator doesn't *get* to determine the narrative, not just because he's the one telling it. So everything is fake, because everything *is* fake — everything outside the film, everything inside it. The theatre, the audience, the world. Not even the dream is real." Winn finds herself trailing off, breathless with something she can't name: joy, awe, horror, dismay. "*Nothing* is real," she murmurs.

Claire hikes an eyebrow, cosmetic-dark against her fair hair. Demanding, as she does: "The *fuck* are you even talking about, Winona, exactly?"

More tired than anything else, Winn decides to take this rudeness as affection rather than contempt. "You sound better," she offers.

"Yeah — I took your advice." Claire lies back on the couch. "Got rid of her. For good. Best decision I ever made." She yawns, red tongue in a red matte mouth; Winn's smile fades, recognizing the shade. "It was her or me, you know," Claire tells her, conversationally. "Much longer under that bitch's tender 'care,' and I'd've called a padded white room home the rest of my life."

"Can she *do* that?"

Claire snorts grimly. "You know she could."

(But: *I don't know what I know*, Winn thinks.)

Then glances back down at her manuscript, only to reap another shock — no slow jolt of dread, this time, but a spike of ice punching quick through her gut. Because there are words there she knows she didn't write, hastily scrawled, in a hand that isn't hers. They say —

> *Claire is not who she seems. Stall her.*
> *Give no sign you understand.*
> *I will get help.*

Thanks a lot, doctor.

I'm on my own, Winn thinks, smiling vaguely as she tries to come up with something more to say but can't, while Claire slyly pretends not to notice; "Only problem is, I don't know what to do next," she continues, a monument to bad liars everywhere. And peeps up at Winn through flyaway blonde hair, head rotating mannequin-style under a fiberglass wig, with every part of her rendered abruptly unfamiliar— even her *nose* looks off, suddenly. Was it always that big, that crooked? Did it always come with that smear along its bridge and down both sides at once, like some ill-conceived attempt at contouring?

Knits her hands like a little girl and pouts, ignoring the obvious bloodstains under her nails, ill-concealed dark splotches flaking away as they dry. And implores, with a little vocal tremble: "What do *you* think, Winn?"

"Maybe a nap?" Winn finally suggests, inanely.

Claire nods slowly, sketches a yawn; "Maybe," she agrees, folding her murderer's hands on her breast and letting her eyes droop closed— tics her head sideways and goes still, breaths slow and even through the nose, a clunky middle-school pageant Sleeping Beauty. A bad parody of slumber.

This isn't real, be careful; no time for mistakes. Help is on its way, supposedly, if she trusts the doctor or her note—what she can only *assume* is her note. That nameless, faceless, oddly persuasive doctor with her hypnotic voice, her impossible-to-recall eyes. Which . . . to be frank, Winn really, really doesn't.

She can't afford to.

Winn rises, carefully, own gaze kept locked on her roommate's "sleeping" face. Steps as quietly as she can to stand above Claire, one hand snagging a kitchen counter knife on the way; scans her up and down, examining the evidence. But even this close, she still can't tell if the dark stuff on Claire's hands is blood. Her hands work the knife's handle, shifting their grip, sweat slickening.

And: "One of the therapeutic side-benefits, with hypnotism," the doctor explains, from Winn's elbow, startling her so badly she almost drops her weapon right on Claire's head. "Sleep comes quick and deep. Some people respond so well they don't even require surgical anesthesia." She smiles down at Claire's somnolent form, caressing her face. "It makes them dangerously vulnerable, of course. But that *is* the risk, when digging out the Stone of Folly . . ."

Winn surprises herself by recognizing the allusion. "Bosch," she says. "Hieronymous Bosch's painting, 'Cutting the Stone'. A doctor in the funnel hat carves into his patient's skull, while a woman with a book on her head watches."

"Yes, exactly. Renaissance philosophers hypothesized the Stone as a physical growth, either causing or caused by madness, the extraction of which might ease a sufferer's self-destructive passions. As if thoughts could turn so unnatural they might literally thrust themselves from the flesh, like tumors." Her gaze turns melancholy, still fixed on Claire. "Wouldn't it be lovely if it were so easy, hm? A quick wrench, one brief moment of pain, then gone . . ."

Winn nods. "But that's not the process, is it? Nothing's ever cured. Nothing's ever *over*." Then, turning towards the doctor: "And what were you supposed to *do* with it afterwards, anyway? Throw it out? Keep it?"

"Grind it to a lens, through which to view the world without comforting illusions?" The doctor smiles faintly. "I don't know, dear. Any or all of the above."

Winn narrows her eyes. "And we only assume the guy in the painting's a doctor, because of what he's doing, but that hat—a dunce's cap, if ever I saw one. One fool operating on another."

"An entirely plausible interpretation. Even with the best will in the world, sometimes conflicting imperatives render fighting damage with yet more damage . . . inevitable. The only merciful option."

She nods to the knife in Winn's hands, then back at Claire. Winn's mouth drops open.

The doctor lifts a hand, forestalling her. "Claire's already made her choice, Winona—either of us could be her victim, next time. And this is your chance to make a different one, expediting the inevitable. To prove you're willing to cooperate in your own recovery, however drastic the requirements."

She steps back.

Winn knows now what Claire felt, before she tried to attack the doctor; she trembles as though someone's shaking her, unable to keep her own body still, to stop what's coming. To *not* turn, lifting the knife, gaze riveted to the doctor's face, approval-seeking: that fixed, red smile, skin greasepaint-white, eyes like staring marbles. Winn imagines plunging the knife into *her* instead, feeling dusty cloth give way, a dummy spilling stuffing. But the blade pulls at her with a will now, sharp steel-edged, like iron to magnet. It can't be stopped.

None of this can ever be stopped.

Not 'til Winn brings the knife down hard as she can, at least, in that very last moment, twisting her wrists to plunge the blade deep as humanly possible into her own gut.

Then: Claire is gone. The doctor is gone. The knife is gone. Winn's midsection aches mildly from the impact of empty, fisted hands on flesh, sudden to be sure, yet hardly painful enough to make her gasp. Around her, the dark apartment is empty too, walls, floor and ceiling all stripped bare, with even the table she once though she wrote at missing and the window invisible under a drawn blind, air smelling of turpentine and dust. No paper when she looks down. No pen.

Nothing.

Not sure if she wants to weep or sigh with relief, Winn steps to pull the blind, flipping it up like a lid. The sky beyond is gray, stained, a clumsily applied coat of primer, seemingly close enough to touch. In the glass, she sees her own face dimly reflected, pale cheeks and dark eyes void-set and floating, a flat mask. Brings her hands up to touch, first just lightly, then progressively harder, grinding heels and palms alike over her cheeks. Feels something smear and distort under that pressure, like wet clay, before she finally claws her fingers and starts to scrape as the reflection in the window warps, features mashing unrecognizably.

Still somehow able to see what she's doing, Winn peels and peels 'til this painted mockery of a face she wears comes away entirely, in sections. Her mind stays empty as she does so, clear like water, undisturbed. And beneath it all there is nothing but a blank space, an empty hole, a single, solitary loop. A bare strip of translucent film with the emulsion scraped away, through which light streams.

As she watches that light first brightens, blurs, then darkens—turns amber, turns brown. It sticks in the frame, catches fire, melts. Runs and runs 'til the whole world's unseen motor burns itself out, at which point it disappears, a blown candle-flame. A single thought in blackness.

Iris shut. *Clack,* and gone.

The frame shifts, pops like a reel-end trailing sparks, before winking out forever.

And then—

THE END.

HAIRWORK

N

O PLANT CAN thrive without putting down roots, as nothing comes from nothing; what you feed your garden with matters, always, be it the mulched remains of other plants, or bone, or blood. The seed falls wherever it's dropped and grows, impossible to track, let alone control. There's no help for it.

These are all simple truths, one would think, and yet, they appear to bear infinite repetition. But then, history is rewritten in the recording of it, always.

"Ici, c'est elle," you tell Tully Ferris, the guide you've engaged, putting down a pale sepia photograph printed on pasteboard, its corners foxed with age. "Marceline Bedard, 1909—from before she and Denis de Russy met, when she was still dancing as Tanit-Isis. It's a photographic reference, similar to what Alphonse Mucha developed his commercial art pieces from; I found it in a studio where Frank Marsh used to paint, hidden in the floor. Marsh was a Cubist, so his paintings tend to look very deconstructed, barely human, but this is what he began with."

Ferris looks at the *carte,* gives a low whistle. "Redbone," he says. "She a fine gal, that's for sure. Thick, sweet. And look at that hair."

"'Redbone?' I don't know this term."

"Pale, ma'am, like cream, lightish-complected—you know, high yaller? Same as me."

"Oh yes, *une métisse, bien sur.* She was cagey about her background, *la belle Marceline,* liked to preserve mystery. But the rumor was her mother came from New Orleans to Marseilles, then Paris, settling in the same area where Sarah Bernhardt's parents once lived, a Jewish ghetto; when she switched to conducting séances, she took out advertisements claiming her powers came from Zimbabwe and Babylon, darkest Africa and the tribes of Israel, equally. Thus, the name: Tanit, after the Berber moon-goddess, and Isis, from ancient Egypt, the mother of all magic."

"She got something, all right. A mystery to me how she even hold her head up, that much weight of braids on top of it."

"Mmm, there was an interesting story told about Marceline's hair—that it wasn't hers at all but a wig. A wig made *from* hair, maybe even some scalp, going back a *long* time, centuries . . . I mean, *c'est folle* to think so, but that was what they said. Perhaps even as far *as* Egypt. Her mother's mother brought it with her, supposedly."

"Mummies got hair like that, though, don't they? Never rots. Good enough you can take DNA off it."

You nod. "And then there's the tradition of Orthodox Jewish women, Observants, Lubavitchers in particular—they cover their hair with a wig, too, a *sheitel,* so no one but their husband gets to see it. Now, Marceline was in no way Observant, but I can see perhaps an added benefit to her *courtesanerie* from allowing no one who was not *un amant,* her intimate, to see her uncovered. The wig's hair might look much the same as her own, only longer; it would save her having to . . . relax it? *Ça ira?*"

"Yeah, back then, they'd've used lye, I guess. Nasty. Burn you, you leave it on too long."

"*Exactement.*"

Tully rocks back a bit on his heels, gives a sigh. "Better start off soon, you lookin' to make Riverside 'fore nightfall—we twenty miles up the road here from where the turn-off'd be, there was one, so we gotta drive cross Barker's Crick, park by the pass, then hike the rest. Not much left still standin', but I guess you probably know that, right?"

"Mmm. I read testimony from 1930, a man trying for Cape Girardeau who claimed he stayed overnight, spoke to Antoine de Russy. Not possible, of course, given the time—yet he knew many details of the events of 1922, without ever reading or hearing about them, previously. Or so he said."

"The murders, the fire?" You nod. "Yeah, well—takes all sorts, don't it? Ready to go, ma'am?"

"If you are, yes."

"Best get to it, then—be dark sooner'n you think, and we sure don't wanna be walkin' 'round in *that*."

A mourning sampler embroidered in 15 different de Russy family members' hair once hung upstairs, just outside my husband's childhood bedroom door: such a pretty garden scene, at first glance, soft and gracious, depicting the linden-tree border separating river and dock from well-manicured green lawn and edging flowerbeds—that useless clutter of exotic blooms, completely unsuited to local climate or soil, which routinely drank up half the fresh water diverted from the slave quarter's meager vegetable patch. The lindens also performed a second function, of course, making sure de Russy eyes were never knowingly forced to contemplate what their *negres* called the bone-field, a wet clay sump where slaves' corpses were buried at night and without ceremony, once their squeamish masters were safely asleep. Landscaping as *maquillage,* a false face over rot, the skull skin-hid. But then, we all look the same underneath, no matter our outward shade, *ne c'est pas?*

In 1912, I took Denis's hand at a Paris soiree and knew him immediately for my own blood, from the way the very touch of him made my skin crawl—that oh-so-desirable *peau si-blanche,* olive-inflected like old ivory, light enough to shine under candle-flame. I had my Tanit-wig on that night, coils of it hung down in tiers far as my hips, my thighs, far enough to brush the very backs of my bare knees; I'd been rehearsing most of the day, preparing to chant the old rites in Shona while doing what my posters called a "Roodmas dance" for fools with deep pockets. Frank Marsh was there, too, of course, his fishy eyes hung out on strings—he introduced Denis to me, then pulled me aside and begged me once again to allow him to paint me "as the gods intended," with only my ancestors' hair for modesty. But I laughed in his face and turned back to Denis instead, for here was the touch of true fate at last, culmination of my mother's many prayers and sacrifices. Mine to bend myself to him and bind him fast, make him bring me back to Riverside to do what must be done, just as it'd been Frank's unwitting destiny to make that introduction all along and suffer the consequences.

Antoine de Russy liked to boast he kept Denis unworldly, and I must suppose it to be so, for he never saw me with my wig off, my Tanit-locks set by and the not-so-soft fuzz of black which anchored it on display. As he was raised to think himself a gentleman, it would never have occurred to Denis to demand such intimacies. By the time his father pressed him to do so, I had him well-trained: *Something odd about that woman, boy,* I heard him whisper more than once, before they fell out. *Makes my blood run cold to see it. For all she's foreign-born, I'd almost swear I know her face . . .*

Ha! As though the man had no memory, or no mirrors. Yet, I was far too fair for the one, I suspect, and far too . . . different, though in "deceitfully slight proportion"— to quote that Northerner who wrote your vaunted *testimony*—for the other. It being difficult to acknowledge your own features in so alien a mirror, not even when they come echoing back to you over generations of mixed blood, let alone on your only son's arm.

You got in touch with Tully last Tuesday, little seeker, securing his services via Bell's machine — its latest version, any rate — and by yesterday, meanwhile, you'd flown here from Paris already, through the air. Things move so *fast* these days, and I don't understand the half of it; it's magic to me, more so than magic itself, that dark, mechanical force I hold so close to my dead heart. But then, this is a problem with where I am now, *how* I am; things come to me unasked-for, under the earth, out of the river. Knowledge just reveals itself to me, simple and secret, the same way soil is disturbed by footfalls or silt rises to meet the ripple: no questions and no answers, likewise. Nothing explained outright, ever.

That's why I don't know your name, or anything else about you, aside from the fact you think in a language I've long discarded and hold an image of me in your mind, forever searching after its twin: that portrait poor Frank did eventually conjure out of me during our last long, hot, wet summer at Riverside, when I led my husband's father to believe I was unfaithful expressly in order to tempt Denis back early from his New York trip . . . so he might discover me in Frank's rooms, naked but for my wig, and kill us both.

Workings have a price, you see, and the single best currency for such transactions is blood, always — my blood, the de Russys' blood, and poor Frank's added in on top as mere afterthought. All of our blood together and a hundred years' more besides, let from ten thousand poor *negres'* veins one at a time by whip or knife, closed fist or open-handed blow, crying out forever from this slavery-tainted ground.

After Denis's grandfather bred my mother's mother 'til she died — before his eyes fell on her in turn — *Maman* ran all the way from Riverside to New Orleans and further, as you've told Tully: crossed the ocean to France's main port, then its capital, an uphill road traveled one set of sheets to the next, equal-paved with vaudeville stages, dancefloors, séance-rooms, and men's beds. Which is why those were the trades she taught me, along with my other, deeper callings. Too white to be black, a lost half-girl, she birthed me into the *demi-monde* several shades lighter still, which allowed me to climb my way back out; perception has its uses, after all, especially to *une sorciére*. From earliest years, however, I knew that nothing I did was for myself—that the only reason I existed at all was to bring about her curse, and her mother's, and her mother's mother's mother's.

There's a woman at Riverside, Marceline, ma mie, my mother told me before I left her that last time, stepping aboard the steamship bound for America. *An old one, from Home—who can say how old? She knew my mother and hers; she'll know you on sight, know your works, and help you in them.* And so there was: Kaayakire, whom those fools who bought her named Sophonisba—Aunt Sophy—before setting her to live alone in her bone-yard shack, tending the linden path. It was she who taught me the next part of my duty, how to use my ancestors' power to knit our dead fellow captives' pain together like a braid, a long black snake of justice, fit to choke all the de Russys to death at once. To stop this flow of evil blood at last, at its very source.

That I was part de Russy myself, of course, meant I could not be allowed to escape, either, in the end. Yet only blood pays for blood, so the bargain seemed well worth it, at the time.

But I have been down here so long, now—years and years, decades: almost fifty, by your reckoning, with the de Russy line *proper* long-extirpated, myself very much included. Which is more than long enough to begin to change my mind on that particular subject.

So, here you come at last, down the track where the road once wound at sunset, led by a man bearing just the barest taint of de Russy blood in his face, his skin, his veins: come down from some child sold away to cover its masters' debts, perhaps, or traded between landholders like a piece of livestock. One way or the other, it's as easy for me to recognize in Tully Ferris by smell as it'd no doubt be by sight, were I not so long deep-buried and eyeless with mud stopping my mouth and gloving my hands, roots knot-coiled 'round my ankles' bones like chains. I'd know it at first breath, well as I would my own long-gone flesh's reek, my own long-rotten tongue's taste.

Just fate at work again, I suppose, slow as old growth—fate, the spider's phantom skein, thrown out wide, then tightened. But the curse I laid remains almost as strong, shored up with Kaayakire's help: Through its prism, I watch you approach, earth-toned and many-pointed, filtered through a hundred thousand leaves at once like the scales on some dragonfly's eye. I send out my feelers, hear your shared tread echo through the ground below, rebounding off bones and bone-fragments, and an image blooms out of resonance that is brief yet crisp, made and remade with every fresh step: you and Tully stomping through the long grass and the clinging weeds, your rubber boots dirt-spattered, wet coats muddy at the hem and snagged all over with stickers.

Tully raises one arm, makes a sweep, as though inviting the house's stove-in ruin to dance. "Riverside, ma'am—what's left of it, anyhow. See what I meant?"

"Yes, I see. Oh, *pute la merde!*"

Tree-girt and decrepit, Riverside's pile once boasted two stories, a great Ionic portico, the full length and breadth necessary for any plantation centerpiece; they ran upwards of two hundred slaves here before the War cut the de Russys' strength in half. My husband's father loved to hold forth on its architectural value to anyone who'd listen, along with most who didn't. Little of the original is left upright now, however—a mere half-erased sketch of its former glory, all burnt and rotted and sagging amongst the scrub and cockle burrs. Like the deaths of its former occupants, its ruin is an achievement in which I take great pride.

"Said this portrait you come after was upstairs, right?" Tully rummages in his pack for a waterproof torch. "Well, you in luck, gal, sorta . . . upstairs fell in last year, resettled the whole mess of it down into what used to be old Antoine's ballroom. Can't get at it from the front, 'cause those steps is so moldy they break if you look at 'em the wrong way, but there's a tear in the side take us right through. Hope you took my advice 'bout that hard-hat, though."

You nod, popping your own pack, and slip the article in question on: It even has a head-lamp, bright-white. "*Voila.*"

At this point, with a thunderclap, rain begins to fall like curtains, drenching you both—inconvenient, I'm sure, as you slip and slide 'cross the muddy rubble. But I can take no credit for that, believe it or not; just nature taking its toll, moisture invading everything as slow-mounting damp or coming down in sheets, bursting its banks in cycles along with the tea-brown Mississippi itself.

Ownership works both ways, you see. Which is why, even in its heyday, Riverside was never anything more than just another ship, carrying our ancestors to an unwanted afterlife chained cheek-by-jowl with their oppressors, with no way to escape, even in death. No way for *any* of us to escape our own actions, or from each other.

But when I returned, Kaayakire showed me just how deep those dead slaves had sunk their roots in Riverside's heart: deep enough to strangle, to infiltrate, to poison, all this while lying dormant under a fallow crust. To sow death-seeds in every part of what the de Russys called home, however surface-comfortable, waiting patient for a second chance to flower.

Inside, under a sagging double weight of floor-turned-roof, fifty years' worth of mold spikes up the nose straight into the brain while shadows scatter from your twinned lights, same as silt in dark water. You hear the rain like someone else's pulse, drumming hard, sodden. Tully glances 'round, frowning. "Don't like it," he says. "Been more damage since my last time here: there, and there. Structural collapse."

"The columns will keep it up, though, no? They seem—"

"Saggy like an elephant's butt, that's what they *seem* . . . but hell, your money. Got some idea where best to look?" You shake your head, drawing a sigh. "Well, perfect. Guess we better start with what's eye-level; go from there."

As the two of you search, he asks about *that old business,* the gory details. For certainly, people gossip, here as everywhere else, yet the matter of the de Russys is something most locals flinch from, as though they know it to be somehow—not sacred, perhaps, but *significant,* in its own grotesque way. Tainted and tainting, by turns.

"Denis de Russy brought Marceline home and six months later, Frank Marsh came to visit," you explain. "He had known them both as friends, introduced them, watched them form *un ménage.* Denis considered him an artistic genius but eccentric. To his father, he wrote that Marsh had 'a knowledge of anatomy which borders on the uncanny.' Antoine de Russy heard odd stories about Marsh, his family in Massachusetts, *la ville d'*Innsmouth . . . but he trusted his son, trusted that Denis trusted. So, he opened his doors."

"But Denis goes traveling, and Marsh starts in to painting Missus de Russy with no clothes on, maybe more. That part right, or not?"

"That was the rumor, yes. It's not unlikely Marceline and Marsh were intimates, from before; he'd painted her twice already, taken those photos. A simple transaction. But this was . . . different, or so Antoine de Russy claimed."

"How so?"

You shrug. "Marsh said there was something inside her he wanted to make other people see."

"Like what, her soul?"

"*Peut-etre.* Or something real, maybe—hidden. *Comme un,* eh, hmmm . . . " You pause, thinking. "When you swallow eggs or something swims up inside, in Africa, South America: It eats your food, makes you thin, lives inside you. And when doctors suspect, they have to tempt it out—say 'aah,' you know, tease it to show itself, like a . . .

snake from a hole . . . ”

Tully stops, mouth twitching. “A *tapeworm?* Boy must’ve been trippin’, ma’am. Too much absinthe, for sure.”

Another shrug. “Antoine de Russy wrote to Denis, told him to come home before things progressed further, but heard nothing. Days later, he found Marsh and Marceline in Marsh’s rooms, hacked with knives, Marceline without her wig, or her, eh — hair — “

“Been scalped? Whoo.” Tully shakes his head. “Then Denis kills himself and the old man goes crazy; that’s how they tell it ’round here. When they talk about it at all, which ain’t much.”

“In the testimony I read, de Russy said he hid Marsh and Marceline, buried them in lime. He told Denis to run, but Denis hanged himself instead, in one of the old huts — or something strangled him, a big black snake. And then the house burnt down.”

“Aunt Sophy’s snake, they call it.”

“A snake or a braid, *oui, c’est ca. Le cheveaux de* Marceline.” But here you stop, examining something at your feet. “But wait, what is — ? Over here, please. I need your light.”

Tully steps over, slips, curses; down on one knee in the mud, cap cracking worryingly, his torch rapping on the item in question. “Shit! Look like a . . . box, or something. Here.” As he hands it up to you, however, it’s now his own turn to squint, scrubbing mud from his eyes — something’s caught his notice, there, half-wedged behind a caryatid, extruding from what used to be the wall. He gives it a tug and watches it come slithering out.

“*Qu’est-ce que c’est, la?*”

“Um . . . think this might be what you lookin’ for, ma’am. Some of, anyhow.”

The wet rag in his hand has seen better days, definitely. Yet, for one who’s studied poor Frank Marsh’s work — how ridiculous such a thing sounds, even to me! — it must be unmistakable, nevertheless: a warped canvas, neglect-scabrous, all morbid content and perverted geometry done in impossible, liminal colors. The body I barely recognize, splayed out on its altar-throne, one bloated hand offering a cup of strange liquor; looks more the way it might now were there anything still unscattered, not sifted through dirt and water or filtered by a thousand roots, drawn off to feed Riverside's trees and weeds with hateful power. The face is long-gone, bullet-perforated, just as that skittish Northerner claimed. But the rest, that coiling darkness, it lies (*I lie*) on —

You make a strange noise at the sight, gut-struck: "Oh, *quel dommage!* What a waste, a sinful waste . . . "

"Damn, yeah. Not much to go on, huh?"

"Enough to begin with, *certainment.* I know experts, people who'd pay for the opportunity to restore something so unique, so precious. But why, why—ah, I will never understand. Stupid superstition!"

Which is when the box in your hands jumps, ever so slightly, as though something inside it's woken up. Makes a little hollow rap, like knocking.

As I've said, little seeker, I don't know you—barely know Tully, for all I might recognize his precedents. Though I suppose what I *do* know might be just enough to feel bad for what must happen to you and him, both, were I any way inclined to.

Frank's painting is ruined, like everything else, but what's inside the box is pristine, inviolable. When my father-in-law disinterred us days after the murders, too drunk to remember whether or not Denis had actually done what he feared, he found it wound 'round Frank's corpse, crushing him in its embrace, and threw burning lamp-oil on it, setting his own house afire. Then fled straight to Kaayakire's shack, calling her slave-name like the madman he'd doubtless become: *Damn you, Sophy, an' that Marse Clooloo o' yours . . . damn you, you hellish ol' niggerwoman! Damn you for knowin' what she was, that Frog whore, an' not warnin' me . . . 'm I your Massa, or ain't I? Ain't I always treated you well . . .?*

Only to find the same thing waiting for him, longer still and far more many-armed, still smoldering and black as ever—less a snake now than an octopus, a hundred-handed net. The weight of every dead African whose blood went to grow the de Russys' fortunes, falling on him at once.

My cousin's father, my half-uncle, my mother's brother: all of these and none of them, as she and I were nothing to them—to him. Him I killed by letting his son kill me and set me free.

I have let myself be dead far too long since then, however, it occurs to me. Indulged myself, who should've thought only to indulge them, the ancestors whose scalps anchor my skull, grow my crowning glory. Their blood, my blood—Tully Ferris' blood, blood of the de Russys, of owners and owned alike—cries out from the ground. Your blood, too, now.

Inside the box, which you cannot keep yourself from opening, is my Tanit-Isis wig, that awful relic: heavy and sweet-smelling, soft with oils, though kinked at root and tip. You lift it to your head, eyes dazed, and breathe its odor in, deeply; hear Tully cry out, but only faintly, as the hair of every other dead slave buried at Riverside begins to poke its way through floors-made-walls, displace rubble and clutter, twine 'round cracked and half-mashed columnry like ivy, crawl up from the muck like sodden spiders. My wig feels their energies gather and plumps itself accordingly, bristling in every direction at once, even as these subsidiary creatures snare Tully like a rabbit and force their knotted follicles inside his veins, sucking de Russy blood the way the *lamia* once did, the *astriyah*, demons called up not by Solomon, but Sheba. While it runs its own roots down into your scalp and cracks your skull along its fused fontanelles to reach the gray-pink brain within, injecting everything which ever made me *me* like some strange drug, and wiping *you* away like dust.

I *would* feel bad for your sad demise, little seeker, I'm almost sure; Tully's, even, his ancestry aside. But only if I were anyone but who I am.

Outside, the rain recedes, letting in daylight: bright morning, blazing gold-green through drooping leaves to call steam up from the sodden ground, raise cicatrice-blisters of moisture from Riverside's walls. The fields glitter like spiderwebs. Emerging into it, I smile for the first time in so very long: lips, teeth, muscles flexing. *Myself* again, for all I wear another's flesh.

Undefeated, *Maman.* Victory. I am your revenge and theirs. No one owns me, not anymore, never again. I am . . . my own.

And so, my contract fulfilled, I walk away: into this fast, new, magical world, the future, trailing a thousand dark locks of history behind.

L AGAN

The sea is so much deeper than the grave.
— Robyn Hitchcock.

*I*N *MARITIME LAW, the terms* flotsam, jetsam *and* lagan *describe specific and distinct kinds of wreckage. Jetsam describes goods voluntarily cast into the sea (jettisoned) by the crew of a ship, usually to lighten it in an emergency. Flotsam describes goods left floating on the water by accident, often after a shipwreck. Both may generally be salvaged, reverting to the original owner only if explicitly claimed. Lagan, on the other hand, is the term for goods that have been marked, most often by a buoy, so the previous owner can retrieve it later. Lagan therefore remains that owner's property and cannot be salvaged unless it can be legally proven that the owner is either dead or abandoned it under circumstances which assured they could not possibly have ever held out any real hope of recovering it.*

"You look like shit," Sean said. "Seriously, mate. Like you haven't slept in yonks."

Draped across the rail, Ric didn't bother to shake his head. "That's 'cause I haven't."

Barely gone noon, the air even below-decks so hot everybody felt mildly feverish. Not that Sean'd be able to tell, really, barring recourse to the 'Net; though he'd bluffed his way on board (with Ric's connivance) by misrepresenting his summer job at Auntie Di's veterinary clinic as some sort of pre-med internship, all he'd had to do thus far was dole out Dramamine, ibuprofen, Polysporin and Band-aids. Oh, and stitch up a few shallow wounds here and there, but that's where a strong stomach and Mum's sewing lessons came in handy.

"Best go down, then," Sean suggested. "Knock a few back, have a bit of a zizz . . ."

"Can't do that, mate." Ric looked at him full on, then—face haggard under its tan, eyes bruise-set, like they'd been boiled. "I do that, I'll have the dream. And then . . . yeah, better not."

Which dream's this, again? Sean thought of saying but didn't.

But Ric was already deep into monologue-mode: ". . . like I'm drowning, or . . . remember the one about cats sitting on babies' faces, stealing their breath? Like I'm being pressed down by something, so hard I'm paralyzed, and it covers my face so I can't breathe, all warm and moist but not furry at all, it's *skin*, flat as a bag, and wrinkled, and naked. Like . . . somebody else's bloody scrotum."

"Ah, Jesus, now I *know* you're not serious."

"You're the one fuckin' asked, you prat."

To which Sean simply shrugged and leant back against the rail, arms crossed to ward off a vague, creeping discomfort. "That's just a night-hag, Ric; bloody sleep apnea, dressed up like the Late-Night Fright Show. Sure you're not speeding again?"

"Been out going on a week, so no." But even total exhaustion couldn't completely root out the essential Ric-ness, same eyebrow-waggling comic charm which'd originally fished Sean in, at least halfway. "S'pose a quick blowie's out the question, then."

"And that'd pay back for me how, exactly?"

"Fresh protein?"

Without wanting to, Sean found himself hovering on the verge of laughter before biting it back, hard. "Thanks, but no thanks. How's about a few Aspirins and a massage, and we call it even?"

"Prick-tease."

"Well, you know me."

Ric shot him a dark look from under equally dark lashes, genuinely too knackered to take further offense. Just as well: Six-two of enraged Melbourne Greek was nothing to sneeze at, the best of times, and Sean really didn't feel up to doing yet another *piss-off-out-of-my-personal-space* macarena with the fucker, below-decks or above-. He one-eightied to look out over the water instead.

Sometimes the ocean seemed a bright-burnt skin they could crawl upon blindly, persuading themselves it was impenetrable, but this wasn't one of those days. The usual salt-haze had boiled off, discovering all too clearly the near-endless soup of part-degraded garbage and haphazard death they floated in: The Great Pacific Garbage Knot's outermost gyre, folding all manner of entropized crap in towards the center, where it could hit, stick, grow by incredibly slow degrees into the loose trash-conglomerate "island" that rumors now reckoned at roughly half the size of Texas.

Around them, "Captain" Shaftoe's folly let out a chorus of groans, like small animals were being pinched between its joints. Dougray Shaftoe himself having only the barest interest in boats for their own sake, it was nameless except for its maritime registry code; between themselves, Ric and Sean had taken to calling it the *Bad Idea*, persisting long after the joke stopped being funny. A full-displacement hull outrigger shrimp trawler from New Guinea, Shaftoe had had it converted to salvage-hauler by removing the refrigeration equipment, freeing up storage space for that legendary cargo harvest he was sure would drift into their laps if they only camped out by the Knot long enough. Chief amongst many things he hadn't really reckoned on, though, was the lingering stench of a million hauls past, which made sleeping on the *Idea* a fairly disgusting exercise in itself, nightmares notwithstanding.

Neither the actual smell nor the general stench of idiocy hovering 'round this venture had seemed quite so obvious back in Port Moresby, where Sean had been stupidly content to stand by as a blind-drunk Ric threw both their oars in with Shaftoe's crew. Still, ridiculous as this all seemed in hindsight—especially from his current perspective, bobbing like a tin-can in the middle of arse-end nowhere with a bunch of similarly delusional losers—at least he hadn't compounded the mistake by giving it up to Ric later on, considering what a birk he'd since turned out to be. And it was the rancid aftertaste of that not-quite-relationship, in fact—liberally cut with five weeks of too-close quarters, and Ric's increasing craziness throughout—which now kept Sean securely at arm's length, unwilling to dole out even a perfunctory clap on the shoulder (*Cheer up, mate! Could be worse . . . somehow*), lest it be misconstrued as a come-on.

"We're all in the same boat, though, aren't we?" Ric demanded, breaking Sean's train of thought. "Like, literally."

"You're right there," Sean agreed. But felt his gaze drawn further down, towards the hatch, where that all-important first piece of flotsam they'd picked up still lay discarded—a dark green, plastic-blend hull-chip marked with the center-set yellow letters EEN and PHOE.

Green Phoenix.

Experimental craft, whole thing's made out of recyclables, Sean had told Shaftoe, running three searches at once, while the rest of the tiny crew loomed angrily 'round them. *They launched, uh . . . two years back, off of California; big idea was to surf currents all the way here, tracing the gyre's path and taking samples of all the garbage that went along with 'em. Been out of contact for . . . nine months, looks like.*

Private venture?

Corporate—ReVive, a subset of Grummacher Pan-Oceanic. WikiLeaks says they set it up as a P.R. dodge, to shift attention off those dumping scandals.

So . . . they'd pay to find out what happened to it, yeah?

Yeah, sure. Probably.

Which gave them a plan, at long last. That little piece of drift was the best "catch" they'd had since pushing off, one way or the other—and it'd certainly stopped that potential mutiny in its tracks, for which Shaftoe'd privately declared himself grateful. As he bloody well should be.

Trouble had started a fortnight back, when Arjit and Sam-I-Am went poking 'round in the hold, only to discover half the crates down there were empty rather than supply-packed—meant for that endless flood of three-year-old jetsam Shaftoe'd been shit-sure would flock their way, they only made it to the Knot and camped out in its orbit. So far—as one might only expect, given the original plan's intensely un-researched laziness—it hadn't exactly panned out; the stuff they did rake from the water tended to be either damaged or worthless, with an occasional side-order of resale-unfriendly randomness. (An entire crate of little party balloons that blew up into funny animal shapes, for example, seemed virtually designed not to attract big eBay bidders, unless one of them turned out to be a nostalgic Nicolas Cage.)

What are we gonna do for food, then? Arjit'd demanded, understandably.

Fish? was Shaftoe's grand suggestion. *Ship's already set up for it, right?*

Yeah. Except that the area was *contaminated*, as befit a fucking two hundred and fifty thousand square mile dump, a rummage-bin toxin-patch culled from here to China; every catch they brought up was half corpses, scales dull and lifting, gills deformed, their bloated stomachs stuffed with degrading plastic leaching fluorocarbons. Sam-I-Am took to sharpening his clasp-knife, while Arjit spoke darkly of how easy it would be to signal pirates, if not simply give Shaftoe (who'd holed himself up in his cabin, where he kept at least two guns) the stealthy heave some night and become them.

Then Sean found the *Green Phoenix* drift while flushing out the bilges, done some satellite uplink-grade asking 'round, and made his pitch. Radar and hard work did the rest—hadn't taken much past forty-eight hours, in the end: A media event, just waiting to happen. The whole of the wreck, or what was left, plus an arse-load of lagan clearly marked with reVive's eco-friendly tramp stamp. Plus, inside one of them, something even Sean could've never foreseen . . .

. . . a survivor.

Above water-level, the garbage piles together in shoals, mortared with its own melt; pollution becomes cement, suture, cobbling a crazy-quilt that daily grows denser. Beneath, the underside spirals down in tails like kelp, great interlocking daisy-chains of current like inverted tornadoes: Turning and turning, an endless fishline loop, to scrape at the sea-bottom.

Under the water, down in the dark; where light fades as it diffuses, where things become slimy and inappropriate, unreadable as some alien alphabet. The mimic-octopus on the off-reef floor, masquerading as either what it eats or fears — burying itself until only two or three limbs are visible, a coiled knot of mock sea-snakes, poison-banded. The sponge angler, further down and dimmer, rooting itself amidst anemone-forests and great shell-shelves — flicking one long spine out and back, out, and back into the oncoming current, to reel in unwary prey. The glass-headed barrel-eyes, prowling restless at Immeasurable Depths — swiveling its nostrils in two different directions at once, negotiating by its nude brain's light, mouth wide for whatever it chances to blunder against.

None of us are what we seem below a certain depth, where narcosis' inevitable prospect transmutes to one immense, all-over kiss, suffocation a blissful blessing. Caught up in this joyful sub-tide, we forget our original forms, grow fluid and slippery, like drowned men's flesh. We degrade by degrees, scatter our bones at random in a broken necklace, and watch them turn to coral.

Even further down, bones are a luxury, far too easily crushed. Here we become elastic, infinitely supple; we drift, exerting no unnecessary effort, reshaping ourselves to whatever comes along. Gelid, we spin ourselves out like ropes, chains of stomachs inside stomachs. We digest, and are digested, in turn.

Thus, hunger itself becomes a form of selflessness, a form of worship. A form of love.

Sean still couldn't figure if it'd been blind luck, seat-of-the-pants cunning, or maybe a fortuitous combo of the two. When they'd first dredged it up, the rig looked like half a car wreck fused with found object sculpture — mucky scribble of knotted-up lead line cross knit with weed, an American flag reduced to sodden ribbons lashing half a trimaran pontoon to one side of a rickety, semi-compacted shipping crate, whole thing stoppered by a massive, partially cracked rainwater cycling tank they only later realized had been haphazardly patched with sail tape, from the inside. Just a random conglomeration of garbage, or so they'd thought 'til they tried to lift it: Impossibly heavy, shadowed internally, sloshing with who knew what. When Shaftoe gave the order, the crate's sodden remnants prized up and away on three, like husking a coconut.

And there *he*'d been, inside: Curled fetal, skin a too soft mess of salt and burn — like he'd been steeping in his own filth for weeks, poached egg-style under that relentless sun. Try to pull him out now, and Sean could already see his hide ruck, bones ground like marbles in a sock from bobbing through twenty-foot waves, meat beneath just a rancid stew. That bright thatch of hair slipping off beneath prying fingers, an ill-glued skullcap.

Sean caught his breath at the very idea, deep. Then gasped, almost retching, as he seemed to feel the whole cobbled together escape pod's funk come in at his eyeballs, ream him from stem to stern; not so bad, really, once you got used to it. Not *so* very bad, at all.

Which was when the man in question had opened his eyes, green-guileless as the sea itself, and looked at him.

They got him down to "sickbay" (i.e., Sean's storage-closet of a bunk), sent Sam-I-Am and Ric back up for a gallon jug of fresh, and started the process — cut away what was left of his clothes, sluiced him down, sponged away the shed. What emerged was sallow yet weirdly fresh-looking, free of scars and hair alike, cool and firm to the touch. No detectable pulse at neck or wrist, so Sean was forced to search further afield: brush his torpid tackle aside, snoozing oyster-slack in the shadow of his equally blond groin's half-shell and feel for the femoral.

Which did indeed respond, albeit sluggishly, as though still underwater.

Then: *Aussie,* his patient'd suddenly observed, mouth not even sounding dry after what had to be days of drifting, and not seeming concerned at all about a stranger's hand in his crotch; it was a soothing voice with vowels worn flat, classic SoCal drawl up-climbing towards the sentence's end, familiar from any one of a hundred TV commercials. *'M I . . . near there, now?*

Closer to Papua the one side, Indonesia the other.

So . . . still in th' Knot, then.

Still, yeah. Don't try to talk.

Then Sean scooped two fingertips' worth of water, let the guy suck it back, and felt his tongue's unexpected heat lave the prints: immediately, his cheekbones burnt hectic, saliva-scoured nerves firing raw, nape sweat-damp. To fend off a blush, he contradicted himself, asking: *You're Grinnage, right? Simon? Navigator, did all the IT work . . . I saw your Photostream on Flickr.*

. . . 'f you say so.

Look, you either are or you aren't, mate. It's not multiple bloody choice.

The guy made a sketchy attempt at a shrug, which worked out more like a ripple. He seemed limp, leached, like all his minerals were gone.

Could be, he allowed, finally.

A cough. Sean looked up to find Shaftoe in the doorway, arms crossed, frowning. Demanding: *What's that even mean, son?*

Means . . . I could be this . . . whoever you said. Or not. Could be you, or him . . .

(nodding here at Sean, who colored again, obliquely embarrassed)

. . . or anybody.

Nemo, Sean'd thought, at the time, same as Cyclops Polyphemus in his cave: curse of a Classical education, though it did make reading MedicalWiki entries a fair bit easier. *No Man. I will eat No Man last, as my guest-gift. Come quickly and help me, brothers, for No Man has put my eye out!*

Shaftoe shrugged once more, like he was throwing off flies. *Well. Whoever you are, you should be grateful, eh? 'Specially to* this *one. He's the bloke found you — your ship, anyhow. Man saved your bloody life.*

Sean gave a dismissive headshake, mumbled something down into his neck, but those mild eyes—washed clean, tide-abraded, like sea-glass—have already turned back his way. They caught him up without prejudice, neat as a flounder's sand-plus-prey suction and swallowed him whole.

Thank you, the man from the sea told him. To which Sean could only reply—

. . . you're welcome.

And now Sean finds himself once more sunk deep in his own dreams — no Freudian rape-fantasies here, no flesh-bag settling over him, sliding a proboscis down his throat and digesting him from the inside. These visions are all numbing cold and softness, dark on dark, the gloom he floats in only further obscured by a silken mesh of movement: Narcosis, shipwreck-hypnotism, the endless waves, amniotic. The lure of the drift. The lure of letting go.

Because: What do I have to keep me here, after all? What did I ever have?

This stinking boat, Shaftoe's folly. These awful people, him very much included. Just crap and garbage, a tainted, tainting mess of air-breathers' detritus. Trash in a soup of trash, under which something else lurks, unrecognized — something tempted slowly upwards by the scent of change, of possibility. Unrealized hungers revealed, made suddenly attainable, the same way bodies fruit, decay sliding fast from waste to potential.

In his marrow, Sean simply knows *these aimless loops of sleep-thought are nothing to fear; quite the opposite, really. Weirdly pleasurable, in a purely perverse way: Circuitous skull-spirals, itch-scratchingly slow, which clear him out so completely he often looks forward to returning to them in progress, even while awake . . . sometimes feels he'd gladly sleep all fuckin' day to do so, if he only could . . .*

(but don't tell Ric that, mate)

Like back when he was twelve, traveling the Great Barrier Reef with his Mum and Dad, and he side-stroked without looking first right into the middle of a Lion's Mane jellyfish bloom: That clench of recognition, filaments already wrapping 'round him from every side in streamers, pale poison-full vermicelli, just beginning to sting him with their multitudinous fine hairs. A caress on its way to becoming a wound.

There at the edge of the shelf, the last clump of brain and cup and stone before the drop-off: Clear shading to blue shading to black, going down down down into nothing. He'd hung above an abyss, spun sugar-caged by luminous mucus, watching the jellies' stomachs pulse like hearts through their sides, and contemplated—in one skipped beat, one breathless no-scream—the utter end of the world.

What's down there, Dad?

Things you've never seen, son. Things you never will see.

(Things you never want to.)

But separate, always, kept down by pressure, gravity versus its lack. No place in our world for their eddying, porous likes, and barely any room in theirs for us: Fragile in a different way, clumsy, blundering in our bathyspheres and our pressurized suits, subject to the bends. Go down too fast, we rupture; come up too fast, we burst. Never the twain shall meet, for long . . .

But we do strew our leavings everywhere we go, and each bit of garbage left behind is a seed, a potential grit-pearl. The ocean adapts to our corrupting influences, shaping itself to what it assumes is a new system of prey-or-be-preyed-upon.

Look, Sean, *Mum said, pointing, her mask-voice a tinny buzz in his ear.* Here's a stonefish, looks like a rock. A skate, trying to look like an old shoe. A sponge grown into the shape of a slipped carburetor—is that rust, or protective color?

And there, where the bombies meet, a jumble of far more intimate human litter . . . is that somebody's femur, somebody's splintered tibia? Or just a thousand-generation anemone colony bleached white sand-on-calcium gray, trying to fit itself into the hole where somebody's trapped and weighted corpse once used to lie?

All this, or none of it, or something else entirely —something new, unknown, unseen. For there is far more sea to pore through, waiting unexplored, than there ever will be land.

Sean came back up gasping, sweat-wet, in darkness. Felt his dreams shrug aside to let him free, silky-smooth and sandpaper by turns, an affectionate quilt of flocking rays —their cartilaginous wings sliding away quick down every limb, a peeled cocoon. An extra pulse seemed to hammer at his breastbone, where the female ray's pectoral disc would lie; when he checked himself in the cabin mirror, sure it was purely psychosomatic, he thought he saw a bruise just beginning to raise, a wine-dark birthmark kiss. As though something trawling sleep's deepest levels had bit down on him, hard, before trying to slide its fertilizing claspers in.

Up on deck, the moon hung low and huge in a star-crammed sky, its outline sketched in burnt-retina heat-haze orange. The planks still held most of the day's heat, beating up right through his flip-flops' rubber soles; sweat had already stuck pits to sleeves before he'd even climbed the ladder, warm as blood and glue-heavy, 'til he could barely tell ass-crack from shirttail.

When he sucked down a long gulp, straining in search of relief, all he got was more of the same, but salt-flavored, mildly decayed. Like he was breathing air from his own corpse's lungs.

"Hey," the man from the sea said, from behind him.

Sean turned, blinked stupidly, blood pounding in his face and pelvis —instinctively made to back up, and rocked against the railing.

Might've fallen, even, if somebody hadn't laid their big American hand (dusted with gold hair on the back, palm still rough with broken blisters) on his, and pulled.

"Should watch out; it's pretty dark. You fell, sharks'd find you a damn sight faster'n we would."

"Too right. Smell bring you up?"

"Nah, that's about the same—just stop noticing it, eventually, I guess. I thought . . . " He gave a cursory look 'round: a bit too quick, barely a headshake. "Thought I might check the rig out again, that thing you found me in. See if anything pops."

"And?"

"Nope."

"That's normal, mate. Given the circumstances."

Another eye-flick, tracing the same static path. "I'm not even trying to *remember*, so much, now—just to, you know, figure it out. How it all must've happened."

"The wreck . . . "

"Sure, and after. Like when your captain asked me: *That how it went?*" He shrugged. "I don't know. I just—woke up, inside that thing. I mean, I *think* I woke up . . . "

"Yeah, well. What else would you've done?"

" . . . I don't know."

Sean didn't, either. So he looked away again, studied what he could see of the waves instead, until his head began to hurt. Thinking, all the while, how immature his long-expired crush on Ric now seemed in the face of *this* yearning—an all-encompassing draw, deep water pull, stronger than any undertow.

Desire as a devouring force, as loss of self, as death-wish. The crazy urge to somehow submerge himself inside this ghost of a man he "knew" only from Google, apparently better than the guy knew himself; to dive in head-first, let all that sun-kissed Yank-ness wrap 'round him and sink 'til he either came out the other side, or smothered.

"Crazy" is right, Jesus.

"Smart to get yourself in there, though, in the first place," he heard himself say, numbly. "Shows presence of mind, and all that. I mean. . . you couldn't've known anybody'd be coming for you, not really."

The guy nodded. "Yeah, that makes sense, what you're saying. But I think . . . I must've hoped they'd come for the ship, anyhow. Cost a lot of money. Not the kind of thing you'd just . . . throw away."

"No," Sean agreed.

"It's yours now, though, I guess. Me, too."

All at once, that pulse was back, hammering twice as hard.

He can't mean what you think.

But: "What *do* you mean?" Sean found himself incapable of stopping himself from asking, shamefaced. To which the guy simply smiled, gently.

"Well . . . you found me. So, I guess —"

(*you get to keep me*)

Speech? Thought? Those five small words seemed to stone-skip through him like a bullet-fragment ricochet, cascading from ear to brain and straight back out again. Exiting through the lips, already opened wide, as they collided with the guy's own and stuck fast: Passing the same lust-flavored breath back and forth, back and forth, like sharing an air-bubble.

Oh God, let go. Oh God, don't.

Don't let me go.

Oh God.

They were the same height, give or take; pretty much the same build, 'specially after all that time on Shaftoe's cargo-before-crew starvation diet versus all that time — how long, exactly? — adrift. Even their hand-span a near-exact match, just wide enough for each to clasp the other's wrists without strain. Yet the contact alone was enough to sap Sean's reserves, dip the empty he'd apparently already been running on low enough he could feel himself vibrate; he clutched at the guy for dear life, tongues twining, holding on. Holding tight.

Because: *If you let me go, I'll fall. And . . . if I fall . . .*

. . . I'll drown, Sean thought, feeling his eyes roll back, his temples throb and sing. Practically goddamn *swooning.*

And time must've passed, without either even noticing. For a moment later he glanced back up to find Ric, looming large — already halfway lunged forward into their all-too-closely-shared personal space, raw eyes bugged 'til his lids started to slant the wrong way.

Uh oh.

A warning seemed in order, but his mouth was otherwise engaged. Besides, the juggernaut was well on its way; all they could do was make room. So Sean side-stepped, tried his best to swing the guy along with him, but only succeeded in turning him so he and Ric could lock gazes: Glazed and crazed to amiably mild, almost stoner-calm, swimming in endorphins. Should've gone over like a bong-hit, defusing the situation, and yet —

Ric simply froze, rigid, riveted. Neither angry nor jealous, anymore, but terrified.

What is he seeing? Not what . . . who . . . I am.

A rush and a push and the deck was cleared: Ric went past at high speed, *Demeter* first mate style, and folded over the rail as if he'd been stomach-punched. Sean grabbed for Ric's shoulder but felt it slip by, sweat-greased; felt the guy reaching down as well, yet saw Ric twist mid-plunge to avoid that grasping, offered hand. A strange cunning lit both irises, made them flash in recognition. Like:

I know you, now — don't see how I couldn't see it, before.

But you won't bloody get me, too.

Letting go, perfectly deliberate, Ric fell into darkness, hit the unseen water below with barely a splash. Sean made to follow, hollering:

"Ric, *fuck*, swim, you idiot! Grab for the Knot! Grab *hold*, you bloody fool!"

No reply, save the lapping waves. And a whisper that might've come from the guy whose strong arms were even now holding him back, making sure he wasn't going after poor, sleep-deprived idiot Ric . . . Ric, whose misfiring synapses had sent him off and running so hard he'd thrown his entire life away like trash, all to escape a damn dream . . .

Nothing out here to grab hold of, Sean. Just garbage soup, and plenty of it.

"Sharks'll get him," Sam-I-Am said from the wheelhouse door, with peculiar satisfaction. Like he'd just been waiting, all this time, for the pleasure of eventually getting to make *that* call.

Behind him, further down the staircase, Sean glimpsed both Arjit (pausing to spit, derisively, while perhaps wondering if he should join this impromptu all-hands-on-deck funeral) and Shaftoe (knuckling sleep from his eyes, dazed and confused, having apparently left his six-guns behind in his cabin), both staring upwards. Then everyone cringed at once, top-lit by the glare, as a flare split the night to illuminate a pair of small, sleek craft coming in dark off either bow, armed to the teeth. Didn't have to be sporting the Jolly Roger to know what *their* game was, either, way the hell out here, where there was nothing worth stealing but the trawler out from under them.

Sean did a double-take Shaftoe's way, wondering if he looked a bit like Ric had, before blurting: "No way in hell even *you*'d've been stupid enough to email reVive already, you stunned fucking cunt."

Shaftoe gulped. "I . . . just asked 'em if they wanted their property back," he managed. "Before the media got hold of it, and him . . . "

"Oh yeah. 'Cause there's absolutely *nothing* dicey looking 'bout an eco-boat that bloody *sinks*, is there? Nothing that reeks of corner-cutting, nothing that says: *I don't really give a toss so long's they stop telling me where not to dump, so please just make sure to drift off-radar when your rig falls apart, and stay there —*"

The guy nodded, slightly, like this was happening to somebody else entirely. "Does kinda seem that way, doesn't it? Man, Sean, you should be in GPA-Marine, or something."

Two steps saw Arjit up on deck next to Sam-I-Am, Shaftoe left wibbling in the gloom behind; he gave Sam a friendly cuff to the shoulder: *You 'n' me, eh? Only two brown boys on a ship of crazy whites!*

Sam-I-Am just shifted stance to ask out one side of his mouth:

"You *in* on this, man?"

Arjit shrugged. "They get the ship, we're home in a month, find a real damn job. Told ya it'd be better, this way."

"Oh, you think? Can't trust pirates, fool! We ain't worth the chain to sink us, to them scallywags."

"Chill, mate. Everything be fine. Just gotta . . . take care of a few things, first—"

Shaftoe, three steps behind as usual, seemed at last on the ragged brink of reacting to Arjit's confession when his former second-in-command pivoted to empty the *Bad Idea*'s own flare-gun—conveniently holstered nearby, for easy distress access—into his face. Though the flare's velocity was far too slow to penetrate anything, the effects were nonetheless startling: A bright red nitrate-magnesium flash, all hiss and burst, bouncing off-center to crush in Shaftoe's beak with a satisfying, gluey *crack* before ricocheting further, skipping down the hallway like a lit phosphorus-brick.

The "Captain" fell back, hair a-smoke, and out of sight—possibly dead, but Sean supposed that didn't much matter either way, now the rocket-exhaust trail had below-decks safely caught on fire. And at this answering signal, a volley of shots rang up from the starboard boat, along with a spatter of cheers.

Sam-I-Am clapped both hands over his mouth and heaved. "Fuck *me*, up, down and sideways—"

Sean contemplated cutting and running, just for a second, but there weren't a whole lot of places left to go. Besides which, the guy—*Grinnage*, goddamnit—

(Simon?)

—seemed spot-rooted, studying Arjit as though he were less threat than vaguely interesting problem, simply one more oddity in a days-long string.

"Got one of those handy for us, buddy?" he inquired, mildly.

Arjit shook his head and pulled a Glock from his waistband, advancing. "Nothing personal, man," he replied. "I mean, you already had the short end, what with that wreck 'n' all. But, see . . . those out there, they only got berth enough for two."

And here it's as though the dream drops back over him, a wall of water slopping down to place five fathoms' worth of highly welcome waver between himself and what happens next: How the guy, glancing back at him, raises a faint gold brow . . .

. . . and Christ-well sheds *himself somehow, flips inside-out, opens wide as a bifurcated cloak of lip, unwrapping a slimy heap of bones and muck that clatters to the boards and lies there steaming, an awful surprise gift. What's left launches itself at Arjit, tumbling from axis to axis, like it can't tell which way is up. As though it's used to dealing with a different grade of gravity, entirely,*

(but that can't happen)

(can't happen, not like that, not like)

(any of it, impossible, no no goddamn *no*)

And: Are there eyes *in those sockets, that same hypnotic green gone shucked and nude, unblinking? What the hell can it have left to see its way with now, if so?*

Arjit's a bastard, not dumb — pumps his whole clip into it, but nothing slows it down. Sam-I-Am, on the other hand, takes one look, and slams the wheelhouse door on 'em both. After's a second's hammering and cursing, Arjit turns right back into the thing, which hits him like a pizza-dough facial: submerges him completely, quick-digesting him from the outside in. Sean can hear him, muffled, through wads of flesh and cartilage, a kitten swung in a bag against unforgiving walls.

Drowning would be a fucking mercy, by comparison.

Eventually, the sounds stop. Sean looks up again, just in time to see whatever-it-is detach from — never mind, some grotesque hybrid of corpse and turd, like what you get when you peel a snake. Then tumble-splat, tumble-SPLAT as it heads for the wheelhouse, targeting that thread-sized crack under the door and squishing itself flat, flatter, so thin its molecular bonds almost separate. The privileges of bonelessness, caught in action.

From inside, Sean hears Sam-I-Am start to scream. But that doesn't last too fucking long, at all.

(oh god, I think it's coming back out)

Re-emerging, the creature flows back over its original sticky core-dump mess and reassembles itself, wetly; everything moves back into place with a series of clicks and pops, "the guy" re-emerging whole from an unrecognizable lump of goo—skin reversed and mainly blood-free, pinky-blond hair only slightly out of place. Those naked eyes pop back into their orbits, open, crinkle slightly.

"Hey," he—it—says.

Sean coughed, wrackingly, mouth gone drier than he'd been in a month. "Are you . . . gonna kill me?"

"Don't think so, no. You want me to?"

" . . . not like that."

A fresh rush of yells from the pirate peanut gallery—might be they saw what happened to Arjit; might be they didn't like it—proved weirdly easy to ignore, 'specially as Sean's brain raced to fill in the spaces, ever newer and dumber questions just rolling straight off his tongue with gumball-machine precision. "You're not . . . him, then. Simon Grinnage. Never were."

"No. I thought I was, but . . ." A shrug. "Guess it doesn't much matter now, really, what I thought. Or didn't."

"So—you just attached yourself to his corpse, that what happened? Grew into the shape of the hole he left, somehow?" Without waiting for a reply: "Is there anything of him still in there at all, in you?"

"Shit, Sean, I don't know. You saw when I—back there—" Sean nods. "—well, much as I'd like to think I'm at least some sort of composite, what came out . . . it felt like bones, to me."

"Looked like 'em, too."

"There you go, then."

Fresh flares went up, spotlighting this odd little triptych: Sean, Arjit's leavings. The thing, unnecessary clothes discarded—Sean couldn't remember where they'd gone—and now clad only in its own smeared blood-tracery, a pattern of red tattoos. More yells from the pirates followed, urgent-fearful, as though they somehow recognized it.

"Don't s'pose you could take 'em all," Sean suggested, only half-joking.

"Unlikely. But . . . " It glanced over at the *Green Phoenix* rig. "Could just get back inside that and hit the water. Did okay, last time."

"*You* could, mate. Simon didn't come off quite so well, though, did he?"

Swapping banter in the face of death, or worse . . . much worse. Yet Sean still can't find it in him to fear, not completely; every breath he draws seems to say it means no harm to him, if no one else. Something chemical, probably, borne on the hot and stinking wind—something it probably doesn't even need, underwater. Pheromones, designed to attract landbound prey by making the thing seem lovable? Or spores drifting up his nose to root in his cortex, then bloom and puppet him consumption-wards, the way Brazilian zombie fungi turn ants into living seeders?

"*I still want to touch you,*" *he tells it, helplessly.* "*Even now.*"

"*Me too.*"

"*Why?*"

"*I don't know, Sean—how do I know anything? I just do. Everything Simon knew, most of what you know . . . what Arjit knew, and Sam-I-Am. And Ric.*"

"*So that was you, then? The dream?*"

It shapes that easy, white-toothed SoCal smile. "Who else?"

On the port boat, someone raises an Armalite's massive barrel, bracing it against their shoulder: The Bad Idea's *off-limits now, apparently, not worth salvaging. Infected, possibly infectious. And they'll get the contract fee either way, Sean can only think, so long as what's left of the* Phoenix *goes down with the rest.*

"Too late," the thing confirms, stepping closer. "But . . . I really do want you to come with me, Sean. I want you. *I think . . . I kinda want to be you . . . "*

(oh)

(oh God, me too)

. . . is what Sean replies, in that last second before the rocket ignites. Or maybe he only thinks he does.

The explosion cracks the deck in half; the prow goes up, stern down, Titanic *in reverse. And as they fall together Sean grabs his long-drowned demon lover by both elbows—its arms come up like a toddler, like a trap. It latches on.*

Together, they step down, holding fast, joined at the lips. Until the trash-strewn waters close, kiss-warm and -soft, over both their heads.

Falling and falling and falling, forever, with nothing left to break against. With no hope of an impact, an ending.

Sean and the thing—heavier than it looked, by far—rode cold currents torn from the ocean's floor, winding upwards to capture the Knot's turnover, its increasingly brisk gyre. They nudged past confused sharks, kicked aside scraps of Ric, barely escaped being grazed or brained by various pressure-driven trawler-bits. They sank through fathoms, sharing air, light and air narrowing together in one last spasm—then winking out, the same way each synapse inside Sean's brain had already begun to flare and crisp and die, like bone-jarred fireflies.

Thinking: *I'll be him, I guess, or he'll be me; close enough. Too close for even him to tell. So it'll be as though one of us survives, anyhow . . .*

. . . as his grip kept on steadily tightening, pulling it ever-closer, bruising it 'til the skin-suit folded back and all he held were Simon Grinnage's bones, before heaving to enwrap him once more . . . smothering him in a heat that was fever and spice and slime alike, pulsing organs fluttering like mouths against every part of him as its spiny heart suckered fast to his breastbone, eating its way inside . . . the mere unfiltered scent of it enough to make his own blood boil in his hemorrhaging eyes, his gouting ears screech like dolphins before they popped and his trouser-caught cock to finally explode, perhaps even literally...

Praying, all the while: *Don't let me go, please. Never let me go. Don't let me drown.*

(*I don't want to drown, not now*)

(*not like this*)

(*not*)

(*without you*)

Down there, in the deep and dark, where everything blended with everything else. Down where trash became treasure, and vice versa. Where flesh was eaten, over and over again, in endless communion; where prey and predator alike became bone, fossil, sand. Where currents bore him away in every direction at once, hoping against hope that nothing was ever lost, only changed. That the ocean, though a cornucopia of miracles and horrors—like death, like love—

(for all that it *had* a floor, one which he might never reach)

—might yet prove to have no real bottom.

Ghost Pressure

"HOW D'YOU LIKE it here, gran?" young Kristle was forever asking her, to which Gavia Pratt ("Not missus, just miss, or nurse, if you prefer") would only reply: "Doesn't rain enough." Which it didn't by a long shot, though the days were certainly overcast, air water-heavy and gray, sinus pressure forever shifting like the beginning of the bends. Still, a lake wasn't the sea and couldn't be; she missed Blackpool, the pier, cold wind and sting of salt, always bracing even with bad tourist karaoke bawling in the background, plus the sound of amusements-with-prizes going off in the distance every thirty seconds like a layered choir of tiny electronic car alarms.

She'd been in Toronto almost six months now, sent by the Hermes Lifequality head office to help structure their primary Canadian outreach, a task which mainly consisted of vetting care-workers, matching them with assignments, coaching debriefers or debriefing them herself. It was a tightknit group thus far, funded through a mixture of benefactor donations and fees from global pharmaceutical companies looking to test new pain-management product variations on subjects unlikely to complain if anything went wrong; eggs and omelets, all that. Did get the job done, though, which was more than she could say for her staff, on occasion.

"What you have to remember is, palliative care's not all about *you*," she told them, what felt like over and bloody over. "Can't be, not and work the way it has to. So be present for *them*, and keep all the chat about your own fine feelings for me, thank you very much—it's what I'm here for, isn't it? One way or t'other, these things do come with a time limit; you'll make yours, you just try hard enough. Or if not, I'll rotate you offsite and find someone else who can, no harm, no foul. That's guaranteed right in the contract, case you didn't think to look before you signed it."

They were mainly soft, this lot, most of 'em; you'd think they'd never seen anyone die at all, 'less it were on the telly. But they did tend to have these very specific *ideas* about the process, nevertheless—touchy feely, broadbase "spiritual" without benefit of church, all candles and incense and white light, total Serenity Prayer faff. Some even preferred to be called end-of-life doulas, if you could believe the cheek: exit midwife, was it? These young girls. Nothing ever good enough.

Like a lot of her peers back home, Gavia'd rotated through a gross of other counselling services before eventually settling at Hermes—Samaritans, Adfam, ElderCare. Everything from emotional distress to right-to-die work for Exit International, though that was on her own time, of course. Her NHS background stood her in good stead, along with the experiential legacy of those wild teenaged years that'd seen her saddled with Kristle's father before she reached the grand old age of nineteen. And now, thanks to the same lovely girl's fine practical judgment about whether or not it was worth reaching for a rubber one drunken night out, she was a great-grandmother at barely fifty: tall, gray, and grim, striding 'round this silly city with her coat barely buttoned, sweating like a human hot flash. Probably would've had to be here anyhow, but she could've stood not to have to change nappies on her off-time while she was.

Right at this moment, though, her phone said 4:05; time for . . . Jaiden, if she recalled correctly. One of the better sorts, a butch little number who dressed like Elvis circa *Heartbreak Hotel*. She got out the file.

"So," Gavia began, "this makes a month you've been with Mister Zukauskas, by my count. How're you getting on?"

"Uh, pretty well, I'd say. He's got late-onset Alzheimer's and Stage Four lung cancer, so it's all about keeping him happy, at this point—

less *un*happy." Gavia nodded. "Stopped eating last week, so we have him on a drip, and we moved from transdermal fentanyl patches to oral morphine; added haloperidol to stop the nausea and vomiting. But now we're past the first three days we're just on a prophylactic laxative to clean him out, and I discontinued that today."

"You're dayshift, yeah? And that starts when?"

"Five A.M."

"So you're off early today."

"I . . . asked the night-shift guy to come in early, cover for me. Sayyid. Because I wanted more time to talk to you."

"Oh, aye? About what?"

Jaiden paused for a moment, seeming to think; Gavia felt the urge to tap her pen, mark off however many seconds it took, but resisted it. Her AA Agnostics twenty-year was coming up fast and she'd been feeling the pull all week, cycling through various coping techniques 'til she could get back to her original sponsor rather than rely on one here, though she took as many meetings as seemed useful, in the interim. Tonight's was at that odd little Heritage building church sandwiched between the DoubleTree by Hilton hotel and the Eaton Centre, but Gavia didn't think she could make it before needing to get home and relieve the babysitter she'd arranged for instead of chipping in on rent, so Kristle could work that ridiculous "acting" job she'd gotten and pretend she was still paying her own way . . .

"You know much about Lithuania, Miss Pratt?" Jaiden asked, finally. Gavia shrugged.

"Used to be Soviet, now it isn't; next to Latvia, I think, or Poland, or both. Why?"

"Well, Zukauskas is from there—his family snuck out around 1952, after the war, when he was like twenty. Came over with his mom, his little brother and his wife, so they've been married sixty years plus. His Dad died in a camp. And I know all this 'cause he told me, right, 'cause he talks *all* the time, like pretty much non-stop, except for when he's asleep . . ."

"Old people do tend to, yeah, even when they're not dyin'."

"Which I get, I remember that from the prep course, the materials. But . . . " Another beat. "Then, last week actually, right before he went all liquid diet, he starts telling me different stuff, weird stuff. Like folklore, fairytales. Except he's not telling them about once upon a time, or some sh—crap, he's telling them about him*self*. His life. His . . . wife."

"What about her?"

"Well, that she's like—a nightmare. By which I mean she's not a person? Like, not even human. That's she's this *thing*, called a Slogutė or a Naktinėja . . ." Jaiden pronounced the words carefully, almost phonetically, with a hint of what Gavia could only assume was the old man's accent: *slow-GOO-teh-eh, nacktee-NEH-EH-yah.* "This creature that, like, comes through the keyhole and oppresses people while they're sleeping. How his mom used to tell him he had to protect himself by getting into bed sideways, like a crab, or she'd sneak into their house and sit on the youngest person in the family 'til they died—"

"Sounds like classic night terrors to me, with a little bit of cats suckin' baby's breath thrown in for good measure."

"Yeah, me too, at first. So I just nod and smile and go 'uh huh,' basically, same way you taught us to. But—he just won't stop, keeps going on and on. And the *really* creepy part is that his wife? She's in the *room*, while all this is happening. Like, right there, in the corner."

"Does she hear what he's tellin' you? Can she even speak English?"

"I don't *know*, Miss Pratt. I mean, I've never talked to her, but that doesn't mean much; she's just always *there*. I actually don't think I've ever seen her anywhere else in the house, or seen her leave the room, either. Just sits there knitting the whole time, and never even looks up."

"Odd she isn't mentioned on the intake form." Off Jaiden's look, Gavia sighed, and spun her the document. "See? Nowhere."

"Well, I don't know what to tell you; she exists. About his age, and little, like this high—" She sketched a figure whose head might come up to Gavia's armpit, at best. "Looks nice, normal. Old lady with her hair pulled up under a scarf. Nothing remarkable about her at all."

"A nightmare," Gavia repeated, and was slightly heartened to see Jaiden smile, at least a little: sidelong, self-deprecating. Like she couldn't quite believe she was still going on about all this.

"It *is* normal, y'know, this," she told her, comforting as her basic personality would allow for. "Clients start flushin' out their heads, by the end; doesn't mean anything, no more than froth from something bein' boiled. And eventually it's all boiled away, froth as well, so you can wash the pot out and start over."

"Uh huh."

"I mean, if it's really bothering you, I *can* see about gettin' you moved—"

"—'cause that's in the contract, right, I know, but . . . I don't; I'm not… That's, uh, not what I'm trying to . . . "

Here she ran down for another few moments, face contorted, puzzled. As though she was sounding her next words through in her head, or trying to decide for herself how the whole thing made her feel. Continuing, finally—

"Mister Zukauskas says he had three little brothers and sisters, to begin with, and she—the Slogutė, his wife—killed them all, or that's what his mom said, at the time. And granted, things were really bad in Lithuania back then, so it could just as easily have been, like, pneumonia, or starvation, or freakin' typhoid fever from drinking water with sewer waste in it, or whatever. But one night he stayed awake while everybody else was asleep and he watched the keyhole, and he saw her come in through it, twisting in the air like a ribbon. And when she tried to wrap herself 'round the bed where his little brother was, he caught her in a trap he'd made out of pages from an old Bible, so old it still had the Book of Tobit in it. And he told her if she didn't agree to marry him and leave his family alone, he was gonna throw the whole thing in the stove fire and burn her up, and then she'd just be gone forever—no heaven, no hell, no nothin'. And I guess she said yes, 'cause they've been together ever since."

"Now, Jaiden—"

"So he's telling me this, right? And then he says he's happy he's dying, finally, 'cause no matter where he ends up, there's no way she can follow him; says all this time he's been suffering, she's waited 'til he's asleep and then pressed on his chest, given him awful dreams and suffocated him 'til he can't sleep anymore so he's had chronic insomnia for over sixty years—and that, that *is* in the file, I know, 'cause I checked." Words spilling out, faster and faster, and the more they did the more Gavia was inclined to simply let 'em 'til Jaiden ran herself down—sit back a bit, narrow her eyes, and watch her go on as long as she needed to. "But he feels bad too, right, 'cause then she'll be free to start doing what she was doing before, back when. So he says to me, 'can you take her?' Like, 'I know you like women. She can be beautiful, she can be whatever you want. It's a hard bargain, but there are rewards.' And I'm just . . . "

"Sounds like clear grounds for a sexual harassment suit, you ask me."

"No, I mean—I don't think he means it like that. It's just . . . I'm getting afraid, 'cause now *I'm* having these dreams, almost every night, and I feel like I'm going to wake up one morning, go into work and find out he died during the night, and then she'll just *be* there in my apartment when I come home, you know? Like she's come to stay with me, forever, and I never even got the chance to say no before she starts in to *pressing* on me—"

Gavia raised her hands, then, fingers spread. Told her shivering charge, voice gentle as it ever went: "Jaiden, love, breathe. Just take a minute. *Breathe*, yeah? It's hardly the end of the world, y'know."

"No?"

"No. Not by a long shot."

Two hours later, Gavia was finally on her way back to Kristle's, still debating the best way to deal with Jaiden's odd troubles in her head. 'Cause it really was *not* about her, so much, as it was about the case: Zukauskas's final process, with its built-in time limit. If Jaiden was still able to see that through—and nothing she'd told Gavia truly gave her to understand the opposite—then there was no problem. The man was terminal, had no heirs to complain about her behavior, let alone his; pretty soon he'd be gone, and all this'd be gone too, along with him. Meaning that though her most cautious instincts might say to move Jaiden on, this current situation wouldn't *last*, unless Jaiden let it.

Working with the soon-to-die was upsetting, after all, inherently so. Reminded people of their own mortality—the ghost inside, their flesh's frailty, senescence in action. Entropy. Universal pressure wearing away at 'em all, same's the sea did the shore, visible in every mirror. Couldn't penalize the poor bint for reacting to *that* cold revelation, could she?

Well, in every strictly legal sense, yeah, she could; had a perfect right to, right there in black and white, uncontestable. But in this particular instance, she wouldn't.

Stopping on the corner of Kristle's side street, Gavia cast a slightly longing look over the local dive bar's way: classic all-day drinkers' haven, the type she'd spent a good deal of her twenties in. Had a moment's clear impulse to go in, order a gin and tonic, then sit there looking at it 'til some poor sod came over to chat her up, at which point she'd simply get up and leave him there with it, as a donation for wasting his time. Last occasion she'd put herself through that rigmarole, playing it out like a ritual from some long-lapsed religion, had to've been . . . five years back, at the very least. So, she supposed Jaiden's little fairytale must've had her feeling a trifle fragile on some level, not that that necessitated doing anything about it.

Felt a cold wind at her back all of a sudden, and not from the weather, either. But: *Aw, get on with you, old woman,* she told herself, scornfully. *Never anything in the dark weren't there in the light, and no mistake.*

So up she went instead, feeling for her keys.

The sitter, Karen, was curled up on the couch with one of Kristle's books, some twenty-quid fantasy soap opera hardback big enough to kill a rat with; she unclasped herself slowly, yawning. "Hi, Miss Pratt," she said. "Kristle called to say she's gonna be late again—they've got her walking lights for set-up, or something like that."

"Oh, aye? Don't s'pose she's bein' *paid* for her trouble, at least."

A shrug. "Minimum wage; still, industry work, right? So that's something."

"Hm, yeah. How much she owe you, exactly?"

"Two-twenty?"

Sighing a bit at the expense, Gavia paid her, saw her out, locked the door carefully behind. Then went into Gavin's room to peep in on the poor little mite, fast asleep and snoring with his chubby fists up in the air, like he was boxing God. The name had been a nice touch, on Kristle's part—almost as though she'd been coached in it, already knowing Gavia would need to stop over for a good chunk of the year, checkbook in hand. Which, by turns, only served to remind Gavia how in some ways, her ever-so-respectable schoolteacher son could be very much like that feckless bloody "entrepreneur" bugger of a father of his indeed; not that she'd more than barely allowed the two to know *of* each other, let alone bond. She still saw the latter up and down the pier sometimes back home, flashing the charm and cadging cash out of punters with a chippie on either arm, looking more like some Vegas preacher than the gangly young rockabilly thug she'd once fallen pregnant by. Ten to one he still had that quote from "Ring of Fire" tattooed on his arm, though, under his nice suits: *I was bound by wild desire . . .*

But enough of that: tea, then paperwork, then sleep. Tomorrow started early, like always.

Waking to dreaming was a dim slide, barely perceptible, like floating to sinking. Then the dark behind Gavia's eyes bloomed up, became a door whose keyhole hung perhaps waist level, perhaps lower, through which a feeble, dreadful light of no discernible hue leaked like poison — and soon enough, something fluttered behind it, visible only from the corner of her eye, giving her to know she was not alone, for all she might dearly wish to be. The knowledge, washing overtop her in one choking wave, that someone — something — sat beside and a trifle behind, unbreathing yet undeniable, with all its considerable focus kept trained at one itchy point on her back: not her spine nor the rhomboideus next to it, neither trapezius above nor serratus below, and not quite her shoulderblade's bony wing, either. Some cluster of nerves, perhaps, unfurling like a knot made from pain to catch and hook, spiral itself deeper, unstring the various parts of her like pegless puppet-pieces. And hurting, hurting, all the way through: colder than undertow or tide, than barely-melted ice, than frozen gut-blood slurry off the decks of fisher boats. Colder even than her own long dead father's heart, when he waited all night in the maternity ward for her to wake up after her caesarian, just so's he could tell her to her face how no bastard's bastard would ever set foot in *his* house, Gavia Jane Pratt...

Something plucking at her now, filtering down through fathoms, a too bright skewer popped in and twisted, over and over again. The squeal of a thousand pigs. Or, better yet —

(the bloody phone)

And up she came again, like a popped cork. Back out into the real world, brow wet, arm already flailing for the receiver.

"Yeah? Gavia Pratt, this is, from Hermes Lifequality. Who? Oh, Sayyid — he's one of mine, yeah. Put him on, please." A second of silence to let both breath and pulse slow as she waited. Then Sayyid's Arabic lilt, more exasperated than upset: "Sorry to disturb so early, Miss Pratt —"

Reflexively, she glanced at the red LEDs of the clock radio: 5:45 AM. Could be worse. Then memory clicked. "Jaiden left you to cover her shift again? Might've let the switchboard know . . . " Trailed off, suddenly thinking: *But that's not like her, really—not after today.*

"I do not think it matters if she arrives or not, very much. Mister Zukauskas is dead."

That set her back. She'd never had much use for the typical euphemisms—"passing on," or "away"—but they were taught not to be so blunt, 'specially in front of other people; then again, that first voice had had an EMT's impersonal professionalism, or a cop's. "What happened?"

A sigh. "I checked on him at three-thirty; he was still breathing at that point, his wife in her chair, as always. I thought she had gone to sleep. Made sure the call button was under his hand, then went downstairs, where I . . . also closed my eyes, but only for a moment, that was my intent. When I woke it was a few minutes past the hour, and when I went upstairs, he was gone."

"The wife?"

"Gone as well. I called paramedics, as per S.O.P.—"

"Wait—not in the house? She's much the same age, Jaiden said; not likely to wander off, I'd think."

"Quite old, yes, but nevertheless. An emotional break? Nothing seems taken, so I've no doubt the lady will return, but Jaiden knows her better than I do, to a degree. Perhaps, if and when she arrives…"

A shadow moved in the hallway, sliding down the wall towards Gavin's room. Gavia shrugged it off, sure it must be Kristle going to check on the boy—then stopped, all at once realizing she could hear Kristle's snores, from the main bedroom.

What is *that?*

"'Scuse me a moment, Sayyid," she said, voice low, and put the phone down sideways 'cross the cradle, not quite hanging it up.

Been a long time gone since she'd gotten herself in (or out of) trouble, but fear's spike brought all the old tricks rushing forwards. She grabbed up that brick of a book Karen'd left behind on the end table— do for a club to the face, in a pinch—and slid soundless off the couch, stalking quiet, balanced on the balls of her feet. Gavin's door'd been shut, she done that herself, but it now stood open. Fingers clenched 'round the book's spine, aching with effort, Gavia lifted it high and was 'cross the threshold in one quick stride, poised to strike at whatever she might find —

But all that greeted her was a woman, completely unfamiliar, plain gray coat belted under her high little breasts like an Empire gown and neither young nor old, at first glance: small-framed yet upright, hair hung down dark in a double curtain, soft as smoke. She stood there staring down into Gavin's crib, transfixed, as though he were something far less ordinary, more precious, than a mere sleeping baby — 'til Gavia made some small noise, at least, alerting her to her presence. And even then, she didn't *turn*, per se; just cocked her head, birdlike, to glance back over her shoulder and smile, very faintly.

"Such handsome boy," this creature told Gavia, accent vaguely Baltic. "*Such* lovely place you have here, with family, even so far from home — *so* very lucky you are, *mažai močiutė*. Your life here is pleasant dreaming, surely."

Grip failing, muscles gone slack, the book Gavia clutched came wavering back down, abruptly too heavy to hold; that black wave swept back up and over in one vertiginous rush, frost and tide and pain, a scraping, keening rush of sound. Memory, swirling headlong into words; Jaiden's voice, cautious but driven, once more telling her how *I'm afraid I won't even get the chance to say no, before she just starts in to* pressing *on me . . .*

But: "Who're you?" Gavia husked, or tried to — abruptly gone all vowels, throat constricted-thick with indignation. "What d'you — what y' *want*, here? Whuh, whaaah . . ."

The woman shook her head, however. Put one scar-white, nailless finger to her own lips — one of six, Gavia now saw, on either delicate hand — before reaching out to lay it on Gavia's instead, bisecting her mouth in mid-protest like a sharp downward cut, a needle-thrust, a still-burning brand.

Not fair, she might well've complained, if only her tongue would allow it; why *her,* for Christ's own sake, of all people, to be selected for recompense—she who'd never even set foot in Zukauskas's house, let alone heard him boast of his ancient crime? Why not Jaiden, who'd worked the contract and listened to the stories, who already knew this fast-unraveling shell of a thing—this pretty nightmare, this swan-queen re-feathered, this selkie without a skin—by sight?

Salt in her lungs, a wet gasp, swallowed under fathoms; pain in her chest, her heart, light and hollow, dank and deep. Kristle'd find her drowned on dry land by sunrise, no doubt, with Gavin suffocated in his sleep nearby and no possible hope of a swap even were she able to beg one out loud, no last-minute offering up of old for new. For nightmares, Gavia well knew, were rarely so logical, and cruel by default.

Better by far to try and fail than not to try at all, though. She could do *that,* at the very least.

Letting go book-first, skeptic and practical Gavia Pratt fell by slow degrees, a tree toppling, doing her level best to broadcast, all the way to the floor: *Not him, me, take* me. *I'll even marry you, that's what you're lookin' for again; marry or burn, either way. Down down down with no attempt at protest, into that ring of fire . . .*

Whilst the woman, in turn—Zukauskas's wife no longer—only let that smile of hers widen in return 'til the whole front of her head fell open, a hole of stars through which only a dim black beach could be glimpsed, far away in the distance: some empty world, stretched out dead and cold under a faint white sun, irregular-shaped and pale-shining as the top of a baby skeleton's soft skull.

COFFLE

If you get hungry enough, they say, you start eating your own heart.
— Margaret Atwood.

IT WAS AN old word, "coffle"—come down all the way from before-time, years on years. Old Gerun, the man at whose knee Ardenne had learned it, used to call it historical. But to Ardenne it was no mystery; every slave knew the thing well, if not the proper term for it: a chain long enough for ten or more, maybe twenty all cuffed at the ankle, set short and shuffling. She'd walked that way a mile or more when only ten, driven to market at whip's stroke by indifferent herders and sold for a handful of meds, like so many others. Like the ones she led now, roped together into a coffle of their own, for which she played driver and navigator both.

That first chain they'd worn unwilling, but this one—this was by choice, a desperate mutual gamble, slim chance of life cheated out from living death. They tied themselves to it by pairs, then followed Ardenne's lead across the sands with hands knotted tight, no doubt hoping to hell she knew just what it was she was doing, all the while.

Ardenne might've hoped so too, by now. But it was a hard enough thing to steal yourself into freedom, let alone go back and steal upwards of fifteen or twenty others more, over and over again.

They'd fled the Rim-town named the Mount at nightfall, when

Ardenne's drugged 'shine had left the pen-guards a-snooze, giving them most of the night for a headstart. The catch-corps chased them hard the first three days as a matter of course, knowing that'd be the best time to catch property in mid-run. But Ardenne had her tricks — some learnt at other guides' elbows, the rest all hard experience — and set dangers in their way they were hard-put to see coming: sand-traps to snare, unexploded ordnance to damage, the same fearful truck of predators and poison that usually kept Rim-towners from the wild. All those bad things from which worse things caged themselves, with stop-gap measures like walls, weapons and other folks' used-up bodies set in between.

Out on the sand, meanwhile . . . there was silence, sanctuary, peace of the self-damned. The tainted, fearful protection of the Patch, that place no sane person chose to go unless they absolutely had to, seeking freedom or death, with nothing in between.

You felt it the moment you stepped out onto the Patch's sands, under the white-burnt sky, humming up through your bootheels like some mournful sound from deep inside the earth itself. Word was a shell hit here, viral-loaded — one of those everything-but-the-sink cock-tails they'd been mixing by War's end, with no time to test it except in action. Those tiny, bloodborne sick-seeds that made it up, those "nanites" first crafted to keep the wounded alive but warped to make them weapons instead, had made this whole area one huge open grave home to a million jostling corpse-husks — a dead horde forever bent on tearing apart whatever live bait came their way, along with spreading whatever awfulness kept them upright yet one body further.

So then the Old Folks dropped blast-bombs, burnt the place down to ash and hot glass. But the nanites remained, sowed too deep to boil away, rebuilding themselves to feed off the self-same invisible fire meant to kill them. They lurked forever, ready to catch the unwary and make them over into ravening monsters; there was no escape, no hid-ing — mere hours in the Patch, and they were in you, poised to take you within minutes of death however you died. Which was what made this ill-fate route the perfect path away from slavery, Ardenne had found, at first only to her own benefit: one everybody else, fled goods squads and catch-corps very much included, would always fear to tread.

Ardenne had been across the Patch five times now, not counting her own liberation-voyage, when she'd run from the Mount's trade-stops alone, barely into her breeding years, with nothing but her last owner's knife and a supply of hoarded food. Which was how, even before realizing her freedom's true vocation lay in helping others make the same trip, she'd already understood in her very bones that the trick was spending your time and miles wisest, reckoning almost to the second how long you could stay Patch-hid without falling ill, or travel ill without dying.

Of course, she'd never had a pregnant slave along for the ride before, especially one so close to her time—but no more than halfway through this trip's first meetup, Ardenne'd been forced to admit that Heba's pleading had already gotten to her, much as she knew it was a decision every one of them might come to regret before journey's end. Luckily, one of the older cook-women—May, her name was, Ardenne reminded herself—had volunteered to play escort right away, monitor Heba's signs, so the others wouldn't have to worry themselves about it. But that would only go so far, once embarked. With every fresh step, the Rim fell behind, farther and farther. Which meant that from now on, they'd all just have to wait and see if the poor girl's get would wait for less sour climes to drop, or die on the way, turn, and tear itself free.

"Keep up," Ardenne told her coffle of fled-goods as they groped along behind her, yoked each to each and sidestepping, to leave as little trail behind as possible. "That's the real rule and regulation here—no time for rest, not 'til the other side. We travel days and nights too, doze in shifts, get as much under us as we can without dyin'. We don't aim to stick around."

"No'm," they replied, almost in unison.

Raising her voice, sharper: "*Mind* me, too, each and every one, or I'll drop your ass quick and move on, leave you to keep the catch-corps busy. I can lose half of you and still feel lucky, 'long as the rest stay moving."

"Yes'm."

"All right, then."

So they moved forward by strides, stalking and slipping, hung grimly on by their white clenched knuckles as the rope wore their palms raw, oozing with blood. The sun overhead burnt low even at its height, hot as flinders, peering through cloud like a veil.

Cliffs rose here and there like exposed bone, low breaks they could huddle against when the winds rose and the sands began to blow. No water worth the drinking, which was why Ardenne carried half her own weight in liquid nutrient, mixed thick enough to chew on. One swallow apiece, every four hours: that was what her teacher had set as standard, so that she kept to. Some argued, but only the once or twice, before sheer exhaustion ground 'em down.

"Keep up," she repeated, as the sun crept horizontal. "Night's long out here, and the sands don't rest. Hands on the rope; don't wander. Piss where you stand, or you'll never find your way back."

She'd left with twenty, calculating to save ten. In the morning there were eighteen.

Ardenne stared down, committing her casualties to memory, making herself recall their details. The rest of the coffle shuffled uneasily, muttering at arm's length.

Kolya, she thought, looking at the man's scarred face. *He tended livestock. Wanted to make the far side, see if his friend who ran ten years back was there. And Etta, who left two of her own behind, a daughter and a son* — the one sold away already at eight or nine years old, for fieldwork; her Master's Number Two Wife took the other, fostered him, planned to raise him up as whipping boy for her own baby. *Good breeder, Etta, two kids into a five-child minimum. And didn't even like men.*

No sign of what'd killed them, but that wasn't uncommon out here. Thirst, heat, pace, haply all three. She tried very hard not to think the other, harder thought that wouldn't keep silent: *Still, more feed-draught to go 'round for the rest of us, at least.*

"You'll have your stones in the pile," Ardenne told them, so quiet it was almost under her breath. "Write your names on myself, I promise you that. I'll read 'em every week, and pour out for you, too—water, blood, whatever's handy. Whisky too, if I can get it, just like all the rest."

The moment passed, her empty prayer said; Ardenne sniffed hard, raised up her head, shrugged to clear it. Then stuck her knife through the dead ones' eyes, to scramble what was behind. The Patch's nanites needed a brain with all its nerve-paths close to intact, so destroying that organ—as much of it as you could, anyhow—was the only real way to guarantee both bringing down the dead who'd already started to walk and keeping the ones due to rise from doing so. Decapitation worked too, but it was a difficult proposition without an axe or the like handy. Simply thrusting your blade through the eye socket worked just as well, especially if you jerked it up and down and swirled it 'round after, like stirring stew. Like *this.*

There was still brain-tissue on her blade when she cut Etta's and Kolya's bodies loose. She led the others on, ignoring the whispers and mutters.

What Ardenne had known of the Patch beforehand she'd learned from Gerun, Old Master's history-man, an educate turned indenture as punishment for some unknown crime. He'd obviously tried to run at least one time since, as shown by the fact he'd been hamstrung and now had to pull himself 'round on his knees with crushed feet fused like flippers, shins all gone to scab. Thus supposedly tamed, he'd been reduced to tutoring those slaves set aside for bed-sale who New Master thought to market on promise of good conversation, and Ardenne'd managed to sit in on his classes just by manning the fans while keeping her head low, playing human furniture.

They had that much in common, just tools for any free-born to use, though Gerun at least got to talk. But the old man'd soon spotted her mouth moving silently, trying to memorize whatever she could and tucking it away for later, so he'd put in an ask for her nighttime company and drawn her a map on the floor, murmuring — in between feigned bout-noises —

See here, that's the Shallows, with enough glass and stone underneath wheels can drive on it without slipping . . . but after this range and this, the Two Horns, that's where it deepens out, where the sandpits come, so they won't be able to follow you much further. Things move and shift in the Reach, gal; gotta feel your way, bring a stick long enough to drive down three feet at least, find those big chunks of glass to step on. Walk sidelong and slow for as long as you can, one to the next, and if you feel the current suck you down, take care you don't panic. You can swim a long time, long as you keep yourself regular. Just remember: the more you thrash, the faster you'll sink . . .

That was the Patch writ small, really — that one line. And Ardenne never forgot it, same as she still kept Gerun's map scribed inside her brain. She'd added to and subtracted from it more times than she could count, since, in memory of the tough old bastard who'd given her the tools she needed to wrest herself free.

Though Ardenne of all people knew slaves didn't have much to pay their way with, meanwhile, she always charged for her services — a low fee, sure, but never no rate at all. Her logic was that when you were born for sale, or made to feel so, cash money was the only way you learned to reckon self-worth; she hadn't had that thought disproved thus far, on any of her ventures. And one way or the other, once the trip was done, she could salve her soul just a little by making sure to hand most of it back at the end, so the trip's survivors had something to start their new lives with.

To the coffle's faces, she pretended to not care to know them beyond their names, if that far. To herself, meanwhile, she made careful note of their details, folding it all away for later record. She recalled every one of her losses, making sacrifice later in their memory: a cairn of rocks outside her home stood marker, even if nothing else remained. For the Patch was a harsh place to die, even in hopeful forward motion, unfit burial-ground for any but the very worst—catch-corps, traders, Masters. Those she'd consign there gladly, leaving them to roam and rot without even her knife's grace, aside from a brief pause to cut their sins into their faces, if she had time to waste on it.

That was the way of it, the necessary methodology, for this to work: make yourself hard, pull scab over wound; be hell-tough, or seem so. Tough as each slave-string needed her to be, no more or less, to see them safely free on the Patch's far side.

"People say this desert's made from bone, ground fine," that one boy spoke up—Reed, the butcher's apprentice—as they sat panting in a glass shelf's shallow shade, sun licking at them through its scratched-up lens like a distant fire. "That true, you know of?"

Ardenne kept herself from sighing, but only just. "Not that I was told. Sand is glass—look 'round, see the lightning-strikes?" She gestured, taking in a bloom of twisted glass marking horizon-distance, black as burnt wood. "Fulgurites, they call 'em. Bone won't grow those."

"Bone mixed with them nanite-bugs might," Heba weighed in, suddenly, making Ardenne remember she had nurse training. She'd been posted in her Master's medical, running machines, helping the doc make sure only good stock came to term and the rest miscarried without damage, scheduling the ones who only ever bred wrong for spaying; three strikes and you're barren, just like at New Master's. "The Old Folks made 'em from germs, too small to see—breathe 'em in, it changes you, meat-deep. Makes your get born different." She swept a look back and forth, narrowing her eyes still further. "Lots of people lived here once, before the bombs hit. Could be, this's all that's left of 'em."

Ardenne gave her a nod back. "Maybe. Wouldn't matter much either way, though—would it?"

" . . . guess not."

"Well, then."

They sat 'til the light dimmed, sun making its way down slow, just past the apex. Then Ardenne stood, shrugging herself clean, and beckoned; the coffle started on its way once more, tracing her steps slowly, while she felt out pits with her pike.

"I saw some kid, back there," Heba managed, panting slightly, next time they paused. "Up on the ridge, hid behind an outcrop. Watching us."

"No kids 'round here," Ardenne answered, not lifting her eyes from the ground. "*Nobody* 'round here, not for miles. Just mile on mile of empty sand and dead folks, and they don't watch, either—they *come*, they happen to spot you. Fast and hungry, and they don't stop."

Most of the rest nodded too, at that. But Heba still shook her stubborn head, one hand cupped around her swollen belly, the other on the rope.

"I know my own eyes," she maintained.

A half-mile on, however, Ardenne found herself scanning the next ridge for signs of anything that might've set Heba envisioning. The heat-haze was up, doubling every line and making it flicker, down to and including the shadow barely glimpsed beneath her own feet; a bright scrim fell over the world, dazzle striking sharp wherever her eye might choose to linger. And there, right there, in the middle distance... *something* was, clear enough to catch and scratch, like sand under-lid: a tiny figure sunk on its haunches with pin-hole eyes in a barely-there smudge of face, head cocked sidelong as a hunting dog's, studying their progress.

"Stop!" Ardenne barked, and the coffle lurched to a halt. She teased free her oculars, raised them up and let the lenses adjust, squinting against the glare.

Too far off for rifle-range, whatever it was, even if she'd had a gun. Even through the viewfinder, its face was still rendered sketchy by sheer distance, all bone-ridge mask around a set of unblinking pits. No gear, so unlikely to be a catch-corps scout — she'd have to pursue it to tell, and she couldn't see much point to that action. So a dead one, she could only assume, but . . . the way it sat there, hunkered down, for all the world like it found them fascinating far above and beyond their simple tastiness, their infection-potential . . .

"What is it?" one of the other boys asked, from behind. "What Heba said, or somethin' else?"

She shook her head. "Can't tell, not from here."

"Dangerous, though?"

That last made her glance at him over her shoulder, frowning. "All the hell over there? Not likely." Then looked back, only for to have what she saw — or didn't, rather — make her scowl more deeply yet; the thing was gone, not a trace left behind.

"Got up and scurried away, moment the sun struck off your glass," Reed murmured, by her elbow. "Just run off, for all the world like it caught you lookin'."

"They don't *do* that," Ardenne snapped, immediately sore at herself for doing so. But Reed didn't seem too insulted.

"No'm," he agreed, "they don't, not the dead things, you're right; not usually. 'Cept for how *this* one just went ahead and did."

Ardenne allowed herself one sigh, as she tucked the oculars away again. She'd heard hearth tales, same as any of 'em, of dead who didn't act dead: corpsewalkers with the cunning of the living, revenants with memory, *intent*. The idea might have scared her if she'd believed it for a second. Like as not, though, Reed's eyes were tricking him in this heat. *Mirage*, she thought, remembering Gerun's word—hell, if they gave out trade every time *she'd* thought she'd seen faces in sand, or ghost cars on the horizon, then she wouldn't have to take fees at all.

They're deluded, drunk on sun, thirsty, sleepless. No shame in it. Why, that one time—

That one time, years back, not her first trip nor her fifth. When she'd let them all stray so badly, become so lost and parched in the process, that when Ardenne had glanced down to see what looked like snakes twisting under her feet, at first she'd just shook her head hard enough to hurt and told herself something similar, almost down to the words: *It's nothing, just the heat, press on, now.* "Go!" she'd called, and they had, trusting her word—only to walk straight into a nest of dead swimming upwards, claws-first, those submerged shadows the ripples their passage made as they tore their way to the surface. And what the coffle's unwary footfalls had started, Ardenne's own panicked yammer soon brought to pass. The dead things started breaching, pulling prey down and spraying up sand as Ardenne stuck her pike in wherever she could, slashing and stabbing, desperate to save at least *some*.

She'd set out on that trip twenty-strong, only to make shore with nothing; lost the whole chain and been damn lucky to escape with her own hide intact. No need to lie about how, either, even to herself: she'd only managed *that* much by being willing to dump and run, to leave the rest behind to keep the dead occupied. By the time she made far shore she was all cried out, exhausted to her very soul in the journey's ruinous wake, so much so she'd swore up, back and sideways she'd never guide again.

It'd been spring when she'd made that vow, hard winter by the time she finally broke it, and she'd tried not to think on it since: single worst six-month of her life, in hindsight, even with every poisonous minute she'd spent enslaved folded in on top. A damn high price to pay, too, for what little wisdom she could claim she'd gleaned from the experience, the gist of which went thus: *if you see something strange, stop, and think on it. Consider it well. Might be more than it seems, and that "more" might cost you dearly.*

So: "Go again in five," Ardenne said, handing Reed their last part-full feedbag to pass on down the line, headed straight to Heba, once he'd taken just the barest swig for himself. *Sweet on her, maybe,* Ardenne thought, tucking the knowledge away. *Have to watch that, we get in any real trouble.*

There was a locker of extra food buried somewhere beyond the next valley, weighted to keep it hid and marked with a whistle, so she could track it if the sand-tide shifted its position; it'd make a nice reward, if they could only manage to catch up to it before sundown. She resolved to do just that if she could, for hope was hard to cultivate, and needed constant watering.

Ardenne counted as slow as she could, studying the ridge throughout, but whatever that figure'd been, it didn't return. Didn't count herself soothed, though, since it well might be all that meant was that it knew how to hide.

"Time," was all she spoke out loud, finally. And pushed up again, greeted on all sides by groans.

Inside the Patch the sky looked different, just as tainted as anything else. Daytimes it glared white, same's the sand below, sun a bone disk hid in mist; nighttimes it grew darker, but never so much as expected. A wind made from light blew back and forth from one horizon to the other, bending, fluttering. Sometimes it threw forks without thunder, while others it glimmered at vision's very edges, teasing the coffle from any attempt at sleep. It bruised their dreams.

It was only an hour past where they'd noticed themselves watched, meanwhile—in the very next valley, a low and level bowl of dust, sand-rimmed on every side—that they finally met up with the yellow-hair girl, that pretty little creature of ill-omen, sending what'd otherwise been as good a run of runners' luck as might be asked for straight to hell.

It was old woman May, this time, who spotted her first, grabbing hold of Ardenne's elbow with a finger lip-laid, head jerked in the right direction. A slim figure decked in rags, scrambling up over the ridge only to half-fall, half-tumble down towards them, face wrapped against the glare but bright hair flying out the top. She lurched half-hearted, far too tired to set any real sort of pace, while the dead things trailed along behind her: their own coffle's gross reflection, rotted close with their dull-glinting bones stuck out every which way through sere, dried flesh. Looked fit to fall apart from the very act of walking, but their joints stayed somehow tight—that was the nanites at work too, Ardenne could only think, keeping each host upright enough to chase, and catch, and bite.

One way or the other, they kept on and the yellow-hair girl likewise, with nothing but a mournful sobbing of breath to mark her passage. No telling how long the chase had lasted thus far, but there couldn't be much left to it by now since the dead things never tired until they fell apart completely. From the hitch in her cries, the girl knew it, too.

"Ain't there nothin' we can do?" Reed demanded, and Ardenne wanted to snap at him: *NO, fool! What'd I tell you a hundred damn times by now, if I told you the once? You falter, better catch up by yourself, 'cause we're not coming back for your sorry ass; trying to save one person's the surest way to lose everybody. There's no room on the rope for more than we already got.* In the Patch, mercy just ran too high a price to indulge.

Unless . . . it didn't.

They *had* made good time, after all, Ardenne found herself thinking; the remaining sacks were still fullish. Might be they could spare the effort. And might be the girl reminded her of someone, too: herself, in similar straits, back when there'd been no one to offer her aid . . . even if she'd been inclined to take it without expecting that doing so might turn her slave again, before she ever got even the chance to live free.

Pits, Gerun's voice said, from the back of her head. *You spot 'em over there too, don't you, gal? Just like I showed you.*

"With me," Ardenne told Reed, already unhooking him as she let her pack fall. "May, hold the line." She threw the old woman the coffle-rope, slotted her knife's blade sidelong through the top of her staff, and shoved her climbing hammer into Reed's surprised hands. "These things go quick," she told him, "so stay sharp. Anything gets by me, put the claw in its head."

"Yes'm."

Ardenne whirled the pike's staff, limbering up, adjusting to its full weight: the new-formed spike on one end plus the hiking weight on the other, each tracing a whistling figure-eight through the air. Then she spun and took off running, far too fast to allow herself a last look-back.

If this's the day it comes for you, there's nothing else to say but get to it. Get it done.

Ardenne was a small woman, but she had her hard work-strength, her cunning. Better yet, she had backup: Reed stayed close and did exactly what she'd said, covering her back. His first blow took the nearest dead thing full in its chest, clothes-lined it so sharp it fell headlong, breaking its own dry neck before Reed even had a chance to crush the back of its head in. Ardenne, meanwhile, was already in midleap overtop the fallen creature—she speared the next one through its temple and tugged it off-course, using it to trip its neighbors, send them flying. The pike gave her reach enough to keep just out of clutching range even when she stomped on the second dead thing's back to wrench it free, then yet once more to separate skull from spine, before whirling to kick the other two straight into Reed's next face-crushing hammer-smash.

Frenzied, messy, wearing work, but it paid off: where they fell, the bodies created a break the other dead things couldn't help but follow, especially once Ardenne started screaming at them. "This way!" she yelled, hoarse, "Over here, you bastards!" As she swerved towards where the sands dipped, almost too shallowly to note, the yellow-hair girl threw herself face-down at Reed's feet and stayed there, peeping up through her fingers; he squared himself to defend her just in case, even as Ardenne ran on and the dead things lurched after, teeth clicking hungrily.

Calculating where the pits gave out by sight, Ardenne took a flying leap of faith and touched down on the far side, teetering a breathless moment — she could feel hard glass under only her foot's front half, toes scrabbling inside her boot for purchase as she gave one last judder and dropped to her knees, safe on solid ground. But the dead things weren't so lucky; they plunged straight in and floundered, brains too parched to recall how to swim. White sand flew in all directions as they struck out less and less effectively, what eyes they had still fixed on Ardenne's tasty form, fleshless lips drawn back in a shared cheated snarl.

Gerun again, in her head: *The more you thrash, the faster you'll sink . . .*

Sink on, then, and fast, you fuckers, Ardenne thought, chest heaving, as she piked herself back upright. *Tell the devil who sent you when you get there.*

By the time the dead things' skulls were sand-hid, Ardenne had already felt her careful way back around the pits' edges, using the pike as depth-gauge. The yellow-hair girl was up on her bare and bleeding feet, hanging tight on Reed's arm, a service he seemed all too glad to do her. They were each staring at the other like they'd never seen another person of the opposite sex before, which made Ardenne struggle to not feel sour, like: *who was it did the lion's share here, again?*

"Thank you," the girl gasped out, as Ardenne drew near. "Thank you, ma'am, sir. You saved my life."

No point in Ardenne even nodding, seeing they both knew it. "Where'd you come from, gal?" she asked, instead. "How long you been out here? No kin along with you, no friends?"

The girl shook her head, eyes downcast, bright tangle of hair hung like a veil.

"Was a farm I first lived at," she said, at last, "back eastwards, on the Rim. Small crops, some tobacco; we did all right, 'til the Trade-towners took it. As for my kin, meanwhile . . . that's them, mainly, you just made an end to. The last of 'em, anyhow."

Behind her, Ardenne heard Heba draw a painful breath, echoed by May as she held her elbow. "Oh, poor soul," the old fool said. "She can come with us, can't she, Miz Ardenne? To the other side?"

Ardenne bit back an urge to snarl: *No, fool, I risked my hide putting down that lot just so we could leave her to starve.* "Need to be careful, if so," she said, at last. "We're behind as it is, by my count—don't want to spend more nights out here than we have to."

"I understand," the girl said, softly, still looking down, while the rest of the coffle stared hard at Ardenne over her bent shoulders. "Got to do as you see fit, to keep these folks alive; might be I been out here too long to trust, for all either of us know."

"I can watch her," Reed volunteered, far too eagerly.

Ardenne scowled. "And do what, she starts to change?" She jerked her head at the knife in Reed's belt, as he flushed. "You ready to do the needful, boy? Seein' ain't the same as doin', no more'n a girl's a cow. Best leave all that to me."

Reed's mouth worked, all sullen. "I've killed humans too, ma'am," he muttered at the ground. "When I had to—was *told* to; don't think you're the only one. Throats slit the same, either way."

Again, Ardenne had to bite back a harsh retort: this *was* a killing world, no doubt, as they all of them had equally damn good cause to know. The words fell away when her eye lighted on the girl, though, still standing there completely unprotesting, no matter what might come next. Though she had wits enough to let the kid fight for her, at least, rather than risk it herself, having already seen what Ardenne was capable of; that alone made her smarter than she looked, by far.

"Well, what've *you* got to say on the matter, gal?" Ardenne demanded. "Stay under Reed here's watch, or go? We're on a clock."

The girl looked up, eyes visible at last through the thicket of hair, narrow and blue as two branding-strike flames. "I'd thank him to put me down, ma'am, turned out he did have to," she said, softly. "No way in hell I'm lookin' to wander this place any longer than I need, let alone after death."

It was a good stance to take, lie or no. And none of Ardenne's business, either way.

So: "All right, then," Ardenne replied, refusing to waste time debating it further. Adding, to Reed: "Find her a place on the rope; watch her close. It's your business from now on, unless you slip, and make it mine."

"Yes'm."

May beckoned the girl to her with a smile and she went willingly, as Reed and Ardenne trailed along behind: light and sure-footed for all her wear and tear, her scored soles, her supposed exhaustion. Watched how she laid her little hand on Reed's as May knotted her in, face lit by worshipful gratitude, and snorted at the sight. *That's him out of my hair a while,* she thought, *and good riddance. Her too, long as she feels she has to keep it up.*

Another gasp from Heba drew Ardenne's glance, finding her now struggling twice as hard to hold herself straight. "Child coming?" she demanded. She studied the sand between Heba's spread legs and skirt hem for spotting, but Heba shook her head.

"Not yet," she claimed, as though saying so would make it true. "I'm in pain, sure, but not—just as yet, no; I can hold it, if I try. We can go on."

No point in calling her bluff 'til they had to, Ardenne reckoned. "Fine," she said. "Damn well better tell me, though, once it gets so you can't."

" . . . yes'm."

"I'll help, ma'am," the yellow-hair girl spoke up, and reached to lay her palm right on Heba's belly. Heba braced herself to flinch, but as the girl made contact, she quieted visibly, like a soothed horse. Ardenne watched along with all the rest as the pain seemed to quit Heba's face in a blink, making her look all at once younger, softer—surprised by the unexpected kindness, as much as the miracle it accompanied.

"That's . . ." Wonderment thinned Heba's voice to breaking. "You don't know me, but . . . what you just did . . . I thank you for it."

"We'd all do the same," the girl answered, shrugging.

Which was her first lie, turned out. Though not her last, by a long shot.

The yellow-hair girl said her name was Bess, which seemed likely enough, though she mostly ignored any questions after that. Ardenne let it go, knowing what it was to have things in her past she'd rather not remember, especially for others' entertainment. Still, the girl had better speak up with any useful knowledge, if it came to that; Ardenne'd have words for her, and more, if she didn't.

Another day crept past, eking away, as they kept their slow but steady path across the sand. Having already hauled up more from the cache she'd planted, Ardenne came to the very end of her last original nutrient-sack, squeezed it dry into the neediest ones' mouths, then rolled it up small for her belt-pack. The sky had clouded over in such a way had the others thanking God, but she didn't like its looks; weather on the Patch tended to be as odd as everything else, and likewise dangerous. She brought her oculars out again and started scanning for fresh shelter, something a bit heavier duty, if it should become necessary.

"Ma'am," Bess said, almost right in Ardenne's ear, "I might know a place."

Ardenne jolted, shamefully. "Where?" she demanded, as much to cover it up as to know.

"There's a crevasse, right near—hard to see, you ain't all but in it. It's deep, though, and the walls're high. I hid there a time or two while the dead went by, so snug they never even smelled me."

"Uh huh. And when was this?"

"Mmm . . . three weeks back, I think. Maybe four."

Ardenne turned to consider her, eyes narrowing. "How long you been *out* here, to know the Patch so well?" she asked. "Never knew anybody to stay longer'n it took to get across, myself, and that don't take nearly a month, no matter how bad you screw it up."

Reed opened his mouth to protest, but Bess gestured him to keep silent, not even turning; her gaze held on Ardenne's, unabashed. "We come out the other side some time back, my kin and me," she said, "but Rim's Rim on every hand and every Trade-towner knows a slave's value, 'specially when you got no paper." Cocking her head: "Or didn't you tell these poor souls that, 'fore they set off?"

Ardenne felt more than saw eyes turn her way, all up and down the rope. She flushed. "I never double-sold no one in all my life," she shot back, between her teeth. "Never will, neither. I go the long way, so we don't pass close enough to attract attention, then I bring my coffles 'round through the swamps right into Sanctuary, the hundred-year free-hold, where there's walls and guns enough to send any catch-corps squad running. Don't you dare think it doesn't exist, just 'cause you and yours were unlucky enough not to make it there yourselves."

Bess nodded, eyes downcast once more. "Oh, you're no doubt right, ma'am, surely—'course you are. We *were* unlucky, seein' we didn't have no one like you to lead us, not in here nor out of it. So after a spell, we just went back, retraced our own steps—easiest way to take cover from catch-corps was in the Patch, for all its danger. Still, if you let me, I'll show you where that crack is, nevertheless . . . to make up for my slights on your name."

Which was how they found themselves already down inside it, under Ardenne's tight-pegged tarp, by the time the storm she'd feared finally blew up.

Down in the crack, while the wind ran high and her coffle worried themselves to sleep in the hot darkness, Ardenne finally had free time enough to wonder over various strange things she'd seen either side of the Patch, and stranger still she'd heard of.

In the Rim-town where she'd been born, her mother's owner—same one Ardenne still called First Master, if only in her head—kept a box with a black mirror in front that answered questions put to it. Useful knowledge sometimes, other times baffling, and if you didn't string your words well enough together in the inquiry all it gave back was a dull line of blinking symbols plus what sounded like a voice, but with no real tone to it: *Uncertain—Try Again.* The box could tell you what wounds would fester and how to cure them, if canned food had gone wrong, where to cut to save a mother's life, and her baby's too. But it also showed pictures and told tales of things that simply didn't exist anymore, or maybe never had, making no clear distinction between good advice and bad. The answers it returned when First Master asked it how best to break a slave but leave them still fit for work made Ardenne's blood run cold.

It lies, she'd complained to the woman who managed the slave-get, once—Hu Shi, that'd been her name. But Hu Shi'd just laughed, and told her: *No, gal, master's box don't lie . . . it can't. Not like us. Remember, though—it knows a lot, but it can't learn, neither. No more than it can tell the difference between what is now, and what used to be.*

There was craft like that almost everywhere, left over from the Old Folks' time—"tech," Gerun called it later on, after she'd been sold to the Mount. Rare as all hell to find any of it still working, and costly, too. But Ardenne had heard tell of other things, as well: some family up north who spoke to each other inside their heads or teased thoughts out of yours and showed 'em to you. Some blind boy who pointed out places to dig, telling you what you'd find, if you did. A man who made even bad wounds close, just by touching 'em; a woman who made her living letting men cut parts off of her, for the sheer pleasure of watching them grow back again.

The very worst thing she'd heard of along that was a girl who could supposedly run invisible hooks through folks' joints and twitch them to her liking, making them dance her tune whether they would or no. She'd made men kill their own friends, their own children, weeping while they did it, and laughed at the sight. Hadn't ever left off laughing, not even when they burnt her alive.

Ardenne knew a good bit about that sort of hate, same as every other slave, and what scared her most about the story was how much it'd made her envy the girl, sick and green with jealousy over her revenge—for really, who wouldn't want the power to make free-born bastards her puppets and order them to destroy themselves on cue, especially those who deserved it most? Rim-towners, traders, citizens, owners . . . Masters . . .

It hurt to think such things might be possible, that similar secrets might lurk behind any shuttered eye, just waiting to be born. But what hurt all the worse, by far, was the inescapable knowledge that if *somebody* out there had ever had that sort of juice, it sure as hell wasn't her.

It was the War that did it, some people said. *Put new craft in folks' bodies and burnt all the old away.* Which made sense, given what Ardenne had seen already in the Patch: nanites had to be "tech" for certain, done sick-seed small. But as Hu Shi told it, there'd been folks like this always, everywhere, hid deep; all the War had done was pull them back up again so they could show themselves in daylight once more without fear, seeing enough had happened already that they now knew their own unnaturalness wasn't the worst thing people had to worry over, anymore.

Wrapped up close and eyes shut, sand piling high around her, Ardenne thought she vaguely heard Heba cry out from further down the rope and Bess murmur to her, comforting. Almost thought she felt something reach down and touch the top of her head, too—oh so softly, for all its touch was both hard and dry, farthest bones of its fingers popped out from the withered meat like slim, dull claws — before skittering away again, so fast she couldn't've hoped to catch it even if she'd wanted to risk scouring her sight to do so.

And in the morning, when the wind died away at last and they dug themselves free, fully eleven more of her coffle lay forever still and silent.

The only ones who stood back up into the thin, red rind of sun the storm had left behind were herself, Reed, Bess and Heba; May, the old cook-woman; Tayle, a big man who'd lost one eye and his tongue to what his last owner'd called "justice"; Vex, a skinny pickpocket whose lock-break skills hadn't been up to the Masters' manacles; and Nia and Nessa, two sisters less than twelve years old who'd been shoved at Ardenne by their weeping mother before she'd been able to say yes or no. Nobody else.

The coffle-rope hung slack between the prone bodies, and when Ardenne checked her pack, she found two pap-sacks punctured, the whole of the rest nutrient-soaked and drying fast. The sight of such ruin made her bite her lip and look away with eyes burning, refusing to give in to the urge to weep while there were even a few people left to ferry safe to their destination, literal Sanctuary.

"Reed, Tayle, Bess, help me lay these folks down," she said, finally, surprised by how hoarse her voice sounded. "May, look to Heba and the girls. Vex, you sort these ropes out, get everybody knotted back on before we go. There's miles to make up, not enough pap and not a lot of time left to do it in, either. Better mind me extra-well, so we can get the rest of you out of here alive."

The women nodded, but Vex kept on staring around, eyes wide. "So many," he husked, as though Ardenne just hadn't noticed. "All of 'em, but us. How?"

Ardenne shrugged, trying hard to keep her mask up. "It happens, boy. Dehydration, scramble-stingers, nanites, some sick-seeds don't show symptoms 'til you drop . . . might be there's some bug in the air down here, we's just the ones lucky enough not to catch it."

"You said you'd see us *safe*," Vex gritted.

"I did. I'm trying to."

"Not half hard enough, by the looks of it!"

"Hard as I can. I won't promise more, or less." Ardenne's voice hardened: "Or would you rather be right back where I found you, slave-born to live and die the same damn way, with no hope but your Master's pleasure?"

"Maybe!"

You're the ones came to me, *goddamnit,* she thought, angrily. But ground out instead, before she said anything she'd regret: "Well, all right, then! Rim's back that way, if all you want's to be *safe*—you can live the rest of your life on your knees, once they cut your cords for running. Or you can stay, suck it up, and have a chance for better."

Vex's fists clenched—but it was Reed who broke in now, catching her off guard, cold and unimpressed. "Them on the ground, ma'am. What choice do *they* have? Now *or* then?"

He wasn't wrong, not altogether. That was what made it so damn hard to fight back, find the words to persuade, if not entirely refute.

"Same choice any of us ever did," she said at last. "I made this run once and got away clean, or clean enough—didn't *have* to go back, not ever. Could have left it all . . . *you* all . . . behind, but I didn't. I chose not to, even knowing that might get me caught and sold again, dead, or worse. Knowing the odds got harder every damn time I came back through, both ways."

Vex spat. "And we're s'posed to thank you for that, I guess—that right?"

"I don't care to be *thanked*, you ungrateful louse; you don't owe me anything. All I've ever wanted was to get folks like you to a better place, one good enough you might one day want to."

"Oh, uh huh. Didn't hurt we *paid* you for the privilege, though, did it? And dearly."

That it was Reed who threw this last in on top, not Vex, made it all the more surprising—and hurtful. "You think you're the only one?" Ardenne snapped back. "Think freedom comes easy, with no risk of failure?" She rounded on them all, catching the remainder of the coffle in her glare. "What you paid for was the *chance*, the gamble it might turn out different for once, that's all—just that, like every damn body else. It was never a sure thing; you thought it was, it was *you* fooling yourself, not me. 'Cause *nothing ever is*."

These last words came out low, ground up between her aching teeth, a sign that Ardenne'd well and truly reached her limit—as both Vex and Reed finally did seem to see. Vex snapped his own teeth shut and looked away, still fuming, but canny enough to keep silent; Reed looked down, flushing, though that might be as much from Bess softly nestling closer into his side as any shame. Ignoring them both, Ardenne fixed pike and started spearing the dead ones through their orbits; punch in, shake it up, repeat, repeat, repeat.

And all the while, struggling inside to tell their details through with each fresh jolt, each back-pull, rusty and sharp like a necklace of nails: Spindler, who told jokes the way other people coughed or spit; Leah, her lips cropped for talking back, who hardly ever laughed at them, or anything else; Liang and Gaw, married a month after ten years hand-fasted while she worked off a bed-girl contract, plus their boy Justin and that baby they were carrying freedom-ward (had Ardenne ever known its sex, let alone its name?) for a pair of still-slaved friends, stuck too deep to pull themselves out in time to make the runners' crew rendezvous . . .

But here the names either stopped or started to run all together, blending into one indigestible, poisonous, impossible-to-choke-down mess—so many, over the years, both before and after. Ardenne found she couldn't tell the new dead from the old, not without looking.

It was just too much, abruptly. Too much, and never enough.

Done at last, Ardenne found herself leaning on her pike and panting, face wet, too tired to wipe the mess of her own failure away; Tayle stolidly saw to laying out the bodies in the corner, Vex half-heartedly helping. Behind her, May and Bess kept hold of Heba's hands while Reed hugged himself, looking away. His anger'd passed sometime back, Ardenne felt, but even if he might now feel badly over his own behavior, he sure wasn't going to say so.

"Might be we should get to movin'," Bess suggested, eventually, her voice soft as ever. She looked to Reed, who nodded, snorted—then looked on back to Ardenne, who met his gaze to find it hard on the surface, yet lightly pleading beneath.

"You good with that?" she asked him, straight out. And waited 'til he nodded, however reluctantly.

"Yes'm," he replied.

Further on, then, fast and faster. Ardenne took a fresh compass read, shook her head straight, pressed them harder than ever. Breaching the crack's lip, they clambered up dune after dune, slipping and sliding, until they found themselves level once more—and wound up making far better time than she'd thought they might. By noontime, the last section of Patch stretched ahead from the low ridge where they stood, what might well be the far Rim almost visible if they strained enough; a teasing promise, maybe. Journey's end. Or yet another threat, familiar in every terrible way, of disappointed hope.

"Can we make it?" Heba asked, hoarse with dust and strain, May struggling to hold her upright. Ardenne shot a glance at the sun—poised for a long, slow fall into dusk, followed by yet more darkness—and paused, reckoning their chances.

"Possible," she offered, finally. "But not 'til after dark, most like, however hard we push . . . and I don't want to risk night travel, not with you like you are, even if you *can* keep up."

"Think I can't?"

"You tell me, gal. Pains are pretty bad by now, right?" Now it was

Heba's turn to pause, and Ardenne couldn't afford to let her. "Don't lie to me," she ordered, though she could catch Reed making a face at her vision's edge. "We're small as it is, vulnerable to weather, heat, sand, and thirst, as well as the other. Turns out we need to hole up while you bring that child to birth, you need to tell us *now*, before—"

May tightened her grip on Heba's hand while Bess squeezed the woman's shoulder, both probably trying for comfort. But Heba just shook her head again, wincing.

"I can do it," she maintained, stubborn as always. "I *will*, don't you worry. Been in worse hurt than this, by far."

"Not in harder circumstances, I'm thinking."

"Maybe not. But all the rest of us were willin' to kill themselves to get here, so why should I be any different?"

"Already said how we're out of pap, too," Vex threw in.

Ardenne just rolled her eyes. "Put it to a vote, then: Those who want to stop for the night, throw up." No hands rose but hers, an impatient flap, surprising her not at goddamn all; she sighed, shrugged. Rolled her shoulders to loosen them, before turning away.

"All right," she said, almost under her breath. "Get gone, and don't look back."

But: "What's that?" Reed barked out all of a sudden, and Ardenne swerved to look, squinting—for the first time in hours, he actually sounded more panicked than angry. At once, she saw that same small figure as before on the next ridge's very top, arms up and body capering, as though trying to get her attention. She couldn't quite swallow her own yelp of surprise, incautiously loud enough to echo sightly; in turn, the thing—whatever it was—seemed to perk up, signaled. It paused mid-shuffle, both hands cocking sidelong—

(pointing, it was *pointing*)

Ardenne whipped her oculars up, tracking direction, back towards the north-east side of the Patch. Saw Reed do the same, face paling once he realized what he'd spotted: sand up-sprayed, engine smoke rising, white against the haze. That furious churn of motion only wheeled things could make, bent in fast pursuit, scoring the desert by fours or by twos, by threes, eights or even sixes. Through the stifling air, the dull thunder of gas-guzzlers slowly swelled, drone becoming a roar.

"Oh shit," Reed let out, mouth gone fear dry. Beside him, Heba half-groaned, half-shrieked; Tayle made a sound that might have been a roar or a moan, as Nia and Nessa clung to him. Bess stood stock-still while May lunged forward to haul on Ardenne's arm, yammering in her ear: "Not catch-corps from back where we set off, they'd never get 'cross the pits, be face first and sunk in a day, just like those *things*! So it's gotta, they gotta be —"

(Rim's Rim on every side, ma'am, you know that)

" —from the far side," Ardenne agreed, doing her best to break the old cook-woman's grip without doing her damage, gentle but firm. "Cutter's Rock, or Ashhallow. Saw us coming, fled goods for the snap-up, just like Bess here said —yeah, I see 'em too, now *let go*. We have to —"

" —*go*, Heba, Bess, go go go *GO!*" Reed chimed in, grabbing both ladies' hands in his. "They'll be on us 'fore we know it, we don't damn well *haul ass and run* —"

—and Bess looked willing enough, sure, but Heba tripped headlong the second one foot slapped down in front of the other; would've broken her own nose, Bess hadn't rooked an arm around her from behind, stronger by far than she looked. Reed goggled as she held Heba's front-heavy form up single-handed, mouth in her ear, crooning: "Don't you worry none, Heba, you're fine, the kid's fine. Stay put, stay quiet, just let me . . . "

Let you what, *gal? Let you WHAT?*

No time for that, though: down on the flats, the pack of vehicles was already fanning out, forming a giant moving sickle to reap them. Those bastards probably had nets, guns, cloth soaked in meds . . . and Ardenne with nothing but her staff, her knife, her fists, and teeth. Nothing but this bunch weighing her down. Small likelihood indeed they'd be able to back her up, if it came anything close to a minute or so's worth of fight before getting stripped and roped, dragged back to town by her heels, all her gear gone to swell some slaving fucker's pockets. Before she ended up right where she'd sworn she never would again, rebranded on the face so all'd know her incorrigible, with not even a hid blade left to slit her own throat . . .

The thoughts hit fast and hard as New Master's whips, making her brain bleed. So Ardenne set her teeth, wound the rope tight, ready to burn tracks — top speed, just zero to whatever from a dead start, with the whole coffle pulled headlong behind her — 'til they ran her, and the rest, the fuck down.

"He's right," she told Bess, grimly, but Bess just shook her shaggy yellow head, and smiled. Saying only one word, right after —

"Watch."

Long after, Ardenne'd look back and think: *It happened so fast.* Which it did, but not so you'd notice, at the time; as she'd so often found before, adrenaline both shrank your field of vision and enlarged it, rendering you temporarily able to take in a thousand tiny things in one small moment. To her left was Reed, still yelling, and she watched him grab for Bess as the latter threw her hands up too, a distressingly familiar move; Bess barely spared him a glance as she made some sort of gesture that bent her fingers the wrong way, an utterly unnatural flourish, and sent him flying as though from a speeding truck. This she then reversed, reeling invisible thread out of empty air before flinging it out again, straight towards the first Rim-towner car.

That car, less than a hundred yards away now — Ardenne focused on it, eyes sharpening, homing in same as her oculars' lenses: there was a man at the wheel and two up top, one on either side, harpoons at the ready. The driver had eyes only on Bess, stare fixed like he saw his own death, but the right-hand harpooner had Ardenne in sight and his mouth was moving, throat strained to shout. Eighty yards, fifty yards, twenty: Ardenne could almost read his lips—

. . . get BACK, AWAY FROM HER, the girl, she's not . . .

(Not what?)

—DAMN WITCH*—*

The word hit like a punch, one Ardenne hadn't heard in years. Not since Hu Shi, and Old Master's box.

Psi's what they called it sometimes, like P-S-I, Gerun told her, from memory. *Tech's craft, but that was craft, too, like the old tales say—from myth and legend, tech of a kind we never had a real name for. The impossible, made otherwise.*

Bess might've seen this warning shout as well, or even heard it. She smiled—bared her sharp teeth, rather, just this side of a snarl— and knotted a fist, white-knuckled, to punch the hot desert air. The rest of the coffle recoiled from the force of it. Beneath them both, Ardenne felt a tremor like snakes massing, swimming upwards; it made her jump sidelong, the rest flung the other way, leaving Bess alone on the ridge as the car gunned straight for her. The harpooners cocked their weapons—

—and another fist broke the sand from some hidden pit they hadn't yet fallen into, sun dried sere, grabbing tight hold on the car's undercarriage. The vehicle slammed up, belly forward, as if it'd hit an invisible wall, before twisting to mash its left-hand harpooner against the Patch's skin and skid on, starting to tumble. The right-hand harpooner tried jumping free, but his own safety-harness held him trapped; in the next second backlash torque flung him hard against the car's roll-cage, and Ardenne saw his whole skull-side caved in by steel, hollowing out one eye socket in a burst of blood, bone, brains.

As that first vehicle flipped further, meanwhile—crashing straight into the next, no time for course correction—Ardenne could still see the same hands that'd tripped it up clinging on, wrists ripped free yet bloodless in the resultant gas-fire's black-red bloom. It set a line of firecrackers off all up and down the sickle's blade, wheels screeching and swerving; a third war-wagon plowed the double-wreck and up-ended itself in turn, far too close to brake, fresh belch of flame licking out. Clouds kicked up as more cars roared to a stop, reversing hard, trying to find some way around the pileup . . .

. . . but Bess gestured once more, twice, three times. And the rest of her army came to her call, more dark shapes tearing themselves up from the Patch, blurry bone-puppets leaping quick and sure for drivers and passengers alike, their fingers hooked into claws. Shrieks rose everywhere, quick-choked—engines roaring like beasts, then sputtering, dying—'til one alone keened high once more, the caravan's absolute furthest vehicle fishtailing 'round, disappearing into dust. Then there was sudden silence, the dust settling, leaving wreckage strewn all across the sand in a carpet of burning metal, the hunched over, sand-crusted shapes crouched down to feed as black smoke streamed into the sky.

A hand touched Ardenne's shoulder, warm and alive, almost diffident. She gasped and whirled, coughing sand; Bess stepped back, palm uplifted, more in entreaty than threat.

"See?" she asked, soft as ever. "Wasn't no danger, not to you. Not from them."

From Heba, further off, her own voice thinned with pain: "Or from *you*, Bess?"

"I never offered you harm in all this time, Heba, not the once."

"Not *yet*, you mean."

Bess inclined her yellow head, queenly as exiled royalty. "Like you say."

Over to their right, another car went up, completing the chain. Bess snapped her fingers. One by one, out of the smoke, those figures shuffled up the ridge towards them, looking steadily worse—and *smelling* so, good God—with each step closer. Some she recognized from that rout on the hill, her pike slashing and Reed's hammer falling, Bess pretending to cower behind; they'd worked their way back up out of the pits, slow but sure, seeing they'd no need to breathe. Others she hadn't seen yet, aside from that small one dancing atop the ridge, who came scuttling down in a clump of sprayed dust to plump at Ardenne's shock-struck feet. Close up, it resolved into a leathery imp in threadbare rags, eyes mere hollow-pitted smudges, lips shrunk flat. To Bess's side this came unbidden to rub its head on her hip, a ghoul-cat with a death-rattle purr; she stroked its straw-stiff hair-remnants, still holding Ardenne's gaze, even as the similarities between what was left of its face and Bess's own became undeniable.

Her coffle, obviously, held together by will alone, by Bess's long-distance direction. No physical rope necessary.

But at the back there were more, ten and seven at the very least. And *those* faces Ardenne sure as hell knew, every last one of them, right to their pierced eyes, to the scrambled brains behind. Right on back to Kolya and Etta, from the very start of this disaster. Blood and gobbets of flesh dripping from their jaws, smoke wafting off flame-scorched skin and cloth.

Don't need nothing *left intact for* this, she thought, numbly, *'cause that's not the way it works. No nanites, just . . . magic, black as any cat sketched in charcoal. Just Gerun's psi. Just* craft.

Bess's unknowable *force* spread outwards in great gulps, a pulsed, meat-greasy exhalation, met by yet more shuffling footsteps, so like the past three days' main noise it stabbed at Ardenne's heart to hear it. Didn't have to look around, either—well-knew the faces she'd spot, if she did. Just the same dead gamblers she'd buried already, their desperate throws gone to waste against a house too innately crooked to even *have* to cheat.

I failed you, she thought, eyes tight, face burning. *Failed you all.*

Reed turned where he lay and puked onto the stony ground, each retch half a sob. Heba swayed, eyes glazed; May knelt beside her, whimpering into her hands, while the rest cowered and shook. Not all, though: one more drew herself up straight at Bess's unspoken command and stumbled forwards as well, came flocking with the other corpses — Nia, in specific, with Nessa left fumbling heart-torn at her sister's sleeve as she passed on by, not sparing her sibling a single backwards glance.

Enraged, Reed exploded up from the dirt, snarl trailing spittle, hands clawed for Bess's throat. But Bess only flicked a hand like she was swatting flies, and glaze-eyed Nia whirled to seize him, dead teeth out, mere inches away from burying her face in his throat. They tussled a moment as Reed struck out, accidentally leveling poor May when she leaped to his aid, sending her reeling into the other coffle's midst; they grabbed her up by hand and foot, all but slavering, though their jaws clicked dry. Ardenne heard her moan like a slaughter-bound sheep while Reed's next hammer-fall crushed the side of Nia's skull in, with a *thunk* that made everyone wince . . . but nothing else. Not one other shred of difference.

As Reed gaped, hammer dropping, Nia hove back in, still snarling; Heba yelled and Tayle gave an answering wordless roar as Vex took his own half-stomp forwards, before recoiling. *"Don't,* goddamnit!" Ardenne heard herself scream out at the self-same time, not knowing exactly who she directed it to yet desperate, *desperate,* to save them all —

But: *"No,"* Bess said, simply, a Master's snap to her voice. And in response, the corpses just *let go,* Nia along with the rest: dropped grip so fast Reed and May almost fell headlong flat, in manner anything but comic, with not a hint of delay.

Carefully, like her bones were glass, Ardenne turned to look straight at Bess, who stood staring back at her mildly, still stroking what had to be her own dead child's head. "Saw a spear-man yelling, on that car, just before it went over," Ardenne told her, "and he was right. You *are* a damn witch."

Bess shrugged, spread her hands. "Never heard it called such before," she replied. "But that'll do, no doubt, if sayin' so helps y'all any."

Things went quiet, after that; the dead things swaying silent once more, like tall grass in a breeze, and Bess waited too, grave-patient.

"How long — ?" Ardenne swallowed, throat rasping, with a nod at what had once been Nia.

"Oh, since the crack, I guess—felt her dim during the storm, then latch on somewhat later," Bess replied. "Pity 'bout it, I guess, with her so young and all . . . " And here she tilted her head, as if struck by a thought: "Might be I could've raised her up t' be a fit playmate for my boy, here, she hadn't lost herself altogether." Bess patted the ghoul-child once more, strands of desiccated hair sifting down at her touch, as her smile faded. "But that's moot, ain't it? He's only one step up from her, if that. Oh, I can keep him upright, keep him walking, fool myself otherwise . . . but whatever he once was, what he could've been, it's gone now, and that's the truth of it. Almost as much as I am."

"What do you—"

"Said it yourself, ma'am—a body can't *live* in here, not rightly, not for long. Not unless they got something else keepin' 'em that way."

"Food? Drink?"

"Those, yeah. Or . . . "

. . . *love,* Ardenne found herself thinking, not entirely knowing why. *Love like nails driven in, bitter-hot, hard and strong as hate.*

"What—" Reed choked, spat dust and mucus. "What've you *done* to her—to them?" He looked 'round at the swaying dead, baffled. "Ruined brain's supposed to keep a body down, everyone knows that . . . the hell you call this, it ain't witchcraft?!"

It was as much plea as accusation, Ardenne thought, real helpless curiosity. Or maybe the curiosity was hers. Either way, it made Bess stop a minute, seeming to think.

"Coaxin'," she said, at last. "I coax 'em up, that's all—leash 'em to me so I can spin 'em back out, see through their eyes, hear through their ears. They do what I want, 'til they can't anymore; take my orders, sound out my path. They're mine; I'm theirs." A nod to Ardenne, now, both low and level: "Like with you and these, ma'am, much though you don't see it that way, or try not to. You said yourself how every trip's a gamble, their lives wagered against freedom's prize. This place, it charges a steep price, always, and blood's the best single payment."

Ardenne didn't bother to deny it. "So that's the trick kept you up-right, while all the rest of your kin fell face-forward."

Like him, she might have added, indicating what was left of the boy by Bess's side, her distant, capering scout. But that sad item saved Ardenne the trouble, hissing at her through its ruined throat and carding the sand with those same sharp claw-fingers, all the while digging its skull against Bess's gentling hand. She could still feel the touch of those claws, from the night in the crevasse.

"They might've made it," Bess replied, "but for those Rim-town-ers, and the way my Momma never would've done what I just did." Her eyes grew distant. "Momma fled the towns, yoked herself to some nowhere man, all 'cause she swore she'd never let herself be used to set dead things 'gainst the living—not on anyone's account, even her own. Took us out here, to the Patch's very edge, so's even if one of us did turn out to have her same bad blood, it wouldn't show so easy; waited 'til the last damn minute to tell what she'd handed me down, too, and only when the proof of it slapped us both 'cross the face." Bess shook her head, mouth tight. "Could've been graveyard queen of any shithole she chose, I reckon, and me right along with her, but that she was dumb enough to believe whoever told her actin' on her own first instincts was a shameful goddamned sin."

Isn't it? Ardenne yearned to ask, though one look more at the corpse-child clutching Bess's skirts dissuaded her. "And your boy . . . was he the same way, before?" was all she let herself inquire, instead. "Like her, and you?"

"Might've been," Bess said, at last. "Might could've been, Momma'd just let me kill them Rim-towners 'fore they had a chance to lay him down. They hadn't, I'd've never known I could bring him back, or anybody else, either. But we'll never know now, will we?"

"You cursed him," May whispered before anyone else could stop her, mumbling it to the sands like she thought they'd argue different, given opportunity. Adding, after: "Cursed us, too." But Bess simply gestured once more, bringing their former coffle-mates shambling over from the convoy crash-site—some broken and crushed, others still smoldering or burnt beyond all recognition.

"Ain't done nothing to *you*, old woman—as yet, like Heba says," Bess told her, coolly. "You'd do well to recall that same fact, I'd think."

Yes'm, Ardenne thought.

Suddenly deeply engrossed in the state of her clothes, Bess stood there a moment more, brushing off dust. "Anyhow," she began again, once re-ordered, "you seen 'em, them ones I let you 'save' me from. They was all used up; I needed fresh, t' keep goin' with. And like Miz Ardenne here says, there's no one does more'n just passes through the Patch, one way or t'other—chasin' and escapin', takin' what they need. The rest's all sand, and germ, and dead things . . . and me."

Ardenne's fist tightened on her spear's haft; she was more than half-minded in that instant simply to lunge upwards and do her damnedest to spike Bess right through whatever she might use for a heart, consequences be damned. But before she could, the boy-thing hissed at her like it sensed her intentions, tensing where it crouched. Ardenne somehow knew it'd move faster than any walking corpse she'd ever seen if Bess was in danger, so she huffed a breath out instead, easing her grip.

Bess didn't even seem to notice, anyhow—just gestured once more, waving most of her puppets back towards the caravan's wreckage (them moving slow, all dried-up skin over bones like sticks, with eyes and teeth equal-exposed to the elements), as those few who hung behind took up guard stances between her and what little was left of Ardenne's crew. Reed, Heba, May and Nissa huddled into one another, but Bess ignored them too, shading her eyes and scowling; after a moment, she closed them altogether, though Ardenne could see the balls move yet beneath thin lids, roaming back and forth, back and forth, like she was dreaming awake. She cocked her head as if perusing some interior manifest, while her revenants crawled over—and pawed through—those few smoking remains the crashes had spared.

"What're they looking for?" Ardenne asked, willing her voice steady. And: "Whatever's left," Bess replied, "though there ain't all too much of that—broke-down or broke up, the most've it, even 'fore the fire got the rest. Only thing worth takin' off 'em now's their meat."

Ardenne's gorge rose in her throat as she realized what the dead things were doing—pulling the Rim-towners' bodies free of the twisted metal, resuming the feast they'd started earlier. More awful yet were the ones who used nails and teeth to wrench free great strips from the corpses, gathering them up rather than setting in to eat themselves; when they turned and trudged back up the slope to where Bess stood, unslinging a small pack from under her skirts, Ardenne realized they meant this bounty as a gift, a tribute to the woman keeping them . . .

. . . well, you couldn't say *alive*, really. Could you?

The thought pushed her stomach over the edge at last, and now it was her turn to twist away and heave up everything until strands of bile trailed from her mouth to the sand, burning the opened crack in her lower lip. It felt like she'd been punched, and she knew the feeling well: that closed-fist connection, head rocking back, numbly ringing. The way her ears hissed, a double cup full of shaken blood.

Bess glanced at Ardenne and laughed. "So there's things even *you* ain't got the nerve to bear, huh?" she said, not unkindly—but didn't get any farther before Tayle lunged silently at her, big hands coming up to grab for her neck. Shock alone saved her life; she threw herself backwards and tripped, falling flat on her ass as Tayle staggered past her. Before he could recover, the dead exploded into movement, with a fluid grace no nanite-walker ever had. Etta grabbed Tayle's arm, Kolya seized him 'round his waist, Spindler and Leah grabbed a leg each, and the boy-thing at Bess's side leaped off Spindler's back to bury its teeth in Tayle's throat. Tayle's roar drowned Heba's and May's shrieks, collapsing into a gurgle as blood fountained out. His struggles slowed, stopped, but the dead didn't let him fall, holding him up as Bess clambered back to her feet, looking pissed. She strode forward and slapped her hand to Tayle's lolling head, closing her eyes.

"No," said Ardenne, shocking herself with how weak and trembly her voice sounded. "Bess, *no,* you hear me? Don't—"

It was too late, though. The lid of Tayle's only visible eye opened, eye itself beneath skewed sideways, and Tayle stood out of the shamblers' grip like a string attached to his neck was pulling him upright. Clinging to Heba's panting side, Nessa cried bitterly.

"Don't what?" said Bess. "Don't do what I do? How likely is it anyone takes *that* advice, Miz Ardenne?"

"Your mother did."

"And look what it got her."

"Maybe so, but what's *this* got *you?*" Ardenne made herself straighten too, steadying herself, using her staff as a cane. "You can call up the dead and make 'em dance. So why *aren't* you out there, ruling every Rim-town you can find? Why play the victim's part with us at all, come to that, 'cept to torment and pick us away one by one, like any damn barn-cat? Why stick around here, same place got your boy killed, unless—" She paused, realizing. "Ah, but you can't, can you? Can't leave the Patch at all, no more than your puppets." Giddy and exultant, she stepped forward, ignoring the carrion figures that twisted towards her—Bess's boy hissing his warning, chin still darkly slick with Tayle's blood. "You ever even try?"

"More times than I can count," Bess responded, unashamed. "Never works, though; don't know why, don't much care. A day away, a few miles outside the boundaries, we all fall sick. First time it happened, took me everything I had just to get back here, and I left some folk I'd been . . . close to behind, to do it." The pain in her voice was startling. Against her will Ardenne thought of her own coffle-ropes, hanging slack. "Might be if we could just go with *enough* on the line, we might all have the strength to support each other . . . "

"No." Ardenne almost jumped with surprise, and even Bess looked startled; they both turned to Heba, held up between Reed and May, her pallid face sweat-shiny but her eyes dark and unyielding. "I've heard tales of . . . gifts, like yours," she said. "What I hear is they take it out of you to use, same as choppin' firewood or haulin' weights, 'cept worse—the more the person does, the more it takes of 'em. An' if it takes too much—" She shrugged.

Reed stared at her. "What's your meaning, Heba?"

Bess sighed. "She means I coax too many folk out of the Patch with me, we'll all of us only die the quicker, Reed. I half thought as much, but . . ." She shook herself, as if to shed water or dust. "Well, this is a fine fix, and no mistake. Can't leave my coax-kin in here or I die, can't take them with me or I die out there, can't keep 'em upright forever by my lonesome—" She put her hands on her hips and looked around, smiling sad, like a friend had just made some bad joke.

The boy-corpse made a sound Ardenne had never heard before from any dead thing: a plaintive, wistful trill, soft and sorrowful. It nuzzled up against Bess, butting her thigh with its empty-eyed head. Bess reached down to it once more, not looking, and Ardenne stood aghast as the other dead flocked in around it as though called, circling in to nestle close—trying to comfort her, or was she merely taking what comfort she could *from* them? Would she even know she was doing it, if so?

"Love's a chain nobody wants to break," Bess concluded, nodding to herself. And all her creatures dipped their heads likewise at the same time, ungainly rotting puppets, forever caught in her grief's unspoken shadow.

Ardenne couldn't think what to say to that, so she shifted grip on her staff, instead; these things might not go down from a head-strike, but if she could take out enough joints that might make them slow enough to outrun. Or so she told herself, too stubborn to think on the bleak truth of their numbers, their speed.

"Looks like you've got enough . . . coax-kin?—to keep going a while, to me," she ventured, at last. "No need for more. We'll go on our way, you go yours . . ."

Bess looked slantwise at her. "No *need?* Miz Ardenne, you should know, best of all: can't ever have too much supply. Not in the Patch."

The flatness in her voice—along with her dead-herd's slow

turning, wide-spread as a rattler's yawn, poised to snap 'round Ardenne's own coffle's last few remaining travelers—wrote her meaning clear. Even in the midst of this ever-stifling heat, it was a sight that made Ardenne's hammering pulse run cold.

No, she thought; "No," she repeated, out loud. "You need more bodies on your line, take me, but let the rest of 'em go. A willing tithe, not a bunch of strangers all fighting you—that's worth something, surely?"

Bess spat. "What d'you think this is, a Trade-town barter-square? Be no kindness to take you and let the rest of 'em wander, 'specially not with her—" a twitch of her head towards Heba "—lookin' ready to drop any minute." She folded her arms. "I *was* minded to let anyone go, in fact, then it'd be *you*, Miz Ardenne. You're the only one who'd make it out alive anyhow, plus savin' you means savin' all you rescue next."

Ardenne wanted to retch again, or scream. But: "Savin' them for *what*?" she demanded, instead. "More fodder for you, once these rot?" She raised her pike high, knuckles whitening, and shook it—a threat of her own, weak though it might seem, in context. "We *all* go, or none of us—and how're you going to keep that boy of yours upright then, with no fresh meat? How're you sure anybody's ever going to pass this exact same way again?"

Bess's gaze flickered back to the ghoul-child, all of a sudden doubt-shaded, while Nessa's sobs rent the rough air; she huddled in Vex's grip, bent near double, impossible to soothe. Ardenne blinked hard against the dust and smoke, eyes watering with the stink of burning metal, melted plastic, cooked flesh—felt the dry breeze whisper past her face, slaughter-hot. Set her own grip on the pike's haft just one degree harder, and waited for whatever might come.

The ghoul-child tilted its head, leathery forehead skin crackling—*contracting*, like it was trying to frown, even if the muscles had forgotten how. Before Ardenne had time to blink it had already skittered 'cross the sand with frightening speed, then stopped abruptly, crouching almost atop Vex and Nessa, both visibly terrified. Nessa froze, eyes wide, as the dead thing sniffed her face and neck, a ratchet-like clicking sound rattling its throat; Vex just sat there trembling, hands fisted, unable to move.

Bess bit her lip. "Ah," she said. "Well. Had to come sometime, I 'spose."

"What did?" Ardenne asked, mouth dry.

"He's a boy, after all, growin' or not. And maybe I ain't the only one thinks he needs *company*."

The quiet words sounded like the snick of bullets going into a pistol-chamber.

"*Not her*."

For a second Ardenne wondered why her own voice sounded so strange — she'd opened her lips to cry those very words, but they'd come out in a gasp of pain, not rage. Her eyes snapped to Heba, the one who'd actually spoken, who was still hauling herself up to as close as standing as she could, arms draped heavy over Reed and May's shoulders.

"You need someone you . . . and *he* . . . can love," Heba went on. "Can love *you* back, for keeping them safe; Nessa ain't ever gonna be that, not when you let her sister die right in front of her. But I know where you can find someone who might, you just see 'em raised right."

And here she paused, one hand ghosting down to cradle her swollen belly.

It took a moment more for Ardenne to catch her meaning, but Bess was already there, scowling in sour disbelief. Demanding, as she did: "Woman, how foolish you think I am? What good's a babe to me, *here*, even if you stayed to nurse it?"

"Stay here, no, no," Heba husked, between pants. "But . . . we're not far here from Sanctuary. She can be born there, grow 'til she's fit to fend for herself, then come back here of her own accord. All she needs is to stay alive, got now."

"You don't know what you're *saying*, Heba —" Ardenne burst out.

Bess held up one hand, sharp and sudden. "Oh, but I somewhat think she does." Heba nodded, swallowing hard. "Let her speak on, coffle-walker."

Ardenne studied Heba, baffled. And Heba did indeed hold forth, feeling her way. What she said rang harsh but true—they all knew it, had *known* it, to one degree or another. Slave wisdom, born bone-deep, never entirely shed. It rang through Ardenne by ever more painful degrees, popping all her old wounds open and making them ache; sutures and prayer, alcohol splashed in the cut. A forest of old wailings burnt down to the roots, only to watch those same those roots burrow deeper.

No scar's ever entirely healed, under all that tissue, she thought. *All it takes's a bout of scurvy to prove* that.

"You all know my posting," Heba reminded them. "Doctor's shed, trackin' slave and free alike to term—catch the bad before it can't be got rid of without risk, then make sure the good don't kill its dam comin' out, or wreck her parts beyond salvage. So when I found I was bound down that same path, I well-knew if I stayed, I'd lose her anyhow—*my* gamble was always on carryin' this life out into the waste in faint hope she'd be born free, even for just a second, for one last gasp before death. So you tell me, Miz Bess: think the idea of losin' her scares me? I lost her the second I saw her on that scan-screen, when Doctor scoped her deep enough to reckon she didn't have no dangler, 'cause that meant that once she dropped she'd be trained up a slave like me, get beat on and bleed, be sold away in turn and bred 'til she died. She ain't *ever* been mine, not really. Which is why I'll trade her away on deposit gladly, you only help me get her out of me someplace where no Master can lay claim to her."

Heba gulped, pausing to wipe sweat from her face. "I'll pay you for my child's life by raisin' her for you. Miz Ardenne and me'll come back and forth 'cross the Patch, tithe a few on the chain to you each time, so long's you'll keep us safe—see that child growin' up all the while, knowin' she belongs to you, that I'll give her over. And finally, when this boy of yours is so fallen apart even your craft can't keep him here no more, you'll have a fit replacement to look forward to."

Bess's mouth ticced at its corner, twitching up, as though she'd just heard a particularly ill joke. "Can't nothin' replace *him*," she said at length, voice a rasp.

"No, ma'am, 'course not. But . . . alive's better than dead, ain't it, when you're still alive yourself? All told."

Bess bit her lip, hard put to argue. Around-about, meanwhile, the dead paused in their roaming and all looked to her as one, still and silent, pointer dogs with their ears up. Stayed that way, timed by Ardenne's thumping heart, until their maker-mistress let out with a single long, slow, unsteady sigh.

" . . . might could be," she said, finally.

Heba nodded. "Might even find a way to leave the Patch, after. Find somewhere else to be at peace, to raise my . . . raise *your* child." She took another shuddery breath. "But you gotta keep us all alive, t'do it. All of us."

"And what surety will you give you'll return, when it's time?"

For a moment, Heba couldn't answer, face crumpling as a fresh wave of pain swept through her. So it was Ardenne's turn now, stepping in as support, her voice worn fatigue-flat, thin but clear.

"'What surety'?" she asked Bess, parroting her own words back to her. "C'mon, gal—you're the one with all the power here, right? Knew all along where we were headed to, I'll bet; got more pairs of eyes than most Masters. Not to mention how Sanctuary's less than half a day's travel past the Rim, so it don't cost you much to set one of your coax-kin outside the gates, make sure Heba and me don't try running." She paused, then added: "But all that's beside the real point. 'Cause sure as bodies in the Patch rise up, *I'll* come back, even if Heba and her babe don't—'cause I've got to, 'cause my job's not done, not by half. And I've no way to hide from you in here; no-one can. Can they?"

Bess didn't even have to shake her head, to that; her folk did it for her, slow and silent. Her boy's lips widened, cracking at the corners, and that crackling hiss of his split the air once more, as though to answer back: *No.*

No, they sure can't.

For the first time Ardenne noticed that Bess's own teeth showed crooked between her fresh young lips, dull browning ivory, the bone inside her somehow much older than her skin; her yellow hair still hung down like gold, shadowing her face once more, a fisher's pretty lure. Might be part of her witch-tricks, same as she'd played the victim at first, out on those dunes—a way to guarantee people didn't truly see her 'til it was too late to matter, 'til they knew her for what she truly was. God knew, Ardenne had seen folk miss far more obvious things before, and with far less cause.

But I know you now, she thought, almost certain Bess could hear her. *I know you, inside and out. Like you know me.*

"A daughter to share your life, in time," Ardenne finished, holding Bess's blue gaze in hers. "Plus, whenever Heba and me cross the Patch, a tithe for you, for your kin; blood for blood, payment for service rendered. Everybody gets something."

And loses something else, she didn't add. Shot a look sidelong and found Heba's hand pressing hard against her stomach, twisting now for an entirely different reason: she understood, all right. Woman wasn't dumb.

Anything but.

Bess tilted her head yet once more, studying Ardenne—amused, but only half; detached, as if her eyes were mere ocular-lenses. "And you, you're at ease with this idea, huh? Coffle-woman."

Ardenne forced a shrug. "More so than with dyin', sure," she said. "Or slaving on forever here for you, after."

"Oh, hardly forever. I'll die too, one day."

Now it was Ardenne's turn to give Bess a cool look. "You'd think so," was all she said, allowing the silence to speak for her. Implying, as she did—

—but that's not exactly proved as yet now. Is it?

Because when all else failed, under worst circumstances, she could still hear old Gerun's voice in the back of her head, tutoring her in the cold equations' bitter logic—a seductive calculus, inhumanly calm, tallying lives spent against those saved. Asking her, words blending into her own until she couldn't pull them apart herself, no matter how she puzzled: *You ready to do the needful? . . . This place charges a steep price, always, and blood's the single best payment . . . It's a killing world out here . . . What they paid for's a chance, that's all . . . In the Patch, mercy's got too high a price to indulge . . .*

All this, all that, all and always. Then, most important yet, this final piece of sad advice meant to keep at least her upright if no one else, for the benefit of fled gamblers still to come—

. . . more you thrash, faster you'll sink, first up to your waist, then neck, then gone. And take them right along with you when you do.

She doubted overmuch she was really fooling Bess or Heba; wasn't even sure she was fooling Reed or Vex, let alone poor Nessa and May. Maybe the only one she wanted to fool was herself. But God help her, Ardenne thought, not that she even believed in one . . . she was, by this point, fuck-almighty tired of a lifetime's worth of thrashing.

Bess's bone-smile broadened, both sharp and hard, but Ardenne met it head on, no wavering. Demanding—

"So: what d'you say, gal? Make your call, we'll bide by it. Not that we got all too damn much of a choice, in the end . . . "

The witch-girl hesitated, just one long minute more. Then jolted as her dead child laid his dry hand on hers, beseeching—a plaintive clicking echoing in his long-closed throat—and straightened to give her answer.

With Bess's puppets to shepherd them, they crossed out of the Patch by nightfall, able to see the glow of Sanctuary's lights against the setting sun over a new horizon of gently rising green hills. Fatigue was leaden in all their bones by then, but not even Heba wanted to rest. As the stragglers from Bess's coffle fell behind, seeming to vanish back into those infected sands that bred them, a last random piece of luck saved their lives as they approached the walls: one of the marksmen stationed over Sanctuary's gate recognized Ardenne's voice in the dark and jumped up yelling, ordering his brothers to stand down. Ardenne had watched those twelve-foot-high metal panes roll open a half-dozen times in her life; this was the first, and only, time the sight made her weep.

Heba's baby was born near midnight, fittingly. Born into dark, and quiet with it, her wide blue eyes already open.

Hard road ahead for you, little girl, Ardenne thought, as the medico handed her over. She folded the child up and jogged her gently as Heba just lay there with lids closed, milk seeping from both her naked breasts and a stained sheet pulled up over the rest. "Don't you maybe want to—" Ardenne began, at last, once the babe started to whimper, only to watch Heba shake her head against the pillow-pad, silent and slow, like all her strength was spent; seemed like as not to die right there, for all the birth itself had looked a fine enough one. Or perhaps like she didn't even want to touch its product, this child held in trust for some-one else, for fear of loving her too much to ever let her go.

"Not yet," she answered, finally, her voice hoarse. "Not . . . just yet."

Nine years later, Ardenne stood on the edge of the Patch, for the twenty-fifth or thirtieth time—she'd long since lost count. Grass and sand mixed under her boots. Out in the emptiness, the rising sun brought heat-shimmer up from the ridged sands and cracked flats. She adjusted the weight of the feed-packs over her shoulder, shifted her grip on her staff, and glanced down at her companion.

The little girl looked up at her. She didn't smile, but she rarely did; she was a solemn little creature, bright-eyed and quiet. Ardenne took her hand and looked out over the sands again. With effort, she brought back every memory she could of all those she'd brought through the Patch over the years, digging through them for consolation like she might dig through the contents of an overloaded pack. She remembered May, dead two years now of simple age and frailty; Vex, who'd proved no more able to break his bad habits than his manacles and been exiled four years ago after his third conviction for theft. Reed, now a fine upstanding tradesman and citizen, who'd given out he might run for Councilor in the next voting, and who crossed the street to avoid her whenever they passed one another; she wasn't altogether sure she blamed him. And Nessa, who lived yet with Reed, though whether as daughter or lover Ardenne had no idea, nor ever wished to know.

And Heba.

Who was her father? Ardenne'd asked the woman, once, fairly sure she knew the answer: a Master, of course. Heba's Master. And Heba'd just shook her head, sadly, before answering—

Who he was don't matter, not now, maybe not ever. I thought he loved me, thought I loved him. Might be he thought the same. But see, he had others . . . more children, more've his own get with women like me, and for all he might've petted on 'em or given 'em sweet names when they was small, it never stopped him sellin' 'em in the end: away from their own mothers, away from him. Away from everything.

Never got their mothers freed neither, I suspect, Ardenne'd said. To which Heba just hitched what might've been meant to be a laugh.

Naw, she replied, finally. *So I guess his love wasn't worth all too much, in the end—not to him, not for real. And not to me, either.*

Heba, dead three years back now and through no damn fault of anyone's, not even her own: her stone gone to feed the pile at Ardenne's door, name-inscribed, re-told with each fresh coffle. Dead half her own child's life, with Ardenne stepping in to play stepparent to the girl whose hand she held, teacher and trainer and mentor.

If you gave your child away, did that make her a slave? Not if love was involved, Ardenne believed. And she *could* love, that girl—Heba'd made damn sure of that, if only by getting her born free. Ardenne'd done her best too, since, to make sure she stayed that way.

We serve the coffle, she'd told her almost every day, not to mention at the start of every trip. *Look out for them, negotiate their way through this unforgiving world. Save those who can't save themselves. And they help us do it, those in there, those dead folk—your brother-to-be, your . . . mother-to-be. All those on her chain.*

The girl understood, as well; Ardenne had to trust in that. *Thought* she did, anyhow. Had heard all the stories, then seen things at a distance, then closer up—close enough to touch, and be touched. *I can take it, Mama Ardenne,* she'd answered back, after all, just the other day. *I know my value. If I'm the price for Bess's craft bent to our needs, I'll pay myself, and gladly.*

And Ardenne had simply nodded, eyes salt-hot, not trusting herself to speak further on the subject. Knowing experience would prove her either right or wrong on that one, soon enough.

At her sight's edge, a flicker of what might be movement. Without her oculars handy there was no way to be sure, but was that a figure up there, on that first ridge—a small shape, hunched down, two dark-pitted sparks just barely visible in its unseen face . . . ?

Well, maybe not. She squinted harder, brow knit, then gave up; gone, if it'd ever even been there. An illusion. A mirage.

Like love, she thought, *or God. All that we swear on, even when we've no proof any such exists.*

(*Love's a chain nobody wants to break,* she could almost hear Bess breathe, at the same time, in the very back of her head.)

"Mind me," she said to the girl, and started down into the Patch with those small fingers knit in hers, their wrists roped each to each. "And keep up, now. No falling back, no falling behind."

"No'm."

"Don't wander, 'specially once we're all tied on. You have to set a good example for the others, don't you? After all . . . "

Your mothers are watching, always. Both of 'em. And me too, for my sins.

The rest of her life stretched out before her in journey after journey, in increments of here to there, one gamble to the next. Names on stones, gone to feed the pile.

Always knew I'd leave some part of me in here, Ardenne thought, squeezing the girl's hand for comfort, not that it made much matter whose, in the end of it. While:

"Yes'm," the girl replied, all innocent duty, squeezing back.

About the Author

Formerly a film critic, journalist, screenwriter and teacher, Gemma Files has been an award-winning horror author since 1999. She has published five collections of short work, three collections of speculative poetry, a Weird Western trilogy, a story-cycle and a stand-alone novel (*Experimental Film*, which won the 2015 Shirley Jackson Award for Best Novel and the 2016 Sunburst Award for Best Adult Novel). Her collection *In That Endlessness, Our End* won both the Bram Stoker Award and the This Is Horror Award in that category for 2021.

GRIMSCRIBE PRESS